SAVED BY THE

SEA LORD

LORDS OF ATLANTIS

USA TODAY BESTSELLING AUTHOR

STARLA NIGHT

Cover by Earthly Charms
Editing by Linda Edits

For inquiries:

Starla Night
starla@starlanight.com
https://starlanight.com

ONE

Today, Hazel Green was quitting her job.

Just as soon as she got the chance to turn in her notice.

Hazel raced up to the customs desk at the Brooklyn Marina, heaved the tote of men's clothes onto the service desk, and panted, "Sorry I'm late. I'm here to pick up my merman."

The customs agent paused her typing. She had the dark brows and unimpressed gaze of a Latina action star.

"I was ready to pick him up yesterday, but I guess the undersea currents pushed him off course." Hazel fumbled her iced nonfat triple-shot caramel latte with whip onto the counter, quested in her documents bag under her neatly printed two weeks' notice, and yanked out the paperwork. "You know how that is. Or maybe you don't. I don't. Anyway, here is his customs application, the verification card from when he was last in the country, his ID, his measurements, his blood type, clothes—"

"You are?"

She straightened. "Hazel Green, program assistant at

MerMatch.com."

The reflection in the tilted mirror behind the desk showed a big chunk of arugula from her tofu curry quinoa wrap stuck to her front teeth.

Crap.

She rubbed her finger over her front teeth. "I was supposed to be here an hour ago, but the express stopped, and I didn't get my boss's call until—"

"Hazel Green?" the customs agent repeated.

"Did you want my ID?" Hazel pulled off her mini backpack—so stylish last season—and searched among the lip balm, sunscreen, aspirin, facial tissue, earplugs, second earplugs, mini notebook, erasable pens, third earplugs, and a hundred loyalty cards that had escaped from her bursting wallet.

The customs agent took her ID and typed.

Hazel texted her boss she'd made it to customs, then scrolled through Slack messages about her Young Entrepreneurs meetup. Gah, it was past one. Could she grab the merman, stash him at a hotel, and get home with time to change before the meetup? There was nothing wrong with her work blazer, but—

Was that a splotch?

Hazel set down the iced coffee that she didn't remember picking up and sipping—although her hand was wet and the ice level was undeniably lower—and smoothed her blazer.

It was a splotch.

How long had that been there?

She rummaged in her mini pack and dabbed the mystery substance with a depleted tube of Miracle Off Stain Remover. The splotch bled out. This was not as miraculous as the ads would have her believe. Of course, she was the one who insisted on an eggshell blazer over a taupe ribbed tank and matching skort, which was asking for trouble.

As a little girl, she'd dreamed of leaving grubby Idaho behind for clean, light, shining wood floors and sipping coffee while wearing a white linen dress. Apparently, she wanted to live in Iceland.

Instead, she lived in a 400-foot square box studio in sweltering New York a few blocks from a market where she could buy, among other things, langoustine, dried fish, and skyr.

It was almost the same.

The customs agent ran a metal detector wand over Hazel's bags and stepped around the counter. "Place your hands on the desk and spread your legs."

Hazel did as she was told. "Um, I'm just picking him up. I'm not a terrorist."

The customs agent waved the wand lightly over Hazel. It beeped at her belt buckle.

"I'm harmless. I swear."

The customs agent returned behind her desk. "Leave everything on the end of the counter."

"Okay, but he needs his clothes, right? The mer usually swim naked."

The agent did not grace her question with an answer.

Right.

Hazel finished her coffee and tossed the empty container, then did as requested. In front of her was a door covered with frosted glass.

"Including your phone," the customs agent said.

What? Augh.

Hazel tucked her lifeline into her mini pack. Her empty hands hung weirdly at her sides. "We're the good guys. I promise."

The customs agent gave her a stony glance. *There are no good guys.*

"We are," Hazel said.

The frosted door clicked and opened. A stout, unsmiling agent looked her up and down. "Hazel Green?"

"Yep."

"This way."

The second agent led her through a narrow maze of fabric-coated walls and into a small conference room. He shut the door to seal her in, then sat and thumbed through his files like a harassed clerk looking through old fines to find the one she'd forgotten to pay.

Hazel perched on the edge of her seat. "I'm really just here to do a pickup."

The agent put on reading glasses and perused her application.

A small window gave a view into another conference room.

Inside, a shirtless man sat facing away from her. He emitted a deadly aura.

The merman.

Shaggy timber wolf-gray hair brushed the base of his neck where it met bulging, capable shoulders. A cord was tied around his neck. A necklace? His angular back rippled with muscles. Iridescent gray tattoos slashed his body in geometric, tribal lines.

She'd met a lot of mermen in this job. The all-seafood swimmer's diet toned their warrior physiques to the peak. And this guy? Whoa.

He turned slightly as though hearing her breathe through the thick glass. The angle of his jaw was sharp, and his nose was honed like a blade.

A frisson of awareness uncoiled in her center.

She held her breath.

Something about this one was different.

The customs agent lowered the application and looked at her over the rims of his reading glasses. "Hazel Green."

She jumped. "Yes, that's me. I've never had another name, except when I was a kid and my softball coach called me Green, which is still my name. Yes."

He blinked.

She laced her fingers. Relaxed. She was totally relaxed. "Anyway, how can I help you?"

"What's he"—the customs agent jerked his stubby thumb at the merman in the other conference room—"doing in New York?"

"Oh, didn't my boss tell you? It's no secret. He's here to find his soul mate."

"Soul mate?"

"You know the story. The mermen are endangered?"

He looked at her like he didn't know the story.

Which was insane because everybody knew.

"Like, a thousand years ago, the mer and humans lived in harmony, but this mysterious Great Catastrophe sank their ancient city, Atlantis, and made the mer go into hiding," Hazel said. "All their mermaids died out, so they had to make a secret pact with women on isolated 'sacred' islands, and everything was fine again until the islands sank or modernized or whatever. Five years ago, the mer got to the brink of extinction, and so the one warrior, Torun, broke their secrecy pact. He claimed a woman from Oregon who was on a treasure-hunting expedition in Cancun."

The customs agent pursed his lips.

"As anyone would," she said. "And that sparked this whole underwater revolution. Most of the undersea world still clings to their secrecy pact, but the rebels founded a new Atlantis by the wreckage of the old and sent up their warriors to meet modern brides. That's where I come in."

"You come in how?"

"I, or really my boss, introduce the warriors to women until they find the one whose soul resonates with theirs. The merman gives his bride his Sea Opal. She drinks the elixir and transforms into a mermaid."

"You ever tried it?" he asked.

"The elixir? My boss gave me some for a headache. It tastes like tap water."

"Tap water?"

"Well, they originally made elixir in the sacred island churches by steeping Sea Opals for centuries, and somebody figured out how to make it a lot faster in an Instant Pot using New York's finest."

"And you drank it."

"Yeah. They sell it as a health drink, you know? Like the Sea Opal powder? They put it in cosmetics, supplements, you name it. The FDA is reviewing miracle cures for cancer and all sorts."

"And you didn't turn into a mer person?"

"Yeah, because it only gives you a health boost unless it's activated by your merman soul mate."

"Activated how?"

"He claims you with a kiss."

"That's it? You get a gem, chug some tap water, smooch a guy, and you get fins?"

"Did you want to try the elixir?" She reached for her missing backpack, then folded her hands again. "I had a bottle in case we run into Lotar's soul mate on the subway home."

"You're carrying it around to shove on some innocent commuter?"

"Only his soul mate. Their souls have to resonate. Otherwise, it's just tap water."

The agent frowned at his paperwork. "So how does that work?"

"Resonance? Your souls vibrate, you know, like a musical instrument or something. Honestly, you should ask my boss about this stuff. She matches people on dates. I just do the grunt work. Filing. Coffee. Grunting."

He did not crack a smile.

She ran her tongue over her front teeth. No more lettuce.

The customs agent tapped his file. "You're sending off the citizens of New York with these mermen from another race and you don't know how any of it works?"

"It's like love at first sight. How does that work? Nobody knows, but it happens."

He didn't look like he believed in love at first sight.

"Well, trust me, it happens all the time at normal dating agencies."

"So you know this MerMatch isn't normal."

"Okay, I said normal, but I meant human-only. The mer aren't that different."

He blinked slowly.

"They're not," she insisted.

God, why hadn't Dannika waited a few extra days to go on her cruise? She'd have already assured the agent that everything was fine and even convinced him to pledge his support for their cause.

"Even underwater, the mer have two legs. They look like free divers with gills. And they shift to real humans on land, you know?"

He thwacked the file. "What I know is that a couple

thousand years ago, they pissed us off and we shoved them back in the water. And that's where they stayed—"

"Except for their secret covenant with brides on sacred islands to keep their population going."

"—until five years ago, they popped out of the ocean and started applying for green cards."

"Well, that was because their sacred islands emptied, and they had no more brides. It's all over Facebook. You can read about it anywhere."

He drummed his fingers on the table. "You know what else you can read about anywhere? That they're monsters who kidnap women."

"That's fake propaganda to make you hate mermen."

"It's not propaganda. It was my morning memo."

"But it's from the Sons of Hercules, right?"

He did not confirm or deny.

"So first of all, the Sons of Hercules are a terrorist hate group. They're being investigated. They started out as a bunch of disgruntled college boys who'd rather blame mermen for their lack of girlfriends instead of washing their clothes and taking a shower."

"Unwashed college kids didn't shut the borders to mermen."

"Right, they switched from sniping to lobbying, and that's been way more successful."

His eyes narrowed.

"Lotar was here before they stopped the visas, so his paperwork is still valid."

The customs agent leaned back and crossed his arms.

"Look." She spread her hands. "This is probably the last time you'll see him. The Atlantis mermen are building a big platform in the mid-Atlantic right over their city. When it's done, we're going to have a giant welcome party. Everyone's invited. All the mermen, any potential brides. Even you."

He squinted.

"And then they won't have to come to the US to meet humans. That's good, right?"

"It's good unless I let him in and he goes and does something on my watch. Then, I'm the schmuck who let him in."

"I won't let him do anything, and I'll be around him the whole time. In fact, I won't take my eyes off him."

The customs agent puckered his lips and scribbled a note on the application.

She patted her pockets for her...no phone.

Ugh.

These conference rooms sure were basic. Industrial carpet, soundproofed walls.

The pen scritch-scritched against the paper.

His wristwatch ticked.

She did *not* turn and obsessively study the merman in the other conference room.

"You can blame me for him being here," Hazel said. "The party was my idea, although I never thought my boss would actually go for it."

He kept writing.

Hazel rubbed her sweaty palms on her skort. "Traditional mer cities hate that their secret existence was revealed. Even after five years, they're mad at Atlantis. So I thought, why not show them what they've been missing? We'll have a big party, invite everyone, and the traditionalists will see how great it is to have families and kids again. So now Lotar has to swim all over the ocean to deliver the invitations. It's an ancient pilgrimage called the 'All-Cities Gyre.' That's gyre with a 'g,' not a 'j.' Like gyrate. Gyre."

He didn't look up. "And what's this guy Lotar doing in New York?"

"I just said. Oh, do you mean literally? Well, I'm going to give him pants." She gestured over her shoulder at the bag she'd abandoned at the counter. "We're going to leave here—hopefully the express is running again—and we'll look over potential brides, set up a couple coffee dates, I'm going to turn in my two weeks' notice, and then—"

"Two weeks? You're quitting?"

"Uh..." *Way to derail the conversation, Hazel!* "Yeah."

"Why?"

She was going to screw up.

Her boss had been urging Hazel to take over the New York office, but Hazel couldn't fill Dannika's Louboutins. She couldn't lobby senators or enchant diplomats. She couldn't even reason with customs agents.

But she was no coward.

And saying she was afraid of being promoted to her boss's position kind of sounded like a coward.

Which she wasn't.

So...yeah, she wasn't cowardly, she was quitting to pursue her dreams. This merman thing was supposed to be a temp job. She was a future independent businesswoman, not an office worker at a dating agency.

Yeah.

But she could imagine what the customs agent would think if she said, *I'm quitting a perfectly fine job before a big promotion so I can be poor and desperate when I start a business. Any business. With no prospects, no safety net, and no ideas. I'm going to be an entrepreneur. Somehow.*

"The Sons of Hercules are a huge reason," she said instead. "When you think the mermen are monsters, remember that the Sons of Hercules sabotaged my boss's airplane. She nearly died. Who wants to work a job where you have to fight terrorists all day?"

The customs agent stared.

Oh.

"It's not for everyone." She laced her fingers again. "So... Is there anything else you need to know?"

"You left his 'leaving' date blank."

"Because it'll be the instant he meets his bride."

"The instant?"

"Oh yeah. Mermen see their brides and then?" Hazel snapped. "They act. If his soul mate can go, he'll leave the next day."

"And if she can't?"

She shrugged. "The All-Cities Gyre takes two years. The platform's supposed to be finished in two years. You do the math."

The agent scribbled and muttered. "And if he doesn't leave, it won't be your problem."

Well, that was true.

Huh.

The door to the merman's room opened. The desk agent emptied the shoulder tote on the table. Her mouth moved, but no sound penetrated the thick glass. She carried away the empty tote and closed the door again.

The warrior pulled out red Bermuda shorts, a blue button-down shirt, and yellow flip-flops. It was the standard uniform for a merman, but he handled the clothes Hazel had folded like an NBA pro palming a basketball. His ordinary-looking hands were actually the size of dinner plates.

Wow.

And every motion was precise. He had a predator's grace. Like how he stood and stepped into the shorts. His lower back rippled and his buttocks flexed with concealed power as he slightly turned and revealed his—

Ooh.

She jerked her eyes away.

Her heart raced.

The mer were totally comfortable nude.

But she had a little respect for privacy.

The agent led her out of the small room, through the maze, and left her at the front counter. "Good luck with your resignation."

"Oh, yeah. Thanks."

The agent departed.

Hazel collected her backpack, document bag, and the empty shoulder tote. Now that the interview was over, her stomach growled. She was starving. Her phone! She ordered another latte from the nearest coffee cart while she waited outside the frosted door for her warrior.

Was it almost three? Already?

Maybe she could skip the office and boot Lotar out at a hotel—

No.

She had to submit her notice today, and she had to do it in person. It would go through their secure office courier and be recorded by the Mer-Human Foundation before Dannika could talk her out of quitting.

Again.

And Hazel shouldn't feel bad about it. She wasn't leaving them in a lurch. They'd have two weeks to find a new program assistant.

She'd work until the very last minute. She'd even work from home. She'd already spent free time she should have used to start her new business reviewing bride applicants and picking out the perfect candidates for Lotar.

Dannika had said he didn't talk much, so his bride would have to be smart, gorgeous, and articulate to convince a bunch of enemy kings to let go of their old grudges and RSVP.

Hazel had poured over the profiles with three high-lighters starring communications majors, corporate sales leaders, and marine biologists. There were so many highly qualified women trying to depart from Hazel's dream jobs to seek an adventure—and of course true love—that she had her pick.

Their accomplishments alternately inspired and demo-tivated her. So many women had made their dreams come true. Why not Hazel?

So, with this two weeks' notice, she was reaching for her dreams.

This was it.

This time, she was serious.

No one would stand in her way of quitting MerMatch.

Yep.

She was leaving the fascinating world of the deadly, gorgeous, tattooed warriors behind her.

Forever.

Hazel took a deep breath and pep-talked herself as the door to the customs office opened.

A rugged wall of tattooed masculinity filled the door-way, angular and powerful. He fixed on her like a shark scenting blood in the water.

She froze.

A shocking wave of heat rolled through her body.

Gray irises evaluated her. Iridescent threads the same color as his tattoos glimmered like secrets only she could see.

He ambled out like a lone wolf, his gray eyes flitting

right and left, seeking and dismissing threats. Capability oozed from his pores. The dark and light streaks of gray hair made him look older and younger at the same time, and his guarded lips concealed mysteries.

He stopped in front of her.

Looked down.

And emitted total, silent dominance.

Throbbing awareness pulsed into her veins. Could he sense it? His eyes caressed her body, and the heat of his nearness prickled her with a strange desire. Hunger licked across her skin with icy fire.

She swallowed. "Hi. I'm Hazel. You're expecting me."

He nodded.

She started to reach out her hand to shake his.

But the mer didn't touch. They had a thing about only touching their brides.

She brushed her hair, her nape, the splotch on her lapel. "Um, nice to meet you."

His gaze softened on her, then fixed on a passing customs agent with sharp awareness.

To her, he was a friend.

To enemies?

He would tear their throats out.

Her phone buzzed.

She jumped and upset her document bag. It tilted, still open, and papers cascaded out.

He moved faster than her eyes could follow. Bag in one hand, spilled documents captured in the other. One paper fluttered past him. He switched hands and snatched the escaped document out of the air.

The whole save was smooth, silent, and took less than a second.

"Whoa." She fumbled the bag and documents from his

deft fingers, never brushing even by accident, and cinched it down. "Thanks. You saved me twenty minutes. Oh." She took the last paper from his hand.

Her two weeks' notice. Still crisp. His midair catch hadn't even creased the paper.

She slid it in with the rest, crinkling it slightly, and snapped the bag closed.

Her phone buzzed again.

He focused on it.

"My coffee order is ready. I skipped lunch." She coughed awkwardly. "Did you want something? I owe you, seriously. I'm running so short on time right now. I could buy you a croissant or a bagel." Or a slab of caribou...

He shook his head.

"Right. Okay." She backed away, tripped on a chair—wow, could she be less cool right now?—flipped around, and stumbled over a garbage can. She hustled toward the exit. "The subway is this way."

He followed.

"Wait, no." She looped away from the stairs. "Never mind. The coffee cart is this way. Haha. Ha..."

He paced her, silent and watchful.

Her heart pounded in her throat.

She was supposed to quit her job today.

She was supposed to leave the mer behind.

She was supposed to find a bride for Lotar who was smart and suave and articulate.

This storm of feeling swirling inside her set off warning sirens.

And one thing was clear.

Hazel wanted the party to succeed.

She absolutely, positively, definitely could not be Lotar's soul mate.

TWO

Lotar was a hunter.

And he had come to New York to hunt.

He was silent and effective. Relentless and unstoppable.

Focused and immune from—

"So." The small female, Hazel, swiftly crossed the hard stone floor, her bags swinging as a kind of defense system. "How was the swim? Pretty exciting? Pretty normal? Just pretty?"

Hazel was pretty.

Bright, fierce. Pure, innocent. Attentive, and yet somehow able to avoid the other humans without looking at them.

No, no. *Do not focus on her.* He had to hunt.

The enemies of the mer grew bolder by the day.

He must remind them that the mer were not peaceful or defenseless.

They would—

"You're so tall. I'm like five-four. What are you? Six-two? Six-three?"

She was small but strong. If she swung those bags, she would give a trained warrior pause.

"Six-four?"

Lotar stretched longer than a juvenile great white shark, stood comfortably in the mouth of the oldest basking shark, or fairly fought the longest conger eel. He had never stolen a trident balanced for a larger mer, although he had taken many who had a shorter reach.

But in human measurements?

Hazel glanced back at him.

Her eyes were a tawny brown shade, similar to the fluffy silk of her hair, and long locks teased her cheek. Her black pupils grew luminous. The longer she gazed at him, the brighter her soul burned.

Almost as if...

He jerked his gaze away and shrugged one shoulder.

"Huh. Wait here." She wove through lounging humans, collected an amber iced drink from the end of the cart, and stopped at a counter to dust it with powders and pierce the foam with a straw.

Her absence was a relief.

How strange that he should tense, coiled, in her presence.

She was not his enemy, although she was an unfortunate distraction.

He focused again on his surroundings.

The Brooklyn Marina was a soaring open space like a clear cavern. Sunlight beamed through the tall windows and reflected off the hard, smooth floors.

Schools of humans pulsed across the space. Their souls shone brightly in their chests. They chattered about boats, sailing, and vacations.

Dim-souled humans scattered here and there. A woman

pushed a wet, mossy stick across the floor. A man stared at a folded print paper and checked a strap on his wrist. The woman at the coffee cart rushed to put food into sacks for the customers.

The Sons of Hercules humans would certainly have dim souls.

They had no affinity for the sea. No love for the mer.

And so it would be easy for Lotar to observe them, hidden, until he identified who, exactly, had attacked his friends and deserved his wrath.

"Ready?" Hazel popped in front of him. "I'm ready."

His heart thudded once. Hard.

Strange.

Hazel did not frighten him.

But she caused a startle reaction. A tingling warning from an electric eel about to paralyze its prey.

"Let's go." She turned on her heels, sipped the cylindrical iced coffee, and simultaneously stabbed her phone with both thumbs. "I'm checking the status of the metro. We'll stop at the office first. I'm on kind of a tight timeline."

Lotar trailed her through the crowds like a hunter weaving through long strands of eelgrass.

"Wow, the Manhattan skyline looks amazing today." Hazel pattered down the steps and through the glass orifice to the outside. "Welcome to New York."

Human machines roared.

The sky was blue. Rock-and-glass dwellings soared for puffy white clouds. Metallic containers called cars growled and rumbled, making his feet vibrate.

And there were humans.

So many humans.

Dim-souled, bright-souled, fast and slow. Angry, aggressive. Slow, avoidant.

The assault on his senses was like trying to wade through a collapsing cliff. He dodged contact, balanced on the low stone ledge close to the growling cars, and stopped with Hazel at the back of a crowd.

"So, what do you think?" she asked.

This city housed his enemies.

And more humans than polyps on a coral reef.

The farther they moved from the marina, the more dim-souled humans mixed into the crowds. Far too many. His plan to observe and stalk them until they led him to the Sons of Hercules needed a change. He had a limited time to deliver his warning before he must leave on the All-Cities Gyre.

Alone.

"Of New York," Hazel pressed. "How is it?"

A car emitted a grating squeal. It pierced his sternum.

He rubbed his chest. "Loud."

"Oh, it was so overwhelming when I first arrived. And I didn't know how to walk fast."

The surrounding crowd pressed forward.

They crossed in front of growling cars and stepped onto another low stone ledge. Her short legs pumped to keep at his pace. "You've got long legs, so you're fine."

He did not feel fine.

How foolish of him to expect this to be easy.

His strength was not in strategy. It was in reconnaissance. He should have grilled the warriors who had visited New York.

But they might have guessed his plans.

His superiors wanted him to find a bride. Together, they would be ambassadors on the All-Cities Gyre.

If his superiors had known finding a bride was the last

thing Lotar would do, they might have denied him the chance to come to New York.

His plan might have been forbidden.

"You've been to the mainland before, right?" Hazel strode brightly at his shoulder. "My boss said you were in Florida for the very first bride matchmaking event, long before they founded MerMatch. A bride pageant. What was that like?"

He did not want to talk with this compelling female.

He had to think.

But she waited for an answer, and he could not fully drag his attention away. "Strange."

"I bet." She smiled like he'd told an amusing story. "Are you excited to meet your future bride?"

"No."

"No? Isn't that the whole reason you're here? To meet a bride to travel with you on the All-Cities Gyre?"

Ah.

This was why he rarely spoke. He was not clever like some warriors. Any words risked revealing his intentions, as dishonorable as they were.

And he tried very hard not to reveal to the Atlantis warriors who had welcomed him and trusted him just how dishonorable he really was.

He tried to fix the problem with more words. "The ocean is dangerous."

"So's the subway, and I ride that three times a day."

Human dangers had nothing on the ocean.

His skepticism must have shown on his face, because she sighed. "Okay, so there are fewer sharks, enemy warriors, krakens, and all that, but I got mugged three times last year! Check this out." She lifted a pink canister clipped to a loop on her back bag. "It's a mace-taser-air horn. I wouldn't use the air horn around you because mer are sensitive to noise, but the next mugger who even looks at me wrong is going to regret it."

Hmm.

The other brides had not ensured their own safety. They had clung, helpless and crying, reliant on their warrior husbands to defend them from the deep.

But Hazel did not seem helpless.

She was small, but she used her bags for a shield and carried a hidden weapon. While texting, she expertly led him down steps and into a tunnel, avoiding hazards without glancing away from her phone.

Perhaps, if she were a warrior's bride, she would handle the dangers...

She suddenly frowned. "Wait. If you're not here to meet your bride, why are you here?"

If he told her, would she help him?

But he could not reach his goal on his own.

She had devised the plan for the All-Cities Gyre. So she had strategic skills and experience.

And what other choice did he have?

He stopped in a quiet corner of a large area with clanking machines.

She swung back, out of the flow of humans, to listen.

"The Sons of Hercules nearly killed second Lieutenant Ciran and his soul mate."

Her eyes flew wide. "I know! Oh, God. Give me five minutes with their leaders in a room and..." She gripped her pink canister again, then her shoulder slumped and she sighed. "I'll prosecute them to the fullest extent of the law."

"I will not." He clenched his fists. "I have come to deliver that warning."

She nodded. "So what's your plan for delivering the warning? You want to make a video?"

"I want to look into their eyes."

They must understand him. He would not allow them to escape a second time.

Hazel pursed her lips. "There's the problem. If we could look the leaders in the eye, they'd already be in jail. All we've found are low-level interest groups and a couple of area lieutenants on notice."

"Take me to them."

"But it won't help. There's a group that meets at the college down the street to drink craft beer and talk about how great they are. Until the government classifies those yahoos as a terrorist group, they can have meetings and advertise, no big deal."

"They will convey my message to the leaders."

"But how? They don't know who their leaders are either."

How was that possible?

"Ever since our security consultant, Starr, began looking into them, the leaders pulled way back," Hazel said. "They don't issue orders or commands. Somebody's running their website, but all that person does is post news and opinion articles to get people angry. It's a real problem."

"They are all the enemy."

"Well, I agree, but it's complicated." Hazel checked her phone. "Everyone arrested for a crime against a merman has called himself a member of the Sons of Hercules. But in comparison to the number of people who attend the meetings, that's like, one crazy person per thousand or something. It's really low. Most are getting together to drink and rage. Only one or two are crazy enough to hurt somebody."

"With no leader, how do they accomplish anything?"

"Well, that's why I said the leaders pulled back. They do have one. Several ones. Somebody's funding the surveillance equipment and the lobbying. Starr has been trying to follow the money, and she's not the only one. When they brought down Ciran and Dannika's airplane, a couple of peons got arrested with incriminating evidence of a bigger structure, and that was a federal crime. We'll get them eventually. It's just a matter of time."

His fellow warriors did not have time. They were being hurt now. "Humans are not taking enough action."

"I feel you. One hundred percent." She pressed her hand to her heart. "Dannika says the only way to stop a group like this is to expose the leaders. Show how crude, small, or ugly they are. The mystery disappears and the organization crumbles. I don't know if that's true, but I hope she's right."

How infuriating. "One member must know something."

"I thought so too until I sent a friend to record a meeting. It was chaos. I couldn't watch the whole thing. My friend told me I'd stopped before the lowest point."

Despite the setback, a meeting was his best starting point. Lotar often noticed small things other warriors missed. He would identify and stalk the members until they revealed the leader. And then he would decide whether to wait for human justice.

"I will go to the meeting."

"Okay." She swiped on her phone. "You just missed the last one. It's New York, though, so there's going to be a meeting somewhere... Huh. Oh. Because it's summer quarter, they're down to once a month, and most are on a long break, so...yeah." She shook her head. "It's going to be, like, a month."

A month?

Impossible.

Impossible!

Hazel shifted her bags from one arm to the other. "That's a long wait considering you need to get on the All-Cities Gyre. I'm going to see that friend tonight, and if you want, he could tell you about his experience. He might still have the recording."

Lotar could not sense souls via a recording.

But perhaps he would catch something useful. Participants' features. Distinctive voices, gaits. Then he could patrol the area until their currents crossed.

"I want," he said.

Her smile flashed.

His body throbbed with awareness.

...Throb?

He was not supposed to throb.

Hazel rummaged in a bag and passed him a small, thin rectangle. "Here's a crash course on how to ride the subway. Keep walking, swipe at the right speed, don't talk to anyone, don't make eye contact. And do. Not. Stare. Got it?"

He nodded.

"Take a deep breath. Let's go." She veered for clanking metal bars, passed her card over a red light, and pushed through.

He mirrored her, and they descended beneath the city.

The sheer volume of humanity made him want to reach for his daggers.

Which he'd stored under the marina per the agreement to climb onto the United States land.

Hazel stopped at the confluence of two tunnels. The other humans waved air at their sweating faces and tugged on their sticky, damp clothes.

All averted their gazes except one young fry. "Look, Dad. His tattoos are shiny."

The father, who had adorned his own skin with multi-colored honor markings, closed his hand over his young fry's finger. "Don't be a tourist."

The young fry leaned against his father, trusting in him, and stared at the iridescent gray tattoos recording Lotar's history and accomplishments.

A second, older young fry stood on the father's other side.

Two young fry.

The father kept his hands on both, protecting them equally.

A sliver of pain embedded itself in Lotar's chest.

He sucked in a breath of warm air—calming techniques were so different above the water—and released it slowly. His heart pulsed in a steady beat.

Most warriors would smile at this display of fatherhood. And two young fry. Such abundance! They would ache for young fry of their own.

Not Lotar.

Only days ago by surface time, Second Lieutenant Ciran had summoned Lotar to a human yacht. "King Kadir and Queen Elyssa have adopted the human tradition of a welcome party. You will convey the invitation personally to all cities."

He had stilled. "All cities?"

"Across the oceans, yes. For too long, we have isolated in our dwindling castles, a slave to the information shared via the echo points or by the All-Council. Now, an Atlantis warrior will spread hope and offer friendship. To reopen the All-Cities Gyre, knowing that no one has completed it in generations, King Kadir has chosen you."

Electricity had sparked in Lotar's heart.

His king had chosen him.

He was worthy.

Or, at least, one king thought him so.

"You are closest to the MerMatch offices in New York," Second Lieutenant Ciran had continued, his green-and-brown irises focused on strategy as always. "Go there first and seek your bride."

The yacht had slanted at an uncomfortable angle. Sunlight had burned Lotar's eyes. "I swim alone."

"Yes, I know." Second Lieutenant Ciran had guessed his discomfort. "A bride will reduce your ability to observe and scout. But consider. Even the most conservative cities will hesitate to attack a warrior with his bride."

"I fear no attack."

"Yes, but on this mission, you must not only deliver the invitation to each city. You must also become King Kadir's ambassador."

"And only your bride can soothe the kraken." Queen Dannika had slipped her arm around her husband's waist and rested her head against his shoulder. Her belly had swelled with young fry. "Since Ciran and I accidentally freed her from her prison, she's dangerous to everyone underwater, even when she doesn't mean to be. She can cause a tidal wave by turning too fast."

Lotar had easily avoided the kraken so far.

"And once your bride embraces her destiny, she can develop the power to heal, shield, or push away danger," Queen Dannika had continued. "You'll even swim faster. The more warriors I match, the more convinced I am that mer are designed to travel as soul mate pairs."

Second Lieutenant Ciran had gently rubbed her belly. "As am I."

Their souls had glowed in unison. Their resonance had been nearly blinding.

Lotar had seen queen powers before. Once, they had been legends. Everyone had assumed them to be lies of ancient times. But queens in Atlantis had performed such feats, healing warriors from impossible injuries and defeating armies by channeling the Life Tree.

And finding their soul mates had made the warriors faster, stronger. More determined.

But he was different.

Lotar had never encountered a situation he was not better suited to handle alone.

"Hey." Hazel glanced up at him, breaking him out of his memory. "Is it true that you know your soul mate as soon as you set eyes on her?"

Her question riveted him.

As did her open face, her cascading hair, her friendly eyes. Her slim shoulders, the curve of her neck he wanted to curl his fingers around, the glistening pink of her lips. Her soft breasts and the hints of curves, from his memory of walking behind her down the stairs—her bare knees, calves, her ankles he wanted to bite. Mark for himself. Claim.

His heart sped.

Until this moment, he had avoided looking at her for very long.

Or very directly.

And now?

Heat pooled in his groin, and his heartbeat localized, thudding with anticipation.

He must close the breaths of distance between them. Tear her bags out of the way, shred her coverings. Press his lips to hers.

Mine.

The brilliant light in her chest resonated with his glowing brighter and brighter. *I am your soul mate. I am your bride. I am your one.*

He had not come here for a bride.

Lotar tore his gaze away. "Sometimes."

"But you have to be face-to-face, right? You can't figure it out over the phone or by video."

He dipped his head in assent.

"And the sacred islands used to have a few hundred brides? But you came to Miami, a metropolis with half a million, and never found yours?"

It was true.

And a reason he'd thought he'd be safe in New York. So, he must be mistaken about Hazel.

His chest throbbed.

He was not mistaken.

Sweat beaded on her upper lip.

He wanted to taste it.

He wanted to taste her.

But he must not.

Because unlike the other warriors, Lotar's heart was not pure. His soul was not honorable. And if he claimed her, their union would not give her strength.

He would take her, drain her, consume her until she collapsed and cursed his name for her terrible fate.

THREE

Lotar's thoughts were thankfully interrupted. High pitched screeching grated on his teeth like the squeal of a wounded kingfish.

Air whooshed and the tunnel filled with connected metal cars. They slowed to a stop.

Doors opened. Humans flooded out, and suddenly the line waiting to enter stampeded away from the car in front of them.

Good.

He ambled forward.

"Oh, no." Hazel grabbed his shirt covering and tugged him back. "Never enter an empty car on a crowded subway. Trust me."

He studied the car as they pushed forward onto the crowded car.

A dim-souled man shouted at a blank wall and clawed at a seat.

Ah.

He stepped over the gap onto the subway car. Hazel

kept a hold of his shirt hem and pulled him down the aisle, squeezing between rows of seated and standing humans. She ducked and compressed her many bags like the eight-tentacled cave guardian squeezing itself into a tiny cave.

Hazel released his shirt and hooked an elbow against a metal pole, rebalanced her many bags, pecked at her phone, and sipped her sweating iced coffee.

The doors closed, and the subway rumbled. Its movement pressed his weight into the metal. A *thub-thub-thub* pressured his ears.

So many heartbeats echoed around him in the small space. An entire mer city's worth of souls glowed in this one car. And although he sensed gazes on him, the other humans diligently avoided eye contact. No one spoke or moved.

Then the car slowed and stopped.

"The subway is experiencing a delay," a disembodied voice announced, and the humans in the subway groaned. "We apologize. Please remain in your car as we may move unexpectedly."

"Of all the days." Hazel tapped her forehead against the pole. "I should have known."

Several more stops and starts followed the delay. At one station, Hazel was near the door when it opened, and a waft of scratchy, irritating air gusted in. Everyone covered their mouths. Hazel coughed, backed away, and waved her hand. "Ugh. That's the mace I was telling you about."

An attack right in the lungs? How effective against humans.

Another passenger passed out small wet squares with a liquid called milk of magnesia. The white substance removed the irritant from her skin and bags but was not effective on fabric. She removed her outer coverings and placed them in a bag.

By the time they reached their destination and exited, Hazel faced him on the busy street with a dilemma.

"I'm off in five minutes. Did you want to go to the office? Pick up bride profiles?"

"No."

"Right, because you don't want to meet any brides. Too bad for them."

For them?

Not for her?

Her thumbs flashed over the phone screen. "Okay, I think we can get a rideshare over here."

He strolled after her. "You have no wish to become a bride?"

"Oh, I work for MerMatch. I'm not a candidate."

Good.

But instead of relief, a squiggly sensation of alarm awoke deep in his abdomen.

"Ugh. Why are all the ride shares disappearing?" She pivoted. "Try this way. I think we can catch one more easily up here. Oh, there is no way I'm getting across town in this traffic."

He followed her across the streets. "Why not?"

"Hmm? Because it's—wait. You mean, why am I not a candidate? Look at me." She stopped at a corner, standing slightly apart from the crowd, and gestured at her body. "Do I look like a bride?"

Yes.

With her soft brown hair brushing her cheeks, her strong arms easily carrying heavy weights for hours, and her chest glowing with fierce devotion, she looked overwhelmingly like a bride.

Mine.

The urge to claim her welled in his soul, flooding his body with heat. He needed to grab her arms and tear the weights off. Unburden her, strip her, kiss her. Start at her crown, work down to her toes and up again, until he knew every inch and she knew he was hers forever.

You are mine.

Her smile faded and brown eyes unfocused. Her lips parted and her chin lifted. Readying herself for his kiss.

His claim.

His heart thudded. Faster and faster. His fingers twitched at his sides.

Their bodies communicated what their mouths would not. And if she looked at him for one moment longer, he was going to forget himself and—

The crowd suddenly strode away from them.

She shook herself and whirled, hurrying to catch up. "Well, even if you wanted to marry me, I wouldn't say yes. You can't start a business underwater."

Huh?

Even if...

But he was not looking for a bride.

Why was he upset?

Everything was wrong. Everything was upside down.

"Ooh, and here's my rideshare!" She hurried to a car sliding perpendicular into a spot a few feet from them. "Get in before someone steals it."

He should not spend more time with her.

Even though watching her friend's video was the only way to proceed against the Sons of Hercules.

He stopped beside her.

"Are you coming?" She waved from the open door. "Hey. Are you all right?"

No.
Definitely not.
Absolutely no.
"Yes," he said and entered the car.

FOUR

Hazel was one hundred percent *not* excited to bring Lotar to her meetup.

Even though her heart wanted to burst from her chest, she nearly bounced out of her mules, and she kept humming the opening to the *Sound of Music*, which was currently showing on Broadway.

Definitely not excited.

Not for the whole rideshare, with her pepper-sprayed blazer tucked into a plastic shopping bag (secured with a twisty tie, both from her mini backpack) and a little tingle in her nose.

Their driver sneezed. "So, you guys new in town? Or what?"

"I'm not. He is." She texted her meetup friends plus Dannika to give updates.

"Yeah? Where you from? Those tattoos—you like an albino Maori or something like that?"

Lotar's gray eyes fixed on her.

Sizzles of awareness fizzed in her belly. "He's from Atlantis."

"Yeah? That ocean city, huh? That makes him one of those mermen. I watch the news. I know about stuff." He sneezed again and rubbed his nose. "Allergies are bad today."

Yeah, his allergy to mace.

Aw, poor guy. "You can let us out here."

"Here? Right here? You got it." He sneezed a third time and pulled over a few blocks from the restaurant.

She tipped the driver hazard pay through the app and set off.

Lotar ambled after her. His gaze was constantly moving, and he missed nothing. He fixed on her with an acuteness that set the butterflies in her stomach aflutter.

But unlike her usual hookups, a merman didn't fall in and out of love. He stayed, pinned by devotion.

Forever.

Goose bumps crinkled up her arms.

She rubbed them down.

Hello. Getting ahead of herself much?

Yes, his iridescent gray gaze sent little licks of fire through her veins, but when a merman found his bride, the whole world knew it.

Ciran had emerged on the docks, back when there weren't as many rules about mermen coming onto land, and he'd moved on Dannika within the first minute. While Hazel had been busy juggling shorts and shirts and flip-flops for the nude warriors and trying not to get too big of an eyeful—and the emphasis was on big—he'd declared to the world that Dannika was his soul mate.

It had been kind of funny to watch her serene, suave boss blush and drop her pens. Dannika had the same capacity to be awkward as Hazel, yet she was usually an articulate, well-put-together, amazing director who dined with senators and spoke with CEOs.

How could Hazel ever go from frumpy wannabe to Dannika-level grace?

But anyway, the other warriors had nabbed their brides right away. If more than five minutes passed, the speed date was over. No match.

She'd finally point-blank asked him. *Hey. Is it true that you know your soul mate as soon as you set eyes on her?*

No one had ever accused Hazel of being subtle.

But a desperate need required an immediate answer.

And Lotar had stared at her for a hot, gorgeous, intense minute and uttered a meaningless answer. *Sometimes.*

But he kept looking at her.

Even now. As she dragged him across town because she'd felt guilty about subjecting an innocent driver to a chemical irritant. "At least there's no pepper spray underwater. Right?"

They stopped at a light.

His quiet voice sounded dangerously close to her ear. "There are worse things underwater."

If he was trying to scare her, he'd have to do it in a voice that didn't sound like it belonged in her bedroom—followed by the sensual graze of his teeth. "Like what?"

"Poisons. Traps. Predators."

"Like sharks?"

His gray-with-silver gaze focused on her. He was the only shark. So near she could almost feel his breath over the humid evening. Wet like his tongue on her. "Worse."

Mm. Teeth.

The light changed, and they crossed with the crowd.

"You are not afraid," he commented.

"About worse? Well, no. It doesn't really affect me."

His lips flattened as if she had confirmed some prejudice.

"What?" she pushed.

"Brides rarely think of defense."

"Beneath the water? Well, yeah, because we've never lived there. Just like nobody knows how to ride the subway at birth."

Hazel led him off the sidewalk and into the aperture of the restaurant, texting her friend they'd arrived.

Pia rushed out and hugged her. Her brown dreadlocks, secured in a Moroccan scarf, smushed Hazel's cheek, and her cute tortoiseshell glasses slid down her nose. "You made it. I saw the delay. And on today, of all days."

"I know." Hazel squeezed her friend and introduced Lotar. "Did you bring the jacket?"

"I brought it." Pia looked up at Lotar and waved with a cheery grin. "The theater just did *The Thick Blue Line*. I had to fit a whole chorus line with leotards and Kevlar."

"Leotards and Kevlar?" Yoshi strode up behind them with his usual thousand-watt grin. Quiet Owen trailed behind. "That's it! That's my new band name."

"What?" Pia hugged the two men. "You're going to start a band? Do either of you even play an instrument?"

Owen, who worked a steady, boring adult job in insurance, shook his head with a blushing smile.

"That hasn't stopped most bands." Yoshi returned Hazel's hug with one arm. His Bluetooth stayed in his ear, and he wore khakis with a polo shirt. "Think of the IP potential."

Inside, Pia stopped at the hostess station and handed Lotar the Kevlar. He was careful to grip the fabric so he didn't touch Pia's fingers.

"This is a bulletproof vest." Hazel grabbed one side of

the vest and helped Lotar shoulder it. Despite a can's worth of Febreze, it definitely smelled like a men's chorus line under hot lights. "It offers some protection from chest shots and air horns."

"Air horns?" Pia repeated and gestured at her ears.

"The sound vibrations hit a merman in the chest. It makes them pass out."

Over the shirt, Hazel's fingers skimmed his pectorals.

They were hard as rock. He had zero body fat and infinite muscle, and all she wanted to do was slip her fingers beneath the mostly dry T-shirt fabric and squeeze.

Mm.

His eyes fixed on her as though he were reading her thoughts. His nostrils flared. A shark scenting not her blood but her arousal.

But still he said nothing.

They followed the hostess through the dinner rush to the table where Erin and Charisma were already sipping cocktails.

Erin had traded a lucrative office career for the massive diamond glinting on her ring finger. Her Coach purse, which sometimes doubled as a diaper bag, hung from the back of her chair.

Charisma was a fashion editor at an international magazine. She wore new designer slacks and a scarf top that had probably debuted on a runway last week.

They all traded greetings and took seats.

Erin waved at Lotar. "Welcome to the Young Entrepreneurs Alumni Meetup."

"Where we're no longer young nor entrepreneurs," Yoshi quipped.

The group laughed.

Their server arrived, and Hazel helped Lotar put in their orders.

"You trust these humans?" he murmured while her friends sipped ice waters and cocktails.

"I do." She didn't bother to keep quiet, and the others listened in. "Way before mermen emerged from the oceans, we all came to New York as finalists in a competition to pitch our business ideas."

"Think Shark Tank for high school kids," Yoshi said.

"And even though most of us went into other careers, we stayed in touch."

"Hazel kept us in touch," Erin said.

Owen asked Pia about her dance troupe audition, but the performance schedule had conflicted with her boyfriend's—who was currently playing the guitar and singing here at this restaurant—so she'd dropped out. "And I got asked to work with top costumers next season. I couldn't say no."

Everyone murmured sympathetically.

Their appetizers arrived.

Hazel dug into a party platter of tangy hummus, spicy baba ghanoush, sweet amba, and spicy schug with toasted pita squares.

She teased Pia. "It sucks when you're too successful and everyone wants to hire you."

Pia tossed a sweet potato fry at her. "You're one to talk! Miss 'I turned down a promotion and quit my job to become a businesswoman.' Of course, if I had your guts, I'd already be in *The Nutcracker*."

"I haven't actually quit my job yet."

"Oh, no? Why not?"

"I was delayed this morning because I had to kick a guy

out of my apartment, and I was delayed this afternoon by, well, everything."

"You had to kick someone out?"

"He didn't respect my rules, so, yeah."

Yoshi tilted his craft brew at her. "Don't let strangers crash for free. You've got to raise capital."

"He wasn't a stranger. He was a friend of my brother."

"Charge 'em," Yoshi said.

"Your room is so cute," Pia said.

"Make your assets work for you," Yoshi said.

"Subletting a studio isn't making an asset work for me," Hazel protested. "It's illegal."

Yoshi rolled his eyes.

"Anyway, most who've crashed were genuine. The instant they're not?" She jerked her thumb over her shoulder. "Out they go."

Lotar's gaze switched from roving the restaurant to focusing on her.

Evaluating her.

And she liked it.

She liked it very much.

Erin tapped her index finger on her wrist. "Oh, Hazel. I've asked around if anyone is interested in going into a Pet Personal Assistant business with you."

"What? I thought you already had a business partner," Pia said.

"She went back to school," Hazel said.

"School? Wasn't that what happened to the woman who was going to help you launch an Iceland Dreams subscription box?"

"No, she went back to teaching."

"Wait, what about the one who was going to teach yoga while you ran a studio coffee bar?"

"Oh, Wake Up and Stretch? Yeah, she moved to Tibet."

Erin snorted. "Where are you finding these people, Hazel? The local swap-and-sell?"

"Everywhere." Hazel fiddled with her napkin. "It's okay. Everyone wants to have a business, but when I draw up the spreadsheet for how much it will cost and how long it will take to break even, they change their minds. Someday I'll find a partner who looks at that spreadsheet and signs up."

"Maybe you should run a business by yourself," Owen said quietly.

"Yeah, but when people work well together, you get this amazing synergy. You can accomplish so much more with a partner than solo."

Lotar's lips compressed. His skepticism was like atomic radiation.

"Doubt all you like," she told him archly. "You're a six-foot-plus warrior, but just so you know, everyone Dannika's matched says working together is way better. And once a bride gets her mermaid queen powers?" Hazel made her fingertips explode outward. "No comparison."

His timber wolf eyes lightened. The corner of his mouth quirked with amusement. "I said nothing."

"Yeah, and that's exactly why you're supposed to be here."

"Oh. Ohhhh." Erin straightened and pointed her manicured finger between the two. "Did I miss something? Are you two...?"

Lotar's amusement faded. He looked down and rubbed his thumbs over his fingertips.

Right.

"No." Hazel gripped her sweating water glass. "Lotar's supposed to meet a bride who does all the talking. She's got to convince a ton of crusty old kings to abandon their traditions, swim to Atlantis, and sing kumbaya. And yes, my boss wants me to spearhead it. I refuse to get any more involved."

"You can throw a party, Hazel," Pia encouraged her.

"I once threw a capstone graduation party that had negative attendance."

Erin choked. "How did that happen?"

"It was so stupid. I accidentally planned it for the same night as graduation."

"Nobody told you?"

"I printed invitations, and everyone I gave them to was like, 'Cool. See you there.' Somehow, they thought I was inviting them to graduation. Like, personally. And the worst thing is I planned the party with two other girls, so it was a joint graduation party."

"What did they do?" Pia asked.

"Overrule me two to one on the color scheme and flavors of the sheet cake," Hazel said.

"True partners." Yoshi lifted his beer in cheers.

"So there I was, sitting with my parents, wondering 'Where is everyone?' when my adviser called. I was supposed to read a motivational quote, and we had ten minutes to reach the stadium which is a fifteen-minute drive away. My dad wrecked the suspension flying over speed bumps. And that's how a graduation party ended with three less people than at the start."

"At least you got cake," Owen said sensibly.

"That was the only good thing. We ran out of cake at the real graduation after-party, so a ton of seniors headed back to my place and demolished my sodas and snacks."

"That sounds fun," Owen said.

"It sounds..." Yoshi pointed his fingers like two guns. "Like a successful graduation party."

"It was the second-worst stress of my life." Hazel pressed her hands flat on the table. "You know I used to work at a call center? Cold calls trying to convince people to want something they didn't want? That's what the All-Cities Gyre is going to be, only underwater, and for two years."

The others nodded, sympathetic again.

"Maybe you just need the right partner," Owen said.

Charisma sipped her wine. "Our magazine is only as good as our writers."

"The writers you can attract," Hazel said. "You attract the best writers because you're the best."

"Are you calling yourself unattractive?" Yoshi asked.

They all laughed at him.

"You could work for us," Owen told Hazel. "It doesn't start out great, but it's steady."

"Thanks. I'll keep it in mind if nothing else comes through."

"Charisma's right, though," Erin said. "If you want to move up, shoot for the moon. Even if you miss, you'll land among the stars."

"Or burn up in the atmosphere," Yoshi quipped.

Again, everyone laughed.

Charisma rested her glass on its stem. "It would be fascinating to see the undersea cities. How exotic. Whoever takes that position will have quite a story to tell."

"A naked story," Yoshi said. "There are no clothes underwater. Your fashion magazine will be uninterested."

"We might be interested." Her gaze flickered over Lotar's tattoos. "These lines have meanings, don't they? We had an issue on tattoos a few years ago. Most of our stories on the mer cover your Sea Opals, their healing properties, and uses in cosmetics and jewelry. Can you shift? Right now?"

Lotar's gaze flickered over the restaurant. He lifted his hand and spread his fingers. The webbing between his fingers increased and tightened.

The table oohed.

His hand was so big.

What would it feel like on her body?

Palming her breasts?

Lower...

"And just think. You'd travel the undersea world as one of them." Erin sighed and rotated her wedding ring. "If I didn't seriously love my husband, I might apply to be a mermaid bride."

"Well, but New York is also pretty cool." Hazel indicated their neighborhood with her fork. "You can travel the world by walking a few blocks. Chinatown, Little Italy, Little Senegal in Harlem..."

Yoshi snorted. "Time to buy up waterfront property for the inevitable Merman Town."

They all chuckled.

"You'd see all the hidden sights." Charisma ticked them off on her slim fingers. "The wreck of the *Titanic*. Undersea Atlantis. The kraken."

Erin nodded.

Exotic travel. Once-in-a-lifetime encounters with whales and other undersea life. Adventure after adventure.

And all wrapped in Lotar's highly capable arms...

Sure, she'd thought about it.

Hazel sighed. "I'd find some way to screw it up."

"Are you actually considering it? You sound a little interested." Pia tried to comfort her. "You'd just be delivering the invitation, right? You can do that."

"You'd be a glorified post office," Yoshi said. "But with fewer rabid dogs and entitled owners."

"You'd be really good at it," Pia agreed.

They were trying to encourage her.

And if she thought about it, sure, Dannika would still have to spearhead the party. Hazel would just deliver the invitations.

Of course, none of it mattered. The only person who was delivering anything was Lotar's bride.

And as for deciding on his bride, Lotar remained dead silent.

These friends made Hazel's soul brighten.

And she worried about the least important part of the All-Cities Gyre. Reaching the cities was the most difficult task. Convincing anyone inside to attend? An afterthought.

Better that no one came. There would be less risk to Atlantis.

Was that the only reason she rejected becoming a bride?

Hazel's tawny gaze flickered to him. "It doesn't matter what I think. It just matters what Lotar's bride thinks."

A hot pulse of longing flooded his groin.

You are my bride.

She had the skills and defensive thinking to survive even the early part of the All-Cities Gyre before she came into her full power.

He tightened his control.

"Well, you'll figure it out," Pia told Hazel. "It might take a while, but you always do."

"And remember, only current and former employees of

the post office can go postal," Yoshi said. "But keep it to yourself. They hate that joke."

Everyone laughed.

Hazel's chest glowed. "Yeah, I'll keep it in mind."

Their conversation changed to other topics. Erin's phone rang, and she turned away from the table to speak to her husband. Her soul glowed.

A male leaned over Pia's shoulder and helped himself to her long crinkly sticks.

"Hey." Her soul light brightened in welcome. "Did you want me to order you something? Those are my fries."

"I'm doing you a favor." He finished her fries, licked his fingers, and grinned. "You want to fit into your cute clothes, right?"

Her soul dimmed. She looked away and tucked her hair behind her ear. "Yeah..."

He dropped a kiss on her cheek, wiped his fingers, and departed.

Owen leaned forward. "Your clothes are cute."

"Thanks." Her soul brightened, and she gave him a sweet smile. A matching light kindled in Owen's chest.

"Hey." From his performance place, the other male snapped his fingers and mouthed Pia's name. "Drink?"

"Oh, yeah." She hurried over with a glass of bubbling liquid.

Owen watched her leave.

Hazel nudged him. "Hey, Owen. Lotar wants to hear about the Sons of Hercules meeting."

Owen straightened and wrinkled his nose. "It was juvenile. Puerile. I wouldn't go again."

"Did you still have the recording?"

"No, I erased it as soon as you said you were done. I only wish I could erase the memory from my head."

"Why?" Lotar asked.

"They weren't nice. Not to themselves or each other. They were nasty in a self-destructive way and preyed on humanity's worst instincts."

"I'm glad you were okay," Hazel said.

"I sat in the back and didn't participate. They barely talked about mermen. I doubt they've ever seen one. They spent most of their time making minority and rape jokes, punching each other, and casually destroying property." Owen lifted his plate and scraped the rest of his fries onto Pia's plate. "It wasn't a pleasant way to spend an evening."

So. The Sons of Hercules truly were disorganized. And yet they had caused so much pain.

"We could probably find a video of a meeting online," Hazel told Lotar. "I bet Owen's not the only one that ever made a recording."

Owen's brows rose. "They would post cringe videos just to make viewers uncomfortable, sure."

Hmm.

When the mer gathered to discuss an enemy, they spoke of tactics. Honor. Grievances. Real strategies to defeat real enemies. Not insults to each other or play fighting.

When a mer drew his dagger, he aimed for the heart.

And the heart was the leader.

Someday, Lotar *would* look into the eyes of his enemies and see their fear.

But now?

The signs of his prey faded, leaving him adrift. Directionless. Without a goal.

Well, that was untrue.

If he did not stay to hunt the Sons of Hercules, he should leave on the All-Cities Gyre.

The Sons of Hercules caused pain on the surface.

But the traditionalist All-Council crushed rebels such as the Atlantis warriors beneath the sea. Would Hazel's party unite the warring factions? He would find out.

"So what are you going to do now?" Hazel asked quietly. "Get started on the All-Cities Gyre? Meet up with brides after all? Sightsee?"

"I do not need to meet with brides."

"Are you sure? I heard those queen powers are nice. And they might come in handy when crossing the ocean."

"Queen powers take time to develop." He held up his hand and ticked off his fingers. "During the early stages, my bride will be vulnerable. She will be afraid. Other warriors might threaten her. She would be unable to defend herself."

"So you need a woman who's smart, cautious, and brave as well as being a great speaker, friendly, organized, and a total diplomat."

How amusing. She described herself.

And he could not argue. The more he watched her, the more capability she showed. She would transition well to the undersea world. Even to the deadly circumstances of the All-Cities Gyre.

A wave of compulsion welled beneath him, up swelling his need to take her. Claim her. Embark on a journey with only one destination.

But he would never fulfill his role as her husband.

She deserved a better warrior than Lotar.

Deserved...but it was very hard to stop the selfish desires from taking hold. He curled his fingers around the soft weave of the cream dining cloth.

"I have a stack of bride profiles back at the office. Or you can look around here." Hazel indicated the other diners. "Of course it would be awkward if you resonated with someone like Erin or Pia, but you're the merman, so you can see soul lights and know if I'm—if someone is your mate."

She should know that he was her soul mate. Even a human could sense that much.

"Erin or Pia?" he queried.

"Erin's married."

Erin lifted her phone with a smile.

"And Pia's here with her boyfriend." Hazel waved at the direction Pia had gone with the other male.

Wait.

"He is not her soul mate," Lotar said.

Hazel's smile faltered. "Well, it's a newer relationship, so you can't say for sure."

"He does not make her soul shine."

"But maybe they have to grow into it. You know."

"No."

Hazel bit her lip. "But sometimes people hate each other and become lovers, or they start out fighting and end up the greatest love story of all time."

"Then they fight a battle inside. Against their own true heart or clouded mind. Not each other."

"Oh, I think they fight each other..."

"Souls must resonate. You may fight resonance, ignore it, run from it, but if you pursue a mate whose soul does not resonate with yours, you cannot ever truly unite your bodies or produce young fry."

"Ah." She lifted a finger. "That's a mer thing. Humans can have sex with anybody."

Oh.

Yes. He had forgotten. "Why?"

Hazel shrugged. "We don't need resonance, I guess. People fall in and out of crappy relationships every day. We don't have your clarity, so things get muddied up real quick."

How horrifying.

The others chuckled gently about bad dates, grudges changing over to passion, and ugly divorces. Owen frowned, lost in thought, and poked a green leaf around his plate.

Hazel strangely accepted this tragedy. "You always start out hoping for the best."

"But you must know." He pressed his palm against the thick bulletproof vest. "And if you force this union, your souls will only vibrate more erratically. Disharmony will fill your heart and tear you apart."

Yoshi chimed in. "That happened to more than a few of my buddies. Where were you ten years ago? You could have saved them a killing in divorce fees."

The others laughed.

Pia sat with a small huff, frowned at the fries, and straightened. "Did someone get me more fries?"

Everyone looked at Owen.

"I had too many," Owen said.

"Aw." She brightened and dusted the fries with seasonings, then ate one. "That's so sweet. You shouldn't have."

His soul glowed as well.

"Hey, Pia." Yoshi gestured at Lotar. "This guy can see if people are soul mates. Guess what he said about your boyfriend?"

Her soul dimmed. She laughed with a pained expression and held up her hand without looking at Lotar. "I don't want to know."

She did not want to know?

"I do not see soul mates," Lotar corrected them. "I only see if another person dims your light."

"No thanks." She cheerfully scooted the fry through the seasonings. "I just skipped an audition I've been in training for over two years, so let's pretend everything is fine."

After a brief pause, the others quickly agreed.

"Yeah, that's right," Hazel comforted her. "Mermen don't know everything."

"Exactly." Pia chomped her fries.

But this was a mistake.

The longer Pia stayed with a male who dimmed her light, the further she would stray from her true destiny. Two years would stretch into five years. Longer. All because she tied herself to a male who dimmed her soul. And if she never left? She would shrink in, darker and smaller, until her light was extinguished.

"You know..." Hazel drummed her fingers on the table. "Maybe I could start a merman dating assistance program."

"That's what you already do." Erin exchanged a small card with her server. The others opened their bags and handed over cards or papers. "You introduce mermen to dates."

"No, no. Couples would hire a merman to say whether their soul lights resonate. 'Is this guy your soul mate, or are you wasting your time?' We could hire ourselves out for first dates, speed dates, bars, clubs. Marriage counselors. So many things." Hazel touched Lotar's hand.

Fire raced up his arm, and his heart thudded hard.

"Did Erin's soul get bright or dim when she called her husband?" Hazel asked, not seeming to notice.

He ground out the word. "Bright."

Erin beamed. "I could have told you that."

"How about me?" Yoshi threw his arm around Charisma, who was sipping her water. "Do I make her soul shine?"

Charisma eyed him. Their souls remained steady, neither dimming nor brightening.

Lotar shook his head.

Charisma smiled into her glass.

Yoshi straightened. "I'd say it's accurate. Hazel, call my firm. If you saved people from expensive divorces, you could print money."

"Oh, I know. How many bad dates have we been on?" Hazel removed her hand from his, letting him relax. She shuddered and signed the slip of paper from her server. "So many."

"So many," Charisma agreed, and Pia echoed her.

"Too bad you've got to go on the All-Cities Gyre," Hazel told him. "We'll just have to stumble around until the next merman gets a visa."

Heat flushed into his pores. The human food he'd consumed churned.

Lotar had been selfish.

So very, very selfish.

Hazel was seeking her soul mate among humans. She had made mistakes like Pia, and she had allowed her soul to be darkened.

And after he left her, she would make such mistakes again.

Because he was her soul mate.

A dim-souled male must not approach Hazel. Touch her hand as she'd touched his. Brush her hair back from her rounded cheek, or kiss...

His belly clenched.

No.

Another male would not brighten her soul.

Another male might damage her, as Pia's boyfriend did. And the longer Hazel dimmed herself and made herself small, the harder it would be for her to grow fearless again and unconquerable.

And she must be that. Because only when she shone as brightly as a star could she claim her true powers.

She would be a phenomenal mer queen.

And leaving her behind was far more dangerous.

"Well." Hazel pushed back her chair, stood, and stretched. "Should we get you to a hotel? It's been a long day. I'll look over the profiles again and you could at least meet a couple brides."

Lotar stood as well. "No."

"Hey, come on. You might meet the bride of your dreams."

"I have."

Hazel blinked. "You've met a smart, brave, organized, great speaker, total diplomat bride?"

He nodded.

"Who's also your soul mate?"

"Yes."

She blinked again, lashes fluttering like she wanted to look around to see who he meant when the answer could not be more obvious.

And then she understood.

Her chest flared. Bright. A star within a sun. Her soul reacted to his, their resonance building as their souls entwined. "You think...? A great speaker? Is...right now?"

He pulled her into his arms.

This was right. It was responsible.

She might hate him someday.

But he did this for her.

Hazel rested her hands against his thick vest. "But...me?"

"You."

SIX

What?

What, what, what, what?

Lotar's fierce gaze scorched her. His hard body was unyielding, like hugging a plank, and the arm that curled around her cinched tight. He had stalked her, studied her, hunted her. And now he pounced.

He thought she was smart.

And brave.

And organized, and cautious, and a good speaker, and...

Yes. He really did.

He...did.

A gush of heat flooded her body.

This total warrior who had so arrogantly assured her he would never bring a bride on the All-Cities Gyre because she couldn't handle the dangers was now equally confident that Hazel could.

He thought she could do this.

Dannika thought she could do this. Her friends thought she could do this.

The only one who wasn't sure was Hazel.

But with the right partner, maybe she could accomplish anything.

Lotar thought so.

And with every cell, she wanted to straddle his waist and say, *Yes. Absolutely. Right now.*

His lips swooped toward hers.

A first kiss—

"What?" her friends cried. "Hold up. Wait, what?"

He tensed, arrested, and his gaze flicked over her shoulder, evaluating the danger.

Her first kiss...

Hazel licked her untouched lips, eased onto her heels, and faced her friends. Lotar released her much too easily. "Okay, I know it's sudden, but that's how it is for mermen."

"Lotar." Yoshi crossed his arms. "I must grill the two of you like you're asking my daughter's hand in marriage."

Erin snorted. "You don't have a daughter."

"Someday I might, and I have to practice." Yoshi pointed at Hazel. "You met him today?"

"Yep."

"And is he your soul mate?"

"We're vibing."

"Vibing, vibing..." Yoshi pulled out his novelty keychain, a small black eight ball, and shook it. "Is 'vibing' good enough? ... 'All signs point to yes.' Well, there's nothing I can do, guys. The fates have spoken. So watch out for crazy underwater homeowners and loose dogs. Because, you know. Postman."

Oh, God.

The All-Cities Gyre.

But Lotar pulled her to his side and looked down at her. She could almost hear him. *Do not dim your soul light.* They would figure out her fear of ruining the All-

Cities Gyre. His fear of taking a bride into the dangerous blue.

Somehow.

But how?

The dinner broke up with more congratulations and requests for postcards—impossible since the spots she'd surface were isolated islands—and Hazel called up another rideshare. Her thoughts pinwheeled.

Was this happening? Was she crazy?

The rideshare dropped them at the familiar steps of her apartment building. She input the security code and led Lotar into the narrow entrance. This building creaked with a stuffy smell, but it had AC, and the prewar tile had a nice old-style charm.

She got in the clattering elevator.

Oh.

They weren't supposed to be here.

"Ah, crap." She held out her hand to stop the doors, but they closed and the elevator ascended. "We're supposed to go to your hotel."

He studied her. The elevator was suddenly way too small for the two of them, and she pressed her back against the metal wall. His soft voice tickled her ear like the first nibble of a kiss. "Is it a problem?"

"It's autopilot. I'm used to bringing friends back to my place. It's not a great place, but for somebody looking to crash for a night, it's okay. The bed's kind of small." Especially considering his height and delicious, looming presence. "It might not be what you're used to."

He followed her out of the elevator and down the hall. She unlocked the triple locks and pushed open the door.

The small studio got great reflected light for its position in the middle of the building, with a neat terrace she was going to grow her own urban garden on someday, a dusting of twinkle lights she'd someday use to make a wall feature, and bunches of succulents atop her freecycle shelves. It wasn't much, but she was proud of it, and it was always neat because...

Her pothos, Phil, had tumbled off his shelf, and dirt sprayed across the floor. The bed looked like someone had thrown a fit in it, and a shredded cereal box cluttered her counter. The smell of sour milk hit her nose.

"Oh God."

She dropped the bag of pepper-sprayed clothes, relocked the door behind them, then hurriedly scooped Phil back into his container—cracked, and she'd liked that thrift store find, what a pity—and put him on the counter while she dumped the half-filled bowl of soured cereal milk.

"Sorry about the mess. The guy who stayed last night was supposed to be chill. My brother and his girlfriend both vouched for him, but it turns out he was a jerk who wanted me to be his hotel."

He'd tried to take her bed and make her sleep on the guest futon, but she'd shut that right down. In the morning, his attitude had gotten worse. And he'd slammed the door when they were leaving, which must have knocked her pothos off the shelf.

Poor Phil.

And he'd had the gall to complain to her brother *and* post on her class's Facebook group. She'd gotten so mad posting what really happened that she'd almost missed her stop.

But whatever. "The bed's a little short for you. I'm guessing you normally sleep in a long. Right?"

Lotar peered out her window as though securing all exits, then prowled back to her. "No."

"Really? Huh."

"I have never slept in a human bed."

A wave of awareness washed over her. "Never?"

He focused on her with sweet intensity. A single, efficient shake of his head sent her heart throbbing.

Pulsing into her body.

Because he was a warrior who'd found his bride.

She swallowed and slowly stood. "So...soul mates. You think maybe I could be yours?"

"No. I know." He looked down on her. "You are."

Dominant intensity crackled off his ripped body. He stood so large in the enclosed space, and she wanted to kiss his neck, unbutton the shirt, find the muscle she'd briefly seen in the customs room, and lick.

But she had to tell him...

Her nose tickled.

The pepper spray, right.

"We should..." Her throat closed. She coughed and cleared it. "You should get a shower."

"Shower?"

"Yeah, this way." She led him into the tiny bathroom, navigated around the toilet, and pulled open the door. She barely fit her knees around the toilet, but that meant they'd fit an entire three-quarters shower inside. For her, it was luxurious. She twisted the dials and aimed the special upgraded rain showerhead she'd bought. "Here's hot and here's cold."

Oh, if he'd never slept in a bed before, had he never used a shower either? She stepped back. "You take off your clothes, and..."

He stood right behind her. For being so large, he was impressively silent. His clothes were piled outside the door.

He was fully nude.

And those tattoos, like his muscles, went all the way down.

Long gray slashes across his abdomen, thighs, calves. Cock. The bulge in his shorts hadn't been her imagination. He was impressively sized, girthy, something to really get her hands around—and currently relaxed. But the longer she stared as the shower pattered and gentle steam fogged the small mirror, his cock lengthened and hardened, as though summoned by her attention.

An answering tingle filled her body.

She'd been excited about a man before, but this felt different. Instead of being swept up in a hazy night of passion, she felt clear-eyed, in control.

And that was kind of scary in itself.

It was much easier to get swept away, honestly.

She unbuttoned her blouse, half-heartedly folded it, and placed it on the toilet lid. The rest of her clothes went the same way. She stood nude before him.

His gaze traveled down her body, crown to toes, and back up again.

And what did he see? The roots she needed to dye again, as soon as she decided whether her next color was going to be mocha latte or mahogany. The old manicure that needed filing and fills. Her not-perky, asymmetrical, side-set breasts, her elephant-skin elbows that absorbed moisturizer like a sponge, her knobby knees scarred with years of diving for softballs in uneven fields, climbing for badminton birdies in rough trees, and unsuccessfully trying to teach herself how to inline skate. The extra five pounds on her belly. The extra fifteen on her butt.

He saw it all without judgment. This was who she was. Totally open, totally revealed. His gaze lifted to her eyes. The dark pupils pulled her in. The iridescent gray threads had overwhelmed what she now saw were ordinary light blue irises.

Her mom had blue eyes, which meant she had half the alleles and they'd have a fifty-fifty chance of having a baby with blue eyes.

"Ah." She cleared her throat and backed to the closed shower door. "So let's wash off the pepper spray and, uh, everything else."

She opened the door for him to enter, and he did so.

"The soap's there." She pointed at the bar. "Lather and rinse. Um, you're going to smell like vanilla and cardamom. I hope you don't mind."

He swept the soap over his skin, efficient and functional, and handed the bar to her. She eased into the shower, closing the door behind her, and edged around his body to get under the water. He eased out of her way, effortlessly moving without their skin even touching. She washed her hair for good measure. He watched her intently, a solid presence taking up most of her shower, but he didn't attack.

Now he was clean and she was clean.

His cock was hard.

He still didn't make a move.

She brushed the tattoos on his sternum. "These have a meaning, right? What does this one mean?"

"It is the symbol of my city."

"Atlantis?"

"My origin city. Syrenka."

She traced the lines up. The snowflake pattern branched into geometric shapes. Smaller hashes and squares divided each square. "Where's Syrenka?"

"North."

The steam of the shower wrapped them in slippery fog.

This moment slipped outside of time.

She was still terrified about what accepting Lotar would mean. The fate of the mermen would rest on her small shoulders.

But she had already decided.

She'd decided when she'd brought him back to her apartment.

The door was there. She'd already opened it.

Now she just had to walk through.

Hazel lowered her hand and forced herself to look up into his deep, watchful eyes. "What happens now?"

"You accept my claim."

"I thought I did."

"With a kiss."

Right. She'd gotten him naked and seen everything but still hadn't shared a kiss.

Hazel did everything out of order.

Whatever. It didn't matter. All that mattered was that she took the next step.

Her stomach filled with butterflies. She was ready. She chose this. She chose him.

Hazel closed her eyes and lifted her lips.

And...

...

Nothing.

She opened her eyes.

Lotar looked conflicted.

A dark frown slashed his brow. His worried gaze fixed on her lips and all his muscles flexed, taut, as he struggled.

When he noticed her question, he blinked as though trying to clear away his emotions, concealing an internal fight behind the quiet, impassive watchfulness.

He'd said she was his soul mate. He knew. And the next step was to kiss...

"Okay, well." She patted his chest. "When you want to do that, let me know."

She turned away to shut off the water.

Lotar's hand closed over her wrist.

He pulled her back, gently but decisively.

Haha, okay, maybe she had misread him. "Oh, hey, you—"

His mouth covered hers in a kiss.

Ah.

The shower pattered on her back. The scent of vanilla and cardamom mixed with sea salt and male.

Heat streaked through her body.

Lotar.

He was all kinds of muscle, hardness and pride, strength and dominance.

His mouth opened, and his tongue sought hers.

She licked his intoxicating male flavor, lapped up every drop, teasing his mouth, delving and swirling, nibbling.

His hand at her wrist tightened and the heat of his body crossed the last inch to draw her against him. Her thigh slid against his, her belly pressed his upper hip, her breasts slid against his chest.

He pursued her mouth doggedly. She teased him, swirling and looping until he released her lips. Then she bit his sharp jaw with little nips and grazed her teeth across his rough chin.

He sucked in a breath.

Yes.

Her nipples tightened to hard pearls, and desire streaked into her center.

He was quiet but expressive. Ready but uncertain.

And that was just fine.

She kissed down the column of his neck, over the cord

of the spiral shell necklace, to his collarbone. So broad, so powerful. Down his pectorals, over the swirling tattoos. Like kissing ice fields, but hot and trembling. This was as meaningful to him as it was to her. After tonight, their lives would never be the—

He caught her wrists, stopping her.

Uncertainty flashed in his eyes.

No, not uncertainty.

Fear.

He stared at her with absolute terror.

Huh?

Had she gotten it all wrong?

———

HAZEL LOOKED UP AT HIM, worry tilting her head. "Are you okay?"

He nodded.

Because he was. He was more than okay.

His soul mate opened her body to him, pressed her soft form to his, accepted, and even covered him with hungry kisses. She wanted his claim. His kiss, his caress, his touch.

It was a dream.

And yet.

His heart pounded as if a pack of angry bull sharks had scented him.

Hazel was so open. So confident in the moment of melding their bodies to create a young fry. Easy and yet serious, playful and yet passionate. She was a pure and beautiful soul.

He must protect her.

From danger, from injury.

From himself.

Her lips curved, her worries fading to a comfortable glow, and she rested her fingers gently on his shoulders. "Then..." She placed a soft kiss against his collarbone.

Yes, he wanted her kiss.

He needed her to desire him.

She kissed over the angular broadness of his chest and descended over his ribs toward his—

May your young fry curse you as you have cursed me.

His hands tightened around her wrists, stopping her at his waist.

This was dangerous.

For her.

He lifted her back to her feet, away from his hard cock.

"Huh?" She frowned, her lips pressed together in a pout, and her hair hung in beautiful wet ropes down her back. "Did you not want to do the whole claim? Mermen usually have a thing about melding their bodies as fast as possible. I'm on the pill, although I guess we'll have to talk about how that's happening underwater, and I have a box of condoms in the cabinet, but..." She frowned. "Or, wait. Aren't you supposed to give me your Sea Opal?"

His mating gemstone.

Curse it.

He had been so certain...

The confession forced itself through his gritted teeth. "I do not have it."

"Oh, yeah? Where is it?"

"Atlantis."

"You left it behind?"

"I did not carry unnecessary weight."

Hazel raised her hand to her forehead, even though he was still holding her wrist. Instead of dimming herself with anger or sadness, she laughed. "You thought you wouldn't find a bride so you didn't bother to bring it with you? Oh, man. Talk about self-sabotage. Can I even still transform?"

"Yes. Of course."

"Of course? I thought it was kind of a big deal."

"It is."

A warrior gave his mating gemstone to his bride as a symbol of his commitment, as part of the ceremony of the ancient covenant, and to increase their resonance.

Where a bride fought herself and rejected her soul's resonance, the mating gemstone refocused her. It was made of the resin of a mer's Life Tree. A pure offering of the sea. And most brides could not resist its soothing, healing shape and color.

But Hazel had already accepted his claim and opened her soul to his. She eagerly united their bodies. When she drank the elixir and they kissed, she would easily transform.

She did not need his mating gemstone. "You can still transform. In Atlantis, you will accept my mating gemstone and complete the marriage ceremony."

"Right, I have to drink the nectar of the Life Tree blossom to make my transformation powers permanent." She lowered her hand. "You guys used to say that the elixir would wear off, but now you aren't worried about it?"

He shook his head.

Several queens had never drunk Life Tree blossom nectar, and their abilities had lasted decades.

Once, no warrior ever questioned the traditions parroted by the All-Council.

But now, rebels questioned many things.

He still wanted to complete the marriage ceremony. He wanted to gift his mating gemstone. He wanted Hazel.

But.

Whatever the meaning of a pill or condoms were, he

could not risk uniting their bodies. He could never risk fathering a young fry.

"So if that's not the problem..." She looked down at his hands, still holding her wrists. "I'm sorry. I forgot that mermen can't, you know." She gestured at his hard cock.

He did not know.

"You know. You can't, um, practice. Or anything. You only react to your soul mate."

Ah. That was true.

"So this isn't just your first time with me. It's not just your first time with a woman. It's your first time getting hard. And here I am, blazing through." She laughed at herself. "The last half hour has probably been a lot of firsts for you. Want to just snuggle?"

"Snuggle?"

"Yeah. Here, I'll show you." She wriggled her wrists. "You'll like it. Trust me."

He released her.

She rinsed her face and hair, stopped the shower, and dried herself with a hanging towel and handed one to him. She spread creams on her face, scrubbed her teeth, and offered him the white paste. "You'll have to use your finger, though. I draw the line at sharing toothbrushes."

He spread the paste on his teeth. It tingled.

And then, treating him much more gently than perhaps anyone had treated his long, lean, deadly body before, she led him by the hand to her bed. There she fluffed the thin sheets and eased him in. "Your feet will stick off the end."

They did.

The bed was a strange, bouncy, creaky rectangle of rustling fabric that urged him to roll to the center.

Hazel hung their towels by a whirring rectangle embedded in the wall near the ceiling. She pulled on a silky top covering with straps and formfitting bottoms that cupped her curves with enticing softness and scooted into the bed beside him, arranging the sheets and fitting her body to his. One knee snugged over his waist. Her head rested at his shoulder. She nuzzled his cheek with her nose. "This is snuggling."

Just touching.

He rested his palm on her buttocks. The material was soft as the tendrils of a fluttering anemone.

She wriggled closer with a sigh. Her bright eyes opened, and she stroked an index finger along his nose. "Does this tattoo have a meaning?"

"The currents I follow and the fish I…" He didn't have the right words. "The fish I resonate with."

"Your soul resonates with fish?"

He shook his head. How to explain? Even warriors didn't talk about this often. "I understand them."

"Their words?"

"Not words. Movements, hungers, needs."

"That's so cool." She traced her finger up across his forehead and down the line of his jaw. "Can anyone read it off your face? Like a social media profile. 'Likes collecting succulents, hoarding supplies for crafts she'll never do, and taking short walks in an air-conditioned mall.' Haha."

Each city had its own unique system of markings. "Only in Syrenka."

"Wow." She yawned and closed her eyes again with a deep sigh. "I can't wait to see it."

A single bolt of electricity burned through his body, a vibrating hot coil.

He had never intended to return. But he must. And worst, he must bring a female.

No, there was still time to change his mind.

He had claimed Hazel with his kiss, but she did not know the true reason for his hesitation to unite their bodies. And when she did know...

In all the annals, in all the stories, he had never heard of a warrior refusing his sacred bride.

He had never heard of a sacred bride *not* carrying a warrior's young fry.

This did not happen.

Tonight was only the first time he could not give his bride what she needed.

And once she realized he would never fulfill her needs, she would leave him.

She wiggled.

Ah, he had tightened his arms. Without noticing, he was squeezing her. Lotar forced himself to relax, and she sighed again.

The day she left him would be cold and hard.

But not yet.

Not yet.

She burrowed closer. "Mm. You know what? It's been a long time since I snuggled with someone. I forgot how nice it was to feel cozy and loved with no pressure. So, thank you. After everything that happened today, I think this was exactly what I needed."

A sharp ache filled his chest.

By degrees, her muscles twitched and relaxed, and she grew heavier with sleep.

His fingers tingled like the white paste she'd given him for his teeth, and then his hand lost feeling.

He endured the numbness, unwilling to wake her.

He'd denied her needs, and this precious female thanked him?

Hazel truly was different.

A small seed of hope unfurled deep within his chest.

Hazel was everything he craved in a soul mate and more. So much more.

Maybe he could tell her the truth.

She would listen. With her bright, sparkling eyes and shining soul, she would let him tell her everything, no matter how long it took. No matter how deeply it terrified him.

She would stay until the end.

And maybe, just maybe, she would understand.

<h1 style="text-align:center">SEVEN</h1>

B*eep-beep-beep-beep...*
　　Hazel woke in an empty bed.
　　In an empty apartment.
With her alarm going off.

Ah, crap.

She rose and stretched. Her feet hit the edge of the futon. She hadn't stored it properly. Oh, yeah. That jerk had made her too late to submit her resignation, so she'd have to do it on Monday...

Wait.

Hazel shut off her weekday alarm. Today was a workday, not a Saturday. Why was she wearing her "pretend you're a rich businesswoman who wears designer bloomers all the time and this isn't TJ Maxx clearance lingerie that Pia tailored one time" which she only wore to lounge with a Moka pot espresso on Saturday morning because they were way too precious to wear all the time?

Oh.

Yeah.

Hey...

Didn't she have a merman in this apartment?

Her phone beeped a low-battery warning.

Crap.

Hazel walked around the apartment. It was a studio, so that didn't take long. Both Lotar and the futon couldn't fit under the bed, seeing as Lotar could barely fit *on* the bed. The bathroom was empty. Her keys were on the hook next to the door, and the door was still triple-bolted, which meant he hadn't gone out the front door...

She opened up her cabinets.

Why? He was a six-foot-plus merman, not a cat.

And he had been so cute last night. She'd gone into her now-we're-going-to-have-sex zone, and when he'd stopped her, the panic in his eyes had been refreshing. Well, not the panic, exactly. Taking it slow with her meant something to him. Most guys she dated rushed for the finish, and she had to fight for her share of fun. She had to remind plenty of otherwise considerate guys to slow down and maybe, you know, actually do some foreplay.

Sex was the ultimate team sport, so Hazel was super picky with her partners, but Lotar was different. They'd figure it out. And as he was her soul mate, they'd have all the time in the world.

Plus she was still so thrilled and grateful he thought she could do this. Go on this All-Cities Gyre. Be a diplomat, like Dannika, and change the world.

Please let me be sensible enough to touch the mermen's hearts and change the world.

But where had he gone?

Her phone rang, and she answered in a panic. "Lotar?"

"Hi, Hazel, I'm sorry to bother you so early, but something's come up, and I'm wondering if I can impose on you," her boss said.

"Oh, Dannika, I am so sorry. I lost Lotar."

"You lost him?"

"I woke up and he was gone."

"Oh. I applaud your dedication, Hazel, but you are allowed to have personal time. Please don't feel that you have to spend your off-hours watching over him."

"But he's not here."

"Well, maybe he's at the hotel breakfast."

"You don't understand. We're not at the hotel, we're at my studio. And I just..." She sat on the bed. Dannika wasn't even in the office to get a resignation letter. She'd lost Lotar. Everything was falling apart. "I think I messed up everything forever. You need a new program assistant."

"You're doing a wonderful job." Dannika's encouraging smile was audible across the phone. "I promise you, Hazel, you're more capable than you know."

Dannika only said that because she couldn't see it from Hazel's perspective. She was much taller, willowy and graceful, from some rich family in Maryland with gardens and peacocks. Her boudoir panties were real.

"Now, I was calling to let you know we had trouble with the cell booster on Sanctuary Island, and so for the next week, you'll be here on your own."

"I can't do this."

"You really can. You ran the whole office by yourself when my plane crashed and everyone presumed me dead, and you did a fabulous job."

Hazel had only done that because the Mer-Human Alliance, the foundation that ran MerMatch.com, had promised they were hiring a new head matchmaker. All she'd had to do was go into the office every day, answer phones, return emails, and direct everything else to the foundation director.

Of course, she'd cried a whole bunch when Dannika's plane had suddenly disappeared, and she'd cried even harder from joy when Dannika turned out to be alive and well with a group of castaways on Sanctuary Island.

"Call in the list of bride candidates you selected," Dannika continued. "I thought your instincts were excellent. Lotar doesn't say much, but when he meets the right woman, I'm sure she'll understand."

Oh.

Haha, that was true.

And that raised a whole other point. "Um, actually, though, I do have to quit."

"Hazel, I love your dramatic flair, but your tone of voice suggests this isn't hyperbole."

"It's not." She rubbed her face. "I was going to turn in my two weeks' notice yesterday, but I got waylaid, but actually—even if I haven't lost Lotar... But supposing I find him again, I still can't be in the office for over a year. Oh. You'll have to find someone else to take over the office. Huh."

"Hazel, if this is about the Sons of Hercules, I want you to know that law enforcement takes a very serious, very dim view of avionic sabotage. When we find the leaders, and we will, they will face charges. And in the meantime, our security consultant, Starr, has done so much for the office."

"It's not that."

"But we absolutely care about your safety. If you prefer to work remotely, or if you would like me to request the foundation assign you private security, I will."

Wow. It was like she was somebody important suddenly. Hazel laughed awkwardly, gripping her hair. "I don't know what to say."

"Say what you need to feel comfortable working for us.

I can ask the foundation to hire another assistant. I should have done so some time ago when your work expanded."

"I still got everything done."

"Yes, and I think you don't realize how exceptional that is. I'll respect your wishes, but Hazel, I don't want to lose you. You're organized, efficient, adaptable. Always willing to try something new. Your passion and big ideas are exactly what we love. And I think you'll be happiest here, either with MerMatch or the foundation, because this is a cause you care deeply about."

Her heart swelled. "Aw." She sniffed. "And then I go and lose your merman."

"Well, we'll find him again. He has a critical job to do, and so do you. I intend to speak with him about training his bride to soothe the kraken."

"Oh. Right." She rubbed her forehead. "There's something else you should know."

"Yes?"

Her phone beeped another warning. "Gah, my phone's about to die."

"I can call back."

"No, no. I'm finding the charger." She put her hand on the usual outlet. Empty. Let's see, that jerk the other day had asked to use it. He'd probably stolen it. She checked the other outlets in case he'd only moved it and she was wrongly besmirching him in her mind. Ah, there it was, in the outlet under the window. So, okay, he was a jerk for plenty of other reasons, but not that one. *Sorry for thinking bad thoughts about you—this time.* She leaned down to plug it in. "There it is."

"Good. I'll tell you, and you can pass it along to Lotar."

"Sure." Her phone hadn't made the charging noise.

"—and his bride."

"Yeah. Uh-huh." She unplugged and replugged it. Still three percent. She traced the wire back to the wall and reseated the charger in the outlet. "Sorry. What did you want me to say?"

"The kraken is a type of squid, you see, sort of an uber-squid in the German sense. The mer sense animals by the resonant sounds of their animal souls, and the music of a squid's soul is a very low, very deep contrabassoon in high G..."

Why wasn't her phone charging? This was an emergency. Her phone was her everything. And she'd loaned her portable battery to Pia so her phone would be charged for callbacks.

Although Pia hadn't actually auditioned. Like Hazel, she had big dreams and small stores of courage.

But Hazel couldn't call her to get it back if she didn't get more juice.

"...and his bride will need to teach this to the warriors in the cities that have ignored our outreach. For their own safety, they must be able to soothe the kraken. The sound is meditative. You might recognize it as a Nepalese Buddhism chant. You know. Ommmmm. Now you."

"Ommmmm," Hazel repeated obediently.

"A little lower. Ommmmm."

"Ommmmm."

"Lower."

"I don't think my voice goes any lower."

"Hmm, well, I suppose under the water you're using different vibrational methods than your vocal cords. If I'm unable to speak to Lotar, pass it along for me."

"I will, as soon as I figure out where he went." And how he escaped from her apartment.

And why her phone wasn't charging. She pulled it out of the wall. It was...

Oh.

Because he had yanked the cord so hard, the plastic sheathing the wires to the charger had split.

That jerk. She was going to take a picture of this and post it to the class Facebook group. She'd think a grown man, an adult, wouldn't trash a girl's...

Hey, wait. Her window was unlatched.

Huh? Had the jerk also unlatched her window? She was on the tenth floor, so it wasn't exactly a theft hazard, but still...

"Yes, and that's why it's okay if you can't quite get low enough. Lotar will have to make sure his bride can make the correct sounds," Dannika was saying.

"That's me." Something had disturbed the dust on her terrace.

"What's you?"

"I'm his bride." She pushed the window up. A gust of warm, moist air blew back in on her.

"You are?"

"Yeah. That's why I have to quit." She stood on her stool and leaned way out.

There wasn't room to stand, although the guard rail was the perfect size to rest a couple of potted plants on and mount a garden trellis. She'd put a pillow out during the fall when it might be pleasant.

Dannika started laughing. "Hazel, you are always full of surprises."

"It's been a morning." There were handprints on the railing. Clean, big prints that interrupted the otherwise uniform dull grime.

No. He wouldn't have.

She crawled out and leaned over.

Nope, still ten floors.

That was like, what, a hundred feet down?

A pigeon flew by making its usual gurgling call. It emitted a white poop that fell all the way down to the dry, barren sidewalk with a distant splat.

If Lotar went out the window, he'd definitely made it all the way down.

"Well, that's wonderful! I'm so happy for you. Oh, Hazel, this is the best thing. You're the one who had the idea for the party. I'm so thrilled you're going to be the one to make it happen."

Her stomach lurched. "Right."

"And I suppose it is essential we get the sound of the kraken right. You're going to be teaching it to an awful lot more people."

"Haha, right."

"This is fantastic. There's such limited time to get in the water and on your way. Speaking of which, please forgive me for the personal question, but it affects how soon you will develop your queen powers. Have you been intimate?"

"Um..." Hazel didn't bother keeping secrets from anyone. She'd spill to her friends in an instant, but discussing this with her boss was like confessing how far she'd gone with the principal's son or something. "Not quite all the way..."

"That's too bad. The sooner you unlock your powers, the better, and from now on, you won't get much privacy. Call the foundation as soon as we hang up here."

"Right now?"

"Oh, that's right. Your phone is dying. I'll call them. You can expect a callback—well, ASAP—and they'll get you on a plane to Cancun as soon as we can rustle up the passports. There's a ship standing by. With any luck, you can be on your way in...hmm, what do you think? An hour?"

Oh.

God.

She tugged her bloomers.

Shower. Dress. Call Pia for her emergency battery. No, no. Do that in the other order so Pia had time to bring the battery to her. Unless she was busy, seeing as it was a Wednesday and normal people had to get to work already.

Then walk out of her life for a couple of years.

Utilities. Rent. That random dental cleaning she had in the next six months, and if she was a no-call no-show, they'd charge her a fee.

In an hour.

Her battery beeped.

"Can I get an extension?"

"We need to move fast. I'm contacting the foundation to send someone over to your apartment right now. You're on the tenth floor, right?"

"Right. Um, but we're still kind of missing Lotar."

"That's another good thing about this. You're his soul mate, so you can sense his presence. Close your eyes and picture him. Lean into the feeling. In no time at all, you should glean a clue to where he's gone."

"I have a slight clue."

"It's already working! Now you follow that feeling until you run into him."

"I don't think I can."

"Yes, you really can, Hazel. Have faith. I know it's odd. As women especially, we're taught our whole lives not to put too much faith into gut feelings or intuition, but the longer you're in the world of the mer, the more you'll trust in yourself and blossom. So turn in the direction you feel and make that leap."

She would if she'd used that get-fit-as-a-dancer DVD series Pia had lent her, but like so many projects in her life, it was on the back burner until she became a successful entrepreneur who had time for personal and physical development.

"Yeah, I don't have the upper body strength."

"I'm sorry?"

"To follow Lotar." Guys had ghosted Hazel before. She didn't bring hookups back to her apartment, so no one had ghosted her quite like this. "I think he went out the window."

"The...window?"

"Yeah, I don't even know how you'd do it. I've never tried before." Somewhere on the internet was probably a video that a shocked passerby had taken of a tattooed warrior clambering down the outside of her building like a marine Spider-Man.

"Oh. Goodness." Dannika laughed again. "You have had a busy morning, haven't you?"

"It sounds like it's just getting started."

A tourist below framed her old building with a camera. Someone bumped into him, and another. He wasn't smart enough to get out of people's ways, which made him a hazard. Then one bumper looked up, stopped, and got out their phone to record.

Motion and light moved beneath her window. Like the reflection of the sun against honed metal.

From a man climbing up the cement mini terraces like a parkour legend.

Even though the situation should terrify her, she felt

relieved. This was a simple mer-human misunderstanding. Lotar hadn't actually climbed out a window to escape.

"Never mind. I found Lotar." Hazel peered through the metal railing. A long trident rested against his side. "He went to get his weapons."

"Even better. They usually stash them in the harbor. This will make our trip even faster." Dannika paused. "Okay, the foundation is sending over an employee. They'll be there in half an hour."

Pia couldn't get over from Brooklyn that fast.

Hazel scooted back into her apartment so Lotar would have all the space he needed to enter via the window, over-turning the stool and stubbing her toe. Ow. "Um, can you ask them to bring a charger?"

"Yes, of course. And don't worry, Hazel, we'll spend as long as you need rehearsing the ways to address the kings of the mer cities, how to connect to their values, and how to avoid offending them, and we'll go over that sound so you can soothe the kraken. You're going to be the first modern human these kings have ever met. And, for as long as my cell recep-tion lasts, I am going to do my best to make sure it's not the—"

Beep.

Her phone shut down.

She held the dead plastic in one hand and massaged her stubbed toe with the other.

Lotar heaved himself over the railing and into the open window in one fluid motion, silent and sure, his muscles clenching. He wore only his boxers. He'd strapped his biceps and thighs with sheathed daggers, three each, for twelve daggers of various lengths and sizes, and the trident he rested in the crook of an elbow with such control that it didn't even scrape the sill.

He stood, barefoot, before her like a Norse god, all rippling strength and power and flashing gray eyes. He'd scaled a building—twice—and hadn't broken a sweat.

Dannika had been about to say "last." As in, she would do her best to tell Hazel how to become smart and clever and articulate enough to banter with royalty, like Dannika did all the time, so that Hazel's first visit with the mer kings wouldn't be humanity's last.

Oh. God.

Lotar would be fine.

But would his race be after they met Hazel?

EIGHT

azel's expression moved from awe to terror. Her soul darkened in her chest.

Lotar's chest went cold, synchronized with her emotions.

Why was she terrified? He carried his weapons now. Did the dangers of their journey frighten her?

She suddenly threw her arms around him. "Sorry. I can't greet you properly. Everything is nuts. Total blur."

Then...his weapons did *not* frighten her.

She released him and disappeared into the bathroom. A gentle shush of her shower started. Her voice drifted out to him. "You can use the door, you know. What happened to your clothes?"

"I do not know."

He had left them on a wooden bench beside a sleeping man to dive into the nearest waterway. Strong currents had carried him quickly to the part of the harbor where he'd stowed his weapons, and an equally powerful crosscurrent had carried him back. When he'd resurfaced, the man had been gone, along with his coverings. Only these thin cloth under-coverings had fallen beneath the bench.

Humans disliked nudity, and their eyes had followed him with too much attention as he'd navigated the few streets back to Hazel's apartment building.

"And I think you're not allowed to have weapons until you leave," her voice continued, echoing from the small room. "Isn't that what the customs guys said?"

"I am leaving," he said.

The shower shut off. Hazel hurried out, towel haphazardly around her, and opened a small door. Inside was crammed a mass of human coverings. She flipped through, tossed them toward a bag, and pulled others onto her body. She dropped the towel and raced around the apartment, muttering as she moved.

"Go bag, go bag...sunscreen? Sure. Definitely aspirin. Sunglasses...wipes...stain stick? Sure, why not?" She yanked open a cupboard. "Have you had breakfast?"

"No."

"Help yourself to anything. I have to unplug appliances. Oh, but not the fridge. Ugh, I should seriously empty that. Look at this mess. How can I leave this for over a year? Oh God, oh God."

This panic led to her dropping things, tripping, causing more problems for herself.

It was not the action of a female who could handle herself.

Hm.

The square metal next to the locked door buzzed.

Hazel dropped more small things into a bag and raced to the square. She pressed a button. "Yes?"

"Hazel? It's Flora. I'm from the foundation."

"Did you bring the battery?"

"Is this like a test? A password?"

"Didn't you get the message from Dannika? I really, really need it."

"Oh. You know you won't be able to take a cell phone where you're going."

"God, don't remind me."

Flora was silent for a long moment. "I was... I didn't see that. Um... Could we get you one on the way? There's kind of a car here. And a private plane is waiting, but we've only got clearance for the next little bit."

Hazel's soul fluctuated, dark and bright and dark again. She fixed on him. Standing in the center of her apartment where he'd been from the moment he'd returned.

Her soul brightened again, steadied by his presence.

His shoulders lowered in response.

How odd. He hadn't felt panicked this whole time. He'd only been watching her.

She took a deep breath, let it out, and spoke into the square. "We'll be right down." She released the button, shouldered her bag, slipped her feet into shoes, and opened the door. "Here we go."

He exited.

She took one last look around her apartment. Her soul dimmed again with worry and another emotion. Sadness? She closed and triple-locked the doors, squared her shoulders, and resolutely turned away.

Panic crossed her face. She patted her pants. "Oh, God, I forgot my phone."

She shoved her bag at him. He held it patiently while she unlocked her door, raced in, returned triumphant with the square of metal and plastic, and locked it all up again. Then she remembered something else, and a third thing.

He studied the construction of the hallway. The mer

rarely swam in these narrow caves. If someone attacked, they'd have no room to maneuver.

"Okay. Take four." Hazel finished locking her door and hurried for the elevator, then halted. "Oh, wait. Maybe I should get—"

"Come." He caught her hand, turning her around to face the elevator again. This panic was making her make mistakes. "You cannot take it with you beneath the water."

"No, but we're going to be on a yacht, so I should—"

"You do not need it." Whatever it was.

"But I might—"

"And if you do, I will get it for you."

She rocked onto her heels and looked up at him. "You will?"

The electrical impulse of panic vibrated out of his core. Into the hand holding hers. Up to his face and down to his toes.

Where had that promise come from?

He must not make vows.

He couldn't be trusted. He wouldn't get her what she needed.

But on this journey, he must provide everything for her.

And so he must.

She expelled a small sigh. "No, I don't. I've just never been on a private plane or a yacht before. I'm sure you're right." She linked their fingers easily. "Okay. Take, what? Five? Haha, that's not right. Whatever. Oh, Dannika's going to work hard getting me into shape. Ugh." And she stepped into the elevator, tugging him after, and descended while her soul fluctuated with new worries.

And he felt...

Released.

She didn't berate him for his arrogance.

The impulses in his body pinged without an escape.

They reached the ground, met the female Flora, and strapped themselves into a car. His trident barely fit.

Hazel and Flora chatted amiably, and Hazel scrawled human script onto Flora's papers, giving her the key along with many pleas to care for something called succulents, especially Phil. She talked Flora into charging her phone to complete conversations with her family members.

Flora escorted them onto an airplane, which soared over the land and sea with a strange motor that muffled his senses. It was afternoon when they landed and drove to a boat, and evening by the time they reached the small atoll that had once formed a sacred island of their first target city, Sireno.

Hazel spent most of the boat ride on the phone with Dannika. Her soul frequently darkened with panic, and she said things like, "I have to do what? But I can't say that? Wait, that's an insult too?"

Other queens had started with the same instability.

But no other queen had been asked to do what Hazel must do.

The white atoll emerged from the sea.

Flora handed Lotar a bottle of shiny Sea Opal elixir. "It's about time."

This elixir would give Hazel the ability to transform into a mer.

His heart thumped.

He carried the elixir inside the yacht to Hazel.

She tapped a long implement against the papers spread out before her on the table. "I'm just wondering if I upset someone—I mean, they're kings, right? Could I start with somebody less important and work my way up?"

He stood at her elbow.

When she finished, he would—

"Oh, is that water?" She snagged the bottle of elixir, cracked it open, and swigged it. "Thanks. I was parched."

Huh.

Usually, there was more ceremony.

But usually, he would give her his mating gemstone, and he did not have that to gift either.

She finished the elixir, replying to Dannika between gulps. "I know, I know. 'Have faith, Hazel.' It's easier said than done. And I still feel bad about burdening Flora with everything. You'd think if I was planning to turn in my notice, I'd have updated my operating procedures."

"That means your heart was never committed to leaving," Dannika assured her, her voice sounding tinny from the phone. "And now look. You're about to be a very important person. You'll go down in history as the first person to circumnavigate the globe underwater."

"So long as I don't win myself a Darwin award." Hazel glanced at him and lowered the phone. "Are we at the atoll?"

"Almost."

"Oh, God." Her soul darkened—which would not help him activate the elixir—and brightened again. She bid Dannika farewell, straightened her papers, and held out her hand. "I guess I'm as ready as I'll ever be."

He must activate the elixir.

He pulled her into his arms and lowered his mouth to hers.

Her soul flared before their lips even touched.

She welcomed him. Anticipated him. Wanted him.

Lotar.

His heart ached.

And then her lips moved against his, exploring and tasting. Enjoying.

He must activate the elixir in her veins by causing their souls to resonate as one.

Their kisses last night had been too short.

He now took this chance to explore.

She meshed their lips, and he traced their shape, suppleness, feminine flavor. The sweet spiciness that was Hazel. She parted, opening to him, baring herself fearlessly.

He pulsed deeper, and she vibrated with a gentle moan. Yielding, entangling, inviting.

Her confident strokes urged him to quest even deeper, to know her more. He took that invitation and filled her, plunging into all her crevices.

She moaned again and clung to him, trusting herself to his capable arms. Her breasts mashed against his chest. Her thigh rubbed his straining cock. Her breathing broke, went ragged.

Her naked desire hooked him in, plunging deeper and deeper until he looked on the abyss of emotion. Hazel was his one. His soul. His mate.

And someday, the mother of his young fry.

He had to pull back before he staggered.

She panted. Her eyes glistened, lips bruised, and her soul glowed like an anchoring beacon.

This was a dangerous kiss that made him lose his mind, forget time.

Forget everything but her.

Hazel.

She blinked, soft and centered, and then she wiped her mouth and giggled, grinning at him with a light as bright as her soul. "Oh. Hi. That was nice. Let's do it again."

Yes, he could do that—

"Guys?" Flora knocked on the wall inside the open door and cleared her throat. "We're, uh, we've arrived."

"Already?" Hazel's soul dimmed. "I mean, great. Haha. Ah..."

Unease seeped into Lotar.

When had Flora opened the door?

He followed Hazel as she repacked her bag, left it with her last instructions to Flora, and went to the railing at the back of the yacht. She stared over the atoll in the sunset. Her worry matched his own.

He must notice everything. Her safety depended on it.

But he was on the land, of course. He would not be so distracted under the water.

Not even pressing her nude body to his for the length of their danger-fraught trip.

Not even by her kiss.

NINE

The sun descended like a big orange ball into the turquoise ocean. Gentle waves rocked the white yacht anchored by the small chalky island tufted with green. Seabirds flew to their nests with farewell calls, and the triple-shot of hazelnut latte, the last she'd probably get in a year, buzzed in her veins.

This was her first time in the tropics. The water of the Hudson was black, and nobody would ever willing jump in, but this looked like a magazine. Blue in every direction.

It was beautiful, serene, and terrifying.

Hazel gripped the shiny gold rails.

This had been her one chance to live like a successful entrepreneur, taking private jets, lounging on millionaire yachts, luxuries at her fingertips, and she hadn't even paid attention because she'd been trying to fix up her life for the next two years.

A loose sort of disappointment warred with the lingering sense of having forgotten something.

Bottled water, keys, phone. She had given those to Flora already. Her hands were empty.

"Are you sure I can't take my passport?" Hazel asked.

Flora laughed. "Where are you going to carry it?"

Lotar stripped to bare skin, daggers, sheaths, and his trident. His muscles rippled and the smooth trident gleamed. He was like a god. A god with a seashell necklace.

Most mer carried a small woven pouch where they stashed things like the Sea Opal they'd give to their future soul mate, but he didn't even carry that.

"You could weave me a seaweed passport holder," Hazel told Lotar.

He rested his trident in the crook of his elbow. "That will drag in the water and slow our travel."

"And that big trident won't?"

He shook his head.

Sure. Whatever.

He moved to the steps.

"It's time," Flora said softly.

Augh.

Hazel unpeeled her fingers from the railing, stomped over to Flora, drained her third—and final—hazelnut latte for a year, and unbuttoned her swim cover. "You know my last road trip was Idaho to New York? We packed my brother's Civic. It was ridiculous."

"I bet."

"My brother drove. We spent all six days in Iowa and Nebraska. Okay, that's not true, but that's what it felt like because day two into the trip, we put in a Lynyrd Skynyrd CD and the player went insane. It stuck on one song and refused to skip, eject, volume change, nothing. We couldn't even shut it off without unhooking it from the battery, which my brother didn't want to do, so we played 'Sweet Home Alabama' on repeat for the *entire trip*."

Flora gaped. "You must have heard it in your nightmares."

"I did. And ever since that fateful time, I refuse to travel anywhere without three sets of earplugs, two sets of earbuds, and a white-noise app." Hazel stripped off her swim cover, folded it, and untied her cute polka-dot bikini top. "And now I'm supposed to travel over a year without lip balm, road snacks, aspirin...? Do you know how many audiobooks I could listen to over two years? What if we get to one of these hidden sacred islands and they have a Starbucks? I'm getting a headache right now."

Of course, she had just drunk three lattes in a row.

Flora laughed and averted her eyes as she took Hazel's clothes. "Well, you don't have to worry about rogue music players. Don't the animals make music?"

"Yeah, I heard it's like white noise. Infinite elevator music." Hazel was babbling to combat her nerves. She handed her suit to Flora.

"You might want to memorize the office number," Flora said. "In case you need anything."

"Oh, I have that." Hazel tapped her head. "Memorized forever."

"I guess you have everything you need, then."

No way. But Hazel made fists of determination. "Okay, I'm ready to drink the elixir."

"You already did."

"I did? Oh. Wait, was that what was in the bottle Lotar gave me? I didn't realize...huh." Gosh, what an idiot she was. She couldn't be that inattentive on the All-Cities Gyre, or she'd pour out historical mer champagne and break priceless artifacts. "I guess that's it. Should I...do I just dive in?"

Flora smiled encouragingly. "We'll wait for an hour, then return to Cancun, and our local contact will check here every week until we hear you've made it to your destination."

In case something went wrong. They couldn't enter the first city, or they had to abandon the whole project.

Okay.

She always had Lotar.

Right.

Hazel turned to take his hand, dive in, and shift for the very first time.

He was gone.

Wait, what?

Flora laughed again. "He's so stealthy. He dove in already."

Gah. Everyone was waiting for her, and she was already behind!

Hazel rushed to the stern, pinched her nose, and jumped.

Sploosh.

The water rushed over her head, warm and enclosing, and her ears popped. Was that normal? It must be normal. She wasn't a swimmer. Hazel bobbed back to the surface and gasped. But Lotar wasn't up here.

Oh, duh.

She gasped and dove.

Would the water sting if she opened her eyes? It might sting, like the chlorinated water at a pool, but she had to see.

Nope, it didn't sting.

And actually, the water wasn't even blue. It was clear, like glass. Really clear.

Colored fish skittered over the reef below her.

It stretched over to the atoll.

And out the other direction, under the boat, like an

endless casino carpet in hallucinogenic colors so bright, they glowed.

Where was Lotar?

Oh, there he was. Beneath the yacht, hovering.

Watching.

His feet had shifted to marine fins, the skin stretched tight between his elongated foot and toe bones, and his gray tattoos shimmered like ghostly messages. His gray eyes nailed through hers, and a strange emotion whooshed through her as if she was looking into the eyes of a wolf, embedded in the wilderness, fierce and snow-dusted and powerful, but she felt no fear. Only intensity from meeting a wild creature in his environment, recognizing each other as equals, and moving on in their own ways.

He waited.

For what?

Bubbles filled her mouth and nose.

She couldn't go anywhere like this. She had to shift.

Right. Okay. She'd heard all about shifting. Seen it, even. She had to suck in the water and shift.

Wait.

Wasn't Lotar supposed to help?

Usually, the warriors helped...

Hazel opened her mouth. *Lotar?*

But what came out was, "Glrglr?"

Bubbles erupted, and water glugged down her throat.

She coughed and sucked water in.

Wet, cold, deadly.

She gagged and choked.

No.

Wrong.

Help!

This wasn't shifting. This was how people died.

She thrashed for the surface.

Arms closed around her.

Manacles. Killing her.

She fought.

The arms tightened, implacable. "Stop."

Water. Darkness. Death.

Let go.

"I cannot let go. You will hit the reef."

Huh?

Hazel stopped fighting and opened her tightly closed eyes.

A big orange chunk of coral stood inches from her forehead.

Lotar's arms closed comfortingly around her.

Oh.

She went lax in his arms. Her body ached from struggling.

The reef stretched out beneath her, glowing with its unearthly aura. Twinkling fish darted between funnel columns and a small crab clacked its claws. A familiar background of noise like the faded mumble and hum of Times Square at lunchtime filtered in. But instead of a rideshare honking or a bodega owner cursing out a would-be thief in another language, the squeals and staccato emerged from the little seahorses clinging to seagrass, or fish with long ombre streamers gaping like she was the strange one.

Cool.

"Watch where you swim," Lotar said softly. "Do not close your eyes."

"*Blurgle.*" She choked on the words. Tiny bubbles soared for the surface.

"Do not use your mouth to speak. Feel the words in your chest."

Right, right. She knew that.

"I...knew that..." Hazel made the strange vibration, sort of ticklish and sort of like gargling, deep behind her lungs. "I forgot."

He released her and floated a short distance back. His body was stiff as a board. He looked grim.

No wonder. It was a good thing she *was* mer, because when she panicked, she swam the wrong way and basically tried to kill herself.

"Thank you," she said awkwardly. "Sorry. I just—where were you? I was asking you to help. Isn't shifting for the first time a big deal? But you hovered there and let me get in trouble. You watched."

He did not meet her eye.

She was arguing with a stone wall. "Why didn't you help me?"

He shrugged one shoulder.

"Why did you jump in? Were you trying to get away before I noticed? Leave me behind?"

"The All-Cities Gyre is dangerous—"

"So you were hoping I'd get so scared that I wouldn't shift and you could go alone?"

Silence.

Great. Their years-long road trip was supposed to start now, and they were like fighting at the end of the block.

He'd said he thought she was brave and smart and cautious and wouldn't be vulnerable.

But now he said the All-Cities Gyre was dangerous.

"Do you even want me to come with you?"

She vibrated the question in her chest, but the vibrations broke, affected by her emotions. She'd been so focused on her not-readiness that it had never occurred to her that maybe Lotar would agree.

He remained stubbornly silent.

Which really hurt, actually. "You don't want me?"

He focused on her. "I want."

Oh.

Thank God.

But... "Then, why did you just watch? I was flailing around, my first time as a mer."

"You jumped in. You shifted." His fingers clenched. "You saw me."

"And I tried to ram into the coral reef."

"I did not realize. Because you moved with confidence. Your soul glowed. You were, for that moment, not a faint new bride. You were a bright, powerful queen."

The noisy ocean faded.

He had not left her to her own devices because he wanted to abandon her. He'd assumed she was competent enough to shift on her own.

Because she *had* shifted on her own. She'd just panicked and hadn't realized it.

He saw her capabilities. He saw her best and brightest moment. And he thought that was normal for her. He didn't realize bashing into the reef was the default. He thought jumping in and being instantly amazing was right for Hazel.

A queen.

And he saw her soul. Which meant that somewhere inside, she *was* a bright and confident queen.

She just had to find it.

Okay, then.

His fingers twitched.

She paddled her stubby human feet to cross the distance between them and took his hand. "I'm not as cool as I seem, but, um, thanks."

Surprise, confusion, and a sharpening focus tightened

his features, drawing down his dark gray eyebrows. His other hand secured her to his waist, and her ordinary feet dangled between his long fins.

He was solid, reassuring, and here. Really here, like a date that had shut off his phone and gazed at her with his full attention.

This was where she belonged.

She would find her future here.

His gaze lifted away.

A low siren, like one of the alert options on her cell phone, echoed across the reef.

His arms loosened.

She turned to face the siren. "What's that?"

The torpedo-shaped gray fish with a white belly veered toward them. Long, narrow, and with a very identifiable hooked top fin.

Almost like...

"A shark," he confirmed.

"Uh, should we run?"

"Why?"

"Because that's what people do when they see sharks?"

But he didn't move, so she didn't either.

The shark veered past with a flick of the current. Its eyes were slit like a cat's and its mouth parted slightly as if it had told a joke and was waiting for her to get the punchline. It continued toward a deep cavern.

Her vision stretched to follow it, even though it felt like she was looking across the Hudson and, without binoculars, picking out every cyclist crossing the Brooklyn Bridge at rush hour. Crazy, crazy, crazy.

A concert of messy grindcore filled the ocean. It sounded a lot like her old neighbor's painful late-night obsession with Japanese noise rock. Massive tentacles emerged from a deep cavern. A giant octopus? The shark veered away from the tentacles and curved toward them for another pass.

Lotar remained still.

She tried to whisper-vibrate, "Is its vision based on movement?"

"No." He vibrated as normal.

Oh. "So we're not hiding?"

"No," he repeated, this time with dry amusement. "The sharpnose is shy."

The giant octopus emerged more fully. Its plus-shaped eyes fixed on her and Lotar.

"It spotted us."

"We sense these animals. They sense us."

"So there's no way to hide?"

"Control your movements, your emotions, your heart." He took her hand and hovered over the reef. "Slow your thoughts. These emit a current. Any shark can sense it for miles."

Ah. "So that triple shot I just finished probably means they can sense me in New York right now."

"Very far, yes."

Interesting.

Hazel spent so much time with mermen that she ought to already know everything, but being here and experiencing it was totally different.

And she'd never allowed herself to imagine. Becoming a mermaid, like starting a successful business, had felt as far out of reach as trying to become smart, articulate, and rich like Dannika.

Four small sharks about the length of her forearm, with the same gray and cat-eye slits, floated out of the reef beneath Lotar.

So cute. "Are those—"

They zipped beneath the sheltering rock again.

She tried to whisper-vibrate again. "Are those baby sharpnoses?"

He nodded.

"They're so adorable."

The larger sharpnose veered toward them again, passing so close, Hazel reached out. Its skin brushed her fingers, rough like fine-grain sandpaper. It zoomed away and back, and Lotar kicked with it, matching its speed and direction effortlessly, like a sort of dance. He paced it to the open ocean. The shark disappeared into the deep.

Lotar returned with a peaceful, yet playful expression, like a wolf that had run with his pack.

So effortless. So free.

"I want to do that," she said spontaneously.

He took her fingers. "I will train you."

Wonderful.

She flexed her stubby human feet. The gills in her lower back were obviously working, and her eyes and vibration-thingy had shifted as well, but the fins and the finger webbing would take time.

Overhead, the yacht's engines started with a burr that scattered the wildlife.

Holy cow. "Did a whole hour pass already? It feels like five minutes."

"Time dilation." Lotar pulled her into his arms and kicked away from the atoll.

She wasn't ready.

Please don't let me screw up.

Up at the surface, the bright disk of the moon reflected. He curved away from it and swam with powerful strokes into the deep blue following the route of the sharpnose.

"Was that a mommy shark?" she asked randomly.

"No. The shark was a male."

Oh, a daddy shark.

Well, she felt better about the journey. There was so much to see and do. The ocean was the final safari, and the Steve Irwin of warriors would guide her. Less chatty, sure, but very competent.

And how about those adorable baby sharks? Too bad she didn't have her phone. She could just imagine Pia cooing. *Hazel, what a cute baby shark!*

Baby shark. Baby shark. Baby shark...

Unbidden, the music started in her head.

Doo, doo, doo, doo, doo...

Oh, God.

Oh, no.

No, no.

"Uh-oh," she vibrated aloud, trying to break the terribly iconic noise.

He tilted his head at her in a silent question.

No.

No.

Please, no?

Hazel had somehow endured four days of "*Sweet Home Alabama*," a great song that her brother's sadistic mid-nineties CD player had converted into torture.

How could she survive an entire year of "*Baby Shark*"?

TEN

I *will train you.*

The promise echoed in Lotar's mind with a strange resonance.

It had popped out.

And the strange thing was how intently he wished to train her.

Even though he had no skill or patience. The wrong temperament.

He kicked steadily into the currents that led him to the Sol Sud, one of the major ocean currents that would take him past their first destination city, Sireno.

Hazel settled herself against his chest, noting and asking questions about the common wildlife. The disaster at the atoll seemed largely forgotten.

It continued to plague him.

Yes, he had done a quick tour beneath the yacht to ensure it was safe for her to enter. Sireno warriors did still sometimes surface here, and although King Jolan had never contributed troops to the All-Council armies to fight Atlantis, he also had not welcomed back any warriors who had left to seek their brides. His true loyalties were an enigma.

One that Lotar and Hazel were about to discover...

Having secured the area, Lotar had returned to the yacht to watch Hazel jump in, thrash, and descend with sharp determination toward the reef.

Yes, he had sensed her panic.

But she might recover by herself, and his intervention would lessen her accomplishment. He must not steal her glory and take improper credit for saving her when she did not need saving.

And when he had stopped her—because scraping against the razor-sharp coral, while not dangerous, was certainly uncomfortable—she had been so angry that he *hadn't* intervened, and his mistake glared even more obvious. Because of course, she was right, he had abandoned his bride in her moment of need, rendering him unfit as a warrior. How could he take her on the All-Cities Gyre when he couldn't even safeguard her in the shallows?

You don't want me?

He did want her.

Against his will. Against his better judgment. Against the obvious unfitness that his inactions had shown.

He still wanted her with him.

She was his.

And in that moment of truth, she'd calmed.

Now here they were.

May the Life Tree save them.

He swerved out of the fast current.

Hazel straightened. "We got off the highway. Where are we?"

"An echo point."

Although it took days and weeks for messages to circulate, the echo points were still the most-used method of communication. Only Atlantis stretched a human wire from the surface down to a "submersible" air bubble, and so only they could pass a message above water in hours.

Once the other cities knew the convenience...well, accepting an electric wire would require breaking the ancient covenant of secrecy.

"What are we doing here?" she asked. "Listening?"

"And announcing our start on the All-Cities Gyre."

"Didn't Atlantis already announce it?"

"As a traveler, I must declare it myself."

Lotar released Hazel to scout. Raiders sometimes used echo points to ambush vulnerable warriors. Alone, he would not consider himself vulnerable, but with Hazel...

A silent thresher shark hovered in the water beneath them.

Ah.

He pulled her into his arms again. Never mind. This echo point was safe.

She stiffened in his arms. "A shark!"

The thresher descended, pushed away by her uncontrolled impulses.

"Ah. It's going away."

"You must be very still. Threshers are the shyest sharks in the ocean."

"So when I befriend it, I've made it." But the shark continued to descend. "Can you show me?"

He released her and lowered into its path, drifting, his senses attuned to its narrow body and long tail fin.

The thresher stopped and rotated toward him. Although shy, it was curious about his presence. Few warriors had shark sense, and he had honed his with years of observation and practice. He floated eye to eye. The thresher stared, eyes dark pits, but much of its senses came from hearing and scent. It descended into the deep, returning to safe waters.

"Bye-bye." She paddled her little human feet toward him. "Do you think I could do that? Commune with sharks? They look so calm floating with you."

"In time." He entwined her again.

"Oh, no. And just when I'd gotten it out of my head again." She squinched up her nose and rubbed her forehead. "Quick. Sing me a song."

"Sing?"

"It's an emergency. You don't even know. A melody, a tune. Hum."

The mer did not sing as the humans did.

But then again...

He vibrated a soft tune as he swam up on the echo point. His father had sung it to him long ago, in a gentler time, when Lotar had fumbled simple ties and cried over broken play-daggers.

"Thank you." She rested her head on his shoulder. "That's haunting yet soothing. Like a mer lullaby."

"It was from my mother."

They floated into the echo point.

In the oddly still water, voices from distant cities echoed.

"*...the kraken. She floats along the Sol Nord. Beware...*"

"*...seen any? The migrations are late...*"

"*...to the shore. The All-Council will execute any warriors who refuse. The ancient covenant must be...*"

He floated into the center. His heart thudded. The announcements of the cities flooded over him. He had spent so much time working alone and silently that it was strange now to announce himself to the undersea world. Hard to find the words.

Hazel vibrated softly, "Did you want me to?"

How thoughtful. But he would do it.

"Hazel and Lotar of Atlantis embark on the All-Cities Gyre." He vibrated crisply, his body stiff with the importance and nerves. "Our destination is Sireno. We journey in peace."

And it was done.

Hazel grinned, lifting her shoulders to her ears, and wiggled with excitement.

As he kicked to leave, his name echoed. He stopped.

"...*The warrior Lotar has no honor. Unsatisfied with dishonoring Syrenka, he seeks to ruin your cities. He is a spy. Turn him away, give him no quarter, he is not welcome...*"

His heart thudded harder. Blood beat in his ears.

"They're talking about you," Hazel said.

He kicked free of the echo point and continued on to the Sol Sud.

His stomach churned.

"That's all a lie. Why say that? Your All-Council guys are as bad as the Sons of Hercules."

He choked. "No."

"Huh?"

"Those words were not from the All-Council. They were from Syrenka."

"Your old home city?" She traced the iridescent gray tattoo on his chest. "Why?"

"They are angry."

"Because you left? Well—"

"Because it is the truth." The vibrations made him ache, but he could not lie to Hazel. "I did as they said. I dishonored Syrenka."

She pulled back and looked at him, interfering with their aerodynamic shape. She touched his jaw. Her fingers trembled. No, his jaw trembled from clenching so hard. He forced himself to relax, but his body hid pockets of tension.

"You dishonored Syrenka?" Hazel asked. "Why?"

By accident. It had been an accident.

But it had not.

"My pride."

"Sorry, not why. I mean, what does that mean? Did you commit a crime? What crime?"

The vibrations rasped in his chest. "I shamed my family."

"Okay." She clamped his shoulders with a little shake. "By...what? Did you kill someone? Maim, hurt? Live in your parents' basement and make your mom wash your clothes until you were thirty-five? Seriously, tell me. I dated a guy like that once. He wanted to move in so I'd wash his clothes. Never again. Oh, wait. You don't wear clothes."

She was trying to distract him from the very real complications of this message.

"Did you insult the prince's prize-winning radishes?"

It was better for her to know now.

He had announced their journey. They must travel together to Sireno. After Sireno was the city of Aiycaya, a city with an established route to the mainland. If she wished to leave him, she could do so.

It was better this way. Before they had united their bodies.

"One day, my brother will rule Syrenka, but I was born larger and faster and..." He was going to say *better*, but that was his pride again. "Quieter. More observant. In any test of skill, I outperformed him. My constant undermining cast doubt on his selection, the future of the city, and his ability to one day rule."

"That's it? I thought mermen barely even had brothers. Because of the lack of brides, you were like under an unintentional one-child-only policy."

"In Syrenka, we are the only brothers. It makes my decisions more unfortunate."

"Yeah, I don't know. I have a brother too, and we competed for everything our whole lives. I moved to New York. He had to one-up me by moving to Alaska. See? We're still competing."

Her brother did not carry the burden of ruling a city.

"I guess he's not a prince." She settled against him again and their speed increased with the water flow. Then she poked him. "Hey. If your brother's a prince, does that mean your dad's a king?"

"He is."

"Wait. Doesn't that make you a prince too?" She poked him in the abdomen. "Am I swimming with royalty?"

"No."

"Are you kidding? Does everybody know? Am I the only one who just found out?"

He shook his head. "In Atlantis, your former city's rank no longer matters."

"Yeah, but still." She rubbed the spot she'd poked. "If your dad's a king, why aren't you a prince?"

"In Syrenka, there is only one."

"But you weren't raised to take over? What if your brother died?"

"Then the elders of the city would choose the next prince. Their choice would not be me."

"I don't see why not. You'd think they'd want the most

competent warrior for their king. But what do I know?" She melted against him. "I'm sorry."

His chest ached.

He held her small body to his. She did not want to leave him. Perhaps it was because she did not fully understand what it meant, and the longer she spent among the mer learning their ways, the more her mind would change.

But perhaps it was because she also found it desperately unfair.

He'd swum his hardest to win a race, returned to his father with his chest high, and been rewarded with a dark gathering of brows because...because why? Lotar should not have won. He'd acted wrongly. Yet his trainer always told the warriors to do their best. When others won through talent or luck, his father had clasped their arms and congratulated them. Only when the winner was Lotar did his smile falter.

"Well, whatever the case, they sound like jerks to bring up old grudges now," Hazel said. "We're not going to spy. We're inviting people to a party. Why would they say that?"

Yes, she must learn much. "Syrenka is known for silent reconnaissance."

"Oh. You're a city of spies?"

"We have more exceptional control over our impulses. Thoughts, heartbeats."

"Well, I don't."

"Depending on how the cities receive this announcement, they may bar my entry." He tightened his grip on his precious Hazel. "You will not only invite them to the party. You will have to convince them to let us into the city at all."

ELEVEN

Oh, man.

Oh, jeez.

Oh, boy.

Hazel didn't totally get the thinking behind banishing a guy because he was good—you don't bench your star player for being a star—but she knew plenty of people throughout history who were idiots, and so she gave them the benefit of the doubt. Like how in ancient kingdoms nobody could be taller or better dressed than the king. And here was Lotar, both pretty tall, and he looked amazing even undressed.

"If I have to go into a city alone, teach me everything you know about mer culture as fast as possible," she said.

"You will never have to enter alone."

"Okay." Thank God. He was bristling with weapons, competence, everything, but she wasn't helpless either. "I should try to develop my queen powers."

He softened another fraction from the icicle he'd been since leaving the echo point to now, almost back to normal hard-bodied firmness. "That will always be welcome."

"Okay, cool. I do want to know about the rest of it. Like,

how do you know which current to take, and how do you use this dagger to hunt, and what are those weird see-through pool noodles?"

He identified her "pool noodles" as a giant fire salp, a colony of see-through jelly planktons that had banded together into a worm. Somehow.

Well, life was a big mystery, but at least Lotar was a patient teacher.

He navigated the currents by taste. A chalky taste meant they were in a current near land, while a metallic taste meant they were heading into the sea. An audible rumble meant there was an earthquake or surface storm that had churned the water and interrupted currents—although not the Sol Sud, which snaked through regardless of such interruptions.

Certain predators and prey moved together, creating underwater islands. A whole ecosystem developed around slower-moving migrations.

But the most fascinating was his skill in understanding sharks.

He'd point them out by magic, and she'd see them out of the dots of other distant fish from much farther away than she was used to seeing on land. Like, the horizon of New York was pretty broken up by buildings, but she still wouldn't expect to pick out strands of hair on the Statue of Liberty from the top of the Empire State Building, and that was really what it felt like.

And there were tons more sharks than she knew. Yes, great whites and makos and hammerheads, but also the blue, lemon, angel, sand, blacktip, bluntnose, and sleeper. It was like taking a walk with an expert birder. She didn't see half of what they saw, but her world was richer for knowing they were there.

"See the dorsal?" he asked. "Up means hunting, down is thinking. Here, it is nonaggressive."

"That is so cool."

He smiled, and the lines by his gray eyes crinkled. The doom clouds he'd carried around New York had finally dispersed in the water.

She felt the sonar clicking of a sperm whale on her body, heard the song of humpbacks, and tracked the days by watching fish moving up and down the water column. Time dilation underwater was real. Five minutes was actually a day, and though she wasn't hungry or sleepy, she'd already seen and experienced so much.

And this was only the beginning.

Finally, Lotar bailed out of the fast current into a slower one. The landscape, which had been rough and rocky, was dotted with coral thickets. They were approaching a great reef. In the distance, a tiny light glimmered like a cell phone screen in the wilderness.

Lotar hovered above coral spires. Japanese noise rock played nearby. Again? Must be another giant octopus.

"We reach Sireno soon."

"Already?"

"That light is the Sireno Life Tree."

Wow.

Her heart kicked, armpits prickled, hands trembled. This was it. She had to convince everyone that they were the good guys, not to kill them on sight, and to come to a party that was her idea.

"My tongue feels like clay," she said.

Lotar's gaze veered from his sharp lookout position to her. His brows pulled together in confusion.

"Like if I try to speak, nothing will come out my mouth," she clarified.

"Do not speak with your mouth." He rested a wide palm on her chest. "You communicate here."

With her heart?

Oh. He thought she had a good heart and others could see it?

That made her feel a little...

Wait, no. "Because I'm underwater so I have to vibrate my words in my chest."

"Yes."

She was an idiot.

But Lotar was with her. This wasn't *Shark Tank*. She could do this with his—

"Stay quiet." He released her and kicked for the ocean bottom, seeming to melt into the landscape.

"What?" She hugged her elbows, bereft. "Alone?"

"Reduce your electrical impulses. I will return." He disappeared to a vague shadow over the landscape.

A goodness to gracious ninja.

Well, he did come from a city of spies.

She drifted on the current, floating inexorably closer to the spires, while schools of gray and silver fish flew past her twittering like strange birds.

Lotar would be back soon.

What should she say to the Sireno elders and king?

Oh, God. Her heartbeat spiked again.

The fish veered away.

Oh, her impulses. She tried to deep breathe, think meditative thoughts, and they veered closer again.

She should have practiced on the way.

Spike.

Okay, don't think about it, don't think about it, don't think about it.

What could she do?

Become a ninja. Practice her powers. Make her fins so she could move more fluidly in the water instead of being stuck with human feet.

She flexed her toes.

Ugh, her nails needed painting. Her toes were stubby and ugly. The index toe went the wrong direction from the rest. Going its own way.

She had so many flaws.

Give up, Hazel.

She stretched.

The fish veered away from her. One brushed her back.

Oh, they weren't veering away from her. They were veering away from something *behind* her.

Noises tugged at her. Like daytime television, or a podcast beyond her hearing.

She rotated.

Tattooed warriors surrounded her with tridents!

Ack.

Where was Lotar?

———

LOTAR COASTED over the healthy reef beneath the floating city.

He dove between thick trunks anchoring the ancient castles to the vibrant, coral-covered seafloor.

The castles bobbed far above. Like all mer cities, they radiated around the brilliantly glowing Life Tree anchored in the very center.

But Sireno's old Life Tree had died off five years ago, and the new one had sprouted up from a different castle, throwing the city off-balance.

If their city was thriving, new castles would have sprung up.

But old cities mourned their absent sacred brides. The castles had dwindled and most had an unkempt, abandoned look.

He found a good spot to anchor and float.

The largest castle close to the new Life Tree belonged to the king. The warriors swimming in and out were advisers. Older ones would be elders. One, two, three...

Hazel was waiting.

He had left her in a sheltered zone cleared of predators. So long as she kept her impulses calm, she would not attract notice.

Impulses such as the jangle of nerves in his belly.

How unusual.

He focused on calm.

Hazel was not in danger. He had made sure of that, but even so, he should return to her. This was enough information. Not as much as he would get, but...

A patrolling warrior swam urgently into the castle.

There had been no call of alarm.

But...

Several warriors exited and swam purposefully toward the region where he'd left Hazel.

No.

Lotar kicked, crossing the reef beneath them, avoiding animals he did not mean to flush out. There was some sort of gathering ahead. And in the middle of it glowed Hazel.

His stomach dropped.

He kicked with all his might.

But he could not reach her in time to save her from the foreign warriors drawing around her with tridents...

Hazel's chest brightened. She pointed through the newly arrived Sireno warriors. "There he is."

The Sireno warriors turned.

And many things became clear at once.

The Sireno warriors held their tridents loosely in welcome.

The foreign warriors around Hazel had their tridents pointed out, protecting her. And she floated with another female. A queen.

"Lotar, look." Hazel waved at the queen. "I was outside the city trying to be quiet like you told me, and who should swim up but Pelan and Roxanne? One of MerMatch's successful, um, matches!"

Pelan, a warrior with black-and-red tattoos, held his bride loosely. Two other warriors from Atlantis had escorted them.

Everything was as it should be for two groups meeting at the boundaries of the city and requesting entrance.

The only one out of place was Lotar.

Curse it.

The First Lieutenant of Sireno, a warrior with purple tattoos introduced as Malem, gripped his dagger, unsettled. "Why are you behind me?"

Lotar hovered his hand over his dagger. "We come in peace."

First Lieutenant Malem's tone flattened. "Clearly."

His Second Lieutenant, Ailan, murmured. "The rumors are true. Atlanteans will overrun us."

The first lieutenant rubbed his chin.

All this was Lotar's fault. Deep, hot shame flared in his belly. No one had caught him out like this since his trainee days.

"Overrun?" Queen Roxanne's mellifluous vibrations soothed the group. "Oh, we're not staying. None of us. We're here on a family visit. Pelan's from Sireno, you know, and we wanted to tell his father in person that I'm in the family way. They"—she indicated Hazel and Lotar—"are doing the All-Cities Gyre. What a funny word, isn't it? Gyre? And they're going to escort Gailen and Iyen from here to Aiycaya because there's safety in numbers, and Gailen's from Aiycaya, which was *not* overrun, but you wouldn't know that from the rumors you hear flying around from that All-Council."

Lotar used her distraction to dive beneath the Sireno warriors and come up in Hazel's arms.

First Lieutenant Malem eyed Lotar skeptically. "Some rumors are true."

"Even one queen is dangerous," Second Lieutenant Ailan said. "Two is a war party."

"We can leave our weapons," Hazel offered.

What was she thinking? Lotar tightened his grip on his trident. The other warriors looked equally shocked and unnerved.

She tilted her head at him as though surprised by his tension. "What?"

"Warriors do not release their weapons unless forced," he told her tightly. "In a city of friends, it is unnecessary. In a city of enemies, disarming means they are imprisoning you."

"Oh. Well, it's okay if they take your weapons, though. Even disarmed, you're formidable. You know. *You* are the weapon."

This line of reasoning did not soothe the Sireno warriors, but it was kind of her to say.

"We weren't supposed to arrive together," Queen Roxanne assured First Lieutenant Malem. "Pelan and I set off weeks ago, and Lotar was supposed to take his time in New York finding his bride, but he's a fast mover on the surface as well as beneath the water, and so this is a coincidence."

"I dislike coincidences," Second Lieutenant Ailan said importantly. "And so does my king. The last time a queen entered Sireno, she destroyed the Life Tree."

"Well, I just know you're not going to threaten my Pelan or Hazel's Lotar, so it won't ever be an issue." Queen Roxanne rested her palm on Pelan's chest and smiled sweetly. Her chest glowed with total confidence. "Right? Are you? You both seem like such nice young men. I'm sure you'll talk things out using reason."

Second Lieutenant Ailan straightened and puffed out his chest. "I certainly—"

"A warrior's vow is his honor." First Lieutenant Malem eyed Pelan. "You left Sireno. You are no longer our warrior. Act like it."

Pelan hugged Queen Roxanne. "I understand."

First Lieutenant Malem narrowed his gaze on Lotar, then pivoted and led them into the city.

Sireno warriors closed in on them.

This city had tried to execute the first warrior to claim a modern queen. Now they were being escorted in at trident-point. Sireno had a new king, but how much had changed?

Hazel trembled with quiet nerves. Her worry pinged on his consciousness.

He snugged her tighter.

No more distractions.

TWELVE

They were in.

This was happening!

Hazel snuggled in Lotar's arms, barely able to feel her fingertips from excitement.

She should really practice what to say.

But there was so much to see, and she was still reeling from the surprise meeting.

First, she'd welcomed the Atlantis warriors.

She'd met them or seen their videos, so they were familiar, but it took about halfway through a hug with Roxanne before Hazel remembered everybody was naked, including her.

How crazy that she barely noticed. Her brain just didn't register it as important.

And then everybody else had shown up, and she'd pointed out Lotar, and the Sireno warriors had gotten downright frosty. Thank goodness Roxanne had smoothed things over.

"You look well," Roxanne told her while floating cheerfully in Pelan's arms, her long fins trailing with his. "Did you lose weight? I love your hair. That color suits you. I think you could pull off red highlights as well. You have the right bone structure."

She was easy to like.

Hazel and Roxanne had worked together until the last year. They'd both gotten their paychecks from the Mer-Human Alliance, although Hazel's came from the dating site and Roxanne's had come from setting up the first-ever mer hospital.

The mer shrugged off almost any injury. They experienced crazy healing powers from the sap of their city's Life Tree running through their veins, but sometimes they got hurt so bad that they needed to touch their Life Tree to survive and recover, and if their Life Tree was a thousand miles away and another mile underwater, that was impossible.

The foundation had set up the hospital back when it had seemed like all the mermen would someday come to New York to seek their brides, before the visa restrictions.

Pelan had been shot by the Sons of Hercules and landed in the mer hospital. The worst moment of his life had turned into the best, and now Roxanne lived with him in Atlantis.

"You look like you've gained weight," Hazel said.

Roxanne's brows rose.

"I mean, in a healthy way. You glow, but not like sweat." Hazel stopped before she made it any worse. "You know what I mean. Have you guys decided on a name? Or is it a boy or a girl?"

Roxanne cupped her rounded belly. "We're going to do the old-fashioned thing and leave it a surprise."

"Oh, so you don't even know if it's twins or not?"

"Just how big do you think I am?"

"No, I mean because Lucy had twins... I just... I'm so excited for you finally having kids."

"Finally? I think a few months in is pretty fast."

"No, because of your age. You... You know what? Congratulations and never mind."

Roxanne laughed. "You, Hazel, are the living end."

Oh, goodness.

Lotar glanced down at her with worry.

Maybe she should focus on the scenery.

It was cool. Dannika and the other brides had described cities, and she'd seen artists' renditions, but it was different seeing it with her own eyes.

The Life Tree floated on a stalk in the middle of the city like the tower at the beginning of *The NeverEnding Story* movie. Its white case glowed like a flower with all the petals drawn protectively around it.

Around it floated these massive shiny bulbs, like frosted glass spheres, anchored in concentric circles to the seafloor.

The purple-tattooed leader, Malem, flew to the largest globe. In the middle, there was a tiny hole, but as they approached, it turned out the hole was big enough to drive a truck through. Or a couple of trucks side-by-side. He gestured mysteriously to the warriors around the entrance, and they moved aside. Everyone swam inside...

Which was down a long corridor...

They popped out in a vast interior courtyard. Doors and windows lined the green, plant-based inner walls. A ten-floor apartment building could fit inside.

Down on the floor, a rich garden of waving plants clustered in vibrant bouquets around a central pedestal. In the center of the pedestal rested a fava bean.

Based on her knowledge of mer castles, that was probably the Life Tree seed. Every citizen got one. And if the

Life Tree died out and one of their seeds sprouted, they became the new king.

Except in a few cases like this one.

More warriors ranged around the pedestal. Tattoos coated their bodies, and Hazel noticed the nudity, but quickly...what, forgot? As soon as she glanced away and back, she lost track.

Malem brought them in front of the main guy.

"King Jolan." Malem saluted and introduced the warriors. "...as well as Queen Roxanne, and Queen Hazel."

Queen?

Crazy.

King Jolan smiled and opened his palms. "My warriors and I welcome you to Sireno. I—"

"Brides?" Behind King Jolan, an elder with a pinched face squinted at them. "Do not welcome them to the city, my king. Warriors who endanger their own brides pose a threat to all reasonable warriors."

First Lieutenant Malem crossed his arms. "That is not very honorable, Elder Runa."

"We did not agree on allowing in females, Malem, and yet you have brought them in. You explain this how?"

"We do not agree on anything, Elder Runa."

"And?"

"That is my explanation. *We* did not agree to allow in females, but *we* do not agree on anything, so..."

The elder pressed his lips together. "You dare compromise the city's safety? And ignore the express wishes of—"

"Elder Runa." King Jolan's smile strained. "He followed my orders."

"But he should have come back and told us the warriors were reckless enough to travel with their brides through deadly open water." Elder Runa jabbed a finger at Malem.

"This is why you should not be the first lieutenant. You have no sense of order."

Malem studied the distant ceiling of the castle.

The elder flushed. "Are you listening to me?"

"Hmm? Oh, well, elders advise the king, not the lieutenants, so I was improving my sense of order."

The elder looked like he was about to explode.

"Thank you, First Lieutenant Malem." The lines around the king's eyes deepened, and although he looked quite young, like, younger than Hazel, he also looked as if he'd grown up real fast. "I am sure there is an explanation."

"Yes. It's necessary to travel with us women these days." Roxanne rested in Pelan's arms. "That kraken on the loose only responds well to us ladies."

"If it even exists," the elder sniffed.

"She does, and you need us to teach you how to soothe her so she doesn't rip out something. Right, Hazel?"

"Yes!" Another save by Roxanne. Hazel swam forward. "I can teach you the sound. Dannika just taught me. You go 'om.'" She made the noise.

Malem and his warriors dutifully repeated her, as did the king.

Roxanne frowned. "Oh, um, I think that's a little too high. It's more like, 'ommm.'"

The warriors dutifully repeated the sound.

Ah. That *was* the chant vibration.

Crap.

Hazel wanted to die. Curl up and die.

Roxanne brought her hands together. "Yes, so if you see a wall of tentacles and three mouths, you'll know what to do."

"Thank you." King Jolan gestured to the gardens behind him. "According to the ancient custom of the All-Cities

Gyre, we serve a filling meal and offer a safe place to rest here in my castle. Warrior Pelan, we were unaware of your decision to return."

"I have not returned," Pelan said.

"It's just a visit." Roxanne hugged her husband. "My parents are both dead, so we're hoping to meet with our last living relatives while they're still living."

"Is my father here?" Pelan asked with confident ease.

"He is out, on the perimeter, searching for signs of the kraken," King Jolan said. "I have already sent a warrior to summon him. If he is willing, you will room in your father's castle."

"Unless he has disowned you," Elder Runa said snidely.

Malem squinted. "Some fathers value their sons. Especially if they have brought a bride carrying a young fry."

"Who should not be endangered by crossing the ocean filled with deadly ancient creatures!"

"So you *do* believe in the kraken?" Malem asked.

"I did not say that. I said that Pelan should be punished for his recklessness."

King Jolan held his palms out in a familiar peacemaking gesture. "Pelan is no longer a warrior of Sireno. Any punishment is the realm of King Kadir."

Elder Runa huffed. "His actions contradict the All-Council. These warriors put us at risk. We have morals. These warriors do not."

King Jolan led them into his gardens, and they floated above the green. Warriors passed boxes with fish fillets and vegetables inside, and other foods. They probably tasted good, but Hazel's stomach roiled. She was hungry and nervous and a total wreck, as if she'd accidentally drunk three hazelnut lattes dusted with caffeine powder. She felt sick and woozy, and her heart was going a hundred miles an hour.

Get it done. Ask. Just say the first word.

King Jolan passed the food.

Maybe she should wait until after dinner.

Or maybe that would be too late.

Maybe she should have already asked.

Ugh.

"Should I invite him?" she asked Lotar, vibrating as quietly as possible. "Now?"

Lotar shrugged in a go-ahead-or-don't gesture.

Ugh.

"Um, King Jolan?"

The king looked over at her mid-bite.

Everyone stared.

"And, um, everyone." Her chest twitched. That must be the equivalent of dry mouth. Oh, wait. Her chest moved again. Hiccups? Oh, God. "I, uh, we're building a platform above Atlantis and it's going to be done in the next two years and we're having a party and you're invited."

He listened politely.

"You're all invited," she said.

Hiccup.

King Jolan chewed his mouthful and swallowed, frowning slightly.

Elder Runa shook his head. "A platform? Such as humans sank during the Great Catastrophe? It is the end times."

The others muttered.

"Really? Because maybe it's the old times. How would you know?"

"It is not the old times. I know."

"Well, you're invited anyway, um..."

"Never," Elder Runa said.

King Jolan rested his hand on his folded knee. "We must balance the needs of our warriors with external threats. Sireno is not growing like Atlantis. We are an easier target for the All-Council, for the kraken, for even typical predators without queens."

The elder harrumphed.

"Well, this is your big chance, though." Hazel stretched her face into what she hoped was a grin. "A big mixer. Your warriors will meet tons of brides. It's going to be great."

King Jolan matched her smile.

Elder Runa lowered his fillet. "Are you aware of how many humans come to our former sacred islands with nets and harpoons? All because one of our warriors made the mistake of taking one of your humans for his bride? Are you?"

"We're fighting the Sons of Hercules too."

"Then we must not increase our exposure." Elder Runa glared at King Jolan. "We will send no warriors. That is the final word."

King Jolan cut a strip of his fillet and ate it unconcerned.

Roxanne looked up. "Well, I suppose it's not a concern for you, is it Elder Runa? Seeing as your great-grandchildren are doing well in Atlantis."

Elder Runa paused, his knife partway through his fillet, then continued with a harrumph.

"And let me tell you, they are adorable. Why, that last week before we left, little Tory was singing her first hunting song, and little Yrun speared his first bigmouth. All the warriors assured me that's very advanced. And they know how to swim up and down the water column, how to cross to the ruins, and how to shelter when raiders are spotted.

They're faster than me. Both of them got their first tattoos, and would you believe they both have two colors, gold and peach, but on opposite sides? Like looking in a mirror. I wish you could see them."

"What about their prank?" Pelan prompted. "At the king's castle."

"That's right. When no one was looking, they hid the king's Life Tree seed. Now whenever one goes missing, there's an outcry, seeing as Atlantis had so many problems with spies and sabotage, but this time, it was those munchkins. Their house guardian, the octopus Benji, found it. The twins blamed the prince, who wasn't even there. You have never seen such goings-on."

"And their first tattoos."

"Oh my goodness, yes." Her eyes sparkled. "You will never guess what they asked for their first tattoos."

Everyone leaned in, including the elder.

"Vegimals," she said. "They're half-vegetable, half-fish characters from the children's show *Octonauts*, and of course none of the warriors knew how to tattoo that, and here we are, in the middle of their first tattoo ceremony and scrambling for someone who knows what the fictional characters look like and can draw them. The prince asked for something ordinary, like his father's heart tattoo, but these two." She shook her head with a laugh. "They're going their own way, and everybody knows it."

Pelan grinned.

"Oh, it's such a shame you aren't coming to Hazel's party." Roxanne paid attention to her food again, although she'd been eating the whole time. Mouths, throats, and tongues weren't required for vibrating underwater. "It would be the perfect time to see your little great-grandchildren, and just think how happy they would be to see you."

Malem raised a skeptical brow at how happy Torun and Lucy would be to see the elder.

But the elder sighed heavily as if he did want to see his great-grandchildren.

The other mer craned to look at him in surprise.

He jerked upright, made his expression pinched and stern, and glanced around quickly. The surprised warriors averted their gazes—except Malem. The elder flushed, huffed again, and focused on the meal.

And so their first city was a total failure, and Hazel had no idea how to fix it.

———

HAZEL'S SOUL DIMMED.

But why?

They had received a welcome from the king, no less, and although First Lieutenant Malem gave him the occasional side-eye, he too did not speak of Lotar's transgression.

Hazel studied the one elder with dissatisfaction.

Lotar offered her more food. "It will be a long journey."

"Thank God." She pushed it away and patted her belly. "I'll work off what I just ate. Otherwise, people will start guessing I'm pregnant or something."

And then she dimmed again.

His stomach rolled.

He still had not told her his problem. And now she was in the presence of Roxanne, a fully realized queen with all her powers and soon to have a young fry of her own.

He really must—

"Pelan?" An older warrior in faded maroon tattoos approached the group.

Lotar jolted. His hands twitched for his daggers.

Where had that warrior come from?

Malem stared at Lotar.

He lowered his hand.

Pelan straightened. "Father!"

His father floated forward, glanced at the irritating elder, and locked his hands in front of him. "You are well?"

"Yes. I survived so many things. And"—he drew Roxanne to his side proudly—"this is my queen, Roxanne."

She wiped her hands on her thighs and rubbed her mouth. "Oh, goodness. You caught me while I'm eating. Well, these days, that's most of the time. Excuse me, I'm pleased to meet you." She bowed, hand on her rounded belly.

Pelan's chest puffed. "She carries my young fry."

His father's chest glowed, and he blinked hard as red rimmed his eyes. He rubbed his mouth. "My son, how can you bring her here? Journeying from safety?"

"We have our guards, and she is a queen."

"I have the magic touch." Roxanne touched Pelan's chest. Her fingertips glowed. A small, jagged scratch sealed to become healthy, unblemished skin.

"How wonderful! I..." His father quickly glanced at the frowning elder. "Ah. Yes. I see. Perhaps we can discuss this more in my castle? Where you may be more comfortable..."

A bittersweet pain filled Lotar's chest.

Lotar swallowed a hard lump in his own throat.

Such a reunion between a father and son touched everyone, not just him, but Hazel rested her hand on his. Even though she could not see souls, she sensed his feelings.

And being comforted by another...that was new.

The meal ended, and the Sireno warriors showed them to the open section of the courtyard where they were to sleep. Hazel followed a house guardian back to its cave and tried to lure it out. Lotar spoke briefly with the Atlantis warriors.

"Curious timing," Lotar told Iyen. "Meeting you here without warning."

The grave warrior studied him as if to ask if he were serious. "We swam flat out."

"Is everything okay?" Gailen asked Lotar. "We heard the message from Syrenka at the echo point."

The Sireno warriors had allowed him into the city. That was all that mattered. "Why are you here?"

"Queen Elyssa worried about your queen's first experience in an undersea city being unfriendly, so we were to arrive first and ease her transition. Good thing your queen is Hazel, though."

Iyen nodded.

"Good thing?" Lotar repeated.

"She knows more about the mer than an ordinary human. Can you imagine if her first time meeting warriors had been an ambush? But she rolled with it." Gailen had always picked up the patterns of words and phrasing of the queens more accurately than the other warriors. "She is resilient."

"Aw." Hazel kicked to them and threw her arms around Lotar's shoulders and buried her face in his chest. "I've tried everything, and I can't get the cute little octopus to come back."

Lotar cocked his brows at the warriors.

Gailen grinned. "Did you try a piece of fish?"

"Fish?" Lotar repeated.

"The queens spoil the house guardians with mer food and they become disinterested in hunting the garden parasites." Gailen held up a hand. "Do not fear. I have avoided feeding your house guardian, and it hunts with proper focus."

"House guardian?" Hazel lifted her head. "You have a castle?"

Her glimmering interest in Lotar's castle—now hers—made another frisson echo through his body. He wanted suddenly to carry her there, now, and lay with her in the greenery as she had once lain with him. But this time, instead of stopping her, he felt an urge to go much further. Her body, nude in his arms, slippery and wet for him. The way her mouth opened to accept his claim and traveled down his body toward his hardening cock...

Her lashes lowered as though she sensed the change in him and was more than willing to acquiesce. Match kiss for kiss, caress for caress, teeth to his lobe, tugging, legs entwined with his as his cock quested for her waiting, wet entrance...

Thank the Life Tree they were not in Atlantis.

"He does," Gailen said cheerfully.

Hazel tore her gaze away from Lotar's lips and, flushed, whirled to face Gailen so her rounded buttocks pressed invitingly to Lotar's waist. "How nice." She glanced over her shoulder at Lotar as though she could only bear to look at him from the side. "Um, what's it like?"

He shrugged a shoulder.

"He does not know because he has spent little time there," Gailen guessed.

"Oh. Is it just like this castle?"

"No." Gailen laughed. "His castle is much younger. It is perhaps three rings deep, and the rooms are barely grown. This castle is generations old."

"That makes sense. Too bad, though. I love the garden."

"It does have a garden. I planted it myself."

Their conversation pushed the other thoughts from his mind, and when he embraced Hazel, he could place her against his heavily armed body and relax.

She nestled between his daggers and trident. "Do you always sleep fully armed?"

"No."

"But it is nostalgic," Gailen said from the other side of Iyen. "Remember when Atlantis was only King Kadir's castle and we all crammed inside? And we were so concerned about attacks, we slept in shifts fully armed so we could swim out in an instant to defend the Life Tree."

That had been a different time.

And he had felt grateful then. Welcomed. Knowing that his skills were an asset, utterly undistractable.

What was wrong with him?

Hazel felt weird leaving Sireno.

Roxanne and Pelan saw them to the edge of Sireno's territory. Together, they just glowed. They were going to stay a few days—which in underwater terms meant a pretty long time—and would return to Atlantis before the baby was due. It caused the one elder to sniff imperiously about overstaying guests, but King Jolan diplomatically ignored him.

Roxanne gave Hazel a farewell hug over her rounded belly. "I'll wear down that elder. We'll send a big contingent to your party. Don't you worry."

"Thank God you came." Hazel flubbed her lips. "What am I going to do in Aiycaya?"

"You'll find your way. Don't doubt yourself too much." Roxanne smiled. "But everyone does, so try to get over your doubts as quickly as possible, and you'll be fine."

"Be honest. Have you ever had a doubt in your life?"

"Yes, of course." Roxanne hugged her again. "I doubted myself so much, I let Pelan go off with another woman. Of course, he was unconscious, and she turned out to be the bride of an All-Council general, so they eventually figured out the mix-up and summoned me. I woke Pelan from his coma with true love's kiss, and Nora chased down General Giru. They're still mortal enemies, but are also lovers? Nora likes a relationship with drama. She can have it."

Oh. Yeah.

"That whole thing was kind of crazy, wasn't it?" Hazel asked.

"It makes every other crisis pass like a dream." Roxanne patted her arm and released her. "And with Lotar as your soul mate, you will conquer anything. Believe."

Well, Hazel really, really wanted to...

Roxanne swam back to Pelan's side with an effortless swish of her fins, while Hazel dog-paddled over to Lotar's side.

They waved goodbye and, on Lotar's signal, headed into the currents.

Gailen and Iyen fanned out behind them. They paused at echo points for Lotar to announce their passage.

More echoes called him a bad warrior, honorless, and a spy.

He said nothing, but regret reflected in his gray eyes.

She hugged him tight. "They're wrong. I know they are."

He stroked her back and they continued on the next leg of their journey.

With the other two guys along, they saw less wildlife. Soaring vistas, but no curious thresher sharks. Distant schools of fish that flew farther to the horizon as though repelled by their presence.

They dropped out of the fast current on the final approach to Aiycaya.

Aiycaya was supposed to be friendly. The city had

reestablished connections with their sacred brides, who had settled on Haiti, and was co-ruled by a brother-sister pair. But the royals had had little contact with the foundation. Hazel had to nail down their RSVP.

She practiced her lines this time, mouthing them silently.

Lotar watched her with concern.

"Just practicing." She rubbed his chest so he wouldn't worry about her. He still thought she was competent, and she wanted him to think that for as long as possible.

So instead, she got to talking with Gailen about gardening.

Unlike her succulent aspirations, he was a real gardener.

"That is why I am going to Aiycaya," he mentioned. "A special herb grows only there, it seems. I have asked the other warriors, and they do not know what I am talking about."

"Except the other warriors from Aiycaya?"

"Well, that is another thing." He glanced at Iyen and Lotar. "Since Aiycaya has reconnected with its sacred brides, the warriors who had not settled fully in Atlantis returned."

"To stay?"

"It is comforting to return to your own people, your own city. Your own sacred brides..." He shrugged. "To support our city and our father with pride is the one thing that Atlantis cannot give us."

"But you aren't staying?"

"No. I will arise to meet the brides, but some things that are broken do not heal." He laced his fingers together. His thumbs bent the wrong directions and did not meet. "I am eager to return to Atlantis."

Now she remembered.

When Gailen had escaped Aiycaya, the patrol had caught him three times. The third time, they'd tortured him, destroying his thumbs so he couldn't make another attempt, but he had, and his final attempt had been successful.

A lot must have changed in Aiycaya. "Did the warriors ever apologize for trying to maim you?"

"Of course not. They followed orders like honorable warriors."

"That's messed up."

"It is the rule of honor." But he returned her sympathy with a sunny grin. "Over this rise, you will see it."

"See it?"

They rose over cliffs, and the ocean floor unfolded around them.

The glistening light of the Aiycaya Life Tree lit the ocean like a beacon in the...not darkness because it seemed like daylight in her mind, but in comparison to the Life Tree, everything looked dim.

Warriors zoomed toward them with loud shouts.

Lotar gestured for Gailen. "Tell them we come in peace."

Gailen nodded and announced their arrival in his language.

They cheered.

One couple swam toward them with an entire aquarium's worth of graceful rays, curious eels, stampeding crabs, and buzzing rainbow-colored shrimp. The rest of the warriors kicked ruggedly behind them.

The couple zoomed in front of her and Lotar and stopped.

It was Faier, a warrior Hazel had spent time with at MerMatch, and his queen, Harmony.

Faier had lost his first city to an underwater volcano and then suffered terrible injuries that had prevented him from wooing a bride, but here he was, beaming, with his equally cheerful wife in his arms.

"Hey, guys." Queen Harmony's Omaha accent was subtle. "Welcome to Aiycaya."

"Hazel." King Faier gifted her with a relaxed grin. The scars that had once rippled across his body had healed, and the normally somber warrior looked bright and healthy. "Lotar. It is good to see you."

"You too!" Hazel released Lotar and gave Faier and Harmony a big hug. "Group hug."

Harmony laughed. "Oh, wow. It's been a while since I had a group hug."

The rainbow shrimp buzzed past.

Faier and Harmony led them back to the vibrant bobbing castles of Aiycaya. English, French, and a lilting language echoed with cheery welcome.

In the center, like in Sireno, the Life Tree glowed with pure, holy silence. It was much, much older though. Mature, like a great winter oak, its barren branches stretched toward the surface, calling down for more brides to join with mermen. Pearly white resin dripped from the tree's crevices, hardened, and tumbled to the dais with tender clinks.

Sea Opals. Hundreds and hundreds of massive, healing Sea Opals.

There was a bajillion dollars' worth of wealth right here.

Which made Faier and Harmony the richest people Hazel had ever met.

They led her to the old castle which Harmony and

Faier had custody of right now. Harmony's brother, King Kayo, was up on the surface.

Everyone circled, floating over the gardens in the courtyard. The travelers clustered together. All the Aiycaya warriors looked to Harmony with quiet respect.

"You're our first traveler on the All-Cities Gyre." Harmony pressed her fingertips together like she was trying to remember a rehearsed speech. "We're supposed to offer you a meal. Faier's got out the best underwater feast, but if you're craving surface food like Nutter Butters or Twinkies, I can't help. We tried bringing it down here, but…" She squished her palms together. "Flatter than a penny on train tracks."

"They do not structure human Twinkies for oceanic pressure." Faier directed Aiycaya warriors to open containers and pass around greens.

"Not even a paste." Harmony took healthy helpings using her dagger. She flicked a bit of fish rind over her shoulder without looking. An adorable little octopus popped up, nabbed it, and whirled it away. "But that's okay. It makes going to the surface exciting."

"It must be so nice to surface all the time." Hazel took the fillet of something Lotar cut for her with one of his long daggers and passed the container to Gailen on her other side.

She'd never thought of getting a dagger. Should she ask Lotar for a dagger? Of course, she had yet to make her fins, and Harmony had those too.

The royals asked about her trip, and she hit the highlights. Faier asked about Sireno.

"Are their leaders still allied with the All-Council?" Faier asked Lotar. "We were never sure."

Lotar shrugged a shoulder.

"So it is still undecided? King Jolan never sent warriors to fight Atlantis, but they were the first city to reject modern queens. As they are our nearest neighbor, we had hoped something had changed."

Lotar shook his head.

"I see." Faier pursed his lips. "It is a conundrum. Should we reach out to them? Or will they call us anathema and attack?"

"It's kind of unfair to call us anathema." Harmony rested her hand on Faier's. Because she was born a mer, she had streaks of iridescent pink tattoos up her forearms. "I mean, we found our sacred brides again, and it's not my fault that my mom kept my birth a secret. She raised me in a landlocked state."

"But I am from Atlantis," Faier reminded her. "And no female mer has been born in a thousand years before you."

"That we know."

He tilted his head in agreement. "The All-Council has no protocol. It is easier to call us anathema than to yield to the changes."

Lotar listened silently.

It was funny. When Hazel had first met Lotar, he had mostly answered in shrugs, but then he'd switched to words and full sentences.

Since descending into the ocean again, he gave orders to Gailen and Iyen and made the announcements at the echo point, but otherwise, he retreated.

Even in this conversation, he faded. Deflected attention from his existence.

But he did not have to hide.

Hazel rested a hand on his knee and addressed the king and queen. "The warriors in Sireno are definitely arguing. The first lieutenant is very pro Atlantis. He hates the super-traditional elder. And the king is in the middle trying to keep everyone from killing each other, but I think if it was up to him, he'd be on our side. So, I'd say they're middle to slightly pro Atlantis." She looked at Lotar. "What did Pelan say when we were leaving?"

Lotar took a moment to answer. "Queen Roxanne is persuasive and will use her powers on the traditional elder."

Faier's brows rose. "Persuasion? I have not heard of that queen power."

Lotar shook his head.

"Pelan meant that Roxanne's good at convincing people," Hazel said, and Lotar nodded emphatically. "And she is. Way before she met Pelan, she was convincing people to build a hospital on a shoestring budget, right? That's not a queen power. It's a superpower."

The royal couple smiled, and Faier asked a few more specific questions of Lotar, who answered them fluidly.

Then they got interrupted by Aiycaya warriors who needed Harmony and Faier, real fast.

Lotar picked up Hazel's hand and threaded their fingers together. "You worry about me."

"No, not really. I thought, you know, you're among friends. You can speak freely. No one's going to judge you for saying the wrong thing. You don't have to hide yourself anymore."

He lifted a brow. "Am I hiding myself?"

"Aren't you?"

His lips quirked, and he massaged her fingers with sweet feather touches. "I must be doing a bad job, because you found me."

"I did." She covered his other hands with hers. "I'll always try to find you if you let me. And your friends will too. We care about your thoughts and feelings. Your observations. Your past. Everything."

He held her gaze for a long, long moment. The ghost of a smile was wiped away. He fought with something deep. Fear? Disagreement?

She squeezed his hands. They were so much larger than hers, but he let her contain him so easily. "It's scary to open yourself up like that, but it's the only way to be loved and accepted for who you really are."

He focused on her hands. She contained him, yes, but she also tried to give him strength. Stability. *I'm not afraid of what's inside. Your secrets are safe with me.*

His frown deepened.

"Hey, guys." Harmony landed abruptly in her eating position. "There was a miscommunication. My brother heard some rumors, I guess, and we assured him that everything's fine, but he's already on his way down here. We have to get ready to surface."

Oh.

Then, Hazel had to hurry and ask—

"Before you ask." Harmony put up her hand and winced. "I know you're here about the party. And, please don't hate me, but...we kind of aren't going."

What? No! "Why?"

"If it were up to me, I'd be there." Harmony rolled her head back and forth with a self-deprecating chuckle. "That's the real reason my brother's in such a hurry to get down here. He's afraid I'm going to commit the whole city because I hate telling anyone no. And he's not wrong. But..."

Harmony lowered her shoulders and looked positively regal. "The warriors of Aiycaya just reestablished our connection with our sacred brides. We must support them.

So, we wish you the best with your party and will cheer you on from afar."

Hazel worried her hands. "But you'd be such a good role model for the other cities."

"I know." Harmony slumped, a girlfriend again, and winced with sympathy. "We would. I totally agree, but things are still a little unstable, especially with our sacred brides, and it's a 'put your oxygen mask on before helping your neighbor' situation. But as soon as we're able to?" Harmony flicked her wrist, and a swirl of shrimp buzzed around the interior of the castle like a rainbow. "We'll be there. I promise."

And just like that, Hazel failed.

Again.

FOURTEEN

"Ugh." Hazel leaned against Lotar. "Aiycaya said no? It was supposed to be easy."

He listened with silent support as he navigated them onto the current for their next destination.

"Sireno was supposed to be neutral. So far, I'm zero for two. What happens when we get to the really hard cities?"

We are lucky to have been able to enter the cities.

"Don't tell me that," Hazel moaned, even though he hadn't told her anything, not even in a vibration. "It's not enough to *reach* the cities. I have to *reach* them too."

Since she seemed to hear his very thoughts, he vibrated them aloud. "You will."

"How can you say that? After what happened? Augh."

He tried not to smile.

Her disappointment was understandable, but Hazel connected so easily with others. She made fast friends with the other queens, brightened warriors she hadn't seen in years such as Faier, and soothed warriors who were facing a dreaded homecoming, such as Gailen.

And then there was what she did to him.

Forcing him to look at his own behavior. Reconsider his past.

And just maybe consider a new future...

"The kids were cute, though." Hazel sighed and rubbed her belly. "Not that I want to have kids right now."

Wait.

His heart kicked as if a predator had spotted him. "No?"

"Oh, don't worry. I totally do want to." She chortled awkwardly. "I know you mer need to have kids. Population crash and all. Not that there's anything wrong with being child-free. I dated plenty of guys who...er, yeah. Anyway. I'm definitely up for kids. Don't you worry."

So she still did want young fry.

Of course she did.

"But there's no need to get pregnant at the start of a years-long road trip. Imagine the morning sickness. Pregnancy cravings. Aches, mood swings, and having to pee all the time. Really weird ones Erin got, like nosebleeds. How do Dannika and Roxanne swim around like that? Of course, they both can make their fins."

She flexed her still-human feet, dragging them back.

Good, but...

Something was odd.

Why had he panicked when he'd thought she didn't want young fry? Shouldn't he have been happy? And why did he feel so conflicted now?

Why did knowing that she wanted young fry relieve him?

"Don't worry." Hazel stroked his forehead. "I know you worry, but we'll work things out, right? Together."

He should not take comfort from her soft, gentle strokes.

But relaxing into her caress eased a tension deep inside his chest.

He could not hide from her.

She sensed the truth.

And yet.

And yet...

"Hey." She pointed to overturned boulders. "What happened there?"

The ground beneath them showed the marks of something recent, large, and destructive scraping over rocks and crushing crabs not yet scavenged. A recent path of destruction.

"Perhaps the kraken."

"Oh, sure. At least I got the 'ommm' sound right this time." She rubbed her forehead. "Ugh. When I got it wrong in Sireno, that was so embarrassing."

Was this the kraken, though? If it dragged its monstrous tentacles on the ground, perhaps...

A ripple, like claws raking through the open ocean, distorted the horizon.

Then the horizon disappeared into a strange fog.

What was that?

Hazel followed his gaze. "What are you looking at?"

He did not know. "Stay here."

"Okay." She hugged her elbows. "You know, the last time you left me, I got ambushed."

"I will not leave your sight."

"That's still pretty far underwater." But her chest glowed with confidence, and she flexed her feet. She trusted him.

Hmm.

Lotar swam toward the ripple. The water had separated like a thermocline, but in a strange place. And it moved. A school of gulper eels shimmered between him and the distortion. They were unaffected.

"I wonder what my power is." Her vibration carried to the edge of his range, and he slowed to stay within it while he investigated. "If the hostile cities come after us, maybe I could shield us from their weapons or push them back. That would be useful. Or if I were stealthier, like you, I could get into the cities and scope them out."

She would never be stealthy. She was too open, too kind, too heartfelt to deaden her electric impulses like a Syrenka warrior.

And that was fine.

He did not wish her to be different. She was better as she was. He would be stealthy for both of them.

Something tugged at his memory.

He should know what this was. From his vast experience, he should know...

Boulders rolled into the thickening fog. The gulper eels tumbled as though something had sucked them into a riptide.

Riptide?

This deep underwater—without a surface weather effect—was impossible. Only a natural disaster such as the movement of the ocean floor, the eruption of an undersea volcano, or the crumbling of a mountain caused such a chaotic current.

There was no animal the size of a mountain.

No.

There was one animal the size of a mountain.

Curse it.

He pivoted and raced toward Hazel.

She was vulnerable. She could be dashed to the rocks. Crushed like the crabs.

He had let her go, again, and she was at risk—

She looked up. "Lotar?"

He barreled into her.

There, on the ocean floor, a cave. He kicked toward it with all his might. The ocean behind him fell away from his fins and the current pulled against him, but he was almost there. Inside, an anchoring rock. He reached for it. His fingers clenched it.

The crushing current ripped him out of the cave and flung him into the center of the storm.

Hazel shrieked.

Lotar pressed her head to his shoulder and tried to shelter her with his body as they were smashed end over end. A boulder cracked against his head. Smaller super-accelerated rocks pummeled him, and needlefish zoomed past. The currents wrenched him in three directions. The ocean itself roared.

It went on and on.

There was only Hazel in his arms, and the numbing pain in his body, and her heartbeat centering him. In all the storm, there was only the two of them.

The noise faded and the current lessened. He uncurled from Hazel.

She blinked. "What was that?"

"The kraken."

"Oh, I didn't see her." Her brows drew together. "I should have made the soothing noise."

"Not her body." He shook his head. His neck ached and the cuts stung, but they were smaller and less deadly than he had any right to expect. Rightly, he should be dead. "Her wake."

"Huh." Hazel frowned and drew a finger along his shoulder. "Ouch."

"You were not hurt?"

"No, you must have..."

Her fingertip glowed, and the stinging eased. His cut turned a dull color as though the healing slightly sped up.

Her brows smoothed. "Hey. I guess I have healing powers, but not very powerful ones. I guess it's lucky that you weren't hurt badly."

That was lucky.

But it did not feel like luck.

He should have realized what he was looking at. His distraction had nearly cost their lives. Should have cost their lives.

Hazel healed him weakly, and he kicked with sore muscles into the best current to carry them to Sanctuary Island.

"I didn't even think about the kraken's wake." Hazel idly trailed her index finger across his scars. "How can we avoid that?"

They could not.

"The other queens use a shield," he told her based on Second Lieutenant Ciran's report.

"Yeah. I guess I'll have to ask Dannika." Hazel rested her head on Lotar's shoulder, and her body suddenly felt twice as heavy as her soul dimmed to black. "But if my power is healing... Ugh. I can't convince anybody to come to the party, and I can't protect us from the kraken. I can't do anything. Is there any point in dragging me with you? I'm deadweight."

He kicked twice as hard with his aching muscles.

She did have a point.

Not the one she thought she was making, however.

Once he had been considered exceptional, and now he couldn't seem to summon even the most basic trainee abilities.

He was not a better warrior with Hazel.

She sensed it as well. "There's a boat to the mainland. I guess you could always leave me on Sanctuary Island and continue alone."

His chest grew heavy, reflecting her dimmed soul, and he struggled harder on his exhausted limbs.

Going alone was what he had always wanted.

He still thought it was for the best.

Didn't he?

FIFTEEN

They reached Sanctuary Island.

Hazel felt like a total fraud. A loser. The worst person ever.

She was about to report to Dannika, her boss, the person she admired most in the world, and share the wasteland of her mistakes.

Lotar had nearly died because she had no real powers.

And she couldn't do the one thing she was supposed to do, which was "the talking" while he escorted her around.

They lifted through the layers of ocean, and even though she didn't sense cold and warm like the old days, the water was lighter and fluffier, easier to move through.

After the echo point, warriors from the city of Lusca met them. Lusca had once celebrated the kraken, but then they'd figured out how to trap her, and everything had gone wrong. In penance for their ancestors' mistakes, these warriors had pledged to follow her and help.

"Beware wild currents," the leader told them. "The kraken has passed."

"Oh yeah," Hazel said. "We hit one of those currents. It *was* wild."

His brows lifted. "You survived?"

"Well, we got banged up, but Lotar kept me safe."

The warrior's incredulous gaze turned to Lotar. "Exceptional."

Lotar looked away.

That's right. He didn't like to be called exceptional. Because every time he'd drawn attention to himself, his father had had to work harder to pretend he'd never existed.

"Don't worry," Hazel told Lotar. "My failures are bringing down the average."

The leader eyed her as if he couldn't tell if she was making a joke.

They continued to the island. Lotar identified himself to patrols and was directed to a cavern lagoon crowded with young mer. The boys peppered them with questions, but didn't listen for answers. Lotar stowed his weapons—except for one dagger, for utility—and the little ones leaped out of the water onto a cavern ledge.

Lotar paused beneath the water with Hazel in his arms. "Your powers will come in time."

Huh?

Wait, had he been thinking about her "bringing down the average" quote this whole time?

She spread her fingers, which did not have webbing, and only the faintest glow emerged from her fingertips. "It's not just my powers. It's the whole mission. I keep going over and over what I'm going to say to Dannika. I went to the easy cities and totally failed."

"I did not think any city would be 'easy.' You shared the message. They did not drive us out. You succeeded."

She wanted to believe him.

"And you will improve your powers because you have a pure and determined heart."

Her chest squeezed. "I do?"

He nodded.

God, she could kiss him. "Oh. Well, um. Good."

He tipped his head as though it had taken this entire journey for him to work up the words to tell her his opinion, and then he surged out of the water in an incredible display of athleticism and landed with her on the floor of a cave.

"Whoa," she meant to say, but it came out gurgled.

And she abruptly bent over and heaved out the contents of her lungs, plankton and all.

About a million years later, she recovered.

One of the island residents, Meg, greeted them.

"I'm the welcome wagon and first aid." Meg flexed her fingers, even though her powers only worked underwater. "But you two look okay. That's lucky. I heard the kraken passed just before you."

Lotar nodded.

"Wow. Okay, now I'm your valet." Meg, a mid-forties mother from upstate New York, modeled a stylish blue sarong with a woven sunhat. The color set off her straight black hair and ethnic Chinese features. "Sarong or sundress?"

Hazel gestured at the sundress and coughed.

"Excellent choice." Meg handed Hazel a towel and the sundress. "It disappoints some visitors we don't still wear grass skirts. Twenty years of being a castaway, and let me tell you, those things itch."

"Death by a thousand grass cuts," Hazel croaked.

"You get me."

Meg handed Lotar Bermuda shorts and a button-up shirt. After they dressed, she led them up the cavern steps into the sunlight.

A grassy headland led down to a glittering white sand beach.

The castaways confined to this island for twenty years were no longer alone. Yachts anchored off the beach. Boys kicked a soccer ball up and down the sand. Beneath waving coconut palms, women and tattooed warriors worked between elevated huts clustered around a busy firepit.

They drafted Lotar and Hazel to assist with the lunch rush.

Meg's mom, the island matriarch, issued directions. "I used to believe in not making guests work, but Dannika convinced me there are no guests here, only future brides."

"Do the Sons of Hercules attack out here?" Hazel asked her. "You're kind of a target."

"No, but we have emergency measures. A baby kraken has taken up residence near the island. Hence why there are no cave guardians nearby."

Huh. Now that she mentioned it, Hazel hadn't heard the telltale sound of noise rock on the swim up to the island. "Where's Dannika?"

Lotar touched Hazel's elbow and pointed.

Dannika's husband, Ciran, strode up the beach, dripping wet. He motioned to them. Dannika rested in a hammock with a sun hat over her face.

Hazel rushed to her. "Dannika!"

Dannika rolled her large belly over and tried to heave out of the hammock. "Oh, Hazel, I am so pleased to see you."

Hazel helped her up and hugged her. "You're still pregnant."

"I know." Her boss rested both hands on her belly. "But I'm due any day. That's what I keep telling myself. Any day now."

Meg's mother called for lunch, welcomed Hazel and Lotar to the island, and everyone clapped. The names of the warriors and potential brides were a blur, but they seemed nice, and Hazel recognized some from their profiles. She stuck close to Dannika while Lotar stood close to Ciran, and while the others chatted about other topics, Hazel told Dannika and Ciran everything.

She'd felt pretty doom and gloom about the trip, but at the conclusion, Dannika reassured Hazel. "Of course it's disappointing our allies won't take this opportunity to strengthen our bonds. I've talked with the foundation and we sensed the Aiycaya group was leaning away, so I'm not surprised."

"I'm disappointed and surprised."

"Because you care so deeply."

"And what happens when we go to the next city? Newas is after this. They haven't let anyone enter their city, and they even tried to kidnap their former warriors from Atlantis."

Ciran studied the blue sky as though he were strategizing.

"Well." Dannika patted Hazel's knee. "You may tell them that if the prospect of meeting their soul mates doesn't excite them, they may instead look forward to seeing their mothers."

"Their mothers!"

"Queen Zara from Dragao Azul has been researching lost brides for years. She's shared the party with the brides she's found. This is a good chance to see their sons all grown up. Feel better?"

"Yeah. I don't know. This trip is so intense."

"Of course it is. You know, why don't you take a week off? Rest, the two of you, and refresh."

Hazel peered up at Lotar. "Can we?"

Lotar looked at Ciran.

Ciran returned his gaze steadily. "As the leader of this mission, only you can answer that question, Lotar."

Lotar frowned.

Ciran took Dannika's hand.

She rested her head against his shoulder. "If you can afford the rest, I'm sure it will give you clarity for the next section of cities." Dannika rubbed her belly with her free hand. "And I'm due any day. You might get lucky."

Aw. Seeing a newborn mer would be amazing.

Lotar stood abruptly and strode down the beach.

Uh-oh. "He's upset."

"He prefers solitude to think," Ciran said.

"No," Hazel said. Something about Ciran and Dannika together had triggered him. Maybe he was upset that they couldn't have a baby until after the All-Cities Gyre. The mer were an endangered species. "This is different."

"I will speak to him." Ciran squeezed Dannika's hand and followed Lotar.

In the distance, Lotar reassured Ciran that nothing was wrong. Then he glanced back at Hazel. The tiniest frown tugged at his lips, and he turned away again.

Yeah, it wasn't her imagination. He *was* upset.

Maybe he didn't want to travel with her after all?

Even if he didn't think Hazel was bringing down the average, she could still step it up.

"Can you teach me how to make a shield?" she asked Dannika.

"Absolutely." Dannika heaved herself out of the chair. "What an excellent idea. You have to be honest and in touch with your deepest emotions, and I think you, Hazel, will be a natural."

Hazel could only pray. *Please let Dannika be right.*

SIXTEEN

Lotar strode into the water and dove.

Finally, he could think.

The dangerous thoughts that had plagued him before he fought the kraken's wake returned with a vengeance.

Hazel looked at Dannika with such admiration. When Dannika touched her belly and spoke of young fry, Hazel's soul glowed.

But that wasn't what disturbed him.

Lotar swam past the broken reef and circumnavigated the island with long strokes. Despite his recent exertion and his still-healing injuries, he needed to move.

And young fry filled this island.

Young fry of the castaways. Second, third, fifth sons. Young fry raised with attentive mer fathers and loving human women. Eager and loud, bright and determined.

Totally different from his trainee period.

He veered away from the island and sought peace.

But even in the deep ocean, his mind would not quiet.

Dannika's hand resting on her belly had revealed the truth.

He wanted to see Hazel glowing, her own body swelling to carry his young fry, excitement and tenderness in her features.

Carrying his young fry...

Never.

Lotar kicked hard.

He must not want a young fry of his own.

He had long ago accepted that he must not have one.

And now...

Now he could not dismiss the idea.

He exhausted himself and returned to the island only after a day had passed. A day in which he had not seen Hazel. A day in which he could avoid his building desires to cup her curves, press her soft places to his mouth, taste her before claiming her with his rigid cock.

He shuddered and veered away from the island.

But Second Lieutenant Ciran saw him, and before he could escape again, waved him to join the gathering of warriors. Adults mixed with trainees and young fry.

"Lusca was closed for so long that you may not know the value of the other cities. Today, we correct that." Second Lieutenant Ciran gestured to Lotar. "This warrior trained in the stealth practices of Syrenka. Watch how he disappears."

Lotar eyed the second lieutenant. He was not a trainer.

Second Lieutenant Ciran grinned. "This should be a fun exercise for you. Exit the reef and return. We will see who notices first."

Ah. Very well.

This was exactly what he needed to clear his mind. Lotar

swam into the ocean. Second Lieutenant Ciran distracted the warriors with a speech about the value of learning from allies. Lotar released his impulses and drifted over the reef inshore.

Reef squid made *doot-doot-doot* noises as they calmly swam under and over him, treating him as part of the coral and helping.

Close to the shore, young fry frolicked in the shallow waves. Humans paddled with their heads above water. Others wore oxygen tanks and blew bubbles.

"I see that no one has noticed Lotar yet." Second Lieutenant Ciran's gaze flicked over Lotar without recognition. "He has certainly entered the reef by now."

The other warriors jostled one another and laughed. "Impossible."

"I do not see him in the ocean," Second Lieutenant Ciran said.

The students studied the open water. They looked right past him.

One warrior nudged another and muttered, "He probably swam into a cave before we remembered to search for him."

Second Lieutenant Ciran arched one brow. "He is probably strategizing how to steal your weapons right now."

The warriors reflexively clamped their daggers and tridents.

Amusing.

Lotar floated closer. He gauged his movements by the reactions of the reef squid, who provided acceptable camouflage. After his recent distractions, it was gratifying to stalk his prey, keeping them oblivious.

He coasted beneath the oldest trainees. A little closer and he would reach the pommel...

Hazel entered the water.

He froze.

Do not think. Do not react. He must not sense her nearness, calling like a siren, clasping his heart and tugging.

Queen Dannika and Queen Meg entered the water after her.

At least their entrance had drawn the attention of the training warriors. They watched the queens, giving him a chance to recover and stretch for control.

Lotar crept closer to the trainee.

The established queens flexed their feet. Their fins unfurled like rippling seaweed, huge and beautiful.

Lotar stopped again, his fingertips inches from the warrior's pommel.

No matter how many times he saw it, it still affected him. Queens in the water. The future of the mer.

The other warriors watched, equally affected.

Still. Quiet. Silence.

Do not think...

Hazel flexed her feet. They doubled in size, skin stretching tight between the bones, small and functional like a trainee's fins.

"You did it!" Queen Dannika and Queen Meg cheered.

"But they're so small." Hazel flexed her feet. "They're nothing like yours. I mean, I always wanted small feet, but this is ridiculous."

"The size of a fin doesn't matter." Queen Meg wiggled her eyebrows. "Only how you use it."

Hazel snorted. "I suddenly have sympathy for the guys that *didn't* comfort."

"But you are making fins," Queen Dannika said. "Ciran told me it's very rare to escape the wake of the kraken without significant injuries. I suspect, like these fins, you are already using your powers, but you aren't aware of it."

"We got pretty banged up."

"Her wake leveled Lusca, Hazel. Crushed it right into the seafloor. And since you have no mortal injuries—which, tragically, is the more common result of the wake—I think you are doing something. We will try to help you realize what you're already doing so you can focus."

"When you know what you're doing, it's super easy," Queen Meg said.

"That explains it. I don't think I've ever known what I was doing." Hazel flexed her fingers. "Okay. Here we go."

Queen Dannika lifted her hands. Her chest and fingertips glowed, and a white shelter twinkled over the trio.

Queen Meg grabbed an injured reef squid. Her chest and hands glowed, and the squid glowed. It jetted away, revitalized.

Hazel lifted her fingers and closed her eyes. Her chest glowed faintly. Her fingertips glowed the same amount. It was significantly weaker than the other queens and quickly faded.

She opened her eyes. "How did I do?"

"You glowed," Queen Dannika said, and Queen Meg nodded. "You're summoning a little power, but you're not focusing it."

"Urgh."

"Maybe open your eyes," Queen Dannika suggested.

"I don't want to see how faint it is," Hazel said.

So, she was aware.

"You could always hunt down your husband and increase your resonance." Queen Meg grinned. "That's my favorite way to charge up my powers."

"Husband?" Hazel said.

"You may have him as soon as he has finished his demonstration." Second Lieutenant Ciran crossed over

Lotar, swimming with long fluid kicks to entwine Queen Dannika. "Your warrior is giving a lesson on stealth." He squinted across the reef. "I believe."

"Oh, yeah?" Hazel vibrated. "When does it start?"

"It has started," Second Lieutenant Ciran said. "Why? Do you see him?"

"Yeah, of course I do." She turned and pointed straight at Lotar. "He's right there."

His heart spiked.

He twitched.

The reef squid fled, exposing him.

The trainees he floated beneath yelped in surprise and fumbled for weapons, unsheathing them far too late.

Curse it.

Lotar darted back, out of their reach.

"Oh, my God." Hazel clapped a hand over her mouth, eyes wide. "You didn't see him? I just wrecked your lesson."

His body shook.

How could his control fail? They had drilled it into him over and over. He must never move. Even after an enemy spotted him, he must drift, motionless and controlled. The instant a warrior looked away, he'd disappear, concealed again.

As in Sireno, his panic had caused a core failure.

Second Lieutenant Ciran laughed. His vibrations of genuine mirth echoed over the reef. "My warriors, you have received two valuable lessons today. The first, I hope, is a healthy respect for the reputation that a Syrenka warrior can murder you with your own dagger. The second is that the connection between soul mates has no barrier. Wherever you hide..." Second Lieutenant Ciran nodded at Lotar, "...she will find you."

And that was the most terrifying of all.

SEVENTEEN

"So, that could have gone better," Hazel told her girlfriends on the satellite phone from the beach paradise. "But yeah, things are going well here. I've failed to get two out of two cities to RSVP, and I have the weakest powers anyone has ever seen, but I can't complain. Except how I'm complaining."

Her friends laughed.

It had taken the whole week to set up the call. Pia and the others gathered for a girls' night at Erin's house while her family was out, and they'd gotten into the wine before Hazel had called.

"But you said the problem was energy, right?" Pia asked. "You have to increase your energy?"

"That's the main part of it, yeah."

"Yoga," Erin said. "Wake up, mat out, music on. Twenty minutes later, you'll be sweaty and feel amazing."

"Or karaoke," Charisma said. "You always had so much energy belting out Shania Twain at two thirty in the morning. Of course, you were plastered."

"And here I am fresh out of yoga mats and alcohol."

"Drunk yoga," Pia said, and they all giggled.

Hearing them laugh and chat made her so lonely. This was a paradise, but things had been awkward with Lotar, and her shield was as weak as her healing.

What was her special talent?

"Perhaps you have equal affinity for all three powers," Dannika had suggested after their third mediocre session together underwater. "Something doesn't stand out to you because you are well-rounded."

"So instead of excelling at one thing, I suck at all three?"

Dannika had laughed. "Try increasing your resonance with Lotar. His confidence will help you increase your power and develop your true potential."

"And by 'increase my resonance,' you mean..."

Dannika had grinned and patted her pregnant belly. "You know what I mean."

Right.

So if she had any chance of hunting him down, she would.

Months had gone by since she'd left her apartment, but it felt like only a couple of days. And with him close by, a sense of coziness filled her, like snuggling under the sheets together while the rain pattered on the window and they spent a lazy weekend inside.

But now?

Well, now she was second-guessing spending another couple of months underwater with the man who wouldn't give her a second look.

It was extra obvious in comparison to how Ciran treated Dannika.

Ciran's gaze followed Dannika everywhere. He stayed close and materialized at her side the moment she looked for him like he was reading her mind or something. He treasured her.

And while Hazel didn't want to be smothered, Lotar was a lone wolf.

Maybe she'd gotten spoiled by the first part of the journey when they'd constantly been together.

Or maybe he was thinking about everything that had gone wrong and decided not to take her on the next leg.

"Hey," Pia broke through the giggles and into her thoughts. "Have you tried theater exercises? I could teach you a couple."

"Are those the weird mouth things you do sometimes?"

"Professional speakers use those," Charisma said.

"Before my husband presents at a sales meeting, he puts Metallica's fastest, hardest album in his earbuds and dances around the executive suite," Erin said. "He did it as a junior right out of college and it stuck as a lucky charm. Everyone loves dancing around when no one's watching."

"Like singing power ballads in the shower," Pia said.

"Ooh! We should have sent you a power ballads album!" Erin gasped. "It's not too late. Here, I'll look up... What's the theme from *Rocky*?"

"'The Final Countdown,'" Charisma said.

"I don't think that's it," Erin said.

"No, no, it's just a power ballad. Also 'More than a Feeling' by Boston, 'It's Raining Men,' 'I Will Survive'—"

"Oh, yes, I love that one," Pia said.

"'My Heart Will Go On,'" Charisma continued.

"Is that really a power ballad?" Erin asked.

"Anything Celine Dion is a power ballad," Charisma said.

Erin and Charisma debated whether it counted while Pia sang the main refrain.

"The *Moulin Rouge* song," Charisma said.

"Ooh, totally," Erin said.

"I did get your package, though." Hazel crinkled the cheesy puffed rice wrapper next to the phone. "I ate so much. The island residents also thank you for your generosity. We're supposed to leave tomorrow, and I don't think it'd last until the Azores."

"We can send you another package," Pia said. "We'll send it early so it'll be there."

"I got the non-food item." Hazel tapped the cardboard package of condoms against the phone. "Ribbed for her pleasure?"

The women burst out laughing.

"I was pregnant on a six-hour cruise, and I do not recommend it," Erin said. "We're thinking of you."

"I appreciate the thought," Hazel said, especially since she'd been off the pill this entire journey. "You know I can't take it underwater."

"Using them all in one night might be a lot, but Owen and I have faith in you," Pia said.

"Owen?" Hazel had enjoyed a couple of girls' nights, and they'd never had a boy there before. "Owen's there?"

"Hi," Owen said from a distance.

"It was his idea to send you the care package," Erin said. "And since Pia broke up with guitar bro, she needs another admirer."

"Haha, you guys," Pia said flatly. "I don't always have a boyfriend."

"Right, now you have a friend who's a boy," Erin said.

They teased her, and Hazel could picture herself there, in the trendy apartment that she'd wanted so much, in the old New York of her dreams.

In the reality before her, the dinner assistants gathered at the firepit.

"All right, well, I'm on tropical dinner duty," Hazel said. "Although having just eaten an entire bag of cheesy puffs, I'm not sure I have it in me."

"You have a strenuous night tonight." Erin laughed, and they all hooted.

She hung up and tapped the condoms box against her thigh.

Hazel didn't have to know every single thought that went through Lotar's head.

But she did have to know where things stood.

Awkward or not, she had to get her answers tonight.

———

Hazel's eyes weighed on Lotar from down the table.

He focused on Second Lieutenant Ciran. "Do you still insist I must take a bride on the All-Cities Gyre?"

"Insist? This mission is fully under your authority." The experienced warrior forced the responsibility back onto Lotar. "King Kadir has agreed. You are the one completing the All-Cities Gyre, so you alone must evaluate the danger and decide to continue with Hazel or not."

His heart thudded. His fingers flexed for his daggers. Undirected electricity churned in his guts. "Travel is dangerous. Hazel has no defenses. Her strongest power is healing."

"So is Queen Elyssa's, and yet she travels often with King Kadir, and fearlessly."

"Not at first."

"Nothing is easy at first. For humans or the mer."

He closed his eyes. "You have no advice?"

"You should have rested this week." Second Lieutenant Ciran laced his fingers. "I once left my soul mate behind. Enemies overwhelmed the island, took our young fry, and imprisoned us to be executed. I would not advise it."

Lotar nodded, although obviously, he had no young fry nor any island to protect.

"Tomorrow you will have an escort back to Lusca. We rotate warriors so all have a chance on the surface. They can also escort Hazel back to the surface if you decide it is too dangerous to continue with her to Newas."

"What about the announcements from Syrenka?"

"Syrenka is assisting the All-Council. Why? I do not know. But you have something the All-Council does not."

"Which is?"

"A queen."

Down the table, Hazel had finally turned away from Lotar and talked to the other queens. She passed a box filled with gifts. Queen Meg's eyes lit up, and she tore a wrapper concealing two long candy sticks. The others made friendly comments about the contents of the box. Hazel laughed and, after another comment, laughed even harder.

He couldn't leave her here. She was so vital.

And someday, she might grow to hate him.

No.

Second Lieutenant Ciran knew his skills and did not hate him.

Maybe Hazel would not.

But if she did...

If he allowed himself to tell her everything and she turned against him...

No. He could not survive it.

He finally said the real problem to his mentor. "She is a distraction."

"She surprised you during the stealth lesson, but in the future, you will prepare for the soul mate connection."

No, that wasn't it. "In me, she causes distraction. Weakness. I do not think. My training stops." He made a scratching gesture over his heart. "I am at war."

Second Lieutenant Ciran smiled. "The weakness is the realization that you are no longer strongest within. For warriors such as us, who have left home cities and fathers behind to join Atlantis, this realization is especially hard. When you embrace that which you are fighting, it will no longer be a distraction. It will be your strength."

Was that true?

Hazel stood abruptly. "Well, I'm going to have to skip *Survivor* night because I don't care what else happens, but I *am* using this Lush body wash before I get back into the ocean for another three months."

The other women clapped for her.

She stared at Lotar for one long, hard moment.

A strong feeling hooked him.

Come.

He had to follow her now, or he'd regret it.

Perhaps this was his chance for clarity.

He rose, bid his mentor farewell, and followed Hazel into the island's interior.

EIGHTEEN

Hazel led Lotar up the path toward the island's outdoor shower.

His body warred with itself.

He wanted to take her. Claim her. He craved her touch. This week, he had endured because he had not allowed himself near her.

Following her into the interior—alone—and fantasizing about drawing her back into his arms brought up forceful images of what he craved.

But he must not.

Hence the war.

Just as Second Lieutenant Ciran had said.

She stopped at the screen and removed her clothing, unveiling her gorgeous body, so different in the air.

His cock flexed against the fabric of the shorts.

He stopped

She hooked a finger. "Coming?"

Come.

He removed the fabric and left the clothing with hers.

Down the steps, she diverted the water of the stream into a shower over her and stood on the wood slats. Her hands sluiced the foaming liquid over her body. She was gorgeous, female, all he wanted, all he would ever want. He drank her in with his eyes, memorized her with his soul. And all he wanted to do was bring her to his body, part her legs, and hoist her onto his hard cock. Take her while she moaned his name in pleasure. Unite their bodies for all time.

But even though his cock yearned to cross the distance, his feet remained firmly planted.

She beckoned to him.

Come.

He must not.

Hazel set aside the bottle of liquid soap on a rock and faced him. Glorious, female. Beautiful.

Determined. "What's wrong?"

She deserved to know the truth. Here. Where she could separate from him easily.

Stay silent.

His body felt like it was being cracked in half. The chitin fractured as he revealed the one thing no mer should ever say to his bride. "I cannot become a father."

———

Lotar looked at Hazel like his world was ending.

I cannot become a father.

Three different urges pulled at her.

Shock, then anger. Why hadn't he told her before? They could have worked through it together instead of avoiding each other.

Most powerfully, she needed to comfort and reassure him. The world wasn't really ending.

It's okay. We can adopt.

Who knew that the mer suffered infertility?

Her cousin on her dad's side had gone through a whole journey, and in the end had fostered to adopt an entire sibling set.

They could...

No.

Warriors only got hard in the presence of their soul mates. Hazel was *his*. As demonstrated by his constant and gratifying reaction to her. When she'd stepped under the shower, she'd kind of been wondering if he'd changed his mind about wanting to be with her, but when he descended the steps with a hard-on that could be seen from space, well, it made her feel even sweeter than the brown sugar scrub.

And nobody gave warriors physicals. If he'd been injured as a child, the magical Life Tree should have healed him by now.

He didn't say he was incapable.

He said, *"I cannot become a father."*

Huh.

And so instead of leaping into the fray, making a ton of assumptions and driving her fragile, conflicted warrior away, Hazel made her most Dannika-like response ever. "Oh? You can't?"

He shook his head.

She allowed herself a step forward. The pleasantly cool shower bounced off her shoulders and sprayed his chest. "Can you tell me a little more about that?"

"I am..." His lips pressed together, and he glared at the rock wall behind her, his shoulders hunched as he relived something. "Not fit to raise young fry."

She took another step. "Not fit?"

"I have no patience. Bad temperament. No protective instinct."

"That's a lie."

"You will curse me. Someday. When I fail my young fry as I failed my father."

"You won't do that."

"I already left you. In danger." His eyes squinted with self-recrimination. "Twice."

Answers poured into her mind.

You saved me.

You protected me.

Everyone makes mistakes.

Or the more logical, *You've never seen a mythical kraken before. How could you know that was the sign? You'll do better next time.*

He was so used to being perfect that the slightest miscalculation set him adrift.

Instead, she touched his elbows. The muscle flexed. Delicious. She ran her fingers lightly up to his chin and cupped his jaw on both sides, forcing him to fix his mesmerizing gray eyes on her. "Do you believe everything you're told?"

His lashes fluttered, but he did not fully blink. "No."

"Then forget the haters. They don't love you."

His gaze turned inward.

She tugged him back. "I'm your soul mate. Which means I know the truth. You're the most patient, most protective, most...most...*fittest* warrior in the entire ocean. And anyone who tells you otherwise can answer to me."

His eyes flickered across her face as if he was studying her for the lie.

But she was telling exactly the truth.

With all she had.

His gray brows lowered, and his gaze focused on her mouth. He finally accepted, even believed her.

Good.

Hazel licked her lips. "But just so you know, if you want to wait a while to have kids, I respect—"

He closed the distance and covered her mouth in his kiss.

Their mouths united, parted, melded. His tongue drove into hers, bobbing and questing, and his arms tangled her in his embrace. He drove her backward, under the spray of the cool stream, and it pattered like a rainstorm, a meeting place of land and water.

Her breasts rubbed across his hard pectorals. Her nipples pearled. Delicious tension streaked to her center and awareness throbbed.

She filled her hands with his rippled shoulders, back, tight buttocks. The hips she had gripped underwater without even thinking about it. The divot for the vee.

His cock slid against her waist.

She curled her fingers around the enticing base.

He grunted in surprise and surged into her hand.

That's right. She knew how to do things that would make his toes curl.

His hands spanned her hips. He took a step forward, planting his foot against a boulder, and settled her onto his bent knee. She gripped his shoulders for balance. He dropped his head to her right breast, circled the areola, and flicked the nipple with his tongue.

Pleasure blossomed, and the throbbing ache in her pussy increased. She scooted forward on his iron-hard thigh, and the slight roughness slicked by water and her lubrication eased the need, but his ongoing suckling and teasing pinches of her other nipple made her clench.

She rubbed her slick fingers up and down his cock.

He made an uncontrollable groan and released her nipple to chase her mouth, a predator fixed on his prey, biting and snapping, savage and sexy. She continued to stroke, harder and faster, and his groans turned to pants.

If he thought this was good, he should see what she could do with her—

He laid her back, balancing her partly on the rock, and lifted her pussy to his mouth.

How—?

His tongue laved her, exploding the ache into a desperate hunger, and each skillful stroke pulled her closer to the peak. So fast. Oh, God. And he looked so magnificent. Other guys made it into a big chore, but he devoured her, showing that infinite patience and groaning as if he were getting off on it as much as she was. She threaded her fingers with his as he sent her over the edge and she arched. Release whipped through her, tumbling her over and over like the riptide.

And then he dragged her down his body, fitted his cock to her still-throbbing pussy, and surged in.

A new explosion of desperate need coursed through her. She grabbed for him, for anything to hold on to, as he pounded his cock deep into her pussy, finding and chasing her deepest pleasure, pounding into her until she curled against him and arched in a full-body, kiss-the-stars, nobody-ever-experienced-this-much-rapture-from-just-sex release. She eventually floated back to Earth. He collapsed on top of her.

The water of the river poured through the slats, misting them.

The actual stars flickered overhead in the deep, dark sky.

Could she have this every day? Yes, please? Gosh, they'd already wasted so much time.

He rested at a funny angle, contorted so his head ended up on her chest, his ear over her heart. She brushed her fingers through his long, damp gray streaks. Lighter gray mixed with darker gray, white, and black, like the pelt of a fierce wolf.

Tamed for her.

Well, tamed because she'd stopped assuming and listened. If only all her important conversations went this well.

Hazel, you have always impressed me with your resilience. You take the most devastating setbacks, grieve like anyone would, and bounce back the next day with new energy that gives me the shot I need to face the new problem. Resilience is something I've long struggled with and only recently started to feel as though I was channeling you.

Haha, her boss was funny.

Lotar took a deep breath and let it out.

Idle feel-good laziness drained away.

She'd been more than ready for this, but had he?

He sat up with a groan and gazed down on her.

No regrets in his eyes.

Thank God.

Just the same tired, amazed, gorgeous gaze. He stroked a love bite and frowned.

She grinned. So sexy. "I should have warned you. My skin shows everything."

He focused on her eyes again. Still no regret—good—and an acceptance, as though he'd been worried for nothing.

Maybe this would turn out okay.

Just maybe.

———

Lotar helped Hazel to her feet and she dragged him under the stream, washing him with the bubbly liquid. His skin was still sensitive.

He took a great handful of the liquid and scrubbed it over her body, the places he'd marked and claimed, her softness. She grabbed his hands and wrapped his arms around her, giggling. "That's ticklish."

Their bodies pressed together. Her giggling calmed and she rested her cheek against his shoulder.

A great sense of wellness flushed through him.

He had taken an irrevocable step with her.

You're the most patient, most protective, most fittest warrior in the ocean.

He had not heard "most fittest" before.

But the sentiment made him hold her just a little bit longer.

When he embraced her distraction, his soul would be at peace and he would experience the greatest strength.

With her faith, he would become capable of anything.

And then she will hate you too.

She wiggled in his arms, and he released her instantly. She looked up at him. "You okay?"

He nodded.

They finished up, replaced their clothes, and returned to the beach. The episode credits rolled, and the warriors scratched their heads while the queens and potential brides chatted about what they'd seen. Nobody glanced at them.

Hazel rose on her tiptoes to murmur in his ear. "I don't think anyone noticed we were gone. You *are* stealthy."

He nodded again, but doubts echoed.

She will hate you.

Because unlike Second Lieutenant Ciran, she can see into your heart. The admiration she feels today will curl into disgust tomorrow.

She squeezed his hand again. "You sure you're okay?"

He nodded a third time.

"Hazel, there you are." Queen Dannika waved her over and rested her hands on her gravid belly. "We were just talking about the 'family' challenge this week. Is it me or does this season feature more betrayals than usual?"

"It's extra backstabby," she agreed, taking a seat at their table. "It's all about the ratings. But after six weeks with a bunch of strangers on a desert island, I'd probably backstab somebody for a chance to see my family too."

"Try twenty years," Queen Angie said.

"And you could be stranded with your mother," Queen Meg said.

Hazel snorted. "Does that make it better or worse?"

Queen Angie squinted at her daughter. "Be careful. I'm the one ordering the chocolate around here."

"Better, of course."

Everyone laughed.

"Question." One bride raised her hand. "For everyone who's not Meg, how did you introduce your merman to your parents? Mine are a little anti-mer, so..."

"I haven't done it yet," Hazel said, settling in. "But my parents know about Lotar, so we'll probably talk next time. But what about when you meet *his* parents? Do I bring a gift? What?"

Lotar edged around the group and crossed the beach to the shore.

Tomorrow would begin the second half of their journey.

And the hardest cities yet.
Hazel would never meet his father.
They would part again.
Before Syrenka.

NINETEEN

Having sex with Lotar changed everything.

They bade farewell to her new friends on Sanctuary Island.

Dannika and Ciran paced them into the ocean for a distance. She'd tried to convince her husband a little exercise would get labor started. He'd indulged her up to a point, and Dannika gave Hazel her final farewell hug.

"Take care of yourself. Your passion and resilience will see you through." Dannika squeezed her and paddled her long, gorgeous fins back into Ciran's arms. "You're exactly who we need on this, Hazel. Increase your resonance and remember: You are enough."

It gave her a warm feeling.

As Lotar entwined her in his arms and they descended, the warm feeling grew even hotter.

His body pressed to hers like a promise. She'd only begun to explore. And she had to increase her resonance, right?

Except this time, half the island's worth of warriors accompanied them. Not exactly the time to say, *Hey, can we take a quick break? I just have to put my soul mate's cock in my mouth. Twenty minutes tops.*

Lotar outpaced the other warriors as if he sensed her silent fascination. At a certain point, he curled his hand around her finger idly tracing his musculature and pressed a kiss to the top of her head. His cock pressed hard as a rock against her waist. So he felt it, all right.

What did guys always have to do? Relax, think deep thoughts, and solve quadratic equations or something.

They descended through the currents, through a veritable deluge of squids, and reached the underwater city of Lusca.

Once, it had been the most feared city in the ocean.

But now, it was kind of bedraggled.

A couple of small castles floated in the wreckage. One single giant castle remained, bobbing on its tether, and it had a big chunk taken out so it was open to the ocean. The Life Tree still glowed with soothing, tinkling comfort, but its stalk was kinked in the middle and the dais floated at an angle, so all the Sea Opals had poured off.

The city rested right on the lip of an underwater Grand Canyon.

"So where did they keep the kraken?" Hazel asked.

Lotar pointed to wrecked structures lining the canyon. "The mirror stone trapped her inside."

"In *there*?"

"She was nearly too large to fit," he confirmed.

What?

"How can she even move through the ocean?" Hazel asked. No wonder there was a tidal wave from her wake. Holy cow.

A welcome group conveyed them to the Life Tree.

"King Ankena and Queen Bex are assisting with something beneath the city," their guide said. "They will meet you shortly to offer food and rest."

Another night in public?

Hazel felt antsy. "We just ate. And rested. We don't have to."

"For the All-Cities Gyre, it is tradition," Lotar murmured.

"Oh, fine."

Lotar eyed her with a hint of amusement and a hardening cock. So at least she wasn't in this alone.

After some time, a trio of warriors approached from beneath the city, and even though Hazel expected a king and queen, it took her a long second to realize one of the three was actually a woman.

"You!" The youngest warrior hefted his trident in a warning. "You. Syrenkan spy. Do not think to reveal Lusca's vulnerability. My mother is a queen. She will tear you to pieces if you even try."

Lotar moved more prominently between Hazel and the young warrior. He rippled with readiness.

"Luk," the queen vibrated quietly.

"Mother." The young warrior stiffened. "I was greeting the foreigners."

The older guy was his father, the king. "Lukiyo, that is not a greeting. It is a threat."

"He's a spy. The patrol told us."

"The patrol reported what was repeated from the echo point." King Ankena gripped the prince's arm. "When you treat your allies as enemies, it weakens your bonds. I taught you better."

Lukiyo's chin wrinkled. "Well then, you should have been here when Grandfather was king." He whirled and swam away.

King Ankena held out his empty hand.

His wife touched his hand, then kicked after her son. Her fins unfurled, and she zoomed off.

That's what Hazel needed. Longer fins and zoom.

King Ankena closed his hand and faced them again. "My apologies, Atlantean warrior. My father ruled quite differently, and he taught my son much hatred in the time we were apart. Lukiyo is doing better, but when we encounter new situations, my father's teachings often emerge."

Lotar nodded—silent again—and drew Hazel into his arms. She rested comfortably against his relaxed body.

"This way." King Ankena led them to the large, damaged, and well-patrolled castle. "Not much survived the kraken's rising, but we offer what we have. This is the first time anyone has attempted the All-Cities Gyre since Lusca seceded, am I right?"

Lotar nodded a third time.

"It pleases me now to welcome you as the first. Of many, I hope. Here." He brought out unique fruits and seasonings, different from what she'd eaten in Aiycaya and Sireno. "Let us feast and rejoice. To new beginnings."

"Cheers," Hazel said, and King Ankena smiled.

Prince Lukiyo returned with his mother later. He looked red-eyed and chagrined, and he was pretty nice to both Hazel and Lotar, even offering advice on where to find the best hunting grounds if they wanted to detour on their way to Newas.

"The Newas warriors always venture outside their city," Lukiyo mentioned. "Especially after Dad stopped Lusca's raids on travelers. But Grandfather never invaded the city, even with his giant squids. What's your plan for getting inside?"

"Winging it," Hazel said, and Lotar nodded.

"Maybe you can break in. If you have my mom's powers."

His mom tossed a fishbone into the air and lifted her hands. Her palms glowed. A wave as powerful and chaotic as the kraken's wake propelled the bone across the castle and embedded it in the wall like a tossed knife.

Prince Lukiyo beamed with pride. "Can you do that?"

Well, she hadn't done the other powers too well, so this was Hazel's last chance to find her special groove. After dinner, she gave it a shot. Practicing with Luk's mother, she got as good at it as she'd gotten at shielding or healing. She could float a drink down a bar, but she would not smash anything.

They passed a restful night in the castle, grabbed a breakfast snack, and hit the watery trail once more.

Prince Lukiyo and two of his friends escorted them to the edge of the city. "See you in a year."

"Unless we have brides already," his friend called.

"And we might take them to the party," the third added. "Bye!"

They whirled and headed back to the city.

She and Lotar carried on alone.

And yet Hazel couldn't drag her mind away from Prince Lukiyo. "His grandfather must have been a piece of work."

Lotar kicked silently.

"I suppose I'll say the same thing in Syrenka."

Silence.

But not the good, companionable kind. Tension vibrated off him.

"So...I didn't want to bring this up before, but we will someday reach Syrenka, and there is a non-zero chance that

I could be pregnant. We should probably discuss custody and next-of-kin and grandparents' rights before we arrive. Um..."

"My father is not like the former king of Lusca. He is honorable."

"Excuse me if I have my doubts."

"He is a great leader. Well respected by his warriors and other cities. That was why the elders chose him for king."

Record scratch.

"Chose?" Hazel repeated. "They chose him for king? It's not hereditary?"

"It is. But if a king dies without a fit heir, the elders will choose another."

So lineage wasn't as important as it was in, say, medieval Europe. "Huh. And they chose your dad?"

"My father was well-respected. He had two sons, a rarity in Syrenka. I remember when he was chosen. Sometime after, he chose my brother as the official prince."

There was that word again, chose. "The prince is always the oldest son?"

"No." Lotar's vibrations tightened. "He could have chosen me. Or both."

But he hadn't.

What a slap in the face.

She squeezed him a little tighter. "I don't care what you say. He still sounds like a jerk."

"The memories are not all bad. Especially before. When he was only a warrior and we were his sons."

But he had to become a king and turn into a jerk. She stroked his pectorals. "What happened to the last king?"

"His prince died fighting a goliath dragonfish. The king followed shortly after of a broken heart."

"Wow. Hey, did you know that they didn't use to

believe in 'dying of a broken heart,' but they did studies, and now they do?"

"It is common for soul mates to die in the same hour. A healthy warrior will sicken. His soul fades and is extinguished. We are linked."

"Right. Linked." She placed a kiss on his shoulder and teased him with her teeth. "Speaking of links—or vibrating? —what am I thinking about right now?"

He twirled in the water, separating them and startling a school of shimmering fish like a flock of birds. He drew them together again. "You will distract me."

"It's important," she assured him, drawing him in with a teasing kiss that worked wonders on his hardening cock. "I've got queen powers, you see, but I can't focus them, so we've got to increase our resonance."

"Mmhm." His skepticism was tempered by the increasingly demanding kisses.

"Yep, and we don't know what's going to happen in Newas, so it's important from a safety standpoint that you fill me up with energy."

He filled her with a lot more than energy.

But as they coasted up to Newas, the danger remained. Hazel was still herself, and she had no idea what was going to happen in Newas.

TWENTY

Hazel was healing something deep inside Lotar.

She needed him—and kneaded him, inside and out—and every time their bodies connected, her bright spirit shone into the darkest part of his soul. And it turned out those dark parts were not as terrible as he remembered. With her, he could face them.

He would not part from her again.

They crossed the currents following whale migrations to Newas, a city new to him, and immediately tested his resolve.

The city nestled in a basin, protected on three sides by cliffs, and unlike cities such as Sireno that allowed empty castles to float in their city, the Newas warriors had pruned their empty castles away. They actively patrolled all parts of the city.

He must review its strengths, evaluate its weaknesses, and make an escape plan should they turn hostile. But how?

Hazel clung to him. "Wow, it looks like a balloon bouquet. Instead of growing in ever-widening circles around the Life Tree, these castles come up from almost the same stem. That's neat. I wonder why?"

"Each city's Life Tree is different in its own way."

How could he take her with him on reconnaissance? This arrangement required all his skills, and he had only barely begun to teach her.

Pop.

She made a noise with her mouth.

The nearest guards looked in their direction.

Pop. Pop.

The guards moved together into a unit formation.

"What are you doing?" he murmured. There was a short time before he had to decide whether to enter the city blindly, and she shortened that time.

"Theater exercises." Hazel stretched her mouth and hummed. "I'm lifting my energy to convince the Newas king we're friendly, the party is going to be awesome, and they definitely want to go. Also that you're not a spy so we can go in together."

The guards approached.

Lotar's guts tightened. He had forgotten the rumors circulating the echo points. Even though he had announced them at every echo point including the one closest to Newas, giving ample warning, and he'd heard the rumors repeated, they hadn't bothered him as deeply as before. With Hazel in his arms, nothing cut quite as sharply.

Unlike Aiycaya and Lusca, Newas had no reason to be friendly.

"And make the best shield so we don't get hurt. All right." Hazel patted his chest. "Ready or not, here we go."

He swam forward with her to meet the guards in the middle of the basin. Before the guards could demand who he was, he announced them, the same as at the echo point.

And it was as hard as at the first echo point, announcing his presence when he spent so much of his time trying to hide it, but with Hazel against his side, waving at the guards, he pushed through.

The guards traded looks.

So, they were expected.

The leader pointed his trident at Lotar. "You may enter, Atlantis warrior. But you." He pointed the trident at Hazel. "May not."

———

LOTAR'S LIPS PARTED, and he looked as surprised as she felt.

"What?" But she'd been practicing her arguments since the last echo point. "Why not?"

"The king refuses entry to a human. Only a fool travels the open ocean with a bride."

Lotar growled softly. "She is a mer queen."

A little shock went through Hazel's veins. A little zip of excitement.

That's right. She *was* a queen. Her powers weren't much compared to the other queens, but she did have powers, and that was more than she could have said months ago. Right?

The Newas head guard didn't blink. "She must not use her powers in the city."

Lotar's fingers curled around her upper arm. "We cannot part."

"He's right," she said. "I always end up in trouble."

"She will not come to any harm," the head guard told Lotar. "My warriors will defend her."

Lotar glared at them, and his unspoken question nearly deafened her.

Who would defend her from the warriors?

Man, look at how far they'd come. Once, he would have tried to stash her in a quiet spot and do the whole mission himself. These past few...days?...he'd changed completely. From the moment he'd stopped avoiding her at Sanctuary Island, they were a team.

And sometimes being a team meant compromising.

"Hey. It's okay." Hazel patted Lotar's arm and wiggled free of his grasp. Her toes extended into little proto-fins. "We don't both have to go. You can give the king the message."

He caught her fingers. "You are also a traveler on the All-Cities Gyre."

"I know. I'll use the time to practice my powers. And power ballads. We're linked, so if anything happens, I'll call. You trust me, right?"

"I trust." He pressed her fingers to his chest. "Do not be deceived by kindness. If you are in danger, act."

"Oh, don't worry. If I need to mace-Tase someone, I won't hesitate."

He released her and faced the warriors. "If she is hurt, I will kill every warrior in this city before you raise a single alarm. Do you understand?"

The warriors straightened, rigid.

The leader sneered. "I thought Syrenka warriors did not waste so many words."

Lotar stared him down. The implication was that he had wasted no words. This was a final warning.

What a sweetheart.

Deadly and loving, like a shark.

The head guard swallowed and ordered half his unit to

block her. The rest surrounded Lotar and led him into the city. He rounded the curve of the nearest castle, swimming toward the glow of the Life Tree inside, and disappeared.

———

Hazel was capable, and Lotar trusted her.

But parting was a mistake.

He instinctively evaluated the warriors and the readiness of the city to defend against a foreign force—the All-Council, the kraken, or *him*—as he followed the Newas first lieutenant.

The first lieutenant stopped at the entrance to the king's castle. "Leave your weapons."

Ha.

Lotar rested his hand on his dagger pommel.

The warriors tensed.

The first lieutenant's nostrils flared. "Disarm."

"Am I a prisoner? Or a guest?"

"You are a..." The first lieutenant gritted his teeth and unsheathed his dagger. "Disarm. Now."

Lotar pulled his daggers from his sheaths and rested them along with his trident on the hard green surface.

There were innumerable ways to take another warrior's weapon. And he knew them all.

The other warriors spread out, giving him a wide berth, as though he were more dangerous unarmed. They led him through the long entrance corridor into the courtyard of the ancient castle.

The king floated in the middle of the courtyard. Elders and advisers floated behind the king.

"This is Lotar of Atlantis," the first lieutenant announced. "Formerly of Syrenka. He is unarmed, as you requested, my king."

"A dishonorable spy." The king crossed his arms. "You realized approaching us by stealth was impossible. That is why we captured you so easily. No one enters Newas undetected. We are not tricked by the overblown reputation of Syrenka."

The king's bicep dagger was slung low, nearly down to his elbow, and he wore a decorative blade on the same side thigh. Both were easy to reach.

If necessary.

"Well, say something," the king demanded. "You are not made of ice."

"My queen and I travel the All-Cities Gyre." Lotar spoke with soft, incisive vibrations. "You have an ancient duty—"

"Bah." The king waved away his message. "You have come to kidnap noble Newas warriors for your anathema city, Atlantis."

"False."

"You lie! You have kidnapped our beloved warrior Tial and keep him under guard. Now you are here to take more warriors!"

Warrior Tial had escaped to Atlantis right after its founding. He was a thoughtful young warrior who had quickly made friends. The warriors of Newas had tried on multiple occasions to kidnap him back, and he had fought his way to freedom.

Despite Tial's firm dedication to Atlantis, the Newas king had continued to send warriors to kidnap him back. Now, he accused Lotar of his own crime.

"Listen, spy." The king raised a bony finger. "You will leave Newas and guide my warriors into Atlantis. We will reclaim our warrior and return him to Newas where he belongs."

Lotar's muscles tightened. "The next city on the All-Cities Gyre is Oria, not Atlantis."

"Refuse and you will die."

Hazel would have reasoned with this king. She would have tried to convince him of the truth.

But Lotar?

"Come to the Atlantis platform in two years," Lotar said softly. "And take him back yourself."

TWENTY-ONE

Lotar must be having a nice, reasonable conversation with the king.

Hazel twirled on her fin-toes and tried not to sigh. She should have prepped him with arguments she'd been practicing on their swim. Not that he needed it. He was a male of few words, but the words he used were perfect.

She practiced her shield. The color was faint and weak. She pushed, and her fingers went through like pushing through a bubble.

The guards studied her with unabashed curiosity.

She flicked her fingers to make the bubble pop and go away. "You know, we're both on the All-Cities Gyre. If you won't let me in, that's like a violation. You're going down in history as the only city that wouldn't let us stay the night. Is that how you want Newas to be remembered?"

Nobody answered.

She felt like the kid left after school waiting for her mom while everybody else had gone home. "Are any of you coming to the party? It's going to be great. Everybody will be there."

They didn't react to her practice speech.

Oh well.

She practiced the other part. "Ommm."

Yeah, that was the right pitch.

It tickled the edge of her range like the princess in *Space Balls* singing "Nobody Knows the Trouble I've Seen." Which wasn't exactly a power ballad.

But since she was bored...

When she'd been in high school, her mom had gotten a pack of old movies, and Hazel had ended up obsessively watching *Flash Dance*. Even though she had no dancing talent, the idea of chasing her dreams—like the main character going from a welder to a dancer—had made an impact. Forget Tom Cruise dancing in his underwear. She was a maniac, maniac...

Hey, were her fingers glowing a little more? Cool.

Hazel hummed that final song, "What a Feeling." Now *there* was a power ballad. She'd loved that so much as a kid. Maybe her friends were onto something.

Dance like nobody's watching...

"What are you doing?" one warrior asked.

Oh, yeah, except like five were watching.

She twirled back to them. "Yeah, I'm practicing for the party where your moms will be."

The warriors murmured.

"Moms?" the warrior repeated.

Another shushed him.

"I told you. Everyone's going to be there, including your mom. All of your moms." She played with the glowing sparkles from her fingertips. Like having a Lite Brite for nails. "Probably. Hey, you want me to teach you a party dance? I was pretty good at the electric slide. And the Macarena."

The warriors stiffened. Faces paled. Jaws dropped in shock. One warrior grabbed another.

She dropped her hands from her waist and didn't even do the hip roll. "Hey, come on. It's not that bad."

A warrior used a shaking hand to point over her shoulder.

Huh?

She turned.

A sideways mountain filled the formerly empty basin. It had the rough shape of Merriam Peak in Idaho, with a sharp point flooding out into a massive body that supported two domed eyes. Masses of tentacles fluttered in front of her. They were uncomfortably large, thicker than California redwoods, and uncomfortably herky-jerky, as if they moved too fast for her to see and she was only getting a strobe effect. They parted to reveal not one, but three squid beaks.

It was the kraken.

Holy moly. Hazel linked her fingers. "Hi."

The creature was Cthulhu on steroids.

"Come here often?"

The kraken's eyes didn't blink. She hovered. A doom blimp. And Hazel was supposed to charm her away before she did any harm.

Right. Okay. Dannika had told her.

"Ommmm."

One of the massive tentacles slithered over the coral and hooked around the anchor cable of one castle. The castle jostled dangerously. The warriors behind her whimpered.

Yeah, that wasn't good.

"Um, hey. How did you sneak up on me? I'm

impressed. You could give Lotar lessons on stealth." Hazel laughed awkwardly.

The kraken toyed with the castle. The anchor creaked. The Life Tree made a discordant noise that echoed like chalkboard screeches in Hazel's chest.

Okay, she had to be awesome right now. Increase her energy. And Zen chants weren't her thing.

"Why don't you take your tentacles back to yourself and, uh, let's talk."

The castle creaked again.

"No talking." She had to get her energy up. Hazel flexed her fingers. Energy. Dance around in her underwear like Tom Cruise. Belt out songs in the shower. Anything before the kraken ripped up the whole city with the flick of a tentacle.

She was a queen.

A...queen...

Queen...

She closed her eyes. *Not enough alcohol.* Hazel pretended to clear her throat, put an imaginary microphone up to her lips, and mouthed the words emotionally as she vibrated one of her favorite karaoke songs. She never got a good score, but nobody cared because they were screaming along with her.

And it was pretty likely that the kraken had never heard "*Bohemian Rhapsody*" before.

She finished all four movements, rocking out as necessary, and it was kind of fun. The castle stopped creaking. She finished and dared to open her eyes.

The kraken had rotated to stare her in the face.

As in, the tentacles had tipped down and the mountain had tipped up. Like, *What in the world are you doing?* if the kraken could talk.

Haha. Ha...

But the tentacle had also released the castle, so that was good.

The one warrior who'd been charged with getting Lotar if anything should go wrong zoomed into the city. Only about ten minutes too late, seriously.

Hazel put on her best grin. "If you liked that, I've got a whole set of favorites I usually do. I could just—"

The kraken whirled and jetted away.

Success!

Or, um, something. Karaoke wasn't for everyone.

One way or another, Hazel had saved the city, which was all that mattered—

And then the wall of water hit.

TWENTY-TWO

"How dare you refuse me!" The king shook with anger. "Listen. The entire city knows you are lying."

The castles made odd creaking noises, and the Life Tree jangled with discomfort.

"You see?" the king demanded.

Lotar barely heard him.

When his mind reached for Hazel, he sensed something like surprise and determination. The creaking stopped, and the city grew quiet. Whatever was happening outside, she was handling it.

"You quaver in silence. Where is the vaunted Syrenkan spy? Where is your stealth that you are so proud of? You will use these skills, if you have them, to lead our warrior back to his home, or you will never leave here alive." The king snarled at him. "Answer!"

Very well.

Lotar had delivered the party invitation. His next move would not please Hazel, but the Newas warriors would be even more sorry they had not allowed her inside their city.

Lotar darted forward, slipping between the guards nearest the king, and grappled him around the neck.

The king choked in surprise.

The guards rushed to where Lotar had been a moment ago, then tracked on his new location with bristling fury.

"Release my king," the first lieutenant growled.

Lotar flicked the dagger from the king's bicep up to his hand and rested the blade against the king's neck. He pressed the thigh dagger into the small of the king's back. "No."

The king froze. "Wh-what do you want?"

"The vaunted Syrenkan spy has doubts about Newas hospitality," he murmured. "You will escort me to the city's edge and apologize for your treatment of my queen."

"Yes. My treatment was wrong. Forgive me."

Lotar tsked. "Apologize to her."

The king gestured for his guards to clear the way. They fell back reluctantly, poised to attack. Lotar eased forward, aware on all sides of how close the guards were, and held the gaze of the first lieutenant, who alone looked as though he was gathering himself to attack. They let him pass. He kept the king between them and kicked slowly backward.

"Now I understand why you wanted her to enter," the king muttered bitterly. "You will assassinate me, install yourself as ruler, and use her mythic powers to lull my warriors into a false obedience."

"Hazel does not use her powers to soothe others." Lotar approached the exit. "She uses her powers to soothe me."

The king made the mistake of catching his gaze. And whatever he saw there made him pale and tremble.

Good.

Lotar preferred not to show his true feelings.

But this one time, he enjoyed letting the king sense the depths of his icy rage.

A warrior burst into the castle in a panic. "The kraken! She is here. She is here!"

His stomach dropped.

Hazel was outside.

The warrior pulled up in front of them. "My king?"

Lotar released the king, whirled, and kicked to the exit.

The king shouted, "Guards!"

He did not feel nervous. Strange. Shouldn't he?

Were they not connected?

Guards blocked the entrance.

He lifted the king's daggers to fight his way through.

"No, not him." The king gestured to the exit. "Defend the city from the monster!"

The guards milled in confusion.

Lotar jetted through, and the guards shouted and swam after him. In their panicked minds, one warrior was much easier to deal with than a mythic beast. But Lotar had to escape before the kraken triggered the castle defenses, and—

The ceiling slammed into him.

Outside, the view tilted. The castle bent. The Newas Life Tree turned sideways in a violent current. The view shrank as the castle sealed itself against the threat.

Uh-oh.

"Back!" the guards behind him shouted. "To the court-yard. Come back!"

But he couldn't retreat to safety.

He kicked and crawled across the ceiling, moving through the rapidly closing entrance tube to the orifice as it closed.

Curse it.

The rest of the tube squished around him, tightening into a choking embrace. He expanded his ribs and held out his elbows to fight the crush.

The city groaned and flattened. His elbows slipped. Spots danced, and his vision blackened...

And the black receded.

The orifice opened a crack. The castle was floating upright again. The tube behind him loosened as the entrance opened.

"To battle!" The king's voice echoed. "Assemble and attack on my command."

Lotar barreled out the orifice—and into another Newas warrior trying to barrel his way in.

"The queen defeated—ah." The Newas warrior pushed past him and jetted down the entry tube. "My king. The female defeated the kraken!"

She did?

Lotar flew through the disorganized warriors and bouncing unsettled castles to the edge of the city.

Hazel floated in the middle of a small group of warriors. A translucent white shield encased them like a bubble.

He gripped the daggers, ready to slash his way to her.

But she saw him, and the bubble disappeared. She laughed. "Oh, Lotar! I defeated the kraken with my 'queen' powers. By which I mean, Queen defeated the kraken. Haha, I'm not making any sense. I'm all shaken up."

She was alive.

His heart thudded hard and loud. He pulled up sharply.

She flew into his arms. "Thank God you're all right."

Her heartbeat matched his.

He crushed her to his chest, careful to orient the daggers so they faced away from her soft, vital body. Her hair swirled around his face like a shield. He squeezed his eyes tight so no one saw this very private, very real moment of relief.

"You won't believe what happened," she vibrated, her hands splayed over his shoulders. "I was trying to remember the words to my favorite karaoke songs, and the kraken showed up without a sound. It was amazing. She's stealthier than you are. And I—"

He lifted her chin with the pommel of the king's dagger and pressed his lips to hers.

All his relief, all his gratitude, was poured into that kiss.

She was safe. She was alive. She was his queen.

He would *never* leave her again.

Finally, the noise of the gathered Newas warriors impinged on his communion, and he pulled back.

Hazel's chest glowed with strength. She smiled, pleased, and squeezed him again. "Anyway, then we got hit with the wake, and I made a shield. It was only big enough to protect the few of us, though. I have to try harder for next time. The city almost flew away." Her lips quirked to the side, and she rotated in his arms to face the others—including the king. "Even though you kept me out, I saved you. You're welcome."

All the other warriors murmured, "A warrior and his queen. She is a real queen."

Second Lieutenant Ciran's words returned to him. *You will accomplish more work as an ambassador by traveling together than by any plot or argument.*

"Hey." She gripped Lotar's wrist and eyed the blade. "Where'd you get this?"

He jerked his head at the warriors clustered around the king.

Her jaw dropped. "You stole it off the king? What

happened to negotiations?"

"They took too long."

She snorted and rested her head on his shoulder. "And people call me the impulsive one."

The king finally swam to the front of the gathered warriors. "You threatened my life. We punish such treason by death." His gaze shifted to Hazel. "You saved the city. We owe you our deepest gratitude and highest honor."

"If you combine the two, you're back at neutral," Hazel suggested. "Which is good because we're a package deal."

"Yes." The king frowned at Lotar still holding his daggers. He waved forth a lower-level warrior burdened with Lotar's weapons. Lotar returned the king's daggers and rearmed himself.

Now, they were starting on true neutral ground. The warriors could chase him and Hazel from the territory.

Or...

"It has been a long time since a warrior has visited us on the All-Cities Gyre." The king still looked pale, but he persevered. "By tradition, I welcome you—"

"Both?" Hazel pressed.

"—both to Newas."

———

Newas was pretty nice after that.

The feast was great. "Finally, a city that appreciates lobster," she told Lotar as warriors handed her a basket of claws and tails. "This is a high-class meal on the shore."

"We understand queens enjoy feeding the house guardians." The Newas warrior pointed out a cute little brown octopus that "walked" across the courtyard on two of its arms, seeming to strut with importance.

She had almost taken a bite. Both the octopus and the Newas warrior stared at her in horror.

Hazel pulled the claw out of her mouth. "Uh, right. My bad. Here you go, little guy." She tossed the claw to the octopus, who caught it with a happy red shimmer.

"We have better food than rock lobster," the warrior assured her, and the octopus hopped on its arms, its malleable expressive body turning spiky and smoothing again. "Quickly! Bring food for the queen. She tried to eat rock lobster."

Oh, the horrors.

She then had to assure everyone that she was not starving, that Lotar had taken great care of her, and it was all a big misunderstanding. But they were even more solicitous, as though she must have endured incredible hardships to have even considered eating rock lobster.

Thirty-dollars-per-tail rock lobster...

Oh, well. The food she did get was delicious, and she had no complaints.

Lotar was quiet that night, and he never let her out of his arms' reach. Which was sweet but also worrisome.

"I didn't mean to scare you. Look." She held up her fingers, silently chanted the opening of "It's Raining Men," and by the time she got to the first hallelujah, her fingers glowed like a nightlight. "I just have to channel my inner 'Dancing Queen.' How crazy is that?"

His brow smoothed. His mouth twisted as though he was smothering a smile, and he finished eating the next serving of food.

After she was stuffed, the king introduced a large, ill-tempered elder. "You will spend the night in the castle of Elder Iliat."

Elder Iliat glared at them.

Huh.

She looked at Lotar.

Lotar drew her against him, careful to adjust her among all his weapons. "Him?"

"He is the highest-ranked elder of Newas and the most important male."

Warriors escorted them to Elder Iliat's grand castle and departed, leaving her and Lotar with the angry-looking guy. Well, Lotar was fully armed. So this couldn't be awkward.

"Here, your sleeping areas," Elder Iliat snapped. "Touch nothing."

A small green octopus peeked out from behind a frond. Hazel waved at it.

"Ignore the cave guardian."

Okay. This was too much. "Are you mad?"

"Of course I am furious." He crossed his arms. "Newas treasures every male deeply. How dare you take my son from me? Now, describe the conditions of his capture."

"Uh...I don't know about any capture."

"Tial. In Atlantis."

"Oh, I've never been there. I saw his interview. I work at MerMatch. Or I did. Lotar?"

He squinted at the angry father. "He is healthy. Well. And free."

Elder Iliat hung on Lotar's every word. "And?"

He shrugged.

Elder Iliat turned to her. "You have seen him? My treasured young fry?"

"Yeah." She hoped that wasn't breaking privacy laws. Or that Tial wouldn't get upset. "But I can't gossip about him. Is there anything specific you want to know? If it's not private, I'll say what I can."

He glanced up at the entrance where the other warriors

had been. "Do not tell anyone I asked this. Do not. I will throw you from my castle."

"Uh... Okay..."

A big smile broke across his face. "How is my young fry? How is Tial? Has he made friends? Has he met his bride? Will he be bringing any young fry home to us? Is he happy? What are his patrols? Does King Kadir recognize his skills? Tell me everything."

Whoa. Talk about a one-eighty. Even Lotar blinked as if he had whiplash.

"Uh, Lotar knows," Hazel said.

"He..." Lotar frowned. "Tial seeks his bride."

"Yes? And?"

Lotar shrugged.

The father looked eagerly to Hazel.

"I haven't met him myself, but he surfaced once in Bermuda, and his interview was fine. Dannika said he was sweet, very earnest, thoughtful."

"Of course, of course, that is him. And the brides? They love him?"

"Oh, absolutely. He hasn't met his 'one' yet, but I'm sure any time—or at least he hadn't when we left, but you know, we've been traveling a long time and haven't gotten any updates. He's definitely happy. Isn't he, Lotar?"

"Yes." Lotar looked relieved. "He is."

"That is my greatest wish." Elder Iliat leaned back and rested his hands on his belly. "I had to help him escape. It was difficult. And the last section of the journey, he had to cross on his own. My heart was in my throat until the king's scouts said they had spotted him in the enemy's camp. And then he settled in that anathema, Atlantis."

Anathema.

Right.

"So you're okay with it?" Hazel queried. "You actually helped him?"

"Yes, of course. You see how it is here. Traditional to the death. 'The kraken will tear us out by our roots before a mainland female enters our city.'" He sounded like he was quoting the king. "That is how it is."

And that had almost happened.

"Why don't you support him in public?" she suggested.

"It is not done."

"Yeah, but didn't I hear you offered a bounty for anyone who would kidnap him?"

"You pressured the king," Lotar said as though he'd just realized something. "Blackmailing me to abandon the All-Cities Gyre and return to Atlantis to kidnap him."

Elder Iliat nodded proudly and tapped his fingers against his chest. "I did that. Yes."

"Why?"

The elder looked shocked and wounded that it wasn't obvious. "Tial must not think I do not care about him!"

What?

Seriously?

Hazel held out both hands. "So you helped him escape to Atlantis to get a bride, and you're also making constant efforts to kidnap him."

Elder Iliat swelled with pride. "Yes. And if I succeed, I will help him escape again."

That was...

Well, it was a lot of work. "You could just tell him."

"Words are meaningless." He waved his hand. "Anyway, you must rest for your long journey. The king will pressure you again to go to Atlantis. I have held my support for the next great hunt over him. He wriggles like a bait worm. So he will chase you from the territory at trident-point."

"Or you could just not do that," Hazel said.

"You are fast, so you will escape."

Lotar eyed him with the same confusion that Hazel felt, so hey, at least it wasn't a mer-human cultural difference. This was a different difference. Haha.

After the Elder left, they snuggled together in a side room, and Hazel had never felt more protected under the shelter of a heavily armed man. Elder Iliat was so blasé about setting the city on them, yet so insistent he couldn't wish his son well and support him. "Geez. I don't suppose your dad has two perspectives like this and saying awful things to you is his way of proving he loves you."

"No."

"Well, maybe by the time we get to Syrenka, he will have changed."

Lotar's mouth stayed in its thin line. He clearly didn't think so.

She nuzzled him. "You've changed."

His brow smoothed, and he snuggled her close to him. Wrapped in his protective arms, she let herself drift.

And yes, they awoke before anyone came after them at trident-point.

Lotar was his usual alert self as they journeyed to the edge of the city, keeping her safe from what they knew—by Elder Iliat's theatrically black, glowering expression—was coming.

At the edge of the city was her last chance to pitch the party. Last chance to avoid another no.

The king approached.

She had to do something.

Now was her last moment to shine.

TWENTY-THREE

Hazel tensed in Lotar's arms, and he felt the same kick to readiness.

But the king's first words were not what he'd expected. "Are you determined to complete the All-Cities Gyre? All the cities of history?"

Lotar nodded, his hand hovering over his closest dagger.

"The All-Council army is in the region to ambush you. A unit came several surface days before you. They are waiting in the ruins of Oria."

That was irritating.

But not surprising.

If he could not stealth past them, perhaps Hazel could create an impenetrable shield...

"Ruins?" Hazel tilted her head. "Why are we visiting ruins? Does anybody live there?"

"Not since the Seven Cities' War," the king replied. "They, along with their two neighbors, suffered most from the lack of sacred brides. Being less robust, they withered or fled."

"Oh. So there's no one to deliver an invitation to?" She patted Lotar's chest. "Easy. We'll skip them."

Skip them...

But then he would not be the first warrior to complete the All-Cities Gyre.

"But then you are not completing the All-Cities Gyre," the king vibrated, echoing his thoughts.

Hazel shrugged. "If it means delivering invitations to empty ruins, I guess not."

An anxious wet-rag feeling twisted in Lotar's gut.

Skipping the cities made the most sense. It disappointed him for no reason. Second Lieutenant Ciran had said nothing about which cities to visit.

But they assumed, like the king and the All-Council army, that he would visit the ancient cities.

"Will you come to the party?" she asked.

The king's brows drew down. "You are still holding my warrior hostage."

"Well, if you come to the party, that's the best chance to meet him. I mean, free him. Of course, if he's already found his bride, she might have something to say about it."

The king looked back at the frowning Elder Iliat. It was a clever ploy. And Hazel was right. If Tial had a bride, she would not go without a fight.

Although the king was looking at Elder Iliat, the warriors reacted as if he had consulted them. The first lieutenant floated forward respectfully and clearly under the charge of the other warriors. "You mentioned our mothers will be there?"

The king frowned harder and looked as though he were about to chastise the warriors.

Hazel vibrated first. "Another queen, Zara, has been

researching them. So if you tell me the name, I'll double-check when we surface in the Azores."

"Alawa," he vibrated quickly, as though he also knew the king did not want him to ask.

"Okay, great. I'll—"

"And Chepi," another interjected.

The other warriors answered behind him, fighting to be heard. Hurit, Karie, Sooleawa, Nadiea. Esoteric ones, modern ones, and all for a culture Hazel didn't know. At last, the deluge ended.

Hazel blinked. "Um..."

"And Brittany," the last one called.

"Haha, I'll remember Brittany," she promised, and the anxious warrior's shoulders lowered in relief. "Uh, Lotar, did you get all that?"

He had.

"Thank God." She laughed again with a bright glow. "And if Zara hasn't found your mothers yet, she can trace them with their names. Plus I'm sure knowing that you're seeking them will motivate your moms to seek you too."

All the warriors brightened.

Even Lotar's chest lifted.

The king's mouth opened and closed, and he tapped his fingers together. He must have been about to order his warriors to chase them from the city, but now that they were doing his warriors a favor, he could not do so. "I need volunteers to escort them to the city's echo point."

There was nearly a fight over volunteers, and many more than were necessary escorted them the extra distance to the echo point instead of at the edge of the city's territory as usual. They used the opportunity to remind him and Hazel of their mothers' names, as well as ask more questions outside of the hearing of their king or elders who were still loyal to the All-Council.

Lotar didn't think about his mother much. She had left before he made permanent memories, like many of the mer. He had never sought her although the surface world was open to him. If he went to her and she was as disapproving as his father...there was no need to seek her out.

Outside the echo point, when the Newas warriors were trying to get him to repeat names one more time, Hazel stopped them with a laugh. "Lotar gets it. He's exceptional, okay? I'd forget in a day—except for Brittany—but if he says he'll remember, he will remember. I promise."

They looked so anxious, but swam away.

His chest tingled.

Hazel approved of and celebrated his abilities. She'd never shown irritation when he exceeded her.

It was possible, just possible, that his mother might be the same.

He floated with Hazel into the echo point.

The news of the ocean swirled around them.

Now was the time to announce their next destination.

But...

A rebellious flare ignited.

He *would* complete the All-Cities Gyre. The All-Council would not stop him. He would leave Hazel and...

No.

This attitude aimed him at trouble. He wanted to test his limits, not endanger others.

He had to reconcile himself to not completing the All-Cities Gyre.

Hazel vibrated, stopped, and motioned him to get out of the echo point.

He kicked out of the echo point and into the ocean to talk without being overheard.

"Where are we going next?" she asked.

It tore at his chest to even say it, but he must. "If we cannot continue on the Sol Nord, we must cycle the opposite direction on the Sol Sud."

"And pass the cities we've already visited? Do we even have time to do that?"

"Perhaps. Perhaps not."

"So can we bypass Oria? Get on a fast current?"

"If the All-Council general is smart, he will station scouts and ambush parties on all routes."

And detouring meant Lotar would not finish the All-Cities Gyre...

Hazel grimaced. "So our only choice is to turn around. Unless...are we sure there's nobody behind us? Can we go over the All-Council? Around them?"

He drew an invisible map for her on his chest. The next cities after Oria were along the coast of her Europe and Africa, and they would circle through the Azores and shoot up the Arctic coasts over to what she called the Pacific.

"The exact route has changed, but this is what King Kadir remembers from the All-Council archives," Lotar finished.

"The route changed?"

"The ocean currents have changed, yes."

"Huh. Why are you so disappointed about skipping cities? If it's changed anyway."

He twitched. His heart palpitated. He had not told her of his unworthy disappointment.

"It's obvious." She rubbed his shoulder. "Or maybe it's just obvious to me. My plans never work out. I get to deal with disappointment a lot."

He rubbed his jaw. How embarrassing. Was he a trainee or a warrior? Such an unworthy complaint.

Such emotions would not distract a real warrior such as Second Lieutenant Ciran.

And Lotar acted as the kind of warrior his father accused him of being. Petty to the point of endangering others, so focused on increasing his own glory, he did not consider what was best for his fellow warriors.

"If the route changed, does that mean you used to visit different cities?"

"The same cities, but a different order."

"Hmm. What about added cities?"

"Added cities?"

"Atlantis is new. The old Atlantis sank so long ago, nobody even knew where the ruins were, right? And we added in Sanctuary Island. Have any more changed?"

What an interesting question.

He had only considered what he'd lost. Not what he'd gained. The plan was to complete the last All-Cities Gyre on record, but that didn't account for the change in ocean currents, or the loss and addition of cities, or even the history of alternate routes.

"But I suppose it doesn't matter if we still have to sneak past the army somehow," she said.

Still, his mind cleared and his heart calmed. He reviewed their alternatives more intently.

"A faster current has opened in this direction." He pointed up the coast of Africa and Europe. "We are taking the weaker crosscurrents to reach the cities in order."

"Oh. Well, can we cut across the ocean and take the faster current?"

But there was no faster route from their current location

—close to this Canadian shore—over to the bulge of the land humans called Africa. "We must go back."

They floated in the current.

"That's too bad. We'll have to sneak past the All-Council. Or..." Her eyes suddenly widened. She pressed her palm to her forehead. "Oh my God. I'm an idiot. It's taken me an embarrassingly long time to think of this. Of course there's a way to sneak past the All-Council! Oh, wow. Oh my God. Please don't fire me. And it will be like a million times faster if it works."

He did not see it.

"How close are we to land right now?" she asked.

"In surface time? A few days."

"Okay, we have to go to the nearest inhabited point. Go back to the echo point and announce we're going to Djullanar."

Djullanar! "No traveler on the All-Cities Gyre has ever cut from Newas and Oria to Djullanar."

"Because no other traveler partnered with a human."

"A land route is impossible."

She patted his chest. "We're not going to walk, Lotar. We're going to fly."

Announcing his destination in the echo point was an act of faith. Then he led her to the surface and followed the coast until they came upon humans fishing from a small dock.

The humans gaped at them clambering out of the water to stand in the snow, nude, Hazel choking up seawater and him with all his weapons. After a short time, more humans arrived with a female elder in a woven, feather-covered blanket.

Once the elder realized they didn't speak the Newas tongue, she repeated one word over and over.

"It sounds like she's saying 'iliat,'" Hazel told Lotar.

The elder nodded intently. "Iliat!" She produced a large white pearl. No, a mating gemstone.

Oh.

"She was a sacred bride," Lotar told Hazel.

"Wow! What are the odds? So you know what she's saying?"

"I am not from Newas, so I do not know."

The sacred bride interspersed "Iliat" with a string of otherwise unintelligible words. She gestured at the sea as though asking why they had come at this strange time.

"Wait, are you saying that you were the sacred bride of Elder Iliat?" Hazel asked. "Does that mean your son is Tial?"

"Iliat, Tial," the sacred bride said happily and gestured at her womb.

"No way! That's so crazy. Seriously, what are the odds?"

"Fairly good." Lotar had taken the strongest current from Newas to the surface, and another strong current along the coast. If any sacred brides remained, they would also be near to the place of strongest resonance, the sea. "And there may be more nearby."

"Lotar knows Tial," Hazel told the sacred bride. "He's from Atlantis. You're invited to our party. Tial will be so excited if you come."

The sacred bride smiled vacantly, clearly having no idea what Hazel was saying.

Hazel put her thumb to her ear. "Is there anywhere around here where we can make an international phone call?"

The sacred bride turned to her human family, and the humans conferenced among themselves. The sacred bride waved goodbye and ambled to the end of the dock, staring out into the misty evening. Her family put Hazel and Lotar into the hard metal bed of a grimy car that Hazel called a pickup truck and had them get out, onto the snow, at a square humming dwelling surrounded by a wire net.

The driver howled to the sky. Lights blinked on inside the dwelling. The driver zoomed away quickly as though afraid.

But the humans who exited the dwelling and crossed to the wire net were even more shocked at their appearance than the sacred bride's family.

Hazel held her hand to her ear again. "Hey! By any chance do you have a cell phone I could borrow to make an international call?"

One male staggered, and the other nearly fell over backward.

A third one shouted from the doorway of the dwelling, "Americans?"

"Just me." Hazel waved.

"Crazy Americans!"

"Fair enough." Hazel hugged her chest and covered her lower area. "I mean, we're naked in the snow, and I'm not even cold. That's pretty crazy when you think about it."

The other two opened the wire net, rolling it on wheels, to let them in. They gave her and Lotar brown blankets and found the phone for Hazel.

"I knew I should have brought my passport," Hazel murmured as she waited for the call to connect. "Oh, Flora? Are you settling into the MerMatch office now? Yes, this is Hazel. We've surfaced on an island off the coast of Newfoundland and we need to fly to Morocco, I think, but I don't have any ID or...you have? Okay, that would be great.

I'm borrowing this guy's cell and I…thanks. Okay. I'll get the name and wait for your call."

She returned the cell phone and collapsed against Lotar. "Even though we just ate, I'm exhausted and starving."

That was normal. Surface needs differed from underwater needs.

After a small meal of plastic-wrapped sandwiches that Hazel devoured, the three humans showed them to a room with a shower and a cot. The door closed, leaving them in privacy.

"Rest," Lotar ordered. "I will wait for the call."

"Just a minute." Hazel slid her arms around his waist. "You know what? Suddenly, I'm not so tired."

His cock flooded with heat. He rested his trident against the wall, within arm's reach, and covered her mouth with his kiss.

And within a human day, Flora called back with instructions. They received clothes and more food, were driven to a human airport, and got onto a private airplane. The flight was so different with Hazel curled against his side, chatting on the new cell phone she'd received or snoozing. In Morocco, they were conveyed straight to the seashore and released.

At the first echo point, they listened for a long time, but he had crossed a month's distance in a day, and even the All-Council army might not have heard his message yet. So he announced their destination again, now so much closer, and away they swam.

"I can't believe it worked." She glowed with excitement, repeating a refrain she'd shared with her friends on the cell phone multiple times. "I won't believe it until we actually get to Djullanar. But if it did...I can't believe my plan worked!"

"It was a good plan."

She glowed and squeezed him tight. They zoomed through the current faster than ever toward their destination.

And her glow matched and strengthened the glow in him.

Even in his unworthiest moment, she had not cursed him.

He'd tried to hide from her, but she always saw through his disguise.

Perhaps, with her, he could be himself.

Perhaps.

TWENTY-FOUR

Lotar must have a lot to think about, and Hazel did too.

Her plan had worked!

They arrived in Djullanar first, startling the warriors despite Lotar's announcements, and this time Lotar refused to separate from her. They had to spend a while in the city's coral jail beneath the Life Tree, but between threats of summoning the kraken—if that was even possible, honestly—and the carrot of promising their moms might attend, Hazel got them released without violence.

They even had a nice meal and guarded rest before swimming on to Rusalka—which followed a similar pattern—and past the ruins of Nerissa, Faier's first city that had been destroyed by an undersea volcano. The molten volcanic destruction was still so sad.

They flew through the most amazing shark-infested waters with iconic *Jaws* great whites, angry bulls, darting tigers, and aggressive white tips chasing them through the clear oceanic sky, but Lotar outsmarted or outmaneuvered them all.

Every time he did something amazing—and she commented on it, or reacted with awe, or asked him to teach her—he looked guarded and slowly, almost unwillingly, forced himself to relax and accept her compliment with grace.

How awful to have his successes used against him. That was the opposite of how things were supposed to be. How unfair.

And it made her super mad at the Syrenka jerks who had treated him so badly.

But he also seemed surprised when she second-guessed herself. Like, he thought she was a lot smarter and more successful than she was.

Maybe her friends were right. That she'd failed all the other times not because she was doomed, but because she settled for the wrong partners.

How funny that the "easy" cities had turned her down and the "hard" cities had committed to RSVP. Lotar was exceptional, so she was becoming exceptional too.

After they passed the wreckage of Nerissa and approached the next echo point, Lotar vibrated to her. "We must decide on our route. Cut west to Dragao Azul and the Azores, or continue north to Syrenka."

Where she would meet his father, the king, and try not to spit in his face.

Lotar tensed.

She mentally promised not to spit in his father's face right away, but Lotar didn't relax. "What about the All-Council army? Do you think they'll try to ambush us?"

"Perhaps on the way to Syrenka. If they passed Dragao Azul, we would know."

Because Dragao Azul was filled with queens and totally on their side. Their warriors would have broadcast any All-

Council army sightings over the echo points. "Could the army have snuck past?"

Lotar shook his head.

"We were going to surface in the Azores anyway. We could hop another flight over the All-Council army and land on top of Syrenka."

Lotar announced their next destination and veered into a deep current toward Dragao Azul.

His shoulders relaxed, his kicks lengthened, and he gently hummed the sweet lullaby he had done for her once to clear her head. Did he even hear himself? When he looked carefree, he was carefree.

All because they were zooming away from Syrenka.

She was no personal relations expert, but it would be great if she could help him. Somehow.

———

"Closure," Hazel vibrated.

Lotar swam along the current toward Dragao Azul, so named because of the plethora of blue dragons that floated near the surface of its sacred islands. "Hm?"

"Oh, I was thinking about times when success got snatched right out of my hands." She pretended to grab for something and opened her hand. Sparkling plankton drifted out. She grunted in surprise. "The ocean is so weird."

She had already succeeded more than Lotar had imagined.

Had he gone on the All-Cities Gyre himself, he would have perused the cities unseen, tossed the message to whatever unsuspecting guard he captured, and counted the mission accomplished.

She had already spoken to—and argued with—kings. She'd impressed warriors of all ranks. And even her powers, weak as they still were, had convinced more than one hotheaded warrior to pause, think, or even fall back.

"When I entered the Young Entrepreneurs competition, my partners and I got the invitation to present our product idea in New York. And we even won."

She still seemed surprised, although he sensed it had happened long ago.

"Only third place, but that was still enough seed money to build a real prototype and test it. We made plans, but I had to spend a couple of weeks on my grandparents' farm, and when I got back, I found out my two partners had spent the money not on tools or materials, but on a high-end gaming PC and a bunch of computer games."

Her soul flared with remembered anger, and she squeezed his shoulders. Then, her light extinguished, and she went limp.

"They wrote some stupid end-of-project summary about how our product had 'failed in testing' and offered me download codes for games that I couldn't even play. I was so mad. They were both already graduated and headed off to community college, so what could I do? Complain to the high school business teacher? It was done. And when I raged at them, they laughed at me."

He held her. "They lacked honor."

"Oh, yeah. You got that right." She expanded her chest, her light brightening to normal levels, and rested her head on his shoulder. "Since we're going to Syrenka after Dragao Azul, I'm sorry for suggesting your dad might be like Tial's dad. You know him. If he cared, he wouldn't try to sabotage your journey with those rumors."

Ah. "My father has never hidden his opinion."

"Well, I originally thought this trip would be a good chance to reconcile, but it sounds like that will be impossible. Reconciling is a two-way street, but maybe you could get closure. What would give you closure?"

"Closure?"

"You know. The fantasy is for your dad to say, 'Oh my God, Lotar, I was totally wrong. I always loved you as much as I loved your brother. I was just bad at expressing it. I feel terrible you went away, and I've missed you every day.' Then he goes in for a hug." She squeezed him. "You know. The fantasy."

His nostrils tingled, and his throat tightened.

How strange.

Even though his father would never, ever, ever speak these words, imagining him doing so, even in fantasy, made Lotar's eyes burn. He could not expand his diaphragm. The strength went out of his legs. He slowed and floated, fighting the unexpected sensations.

"Lotar?" Hazel cupped his face. Her brows lifted, and she hugged him tight. "I'm here. It's okay."

He closed his eyes, but the burning would not leave. It flooded his cheeks and wrinkled his chin. He pinched the bridge of his nose.

Did he cry? He would know on the surface, but here, the current carried away the tears. Grief, for the mer, was swallowed by the ocean.

Eventually, the waves of pain receded. His muscles went limp, and he felt heavy.

Hazel stroked his hair and hummed his childhood song, the one he'd used to soothe her.

And it was soothing.

She would be a fine mother to his young fry.

Which she also believed he deserved and would teach well.

The pain flared again. He held her, absorbing her comfort, not even aware of how much he had ached for this until she'd come and squeezed him and it gushed out. Unspoken wishes flowed out in a river of sparkles on a silent current far from home.

Eventually, he recaptured his control, pressed her to his chest once more, and kicked to their destination.

"That..." He had to control his chest tension and tried again to communicate with vibrations. "...will never happen."

"Yeah, I know. It was nice to imagine, though, right?"

It had not been nice, but it had been what he'd needed. Lancing the old injury to release the sickness trapped inside. Peace settled in his heart for the first time, even though his chest still throbbed like a freshly opened wound. Her gentleness soothed him like a balm. She was not a traditional healer, but she was exactly what he needed to heal.

"So we're going to have to see your dad," she continued, "and even though the fantasy outcome's pretty unlikely, what can you do to get something out of your meeting?"

"I need nothing from my father."

"I mean for yourself. You tense up whenever you think of Syrenka. Say that your dad hasn't changed. You deliver the invitation, and you could also tell him...what? What would finish this off, close it for you so the next time you think of Syrenka, you feel okay?"

He shook his head.

"There's nothing you want to say? That's okay too. In my case, I couldn't sleep at night and hated those guys for weeks. I wished for awful things. I wanted them to die. And then they did."

"Wronged humans executed them?"

"No, it was a dream. In my head, I wanted them to die so badly that I had a vivid dream that they died in a car accident. There was a funeral. The papers asked me to write their obituaries because of the Young Entrepreneurs. Everybody was crying, and instead of feeling vindicated, I felt guilty for causing their deaths with my telepathy—because it was a dream, so dream logic applied. I woke up with tears running down my face."

"Do not grieve for dishonorable males."

"Oh, I know. And it wasn't even real, but it showed me that I really didn't want them to die. I wanted recognition of what I went through and an honest, heartfelt apology."

"But they would not give it."

"Right, so I wrote out a 'closing statement' with all my anger, my disappointment. The things I should have said when I confronted them instead of freaking out and screaming. It was very cathartic. And ever since, whenever I get stuck in a place where I can't get closure—because the person who wronged me is gone or they won't care—I write out a closing statement. It gives me peace." She paused. "Of course, that's usually after I scream incoherently and cry with shame later to my girlfriends. But eventually, I write the statement, and I get peace."

A closing statement?

Hmm.

Hazel did not ask for him to produce it on the journey to Dragao Azul. She gave him the space he needed.

But he must say something to his father.

And her fantasy words had broken something loose inside him.

He had until they finished Dragao Azul and surfaced at the Azores to figure out how to proceed.

Because Hazel would come with him to Syrenka.

He needed her now more than ever.

And he must know his plan before they entered the city.

TWENTY-FIVE

Warriors did not meet them at the edge of the territory belonging to Dragao Azul.

Lotar swam out of the fast currents and pumped his fins over the rugged seafloor. The bright flashes of coral marked the territory's farthest edge. Fish glimmered, and the rocky floor filled with vibrant life much sooner and thicker than he expected.

Three twinkling lights appeared. Bright like stars. These were the souls of warriors. Not a single unit, but a whole group, vibrating with noise and energy.

He slowed to a stop.

Hazel craned her neck. "What's that?"

"A war party. Or..."

The tones changed. The bright spots moved chaotically, and vibrations crossed the distance. "Hi! Hello! We've come to meet you! Hello! Welcome!"

Hazel grinned, and her chest glowed brightly, resonating with the other queens. "A welcome party."

The queens waved. Their warriors paced them, a proud and sedate guard. Lotar released Hazel to greet the others properly. The group enveloped them, and the queens talked over each other while touching Hazel's arms, welcoming her after the long swim, saying she must be tired, or maybe starving, come this way, and they'd planned to meet her but everything took so much longer when you had kids, you know. Three young fry paddled around with shrieks.

They turned *en masse* to the distant Life Tree.

Lotar collected Hazel and kicked to the edge of the group.

Everyone asked questions at once.

"Wait, guys, wait." The youngest queen held out her arms and quiet descended on their group. "We forgot to do introductions. I'm Milly. That's Jen."

Queen Jen enveloped Hazel in a warm hug. "You must be exhausted."

"And that's Sydney," Queen Milly said.

"My turn." Queen Sydney nudged Queen Jen out of the way with her hip and enfolded Hazel in an even more generous hug. Her kinky hair glittered in a sparkly halo. "Welcome, girlfriend! You're going to love it here."

"Thank you." Hazel examined the sparkles. "How in the world did you do that?"

"Okay, so, step one is to give up on your hair routine. Step two, grow an afro."

"Step three, be fabulous," Queen Jen chimed in. Her curly black hair was shorn close to her head.

"And then?" Sydney pointed at her sparkles. "Magic."

"Oh my God. I love it." Hazel flexed her feet. "I'm still struggling with the foot thing."

The queens made sympathetic yet encouraging noises and promised she would get it soon.

Queen Milly continued the introductions. "This is my husband, Uvim."

A quiet warrior with amethyst tattoos nodded to Hazel and Lotar. His young fry silently kicked by his side.

"Dosan is Jen's husband."

"And our young fry." Dosan captured his son before the young one yanked his mother's close-shorn curls. "Watch for the hands. He is strong for his age."

His young fry squirmed.

"And Xalu is Sydney's husband," Queen Milly continued.

The final warrior was large and broad, with tattoos the color of smoke and a deep, resonant vibration. "Welcome." His young fry nestled in one arm and studied them with curiosity.

"You must have seen a lot," Queen Milly said as they swam. "I've been wondering. Are all the cities like this?"

Hazel looked at Lotar. "Nobody else sent a welcome wagon."

He nodded.

"Well, we swim here every day." Queen Sydney gestured to Queen Jen. "We're walking buddies. Just like in the old neighborhood."

"Jen and Sydney were already best friends," Queen Milly said. "They met their soul mates because of a snorkeling trip. I was their dive instructor. Can you believe it?"

"Uh, yeah," Hazel said. "Sure. Why not?"

The women laughed. Queen Jen and Queen Sydney whirled around each other, showing true synchronicity of mind.

"It was my honeymoon," Queen Jen said.

"Which she took *without* her husband," Queen Sydney said. "Because he was a dirty, lying, cheating—"

"And I didn't marry him," Queen Jen continued, "but the tickets were nonrefundable."

"So she roped me in, and she's been roping me ever since." Queen Sydney twirled to her husband, Xalu, and nestled into the smoky warrior's capable arms. "And now I'm a queen."

Her chest glowed.

The other women's chests echoed the brightness, their friendship amplifying their powers, and they all smiled. Queen Jen giggled, Queen Milly snorted, all three laughed, and a glittering brightness shone from their group, showering the land.

They reached the main city, Dragao Azul.

This city had been the birthplace of King Kadir and First Lieutenant Soren. Once, it had been a traditional city loyal to the All-Council, but since embracing queens, it had flourished. And more young fry flew through the city. Elders shouted to warriors, trainees formed behind trainers, and the usual sounds of a traditional city mixed with the very untraditional sounds of the queens laughing, greeting warriors, and even singing.

How unique.

Atlantis had drawn together the warriors of all cities in what was sometimes an uncomfortable melding that constantly had to strive to create new traditions to make the disparate warriors work together.

Unlike Aiycaya, which had lost its sacred brides for a generation, Dragao Azul had continued to grow slowly. There had been no breaks in tradition. Many cities could become like this once they opened to modern queens.

"Have you gotten to see a Life Tree up close?" Queen Milly asked Hazel.

"Not really."

"Come check it out."

Queen Sydney flew with her. "You can scoop up the Sea Opals and bathe in riches. It's opulent."

"You'll feel so refreshed," Queen Jen said.

"Like the queen you are," Queen Sydney said.

Hazel glanced at Lotar. They had traveled together for so long that her checking with him was natural. She trusted his opinion, and he trusted her to accept it.

This city was vibrant, energetic, and safe.

He released her easily. She swam with the other queens, her fins small but mighty in comparison to their beautiful flowing tendrils. The young fry played with them, darting beneath the branches of the Life Tree and squeezing through too-tight gaps, shaking the branches so the hard, pearly-white resin rained down.

"It is a beautiful sight." Dosan echoed his unspoken thoughts. "One that has never happened in our city."

"Perhaps," Uvim said quietly. "Before."

Before the Great Catastrophe, when queens had ruled beside warriors and mer and humans had been friends.

"We should have fought for Kadir's change generations ago," Uvim said.

From the Life Tree, the women squealed and suddenly hugged Hazel.

"We're going to be there," Queen Jen promised.

"Oh, heck yeah. We'd never say no to a party." Queen Sydney danced in place.

"We're still figuring out who's *not* going to go," Queen Milly said. "Put us down for yes at least twice."

All the women laughed.

Hazel's chest glowed. She peered at Lotar and grinned.

He understood.

"We will represent Dragao Azul," Uvim said.

"This is the future. Cities ruled by the All-Council will see it." Dosan's mouth quirked. "Someday."

Xalu turned to Lotar. "You know other cities. Do they understand what they have lost? It is hard to guess from echo points. Much seems untrue."

"Like the rumors about you," Dosan said.

Ah.

His heart palpitated. Tension pinged into his fingers and toes.

He had never confessed his shame to anyone before Hazel, and here he was, working up the courage to confess it to strangers.

Uvim and the others waited patiently, as though they sensed the struggle no matter how he tried to outwardly appear calm.

"My brother is Syrenka's prince," Lotar forced out. "But I showed more skill. It endangered his succession."

A long silence followed.

Xalu's brows drew into a heavy frown. "They expelled a second prince? When a city should treasure every warrior? How archaic."

"They did not expel me. I left."

Xalu traded glances with Dosan and Uvim. All three warriors regarded him with something approaching sympathy.

Uvim reached out and clasped Lotar's biceps, careful of the sheathed weapons. "Honor us by joining our feast."

The other two warriors nodded.

Another hard lump formed in Lotar's throat, so it was lucky he could give his thanks by vibrating. "The honor"—to be among these good warriors, these caring fathers, these kind males—"is mine."

Uvim's lips curved into a slight smile as though he heard

the words Lotar could not express, and he led Lotar to the castle for a welcome feast.

His queen, Milly, zoomed to Uvim, their young fry squealing in her arms. "Hazel does karaoke! Do you know what that means?"

He shook his head with a tolerant smile and hugged them both close, clearly used to their enthusiastic attacks.

"Dance party! Oh, man, we have to practice. I've only done karaoke, like, once in college, if that. This is going to be the best! I cannot wait."

Hazel curled against Lotar's side, concern tempering her bliss. She rested her palm on his chest. "Are you okay?"

The other queens and young fry swirled around him. Elders shouted about logistics for defending the emptied city during the party, and trainers barked at trainees. The mix of new and old, traditional and untraditional, cracked open his heart a little more.

Hazel revealed herself to all. She made herself vulnerable without hesitation.

Lotar had never done so.

But he must consider doing it more. It was good to speak his thoughts.

"Yes." Lotar pressed his lips to hers. She giggled in surprise and melted against him, yielded to his tasting and teasing. "I am very okay."

For now.

Things were going super well.

Lotar looked peaceful for the first time, everyone in Dragao Azul was raring to go to the party, and if no one else showed up, it would still be worthwhile. Plus this was the future Hazel someday looked forward to: hanging out in Atlantis with her new best girl pals, laughing at each other's jokes and finishing each other's sentences, while also being a mom to a kid everyone in the city loved and being completely supported by her devoted husband.

Also, bathing in a tub of million-dollar Sea Opals. Just because.

Jen, Sydney, and Milly got it. They lived underwater full time, so they never really felt their wealth, but they knew about it. They were rich.

Yeah. That would be awesome.

And they also allayed her fears about being pregnant underwater.

"It's not like on the surface," Jen reassured her, while Sydney and Milly nodded. Then she frowned. "Well, I think. I've never been pregnant on the surface, but all three of us had the same great experience, so it must be different."

"You will feel like you can kick major butt," Sydney said. "Like you can face down sharks with laser beams."

Nobody had puked their guts out for months. Nobody had gotten weird nosebleeds or fat ankles or joint pain. Nobody had gotten weird cravings.

"My glam has never been better." Sydney patted her magical glowing fairy forest afro. "Every day is a good hair day."

"The only thing," Milly said, interrupting the cheery recitation, "is that you might get a jolt or a stabbing sensation right when things are, uh, kicking off. If you know what I mean." She patted her abdomen. "So don't freak out and think you're dying. Don't scare your husband or start making out your will. It's just a weird cramp."

"From implantation," Jen said clearly. She was the practical, levelheaded one. "Of the ovum."

"Right." Milly squeezed her eyes shut and grimaced. "And don't freak out. It's embarrassing."

After a nice feast and a rest, the welcome party guided them back to the edge of the city.

Milly conferenced with them as a farewell. "Now, you've met Zara before, right?"

"We've talked on the phone."

"Then you already know she can be a little abrasive." Milly bit her lower lip. "Don't hold it against her too hard, okay? We had a wretched childhood, and the only reason our criminal 'parents' didn't traffic me into literal slavery is because Zara sheltered me from them. And after she finally found love and happiness with her mer husband, traditionalists ripped her away and forced her to the surface, where she nearly died. So she's less a 'glass half empty' person than a 'I can crack the glass into a shiv to protect my family from the enemies lurking outside' person."

"I've talked with Zara," Hazel repeated. "And if I went through what she'd gone through, I'd also have PTSD. But she didn't seem that bad."

"Good. I only see her every six months because she's mostly on the surface." Milly rolled her lips between her teeth. "Zara was my whole world, and I want everyone to see her how I do. That's all. Thanks, Hazel." She swam back to the rest of her group and waved. "See you in Atlantis, Lotar."

The whole group waved, and it was an amazing sight of chaos, laughter, noise, and, well, awesome.

"What a send-off." Hazel nestled against Lotar.

He smiled.

They zoomed along Dragao Azul's well-traveled route up to the ancient sacred islands now known as the Azores.

Humpback whales soared beside them, their beautiful eerie songs deeper and more orchestral, as though what she'd heard in tinny mono above the surface she now heard in surround sound.

They surfaced at dusk among a cloud of small blue-striped creatures with feathery fingers and toes like a watery gecko with stinging spines. He warned her not to touch. Then he navigated around a school of frilly Portuguese men-of-war, and he was pretty blasé about their stings, so she paid a lot more attention to the blue gecko things.

They met a Dragao Azul warrior stationed as a liaison between the city below and the Azores above. He led them over surface currents toward their chosen island, and as the twilight turned to night, bioluminescence sparkled after their strokes like turquoise fireworks.

The Dragao Azul warrior got them clothes—two pairs

of Bermuda shorts and T-shirts—and led them, dripping wet, onto an empty beach. He opened a lockbox and used the cell phone inside to call Zara.

Zara was on another island, but she arranged a car and hotel for the night.

"Queen Zara and Warrior Elan will join you tomorrow." The warrior locked up the phone again. "I will wait with you. Beware anyone who offers you a ride without knowing your name. The Sons of Hercules are not welcome by the humans on this land, but be vigilant."

So they were a problem here too.

Hazel thanked him, and when a car came to pick them up, the Dragao Azul warrior recognized the driver and confirmed it was safe. He bid them farewell to return to his station. The driver had covered his seats with plastic—so this wasn't an unusual request, obviously—and dropped them at a Spanish-style villa.

The driver wore a coat and hat and shook his head like they were crazy for walking around in shorts and a T-shirt, but she didn't feel cold.

Another perk of being a mer.

The receptionist let them into the villa without a question, and they enjoyed small cakes, fresh cheese with chips, and other snacks. Hazel peeled off her dripping clothes for a shower. Lotar joined her.

She bumped his growing hardness. "Why do we always do sexy things in the shower?"

Her gray warrior shrugged.

She slathered herself with a bar of nice lavender soap.

His gaze trailed over her breasts, her belly, and down to her vee. He made her tingle and throb with awareness. How funny that she could be naked with him for months underwater, but five minutes of nudity on the surface and everything was sexy again.

She paused, the bar on her taut nipple. "Are you just going to watch?"

An adorable grin flashed across his face, and he sauntered closer. "What do you want me to do?"

She pressed the soap to his chest. A dusting of gray hair enticed her down his washboard abs and toward the hard, ready cock springing from a thick mat of gray curls. "Scrub-a-dub-dub. Do you feel dirty? Haha, so dirty..."

His mesmerizing eyes captured hers. He licked his lips.

Heat throbbed into her breasts.

She lifted onto her toes and kissed him.

He dedicated himself to her kiss, sucking her tongue into his mouth and releasing her again, rough and hot. A wave of sensual need awoke her pussy with a throb. His wide hands kneaded her breasts, fitted her waist to his, gripped her hips. His cock prodded her belly.

They had united so many times under the water, and her first instinct was to wrap her legs around him and let him pound her straight into a mind-shattering orgasm.

But she tore her mouth free. "I want to suck you."

He paused, uncertain.

She curled her fingers around his hard length. "You're going to love it so much. Trust me."

He closed his eyes and thrust into her hand. So responsive, so much fun. Then he focused on her, iridescent threads in his irises gleaming silver amid the gray. "I trust."

"Good." She pressed kisses to his angular cheek, nibbled at his hard jaw until he groaned, and kissed down his dynamic wall of muscle until she knelt before him. His cock flexed in her hand, long and swirled with gray tattoos like the rest of his body, to the broader tip. She clenched the base nestled in gray and teased her tongue up the vein of the shaft to the sensitive head.

He made a sound and leaned forward, resting his hand on the wall above her head.

Nice.

Hazel stroked from stem to tip and back, then drew his head into her mouth.

He groaned louder.

Her pussy ached, throbbing with reaction to his guttural pleasure.

She wasn't a porn star or anything, but she'd always tried hard and was a little proud of what she could do. She bobbed, slurping and sucking and stroking, coating him with their juices. He tasted like salt and heat, like the ocean before a storm, and his moans lashed the walls, bringing her to the rim of her sensual pleasure. He was almost there... almost there...

He pulled her off and smothered her mouth with his kiss.

Rough, violent, uncontrolled—bruising in the best ways —he bit her lips, her collarbone, her breast. The wild frenzy made her convulse. Her thighs squeezed. She needed his touch, his tongue, his cock—

He dropped her to the floor. The shower he'd been blocking cascaded over them, pattering like warm rain. He parted her legs, suctioned her inner thigh, and kissed her pussy.

"No." She grabbed his hair.

He stopped, chest heaving, and rested on an elbow, hovering over her feminine place.

In her ordinary life, she'd be grateful that a guy was taking the time to repay her favors.

But with Lotar, she made demands. "I wasn't done with you yet."

He lifted one brow.

Yes, she would take on his challenge. He would experience a mind-bending blow job or else.

His lips curved into a smile. He gripped her hips and rotated her in the space, angling her body so he was lying on his back and she was flying over the top of him, sixty-nine. Her knees rested on his shoulders. Her elbows landed astride his waist. He controlled her, muscles flexing from position to position, like iron.

She wasn't tiny, but when he held her, she was.

And she hadn't been successful until she partnered with him. He made her believe.

And now she believed she wanted to rock his world.

She curled her hands around his cock as he kissed up her inner thighs to her quivering, aching, needy center. She plunged his cock into her mouth as he stroked her nub. The aching need intensified, pleasure mixed with want, and she moaned with his cock in her mouth, breaking the seal—but her sounds of pleasure ratcheted up his tension, and his cock tugged in her hand.

He licked her, suckled her, pleased her stroke for stroke until she was a gooey, throbbing, aching mess. She needed him. She needed him right now, and he had yet to—oh yes. Right there. She forgot his cock and panted, whimpering, as he pulled her out of her concentration and drove her right to the top.

He intensified his strokes, pounding and insistent, devoted as he was to her.

He was her perfect partner.

Her soul mate.

Her one.

Pleasure whipped through her, throwing her over the top and making her orgasm so hard, she shook.

And he flexed as she lost control, striping her and the shower in his release.

She rested her forehead on his bent thigh. His still-hard cock flexed in front of her like an offer. Did she want another?

Well, the last one had been amazing, and Lotar was nothing if not exceptional. So, heck yes. Why not?

Hazel pushed herself upright and wriggled on her knees down his body. She pulled her wet hair out of her face and looked over her shoulder.

Lotar watched her with predatory fascination, intent but also fully controlled, intrigued.

"That was great," she assured him, and a cocky gleam shone in his eyes in response. "Now let me teach you an advanced move."

Again, she'd hooked his intense curiosity.

She faced away from him, straddled his thighs, and fitted his cock to her slick, throbbing entrance.

He rose on an elbow.

She lowered herself onto his shaft, sliding him inside until her butt rested on his abdomen. He filled her so deeply. It was wonderful and terrifying how her body adapted to him. She changed the angle until his cock pressed against her most shuddery pleasure spot, and he moaned with a sharp need that matched the hunger in her body.

Hazel lifted to the tip and sat again, thrusting him in and out of her channel. His moans turned to grunts and growls. Although he was normally so silent, in sex she brought out an inner animal, and his reactions made her clench with throbbing heat. And it was fun.

He curled forward and gripped her hips, grinding his cock into her.

A wave of pure pleasure shuddered through her.

She was supposed to be riding him, but he held her in place and drove in harder, hotter, more perfect pleasure. She wriggled and cried. Each thrust pushed her closer to the edge. Each pulse into her spot sent a matching pulse of fulfillment and need cascading through her body. He slammed his cock into her, utterly out of control, and she arched her back as all the muscles in her body tensed and abruptly released. Pleasure gushed over her, a more intense orgasm than she'd ever experienced in her whole life.

He surged into her with a final groan, release racking his body, and then he slowly, so slowly, lay back on the shower floor. His chest rose and fell.

She slid forward so he was no longer pinioning her, then crawled to his front and collapsed.

And still the shower pattered down.

His chin trembled. Ever so subtly.

He was so sweet.

This was so nice.

She could lie in his arms like this forever...

Twinge.

What was that? She rubbed her belly.

A ghostly sensation of a cramp?

Huh.

Sometimes sex was so good, it was toe-curling, but it wasn't usually cramp inducing.

Unless...

She traced the line of his jaw. "You know, if we keep having this much mind-blowing sex, I'm going to end up pregnant before we finish this road trip."

He curled his hand around hers, kissed her fingers, and

nailed her with his steady, intent gaze. "I do not fear that at all."

———

HAZEL'S GAZE SOFTENED, and she rested her head on his shoulder. "Good. I just... It's probably nothing, but I thought you should know."

A deep sense of peace filled him.

He shut off the liquid and carried her from the shower, dried her with the towel, and completed the nightly rituals. She curled against his body—such a different sensation on the surface, her weight pressing him into the bed, her damp hair splayed across his shoulder, and her breathing soft and soothing. He rested his cheek against her forehead.

The Dragao Azul warriors swam confidently with their young fries nestled against their mates. The queens casually shielded themselves, healed, and pushed as needed without seeming to think about it.

Hazel was mostly there. She summoned power when she focused. Her fins were smaller and stubbier than other mer, but they still functioned.

And he had always felt physically capable of caring for his bride and his young fry.

Most importantly, Hazel had seen he was capable also.

She had recognized his abilities and celebrated them. She trusted him.

He would be worthy of that trust.

And with her by his side, he would face down his father and the other warriors of Syrenka.

Unease coiled in his belly.

Hazel would not change her opinion. She would not hear their words, nod slowly, and say, *Ah, now I see. Lotar was wrong all this time. He made it sound like you were the unreasonable ones, but now I understand the truth. I no longer want to bear his young fry or join with him.*

The coil vibrated with sickly energy.

No, Hazel was stronger. She was his soul mate. She would hear their accusations and still take his side.

She would.

Surely.

He held her a little tighter, and even though he was exhausted, he studied the ceiling for a long time, counting her breaths, promising that this would not be the last time he heard them so close or that she trusted in him so completely.

They both slept well, and in the morning, Hazel arranged their flight to Syrenka.

The unease simply would not leave him. Hazel asked several times if he was okay. He brushed her cheek and took comfort from her. She went into his arms willingly, and they united bodies with tenderness until finally, he was able to sleep.

When he awoke again, it was evening. Voices sounded in the main room. He pulled on his damp human coverings and exited.

Queen Zara sat in a chair facing Hazel. Her powerful soul light burned in her commanding chest.

Behind her stood her husband, Elan. Large, well-muscled, and covered in aquamarine tattoos, the former First Lieutenant of Dragao Azul had been blackmailed into leading an army against Atlantis. Now, he had thrown off all ranks and existed as a father, husband, and simple warrior.

Elan's gaze lifted to Lotar. Recognition and cautious respect filled his face.

Their young trainee, Zain, scratched human letters onto a pressed-fiber book. He concentrated hard, his tongue at the corner of his small mouth while he gripped the long writing stick.

Queen Zara's brown gaze crackled with fury. "Lotar. I know you have a history with my husband. Are you going to have a problem?"

They had once faced each other in battle. Lotar had captured Elan from the enemy camp—stolen the general from beneath his very army—and delivered him to Atlantis for judgment. At the time, Lotar had been so enraged that he'd wished to execute Elan, but King Kadir and First Lieutenant Soren had been wiser. Their decision had led to Dragao Azul rebelling against the All-Council. And today, Elan met him as an ally.

Lotar dipped his chin to Elan, and the warrior nodded back.

"Good." Queen Zara folded her hands. "Hazel, finish what you were saying."

Hazel straightened and cleared her throat. "Right, so I was saying that we've got RSVPs from warriors in most of the cities we visited, and as soon as I mentioned you were announcing the party to the old brides, they got super excited to see their mothers. I wrote down the names I remember, but Lotar knows the rest. Here, Lotar, tell me so Zara can look up if they've agreed to come."

He took a breath.

Zara held up a hand to stop him. "Forget it. After four years, I can confidently tell you that none of them are coming."

Hazel's soul light dimmed. "None? At all?"

"And they're going to be angry that I asked. All the brides who want contact have already approached the foundation. So you can call Mel and ask her for the list. Anyone I've hunted is angry, furious, to be found."

"Why?" Hazel lifted her palms. "The secret's out. They can meet their grown-up kids, revisit their old husbands—"

"Revisit their old trauma." Queen Zara leaned on the armrest, regal and certain. "When the Dragao Azul warriors took my newborn son and forced me to the surface, my last vision was of Elan being beaten nearly to death because he would not stop fighting for me. For us."

Hazel lowered her hands.

"The old sacred islanders had traditions," Zara continued. "A support system. That's all gone. And the mer didn't care. They cry about having lost their sacred brides, but the sacred islanders lost everything. The mer took the few brides who remained, used them to produce an heir, and then forced them to the surface to suffer on, alone."

It was hard to hear.

Hazel tried again. "But now things are different."

"How?" Queen Zara's rage flared. "The All-Council is still in power. Their armies still roam the ocean enforcing their traditions. And even if the All-Council does admit they were wrong and apologize, that won't unbreak the women who've been broken."

Zara pressed her hand to her heart.

"When Elan escaped with Zain a year later, I couldn't bear to look at them. And so when I found Elan's mother and she refused to meet him or her grandson—because facing what she'd lost would become too painful—I got it. I understood."

Elan gripped the back of the chair. He had lived through it.

"I'm going to continue tracking down the brides because someone needs to witness for them. Some need me to look them in the face and say, 'I know you went through that. I see and acknowledge you. I can't change the past, but I can be here for you now.'"

Queen Zara gestured at the paper in Hazel's hand. "So I'll take your names and I'll add it to my research stack, but as far as any of them attending, don't hold your breath."

Hazel's soul light darkened even further. She stared at the list. "I told all those warriors they might see their moms. I thought it was possible. I feel like I lied."

"You did." Queen Zara was unrelenting. "So my advice is to watch what you say. If you think you feel bad, imagine how they feel."

Hazel rubbed her chest.

"These women have been through enough. Don't set them up for any more disappointment."

TWENTY-SEVEN

"**I**s there even any point to this?" Hazel vibrated, her chest as dim as it could be and still emit light. "I mean, really?"

Lotar kicked in the Arctic current, his senses on alert, seeking signs that the All-Council army had come this way —and was lying in wait to ambush them before they reached Syrenka. "We swim as ambassadors of Atlantis. We do not know the future."

"But I lied to all those warriors. Like Zara said." Hazel pressed her forehead to his shoulder and wriggled unhappily. "Ugh. I wish I'd never come up with this idea. Or I wish Dannika would have come instead of me. She wouldn't have lied. She'd have said something neutral and yet wise so it would convince them to RSVP without lying. Not even an accidental lie. She talks, and everybody listens." Hazel wriggled again. "This is all my fault."

He squeezed her and nuzzled her. Her soul light slowly brightened.

Good.

Although, he did not mind comforting her.

It took his mind off what was coming.

In Syrenka…

"And I'm supposed to be supporting you." She lifted her head. Her soul almost bounced back to normal. She frowned and pointed. "Hey, isn't that a sign of the kraken?"

A group of rocks had overturned as they had after the kraken's wake passed between Aiycaya and Sanctuary Island.

He slowed. Another cluster of rocks lay piled on bottom-dwelling fish carcasses.

"I thought she normally stayed in the Atlantic," Hazel said. "Around Lusca."

"Yes, Syrenka has no tradition of the kraken. She did not range so far before her imprisonment."

"I guess nobody tells a kraken where to go." Hazel hummed one of what she called her karaoke songs. "Can we find signs of the All-Council army, or has the kraken already erased them?"

A good question.

A honed staff jutted up from one of the rock piles. Lotar rolled out of the current and circled to the staff. It was the carved end of a trident. He rubbed off the fine layer of dirt. Broken tines, but it was a new deposit.

"Yes," Hazel said, answering her own question. "Huh. Is one chasing the other? Like the army is chasing the kraken, or vice versa?"

How interesting.

He must watch for both.

And not become distracted.

The familiar pathways, even altered by the passage of a large undersea creature, filled him with an acute sense of location—and nerves. He was exactly three surface days from the Life Tree. The signs of the army and the kraken faded into the untouched ground, and still he traveled on. Now, two days away. Nerves uncoiled like electric eels squiggling out of their burrows, biting into his joints, making him jolt.

And yet it was home.

In this canyon, he'd speared his first ice snakefish. His brother had announced his kill jubilantly, taking care with the jutting fangs, and his father had bound Lotar's lacerated shoulder, so proud. That field was where he'd collected a long bone to make his first improvised spear, honing it under his father's watchful eye.

There was the gaping cavern where his trainer had made him re-race the length over and over because someone had insisted he'd cheated, and his brother—now a prince— had floated, pale and silent, beside their skeptical father.

Homecoming was a complex feeling.

"Are you okay?" Hazel asked quietly.

The nerves vibrated like eels shooting off electricity.

She splayed her palm across his pectoral. "I'm here."

Yes. She was.

And no one would take her support from him.

He hoped...

He flew over the rise to the edge of Syrenka's territory and slowed. The final echo point sat within Syrenka's territory, and so he would announce their arrival to the patrols he expected to see—especially if an army and the kraken had passed nearby.

The empty floor revealed no one.

Arctic crabs scuttled in a vast migration. The first ridges of coral, sustained by the Syrenka Life Tree, glistening in the impossible distance, proved this was still the territory's edge.

"Hey, it's funny," she vibrated quietly, "but I've been so

focused on your dad, I forgot to ask you about the city. What are we going to run into? Is it traditional like Newas, or at war with itself like Sireno?"

"Independent," he vibrated back just as quietly. "In other cities, if a king is unfit or there is a problem of succession, the warriors ask the All-Council to mediate, but Syrenka has never let the All-Council take over. Our elders developed their own solutions because Syrenka prefers unfairness over subservience."

"An All-Council army so close must make them nervous."

"It will be unwelcome." His father and brother could be conferencing with the elders right now on how to react.

A zing of nerves electrified his belly.

He stilled the inner eels using old techniques.

Hazel also stilled, mirroring him, and even her soul dimmed—not, with fear or sadness, but intentionally for stealth. She had learned much in their time together. In any other case, he'd be proud.

Lotar crept into the territory.

He had no desire to frighten the patrol. As soon as he saw the guards, he would announce his presence.

Deeper and deeper into the territory they journeyed.

Where were the patrols?

Had something happened?

An elder rested on a jutting square boulder, staring at him.

Lotar fought the urge to bolt. He had been spotted.

The elder's lips quirked, but he said nothing. His trident rested at his side, and his long fins dangled. The oyster-colored tattoos made a ghostly pattern on his equally pale skin.

Ah, at least he'd been spotted by a friendly face.

It was his father's eldest friend, who had always tried to mediate his father's anger and who had privately affirmed to Lotar that he would not face the same judgments in other cities, which had given him hope and led to him eventually leaving.

Lotar kicked to the old male whom he'd once considered a measured friend. "Warlord Yashu."

"The prodigal warrior returns." Warlord Yashu rested his trident across his knees. "I thought perhaps you would sneak in unannounced, and so I came to wait for you."

Hazel bristled. "We announced ourselves when we left Dragao Azul. There were no echo points between where we entered the water and here. Plus you have an All-Council army running around that you might not want to show up at your doorstep. So we weren't 'unannounced.' We were looking for the guards."

Warlord Yashu clenched the trident. "And this is...?"

"Hazel." Lotar straightened like a warrior before inspection. He couldn't help it. "My bride."

Warlord Yashu's brows lifted. "Bride? You travel the All-Cities Gyre with your defenseless bride?"

His tone dug uncomfortably into Lotar.

But that was a normal response. Travel was dangerous. Especially for a single warrior. And to take a bride with him—

"Yes, he's traveling the All-Cities Gyre with his bride," Hazel snapped, her hands clenched into fists. "Which you would know if you'd listened for any of our announcements. The whole ocean knows. Nobody was surprised from Newas to Dragao Azul, and here you are, acting shocked."

Warlord Yashu blinked. "I had heard rumors but did not believe they were true. I see now that was a mistake."

The tension in Lotar's spine relaxed. He rested a hand

on Hazel's fist. She was trying so hard to protect him, leaping to his defense. He should have told her a few warriors, such as Warlord Yashu, were on his side.

"We intended to announce our presence at the inner echo point," Lotar affirmed. "Or to the first guard, but instead, we saw you. It is dangerous here. Are you alone?"

Warlord Yashu tilted his head in amusement. "Am I?"

A warrior melted out of the coral to Lotar's left, too close to Hazel. Another melted out of the coral to his right, trident nearly touching Lotar's ear. A third rested at the base of the square boulder, trident pulled back to throw at Lotar's unguarded chest. Another floated behind him, and yet another above.

A classic trap. Place an obvious warrior in the center and wait for the target to sneak up on him, never realizing he entered the snare.

Hazel squeaked and hugged Lotar. A white light flashed out and surrounded them in a bubble, shoving away the nearest tridents.

The Syrenka warriors grunted in surprise and kicked back, giving them a wide berth. They formed a protective shield around Warlord Yashu.

Warlord Yashu's son, Anik, straightened. "What is this? Some exile trick?"

Unlike his father, Anik had never had a kind word for Lotar. His pale limestone-green tattoos coated his well-muscled, well-armed body with more numerous honors. They had rewarded him in Lotar's absence.

"My bride," Lotar repeated with a harder edge. "Queen Hazel."

"And I'm not defenseless." Hazel glared at them. "I have powers you've never even heard of. Don't try anything. I mean it."

The warriors stared in silent defiance. Part rejection because she was with Lotar, but part curiosity because she demonstrated her powers brightly.

Hazel vibrated quietly to Lotar. "So who's this guy?"

"He is Warlord Yashu's son, Warrior Anik."

"First lieutenant," Anik snapped.

A promotion?

To first lieutenant?

It hit Lotar like a slash. After the first lieutenant announced he would retire as soon as Lotar's father selected a replacement, Lotar had vied for consideration. They had chosen his brother as prince, so the next closest role was natural, but his father had never understood Lotar's wish to support his brother. Any success had only been more evidence to his father that Lotar wanted to take his brother's place.

But now Lotar corrected himself. *Never let the feelings show.* "This is First Lieutenant Anik."

"Great." Hazel looked past him. "And the other guys?"

Lotar identified the other warriors. Males who had trained him or trained with him, each evoking a fragment of his past that set off the electric vibrations of excitement and shame. Hazel remained taut, her fingertips and the shield still glowing.

"Okay. Now that we've got introductions out of the way, I guess you should make the announcement."

Huh? "They know who we are," he murmured.

"No." She flicked her fingertips at the warriors. "We're doing this the formal way. This isn't a social visit. We're here on business."

He knew it wasn't a social visit.

She met his gaze with hard determination. "We're travelers. On the All-Cities Gyre. *From Atlantis.* Announce us."

It was that important to her.

Very well.

He vibrated as loudly as if the warriors were the usual distance away. Their names, their mission. And as he did, another piece of tension smoothed over. She was right. It did not matter that one of his former antagonists had taken his coveted place. He was from Syrenka, but he would not stay. His home city was Atlantis. Syrenka was just a city filled with warriors he used to know.

He finished his announcement, and First Lieutenant Anik stared at him as if he didn't know what he was looking at. He had expected something else. Someone else.

Had he thought Lotar would return a broken male? Scarred, exiled, starving? Unable to find a new place to belong?

Instead, he was a trusted ambassador. He owned a castle. Enjoyed great respect from his fellow warriors. Possessed a smart, fierce, powerful bride.

No, he had not returned desperate or broken.

He murmured to Hazel. "You can drop your shield."

"I will when those guys in the back drop their tridents."

Hmm. He was so used to Syrenka warriors threatening him that the weapons, which would have bothered him in any other city, hadn't pinged his awareness.

Distraction. He needed to work on his distraction.

First Lieutenant Anik narrowed his eyes. "Why were you creeping into Syrenka's territory?"

Hazel made a strangled noise.

Lotar bent his head to her. "Mm?"

"Was he not listening when we told Warlord Yashu the

whole story literally five feet from his hidden eardrums? Or is he a total jerk who thinks he's going to catch us in a lie?"

Good questions. Lotar tilted his head at First Lieutenant Anik.

First Lieutenant Anik frowned. "What is a 'total jerk'?"

"Somebody who should know better," Hazel snapped. "I thought Newas was going to go down as the city that disrespected the All-Cities Gyre, but it looks like it's going to be Syrenka. And if the kraken comes by, I'm not sure whether I'm that motivated to save you."

Warlord Yashu vibrated from the side. "I had heard another rumor... Can your bride summon the kraken?"

"Soothe, yes," Hazel said. "Summon..." She looked at Lotar for how to answer.

In a friendly city, she would tell them her truth—that she had never tried—but she did not consider this a friendly city.

And considering this welcome, with tridents still out, he was beginning to agree. "I want to speak to my father."

First Lieutenant Anik glanced at Warlord Yashu, who nodded. The first lieutenant gestured to his warriors. They lifted their tridents and escorted Lotar and Hazel to the city.

TWENTY-EIGHT

It is a very silent, very awkward swim into the city.

Well, for Hazel. The guys acted perfectly fine not saying a word.

That Warlord Yashu flickered in and out of her consciousness on the edge of the group. He must have suffered a stroke, because while he frowned normally, he smiled with only half his face.

The others kicked like ghosts over the thickening coral forest. Other warriors flew in to flank them, each one silent as an owl's wings, and even their tattoo colors were muted. Midnight-sun yellow, shadow gray, white-cliff beige, seagrass husk, tan. They greeted each other with hand signals, trading information with subtle glances.

And she'd thought Lotar had little to say.

Syrenka was a rugged city gripping to life in the hard, uneven rock. The ground was flat and tilted, like sheets of ice, and the coral forests beneath the Life Tree clumped like snowfall. The main city anchor of the Life Tree extended up, and the surrounding castles jutted at variable heights.

The castles were shaggy like mammoths, the water even woolier than the deep oceans.

The great barren oak of the Life Tree was the same.

Slender gray sharks swam with them to the city, their sirens muted, and she wanted to ask what kind they were but she also didn't want to distract Lotar.

Whether good or evil kings, traditional or new ruled a city, the gleam of the Life Tree was meditative and the tinkling wind chimes of its tumbling Sea Opals clinked with hope. Hazel's anger—which had been pumping her blood hot since that warlord had sneered at Lotar—slipped away.

They'd entered the water near Murmansk, the northernmost point of Russia, but Lotar had said it wasn't the closest shoreline point. It was just the easiest to enter currents he thought would avoid the All-Council.

The leader, Anik, made her and Lotar wait at the first ring of castles. The Life Tree's highest branches glimmered, but the grandest castle obscured the dais.

An old warrior swam to meet them. His hair and tattoos were snow-colored, and like the rest of the warriors, he was taller and more angular than Lotar. Based on how everybody deferred to him, even though Hazel couldn't hear a single word vibrated, she was pretty sure he was the king.

He approached with an entourage.

Lotar straightened as though trying to make himself taller.

She'd never thought of Lotar as small, but compared to everybody else in the city, he was barely average. She was the short girlfriend at a basketball player's family reunion.

The king stopped in front of them.

This man had been so hurtful. So damaging. And she had a lot to say to Lotar's oh-so-fragile brother too.

"Lotar." The king's eyes were rimmed in red, and his

vibrations had a strange roughness. "You have finally returned."

Finally? Huh. Maybe this was an emotional reunion after all.

"Father. No, King Falki." Lotar's chest expanded, but he forced himself through. "We are traveling the All-Cities Gyre. In exchange for a meal and a rest, my queen, Hazel, will teach you how to soothe the kraken. And she has a message on behalf of my king."

His father frowned and looked at Hazel.

"His king is Kadir," she said, in case there was any misunderstanding. "King Kadir and Queen Elyssa formally invite the warriors of Syrenka to attend the reopening of the Atlantis platform. It is a place of friendship, built with human and mer hands, and so it's going to be a great place to meet brides..." She almost said *and mothers*, but stopped herself. They had enough problems. "And, uh, have a rocking good time. Can I put your city down as yes to attend?"

King Falki's gaze returned to Lotar. He waited for something.

"If you say no, I will still teach you the meditative tones to soothe the kraken," she assured him. "In fact, I can teach you before you give your answer."

Lotar nodded, still stiff, as though preparing for a dressing-down.

King Falki shook his head. "Then you are not..." He shook his head again. "You are not here to celebrate?"

"Oh, the party's not for over a year," Hazel said. "We'll celebrate plenty then."

Her answer clearly confused him. He focused fully on Lotar. "And you? Do you not celebrate?"

Lotar's eyes widened a fraction. Emotions inundated him, but he controlled them. Barely. "Celebrate what?"

"Your brother's misfortunes."

Lotar looked at Hazel.

She shrugged.

"You have not heard?" King Falki asked Lotar. "Oska swam into blackthorn coral, and a spine pierced his heart."

The color drained from Lotar's face. He went limp.

Hazel grabbed him, although he was floating yards from the ocean floor so it wasn't as if he was going to faint. "His brother's dead?!"

"Dead? No. Not yet." His father grasped Lotar's elbow and dragged them around the castles and across the gleaming center of the city to the glowing Life Tree.

A merman slumped against the base of the tree.

A healer knelt on the mound of Sea Opals beside him and replaced a poultice. From beneath the poultice radiated red poison lines.

The healer pinched a small shard of something in his hand as their group approached. "Another sliver, my king. I keep finding them. It must have embedded itself so deep that more keep flowing up. I do not know if we will ever find them all or how long he will survive."

OSKA LOOKED SICK TO DEATH.

No.

Lotar released Hazel and swam toward his brother.

"Stop him!" someone shouted.

First Lieutenant Anik blocked his path and pushed Lotar back with the trident, piercing his skin with a warning. "Back. *Traveler*."

Hatred seethed for the first lieutenant. Lotar reluctantly floated back until he was even with Hazel.

Lotar turned to his father. "When?"

"Oska could pass at any time."

Huh? No, Lotar had meant—

"But you should know." His father's chin puckered, and the red rimming his eyes grew darker. He swallowed and vibrated with great difficulty. "You should know that when Oska dies, you will not become prince. The elders will choose another. And it will be a noble, honorable warrior who has never abandoned his duty, such as the first lieutenant."

A much sharper pain than the first lieutenant's trident stabbed his chest. Even on Oska's death night, Lotar was not allowed to care about his brother.

"What. The. Heck."

Lotar pushed aside his feelings, quelling them as he always did, and turned calming hands to soothe his bride. "Hazel."

"You think that's why we came here?" Hazel raised her fists at his father in a rage, insulting the whole city and accidentally challenging his father to a duel.

His father looked startled out of his grief.

Lotar grappled with her, starting with the fists.

She tried to pull free and vibrated over his shoulder, very much as though she did want to duel and wasn't making a human mistake. "What kind of a father are you?"

"Hazel." Lotar drew her hands together, forcing her to look at him. "He is the king."

"And your father." She bared her teeth, giving expression to the deep current of shock and rage he was so desperately trying to suppress. "I know grief does weird things to people, but accusing you of being a greedy, fratricidal maniac because we arrived right after a tragic accident and forgetting entirely that, hello, we're doing the All-Cities Gyre, this is literally the next city, is the limit."

The shame seeped away. Hazel strengthened him. He pressed his lips to her forehead, and she brightened. They were linked as one.

She glowed like a nova as she snapped at Lotar's shocked father. "We're not staying. You've made it abundantly clear for Lotar's whole life that he will never be good enough. We're supposed to stay one night because of the Gyre, but honestly, I'm fine with leaving right now."

Lotar stopped her. "Can you heal Oska?"

She casually brushed the cut on Lotar's chest. "Was your brother a jerk to you too?"

"No."

"Okay, well, good." Her fingertips glowed, and the cut sealed. "I should have no problems healing him."

His father's gaze stuck on her glowing fingertips. It lifted to her face. "You can heal my son?"

"My king." Several elders jostled for his attention. "You cannot trust her. She is with Lotar. And a human."

"She is a queen," Lotar corrected.

"That is worse! Do not let her close, my king."

The king looked through the crowd to Warlord Yashu.

Warlord Yashu studied Lotar with a serious expression. "Ah, my king... If she is merely a human, she can do neither good nor harm. If she is truly a queen, you must decide the risk."

His father waved them forward.

They swam toward Oska.

First Lieutenant Anik lifted his trident to Lotar's throat, stopping him. "I vowed to protect Prince Oska. Do not approach."

Rage spiked in his heart.

Someday, somehow, Lotar would thrust his trident into the smug warrior's chest.

Hazel waved at his father. "I have to be next to him. Like this." She brushed her glowing fingertips over Lotar's ear. A scratch he hadn't even noticed was soothed, the itch gone.

His father waved her forward. "Let her through, Anik."

"She is with Lotar, which makes her dangerous to Prince Oska."

"Lotar will remain back. She will go alone."

Hazel looked up at Lotar.

He held her hand to his chest. The disrespect to him didn't matter. Only his brother mattered. She would heal his brother and they would leave Syrenka.

He released her. She swam to where his brother lay slumped at the base of the Life Tree.

———

HAZEL SHIFTED her small fins to feet and bounced across the clinking Sea Opals, strolling across a multimillion-dollar carpet, and knelt by Lotar's brother.

The mer healer rested on Oska's other side.

His brother had an angular build, like Lotar, but sucked in and weak, as though he'd lost too much healthy muscle and body fat. His tattoos were sable instead of gray. The same seashell necklace hung from his neck over the bandages covering his heart.

Red streaked from the seeping chest wound. It looked pretty bad, but Queen Elyssa had once healed King Kadir from a trident through the heart, so anything was possible with the mer.

Hazel rubbed her hands together. She was a queen. A dancing queen. The seventies music rose in her mind, and it was *way* better than "Baby Shark." She reached for the injury to channel her magic—

"No." The healer blocked her. "You must not touch."

Her heart skipped. "But it's how I do the healing."

"You are not his bride."

The mojo receded from her hands as she struggled very hard not to roll her eyes. "Obviously. Okay, wow, I'm so used to coming across mer that understand humans, I forgot how it is in cities where we haven't had contact. My healing powers are weak enough as it is. I know how touchy you guys are, and I get it, I do, but it's just how things are."

The healer looked at the king.

He nodded for her to proceed.

The healer backed off and watched with a frown.

Okay, now she had to get her mojo back.

She rubbed her hands together like Mr. Miyagi in the first *Karate Kid*, but this time, the song that came to her was the one that Lotar always hummed. Soothing and nice. She hummed it as she reached forward and covered the poultice.

Her hands glowed.

Oska's chest glowed.

And then his chest moved as though he were taking a deep breath, except he was underwater. His lashes fluttered, and he struggled to focus. "Mama?"

Shocked mutters sounded behind her. The healer shook with excitement.

She lowered her hands. "Not exactly."

"Oh." Prince Oska lifted a hand and rubbed his bleary eyes. "Who is..." He focused behind her, and his expression cleared to hope. "Lotar?"

Lotar floated behind First Lieutenant Anik's trident. Relief filled his face.

They were friends.

That was—

"I knew you...*ung*." Prince Oska convulsed in pain. He hunched over clutching his chest. His vibrations tightened, and he forced the hissing words out. "...you...betrayed...me..."

Oh, no.

Hazel clutched his shoulders. "Oska?"

The healer shoved her back and the king elbowed her farther out of the way. She drifted past Anik to Lotar.

"Son?" The king wiggled Oska's taut arm. Every muscle in his body clenched. "Son."

"...you...betrayed...me..."

Prince Oska collapsed.

His brother's words echoed over the stunned city.

First Lieutenant Anik frowned as Prince Oska slipped back into his coma. He leveled his trident on Lotar. "What does that mean? 'You betrayed me.' How did you betray Prince Oska?"

Lotar shook his head.

"What did you do? What do you know?" First Lieutenant Anik's nostrils flared.

The other warriors gathered, summoned by the accusation. They lifted their tridents.

And while his father was busy with his brother, who had made the utterly confusing accusation, he was alone. Just like before.

"Hey." Hazel kicked past the first lieutenant and hugged Lotar's side. "He said he doesn't know, all right?"

He was not alone.

"Not all right. Prince Oska said Lotar betrayed him." First Lieutenant Anik snarled. "You must have stabbed him with the coral."

"How?" Hazel demanded. "When was Prince Oska

injured? That's what he was trying to ask, by the way, when your king jumped down his throat."

The first lieutenant blinked, confused that she was trying to change the subject. "But…"

"When?"

A different warrior answered. "In surface time, three weeks ago."

"We were in Dragao Azul."

"Horta," Lotar corrected, because he had more experience with underwater time dilation.

"We were in Horta," Hazel said. "Witnesses saw us at the villa. Ask Zara or Elan. We had to take a flight, so we have plane tickets. Everybody at the airport saw us. We had to change planes. We're on camera in tons of places. There are company receipts for the overpriced croissant sandwich I ate."

"You…you used your powers. To…"

"I thought you said he got stabbed with a blackthorn coral spine. It was an accident."

"Only an untrained young fry stabs themselves with blackthorn coral by accident."

"Okay, how does this work?" Hazel tilted her head. "You think I somehow used my powers to remotely stab a man I've never met in a city I've never been to from a thousand miles away? Even if I wanted to, I couldn't. My powers don't work in the air."

The king and the others backed away, giving Lotar's brother space. They turned and listened to the end of Hazel's argument.

First Lieutenant Anik still held his trident at Lotar's throat. "But my prince said you betrayed him."

"Yeah, well, he also thought I was his mother." Hazel

finally stared down the first lieutenant. "He's been in a coma for three weeks. He's delusional."

First Lieutenant Anik traded glances with the other warriors. No one had any response to her logic. He lowered the trident. The other warriors backed off.

She huffed. "You need to quit blaming Lotar instead of looking inside for the real source of your problems."

The first lieutenant glared at her from the corner of his eye. He did not like her truths.

Lotar pulled her closer. He would defend her from anyone, armed or not.

His father looked even more exhausted. He scrubbed his face and gestured. "He has better color. You have delayed the inevitable. Despite...everything...I thank you."

"Okay, well, 'despite everything,' I can try again," Hazel said.

His father frowned. "You can?"

"Queens have pulled plenty of warriors back from the brink of death. If my natural talent were healing, he'd be fully awake, explaining his cryptic words already. After I recharge, I'll give him another shot."

"Recharge?"

"Eat. Sleep. Increase my resonance. Not necessarily in that order."

The king nodded, much subdued, and brought them into his castle. It was strange to be served a feast when Lotar knew himself where to collect the food, and it was also strange to be served the best meats like honored guests. This disorientation must have been what Pelan and Gailen had felt returning to their origin cities.

His father even brought out a massive side of conger eel and sliced off long cuts. The exotic flavor was like a celebration.

Almost.

"That blackthorn coral is nasty stuff." Hazel chewed the rib with her usual enthusiasm. She had never turned down a meal. "You'd better show me what it looks like. I don't want to get a scratch and kill myself."

"It is not usually fatal," he told her. "Even if it breaks off in the blood, a skilled healer can trace the path of the infection and remove the slivers."

"Wow. Bad luck for your brother."

Yes. Bad luck...

First Lieutenant Anik swam in and out of the castle. He acted panicky, and his gaze continuously returned to Hazel and Lotar with simmering, barely suppressed rage.

If the prince died with no heir, the most logical replacement was the city's first lieutenant...

But even the worst healer could remove the shards of blackthorn coral in one or two tries. And the Syrenka healer was a competent male. Had he turned bitter with malice?

The way his brother had convulsed—it was as if a new blackthorn coral had struck. Such as if there was still a deadly chunk inside.

Who else could be guilty?

Was it a plot or an assassination?

Lotar studied the warriors. Oska had always been well-liked, and his father had always treated his other warriors fairly.

Much had changed in the years Lotar had been away.

The feast ended.

His father led them across the city to his old castle, the one that had belonged to their family before the elders had chosen him as king. "Rest here. Do not leave. We will post guards. You understand."

Hazel eyed his father skeptically, but Lotar accepted the order and turned away.

"Lotar." His father's jaw worked. "I regret the manner of our first meeting. Before Oska's injury, we had planned to welcome you on the All-Cities Gyre. If he...when he awakes, I will have to confess that I failed him. I did not greet your return as we had planned."

Was his father actually apologizing? To Lotar? Truly?

"So let me get this straight." Hazel clenched Lotar's shoulder. Her smile was sharp enough to leave a mark. "You're not sorry for everything you said. You're just sorry it's not what Oska wanted?"

His father nodded.

"That's what I thought. How nice of you to worry about Oska's feelings. I would hate for Lotar's feelings to even cross your mind."

His father blinked. "Lotar's feelings?"

"It's amazing he still has any, right? But don't worry, I have enough for both of us."

His father looked confused. "You?"

Ah. Yes. Reassurance flowed into Lotar's heart. He closed his hand over Hazel's. "Father. I too am sad at the manner of our greeting. But thank you for telling me another one was planned. Perhaps someday, we will visit Syrenka again."

"But don't hold your breath," Hazel said.

"Hold my...breath..." His father rubbed his wrinkled forehead. "You sound like Irina. Oska and Lotar's mother. She taught me many surface phrases, but this one... I do not breathe, so I must always hold my breath."

He looked old at that moment. Old, weak, and close to tears.

And yet he was Lotar's father. Lotar would always crave a nod of approval.

His father frowned and tapped his forehead as though shaking loose something else he and Oska had discussed. "I did not ask about your bride. She is not from our sacred island, is she? And yet she knew Irina's song. How did you meet?"

Hazel snugged Lotar closer. "Do you really care, or are you looking for another reason to look down on Lotar?"

His father's brows lifted. He genuinely hadn't considered hurting Lotar. "Forgive me. I do not mean to accuse you. I am tired. I have not slept since Oska was injured. And I hope you know, Lotar, that despite being my second son, I have always wished you well."

Hazel tensed.

Lotar caressed her shoulder, and she quieted, silently respecting his wish.

Although he always desired his father's approval, Hazel was his life, his heart, his peace, his strength. And so long as her soul shone bright, his was steady. His father might never give him what he craved.

But that was okay. Because Hazel gave him all he needed to be whole. "We should talk after you have rested."

"After?" His father pursed his lips. "Yes. Very well. I have some things to say. If I were not so tired, I would tell them now."

"Go to Oska, Father," Lotar told him gently. "He needs you more than I."

His father nodded, swam a few strokes away, then looked back at Lotar as though reevaluating him.

Lotar had never spoken to his father so directly. He'd never looked him in the eye and faced him, not as his second son, but as a warrior.

His father turned and kicked to the tinkling Life Tree.

Lotar nodded to the guards stationed outside and swam with Hazel into his old castle.

The castle had frozen in the shape of his memories. The garden was the same shaggy mess, and the destructive cuts he'd made in the walls practicing with tridents had hollowed into permanent moldings.

Nostalgia crashed over him.

Here was where he'd grown up. Here was where he'd been a simple young fry, Oska had been a simple trainee, and their father had been a simple warlord.

Hazel peeked into the corridors, curious. When he caught her eye, she slumped. "I don't know how I got through dinner. Thank God for awkward silences. If any of them had said even one word in my direction, I swear I would have unleashed some very undiplomatic things. I barely reeled it in for your father. If I'd said everything I want to say, we'd probably be kicked out right now. And I don't want to leave yet."

"Because of Oska." He drew her into his arms and soothed her sweet, fiery brow.

"You get me." She leaned into him. "Something's rotten in the state of Denmark."

"Denmark?"

"From *Hamlet*. It's a Shakespeare reference. The uncle kills Hamlet's father and marries his mother, so Hamlet goes on a war of revenge, and everybody dies."

"An uncle requires two brothers, yes? If Oska has a young fry, then I am the uncle in Syrenka."

"Haha, oops! It means someone's plotting a murder." She teased her fingertip across his pectorals. "I think it surprised your father that you talked back."

"You are a good influence."

"I try. Although I did snap at, oh, every single warrior in the city."

He had needed her to do so more than he had realized.

"My father has always been fair." He smoothed locks of her wild brown hair. "And having two young fry when all others had one was unfair. So in the beginning, he announced my failures and reacted harshly. The other warriors would believe I was a disappointment and feel happy, not jealous, they only had one young fry son. But I hated to be disciplined, even though I knew the reason, so I worked harder than any other trainee to give him nothing to criticize."

"But that failed because he had to criticize something. If not your failures, then your successes, huh?"

"Yes. But..." And this was the hardest part. "He was kind to me in private. Until...after he became king, he changed. I think he started to believe his own words."

"Augh!" She whacked his pectoral. "I should have melted down on him. I missed my chance. He should have just loved you."

"He had to protect us."

"Well, he did it wrong. When we have kids, you will never say that you can't love one of them. You're going to say 'I love you and I love you and I love you and I love you.'"

Hazel thought they would have four young fry.

How adorable.

"Love is like the ocean." She rubbed her palm on his chest. "It's not a little pebble you have to guard. It's infinite, and it stretches as much as you need to fit everyone. All right?"

He pressed his lips to hers. "All right."

She twitched in surprise, then melted, teasing and tempting him. While they kissed, she vibrated in her chest.

"I warned you before, but are you sure you aren't afraid of being a father?"

"I no longer live by the words of mine." He touched his seashell necklace. "When we leave, I will stop by the pools and collect a shell for my young fry."

"Oh? I noticed only you and Oska have those shells."

"Our mother gifted them. I do not remember her. Oska might, but she told my father I had a strong heart."

"I like her already." Hazel twisted the shell to study it. "Hey, do you think she's coming to the party?"

"Syrenka still has contact with our sacred brides, although our ceremony has dwindled to a few times a decade instead of annually."

"Well, I'm glad you're resolved to have at least one child. Because I kind of have a confession." She pressed his hands to her abdomen. "The queens in Dragao Azul told me about their pregnancies, and some of the things they were saying happened, and...well, I'm pretty sure, um..."

He pulled back and met her gaze. What was she trying to say?

She lifted her shoulders to her ears and grinned. "I'm pregnant?"

Shock rocked him.

She carried his...

She...

"You carry my...my young fry?" His vibrations choked up, and he had to ask again.

She held up a hand. "I mean, I'm not sure and all, but there's a very good chance that I could be, you know."

Lotar would be a father.

Like his father.

Not like his father. Like Hazel said. She knew he was worthy. He enjoyed teaching her. He enjoyed training the

Sanctuary Island trainees and young fry. He would be patient, careful, fair. So very, very fair. Protective. Kind.

He rested his hand on her gently rounded belly.

She rested her hand on top of his. "Turns out it's not all from the jelly donuts. Which I haven't eaten in about, oh, forever."

He pulled her in and kissed her.

Hazel was his one. His love. And he had fought his fears, but he would never fight her.

She stroked his shoulders.

They made love in the courtyard of his old castle. In the place he had always imagined he would bring his bride and raise his young fry. And it was nothing like he'd imagined, but they made it their own.

She nipped his lips, and he returned with gentle strokes. She curled her hands around his cock and urged him to lose control, as he normally did, and he could not stop sweetly kissing her cheeks, her collarbones, down to her breasts. Flicking her nipples with his tongue, he cupped her buttocks, and she pressed into his touch. Sumptuous and slow, he lowered to taste her feminine flower and bring forth her needy moans among the dirt and the fronds. When he finally rose and fitted his cock to her entrance, she wrapped her arms and legs around his torso in understanding. He took her slowly this time. Pleasure built as their bodies united, leaping and diving, over and over. They rolled, but no matter who was on top, he surged into her, infinitely in control. Only their joining held meaning. She was his future. His bride. His everything.

Her face transformed in bliss, and her arms spread as though she were flying. His soul flew with hers and his body shuddered, releasing his seed deep into her warmth. She collapsed on him, and he reflexively caught and held her.

"That was amazing." She kissed his lips and settled against him, her soul glowing with renewed strength. "I'm so glad I met you. Nothing will ever be better than right now. Nothing."

He curled his hands around her waist, snugging her safely to him.

And yet this was not the Syrenka of old. There was a traitor. And they must not endanger Hazel.

If anything happened to her...

They beat Elan nearly to death. Queen Zara's furious gaze crackled in his memory. *They took my newborn son and forced me to the surface, still bleeding. I nearly died.*

King Ankena looked regretfully after his son. *After I defied my father, he stole my son and raised him. Although it was only a few years, my son still struggles with the hatred he was taught. It is my greatest regret.*

And Queen Zara again. *No one cared about the brides. The mer made them produce, stole their children, and forced them to the surface.*

He hugged Hazel.

There was still time. Time to stop his brother's assassin. Time to heal Oska.

But...

If danger threatened, she would go.

He would protect Hazel.

More than he'd protected his brother.

No one would ever take their young fry.

No one.

THIRTY

Shouts echoed through the castle.

Lotar awoke in an instant.

"In there," a warrior vibrated outside the castle. "Get them out."

Danger was coming.

The guard, an impassive warrior, saw he was awake and stopped at a respectful distance. "You must come."

Hazel awoke with a yawn and a stretch. "Huh? What?"

"The king summons you to the Life Tree," the guard vibrated.

"Already?" She finished her great yawn and obediently kicked to Lotar's side, scrubbing her eyes and shaking off her exhaustion. "I could use another few hours."

"There is no time," the guard said.

Lotar's stomach dipped.

The guard concealed something. He turned and kicked out of the castle.

Lotar flew after him, his senses on the highest alert.

Hazel became more alert as they wove through the rings

of castles and approached the Life Tree. A crowd had gathered.

His brother labored to breathe, his chest rising and falling unevenly. The red streaks now shot over his whole body. Dark shadows pinched him. Death clawed at his heart.

The king knelt at his side and shook with sadness.

"What happened?" Hazel murmured. "Is that normal after blackthorn coral?"

"No." The healer floated in the crowd. Oska's sickness had gone beyond his abilities.

"Where was the guard?"

"Here." The healer chewed on his lower lip, angry but also pensive. "Prince Oska was, and has been, under guard since his first injury. I have never had a warrior collapse this completely from blackthorn coral. And to have it be the prince..." He glanced at Hazel, and his eyes narrowed with suspicion on her fingertips, but he pulled his gaze away and focused again on the distant patient. "It is vexing."

Hm.

"Someone did this," Hazel said.

Her vibrations crossed the open area.

His father jerked and whirled to her. Rage contorted his trembling face. "You did this!"

She stiffened in Lotar's arms. "Me?"

"You pretended to heal him, but you killed him."

"Wait a minute. I *did* heal him. You saw me."

"I saw him convulse. And now this." His father pointed at Oska's chest.

They had pulled off the poultice. In the center of the injury was a small handprint.

"The heck?" Hazel kicked forward. "What is it?"

Lotar shadowed her, and the guards kept their tridents close, but allowed them both through.

"Your hand," his father sniped.

"What? That's not me. Look." She held up her hand. "It's the wrong size. They made my middle finger shorter than the rest and forgot my thumb."

"He is deathly ill, and your hand burned him."

"I just told you—"

"Silence!" His father rose, his soul black with rage and grief.

Lotar pulled Hazel behind him protectively. "Father. Calm."

"I was starting to believe that I had been mistaken about you." He jabbed his index finger at Lotar. "But you have only ever wished your brother ill. And so you ordered your bride to hasten his journey into the blacknight sea. Well, you can both get out! Before I have you executed for treason."

This wasn't right.

If he left now, Lotar abandoned his brother to an assassin. His father might never see beyond his hatred of Lotar to realize that someone else was endangering Oska.

But Hazel's safety took precedence.

Hazel and his young fry.

Lotar backed away from his seething father, through the stiff, silent, accusatory glares of the other warriors of the city. Hazel clung to his back. She trembled, not from terror, but from suppressing the logic even she must know would fail to reach his father.

"My king." Warlord Yashu floated gravely at the edge of the dais equidistant between Lotar and the king. "I have long held my counsel when you have spoken to Lotar in this way, but in this time of confusion and tragedy, I cannot remain silent."

Hmm?

Warlord Yashu was publicly taking his side?

"He is innocent of any wrongdoing." Warlord Yashu gestured at Lotar's brother. "He cannot have injured Prince Oska from the surface, and it is obvious from his actions he cares only for Oska's recovery. If you banish him, I believe you banish an innocent warrior."

His father stared as if his oldest friend had announced an intention to capture and keep the kraken as a house guardian. "This is your belief? But he brought a female who injured my son."

"I did not," Hazel insisted.

Lotar squeezed her hand.

Warlord Yashu lowered his head. "I do not know the powers of queens. In the myths, they are incomprehensible and vast. Lotar's bride confessed she has limited control. Perhaps she made a mistake."

"Which costs Oska his life!"

"But a warrior cannot deny his soul mate, no matter her intentions. An honorable warrior believes that every warrior he meets is also honorable. And so, of course, he would also think the same of his bride."

His father pondered the words for a long, hard moment. "Lotar. As you know, I place a great deal of value in Warlord Yashu's words. Especially now, when I am not..."

He gazed over his shoulder at Oska, squeezed his eyes shut, and returned a hardened focus on Lotar.

"But if you desire to grieve here during your brother's final hours, I will overlook these mistakes. So long as you send your murderous bride to the surface before she finishes her dark task."

His heart pounded.

The ocean stilled.

"I can still heal Oska," Hazel protested.

"Get her away from here." The king turned away in disgust.

Guards surrounded them, waiting on Lotar's move.

"He's not dead," she said. "I'm recharged. I can heal him."

Lotar must find the real culprit.

Until he stopped the poisoning, Hazel could not heal Oska.

And every time she failed, his father would grow more dangerous.

Hazel would be safe on the surface.

She would be safe.

"Lotar, tell him." Hazel clung to his shoulder. "There's a traitor here, but it's not me."

He turned slowly and removed her hands.

She gaped.

He untied his necklace and pressed it into her hands. "I am sorry, Hazel."

Shock gave way to hurt. Her soul blackened, and it nearly undid him.

Then she flared with rage. "You jerk! How could you?"

The guards moved her along without touching her, without even raising their tridents. They were experts at herding targets. They forced her across the city and around the first row of castles.

He turned his back on her screams.

"This isn't how things end. I'm coming back for you. You're going to be sorry. Lotar!"

He welcomed her return. By then, he would have caught the traitor, and she would understand.

He did this for her protection.

———

Hazel kicked hard for the surface cursing the whole way.

She'd awoken in Lotar's castle dreaming about carrying Lotar's baby and how sweet he could be...

And then he'd coldly sent her to the surface.

"I will never forgive you!" she shouted into the current. "You jerk! You idiot! You cold-blooded reptilian fishman!"

One warrior who silently escorted her to the surface glanced back at her.

"What?" she snarled.

He turned around. Then, as though he couldn't get the question out of his head, he fell back. "You told First Lieutenant Anik that a 'jerk' meant someone who should know better, but now you use it against your soul mate, a warrior who knows everything about you."

"Yeah, he knows about me, but he just has to do everything on his own. And after we came so far." She grabbed her hair and yanked. "Argh! He knows I'm not the traitor. He decided he'd be better off searching on his own. Which I blame you for, by the way, since you guys always made him do everything on his own, and now he doesn't know how to work with a partner."

The escorting warriors traded skeptical glances.

"And who's going to heal your brother after you find the traitor and I'm still on the surface?" Hazel demanded from the Lotar who was not here. "Hello? Augh! I can't believe you'd do this to me. After everything we've been through."

"You are the traitor," one warrior in the back said smugly.

"Oh?" She swung to face him. "And how the heck can I be the traitor, genius? I haven't even been here."

"You made Prince Oska worse."

"Yeah? Well, who made him sick in the first place?"

The quintet of escorting warriors pondered her question.

"Lotar, perhaps." The smug warrior wasn't so smug now.

"Literally how could he have done that?" Hazel demanded.

"He could have charged another warrior, his secret friend, to attack the prince."

"Then his 'secret friend' is the traitor, and you still have a traitor. Do you guys think *anything* through, or do you rely on spying and eavesdropping to figure it out?"

"We are not Undines," the smug warrior said. "We need not float and think."

"You say that like it's something to be proud of." She shook her head at the lot of them and faced forward again, swimming for the surface for all she was worth. "Who was on guard duty last night?"

"I was," a slender, angular warrior with avalanche-blue tattoos said.

Everyone looked at him.

He hunched uncomfortably. "And other warriors."

"Like who?" his smug friend asked.

The guard listed off the others who had been on shift with him. It sparked a mild discussion about potential alternative traitors, but they eventually looped back to her as the only one with strange powers and a "dark task."

"But you are the one who is not smart," the smug warrior said. "Even if you murder honorable Prince Oska, you will never be the queen of Syrenka."

She flubbed her lips. "I would not be the queen of Syrenka if you begged me."

Their brows rose. Then skepticism narrowed their eyes.

"Did Lotar ever, ever, ever, ever, ever even say he wanted to be a prince? Or king, or anything?"

"Yes," the smug one said. "Many times."

"Oh, yeah? Describe them."

"When he beat Prince Oska at the race. He did so to be chosen as prince."

"Did he ever *say* that?"

They searched their memories. Silence pervaded the latter half of the interminable swim.

Finally, the smug guy dismissed her. "The real traitor is you. Only a traitor would try to convince us she was not. Prince Oska bears your handprint."

She could scream. "My fingers, which were the wrong size, and not my thumb. When I touch someone to heal them, I give whole-hand coverage." She reached out to demonstrate on one of them.

They darted back.

Oh, whatever. She demonstrated on her chest. "Look. All four fingers plus the thumb, but that print had no thumb, which means the real traitor is an idiot who doesn't know what a hand looks like."

The smug warrior pulled his lips to one side. "Perhaps your thumb has no queen power."

"What?"

"Perhaps only your fingers glow with the resonance."

"My thumb has resonance. My thumb is very resonant. Look." She flooded her rage energy into her hand, and the whole darned thing glowed like a torch. "See? The glow comes from the whole hand."

They scattered as if she was going to fry them with a death touch, which wasn't even a queen power.

She dropped her hand with a moan and extinguished the light. "God, why am I arguing with you? You're the ones who are like, 'Lotar is too good, we have to knock him down so he leaves us forever.' Jeez. Which let a traitor run free in your city, killing off your prince and who knows who else. God."

And Lotar was going to try to stop it on his own.

Like always.

The warriors escorted her to the crashing whitecap waves, and the smug one ordered, "Go to the shore."

She peered through the furious water. "You're not going to dump me, are you? I could die, you know."

"This is where we always return humans," the smug warrior said. "You will find them. Do not linger in the water, though. A human sailor will harpoon you for a fish!"

They all laughed as if that were hilarious.

Gross.

They zoomed off, leaving her alone.

She fought the waves over the rough slope and stumbled ashore.

Snow and arctic ice covered the rocky shoreline.

This must be the North Pole.

And it was only a fraction as cold as Lotar's heart.

THIRTY-ONE

otar's gut churned.

He could hear Hazel's shouts long after she left. Her anger, bright and furious, echoed even though she must have reached the shoreline of the ancient sacred brides by now.

All the curses he had most feared hearing, he had finally caused her to cry.

It was for her own good.

She was on the surface.

She was safe.

But...

A very small, very real pit in his stomach warned that he had gone too far. He had pushed her, tortured her, broken her. The other warriors had called his good actions bad, but in this case, he had truly wronged her, and her accusations were real.

I will never forgive you.

The words lanced him.

He had done it. He had done it to her.

To himself.

He lingered near his father, keeping vigil, and studied every warrior who passed.

Although he was no former Undine like Second Lieutenant Ciran, he had to consider how he would have committed this crime.

The traitor must have poisoned Oska after Hazel's healing, during dinner or their rest.

First Lieutenant Anik had entered and exited frequently. He had looked panicked. And now he was nowhere to be seen, absent on a quest when he should be close to the prince he had pledged and failed—perhaps deliberately—to protect.

Warlord Yashu waited patiently with the other elders.

His brother was a fighter. He did not die quickly. Despite the new poisoning, he carried on, his soul sometimes only a flicker within his chest, and other times it appeared to go out entirely, but he would rally with a gasp, making the watchers jerk with fright. Except for their father, who gazed on with unshaken devotion.

Under so much scrutiny, Lotar could not move much, but he did approach the guards under the guise of changing positions and vibrated quietly. "Did you watch over my brother after the healing?"

The guard's jaw flexed. "If you think I did not do my duty, say so to my first lieutenant. Unlike others, he acts with honor and would never bring in a stranger to betray us."

Hot anger flashed over Lotar.

No. He must control himself. This should be a familiar pain.

But since bringing Hazel into his heart, Lotar had found it increasingly difficult to endure the old insults.

The healer broke through the crowd and knelt at his

usual place. "My king, I have identified the new poison. And I have a treatment."

Lotar's father dragged his heavy, shadowed gaze up to the healer. He had been through too much to react now.

Lotar floated at Oska's feet. "What is the poison?"

"A rare one from a mussel shell that thrives only near Djullanar." The healer used a small paddle to spread a thick amber resin on the odd print. It foamed. "There. It is working. Now, he will still suffer from the earlier effects, but this antiseptic resin neutralizes the main toxin. It may even have a small effect on the blackthorn coral."

The king's shoulders slumped. "Another delay."

"Yes. Perhaps."

His father rubbed his face, massaged his temples, and glared at Lotar. "You entered Djullanar."

Lotar braced for the accusation.

But his father frowned. "Your bride could have touched the mussel. Gotten its shell on her hand and..." He gestured with an open palm at Oska. "An accident."

Surprising.

"Oh, no." The healer laughed in a dry way that held little mirth. "She could not have done this by accident. This type of poison requires careful containment. The mussel shell is ground up with several toxic plants. It is dangerous to create and carry. The Djullanar warriors apply it to rocks for their slings using special tools or they become painfully sick. The onset of illness is immediate."

His father frowned. "She is human. Her tolerance is different."

"Not that different, my king."

"You do not know the powers of queens. None of us do."

Lotar did.

And the healer seemed to think he did as well, but he glanced at his king's black expression and focused silently on applying the resin. Oska's jagged pulls of water stabilized and evened. The darkest shadows left his cheeks.

The healer had bought Oska a little more time.

More time for Lotar to find the assassin before he struck the final blow.

"My king." Warlord Yashu approached Lotar's father. "You look as unwell as the prince. Please rest and eat."

King Falki shook his head. "Thank you, my friend, but I will remain until the end."

"Until the end." Warlord Yashu lowered his head, a deep pain echoing in his soul. He floated back to his rightful place with the elders and bowed his head in respect.

Oska could have no better guard.

Lotar approached the armory and asked to see the training daggers.

"Training daggers?" The trainers glanced at each other. "You wish to train now?"

"Revert to a young fry?" one asked. "You do not need training daggers. The weapons on your sheaths are dangerous enough."

"Perhaps ones that have been used recently," Lotar said. "The most popular ones."

They shrugged and brought over the case. No blades gleamed with the glassy sheen of the poison.

What was the next possibility?

A traitor had three problems. Carrying the poison to the Life Tree unseen. Applying it to Prince Oska, under guard, while no one noticed. Getting rid of it after he showed the effects.

Which were instant and very noticeable.

Getting rid of it...

Lotar flew down the stalk of the Life Tree.

The villain would not have had much time. How could he have painted a whole hand on a convulsing, groaning, tortured prince without anyone noticing? Someone had noticed, and he'd broken off before completing the thumb. If grief did not blind his father, he would hear the healer and know that a human, Hazel, could never acquire this unknown-to-her poison, much less use it right in front of everyone. Lotar was an obvious suspect, despite never actually touching his brother, but not Hazel.

So the poison must be in a protective bag. Like a waist pouch.

But it would be dangerous to carry. What if the traitor had only shoved the vial inside without being able to carefully contain it? Or what if it bounced open against his waist? It would seep through and poison him, and everyone would know.

Keeping it would be far too dangerous.

But while everyone's attention was on the prince, it would be easy to drop it off the dais. Maybe while disturbing a few mating gemstones, so their fall masked the true poison.

Mating gemstones piled around the reef. The coral grew over and around them, absorbing life-giving energy from their surfaces.

He cast his gaze over the familiar reef. Nothing caught his eye, so he started at the Life Tree and swam in a spiral outward, until...

A small dark spot flickered at the edge of his awareness like a shadow.

Ah.

Lotar swooped down to it. A woven seaweed pouch. He used his trident to manipulate the bag. Inside was a long stick like the drawing implement young trainee Zain had used to write his human letters and a small bowl with an imperfect seal.

There must be a way to identify the ownership.

If not, it might cut through his father's confused thinking and prove that there was a traitor who was not Hazel.

Lotar carefully looped the band on the tip of his trident to swim back to his father.

"Freeze."

First Lieutenant Anik materialized from the coral. The other guards surrounded him.

"He collected the poison pouch. He is the traitor after all." The first lieutenant's expression was unnaturally euphoric. "Take him to the prison and inform the king."

Curse it.

Lotar dropped the poison bag and followed their directions. His heart raced, but his thoughts moved faster.

He should have known.

The first lieutenant was the traitor.

He had set this trap.

And Lotar had swum right into it.

THIRTY-TWO

"**Y**ou are going to be in such big trouble," Hazel muttered as she stumbled and teetered over the sharp rocks up to the hard, icy shore. "If not from me, then from somebody else, when I'm not there to help you."

The frigid wind whipped away her words.

And the snow and ice were brutal on her feet. Sure, she hardly felt cold water, but the bone-deep ache on her pinkie pigs was unrelenting.

"How could you be so arrogant? I am so. Mad. At you."

She should have seen it coming. As soon as she'd confessed she might be pregnant, he'd freaked out and treated her differently. She'd thought he was being sweet. No, he wasn't being sweet. He was wrapping her in bubble wrap and sending her to the surface as if he'd forgotten the whole point of soul mates was being together.

This was the kind of crap people with complicated relationships, like Nora and that loyal All-Council General Giru, must enjoy.

Not Hazel.

"I can't resonate with you if I'm not close enough to your resonance." Hazel trudged through the aching snow to the highest point to get her bearings. "Jerk."

Right in front of her stood a reindeer.

Okay. "Where's the nearest sign of civilization?" she asked.

The reindeer stared like a deer—er, reindeer—in headlights.

"Houses? Cabins? Yurts?"

Nothing.

"Do you speak English?" she asked the animal, which very clearly didn't speak English or anything else. And she totally knew that, but she had to catch a break sometime, and asking a wild animal was better than asking the rocks or the big old trees. "Come on, Prancer, point me in a direction."

Its ears flicked back and forth. It ambled past her, picked up its hooves and minced a little faster, and then raced away into the snowy woods, leaving a shower of brush and snow behind it.

"Well, that can't be good." She took a few steps after it. The snow plunged up to her knees. Ouch. Cold.

A modern roar echoed over the snow, growling louder and louder, and a snowmobile bounced into view. The driver was fully bundled in a thick long coat, boots, gloves, hat, scarf, and goggles. He—because even through the bulk, she calculated it was a guy—glanced her way, did a double take, and crashed into the brush. The motor stalled, started again, and he piloted a now messier snowmobile out from under the heavy branches.

She waved with both hands. "Hi!"

He jabbered at her in a foreign language. Lots of words

and gestures to express deep sentiments, like, did she know she was naked and it was freezing?

"Yes, I know." She waded toward him, breaking through the top layers of snow. "I'm sorry to bother you, but could you possibly help me make an international phone call?"

He shook his head while jabbering more.

"English?" She gave his frosty goggles a hopeful smile and held her hand to her ear. "Cell phone?"

"Ja, ja, sell phone," the man repeated, and patted the seat behind him.

Well, good deal.

She clambered on behind him and grabbed his scratchy wool coat. The motor growled, and they whirred off across the landscape. Wind, snow, and brush whipped her bare skin. He hadn't offered his coat, but maybe he figured she was a nudist by choice and must be more used to the elements than him.

They pulled up in front of a perfectly pleasant square wooden house, like the kind she might have seen in any rustic tourism magazine advertising off-the-beaten-track stays in Eastern Europe. The driver led her inside without knocking. A couple of blue-eyed men with light brown hair blinked at her in shock while the driver rattled off something.

"English?" she asked hopefully.

The men looked at each other as if each was hoping the other one knew it.

"Cell phone?"

The driver jabbered, waved his hands emphatically, got back on his snowmobile, and zoomed down the road.

She stood awkwardly in what looked like a warm tiled kitchen. At least her feet weren't going to freeze off anymore.

Her stomach growled.

"Um, anything to eat?" she asked.

One man brought her a wool blanket, which she wrapped around herself like a toga, and the other put a strangely shaped kettle on the gas burner. They ushered her to a chair and put a plate of bread and cheese—oops, not cheese, more like a pig-flavored jelly. Lard?—in front of her along with a steaming cup of bitter, herby tea. The men loitered outside the kitchen murmuring and glancing at her as though terrified. The front door opened from time to time, and more strange men piled in, gaped at her, and left.

Well, she was in a house getting fed. This would all be fixed as soon as she figured out...

Figured out what the heck she was going to do now that Lotar had abandoned her.

Her chest heaved.

It was a hiccup. Not a sob. Definitely not a sob.

Yeah, she understood why he did it, and she knew it was coming from the best of intentions, but at the end of the day, she was still naked in some stranger's kitchen because the man she'd intended to marry, *her soul mate*, the father of her future child had kicked her out. Unilaterally. Which meant without even discussing it with her.

He'd made a serious decision that had affected her life, both their lives, and expected her to deal with it.

Like finding out your fiancé spent your wedding savings on a once-in-a-lifetime *solo* trip to Asia, or your best friend borrowed your grandmother's wedding ring without asking and lost it, or...

Or your business partners took the grant money you'd earned and bought a gaming PC and laughed at you for thinking you'd use that money to accomplish something.

She hiccupped a few more times, sniffed down what

was definitely not uncried tears, and puckered her lips over the bitter tea. Not because she was stuck a thousand miles from home, naked, pregnant, and alone.

A man with a uniform and a trimmed mustache sat across from her. "Amerik? Ingles?"

"Amerik?" She wiped her nose and cheeks on the edge of the blanket, accidentally flashing him, and he politely looked away. "Ah, yeah. America. I'm American."

He nodded, still looking away, and pulled a chunky black car phone from his pocket. He pressed something and handed it over to her. "Amerik. Mobile telephone."

"It's a cell phone. Oh my God, thank you so much." She clutched the precious heavy object and dialed.

An automated female voice chastised her in a foreign language.

The man frowned and took back the cell phone, pressed buttons, and started the call again. "Code. Amerik. Code."

"Code? Oh, the country code. Sorry." She pressed it and redialed the office.

It rang and rang and finally sent her to an automated message about hours.

God, what time was it?

She'd caught Flora during office hours both times before. Now, when it was really an emergency, she had no after-hours contingency.

The man stared at her as though wanting to know when she would give his cell phone back and get the heck out of his neighbor's house.

Cavalry. She needed cavalry.

Hazel barely knew anyone's phone number. Who knew phone numbers in the age of cell phones? But there was one she'd dialed or put on enough résumés for character references that she could pull it up. The phone rang and she silently prayed. *Answer, answer, please answer...*

Pia did not answer.

It was a guy. "Who's this?"

"Oh my God, I'm so sorry. I was looking for Pia. I must have misdialed." She pulled the phone away and handed it back to the guy because she still hadn't figured out which button ended the call. There were no red or green phone symbols. It was a total mystery.

"Hazel?" the guy asked. "Is that you?"

Ah!

She squeaked and lunged across the table, startling the man into dropping the phone before he disconnected. "Hello? Hello?"

"Hello?" the familiar voice said. "Hazel, I can hear you."

"Oh, thank God." Wait. "Owen?"

"Yeah, here's Pia." The phone crackled.

Pia's sleepy voice came over the line. "Do you know what time it is?"

Hearing her friend's voice, familiar in this crazy land, sent Hazel into a hiccupping fit. "Pia, I am so glad to hear your voice. I tried calling the office, but they're closed and Lotar kicked me out of his home city after his dad accused me of being a witch and I'm stuck somewhere in Siberia naked and alone and pregnant." She took a huge, blubbering, sniffling breath and let it out with a high-pitched whine. "Help me."

"Oh my God, Hazel." Pia sounded a lot more awake. "Um, what do you want me to do?"

"I don't know. Look up the number for the foundation or something. Find someone who can speak..." She looked at the man, who gazed back at her with serious intensity, as though he were trying to listen with all his concentration. "Any arctic language."

Pia rustled, making comforting noises to let Hazel know she was still on the line.

Hazel sighed, the first rush of relief from at least reaching out to one friend still on her side. "It's not the glamour of the post office, I'm telling you."

"Oh, yeah, I never thought the post office was all that glamorous."

"You were right."

"Okay, Owen found something. The New York office of MerMatch closed. They moved to Sanctuary Island, but they planned this? And now the only office is in Miami."

"That's the foundation."

"Yeah, okay. That's what Owen says too. He's trying to call...but there's no answer. We'll try again in a few hours when they open, but they also have an active Facebook page. If you have internet, maybe you could reach out?"

"I don't think so."

"Hm, okay, Owen's looking into it..."

Hazel tapped her fingertips on the table. The man stared at her like he was willing her to end the conversation, but how could she end it without anyone knowing where she was?

A plump woman with gray hair put the kettle on again.

"So, Owen, huh?" Hazel mostly said it to make it look to the man like she was still having a conversation. "When did that happen?"

"Ah...it's kind of complicated."

"Well, congratulations. I like him way better than any of your exes. I hope he doesn't leave you naked and alone in a foreign country after getting you pregnant."

"Yeah," Pia laughed, "I seriously doubt that. Oh, he's

saying something. Yeah?...Okay, I'll tell her. He says he got motivated when Lotar said my ex wasn't my soul mate."

"That was obvious," Hazel agreed, ignoring the pang from Lotar's name. "Your soul mate would *never* steal your fries."

"I know."

"And call you fat. In the same sentence."

"I know!" Pia sighed aloud. "After that night, Owen started a campaign to make me see that I was worth more than these fry-stealing musicians thought. It took me a while to come around, but... Oh, hey. I have an audition on Thursday! It's for a dance. It's coming up a little too fast, I haven't quite had enough time to get back in my groove, but I'm going for it. And if I don't get it, I'll get the next one, or I'll write my own and perform it solo off-Broadway."

"Double congratulations." Hazel could just imagine her friends in Pia's apartment, Pia in her robe huddled around the phone, Owen nearby being his stable, steady presence. "And since Owen won't have a performance, he can be there to watch."

"Shh." Pia giggled. "You'll give him ideas."

"I'm sure he doesn't need them," Hazel said, but Pia was conveying her statement to Owen, and Hazel had to let it go.

Everything was the same back in New York, and yet everything was different. The world turned. People changed.

There was no expiration date on dreams. One of her guru mentors had said so once.

But right now...

Hazel didn't know.

The man leaned forward and opened his palm.

Time to say goodbye. "I've got to go, you guys. Tell the foundation to call me."

Pia promised they would, and Hazel hung up.

The man took the phone with a grimace.

The older woman leaned against the counter drinking tea. She peered into Hazel's empty cup. "You want some?"

Oh, God. She spoke English. Her accent was slightly British, slightly Nordic. Maybe Finnish?

"That would be great," Hazel said, and the woman poured from a chipped ceramic teapot into Hazel's cup. "Um, what is it?"

"Earl Grey."

"What? Are you serious?"

The woman laughed. "You think it's a woodland potion? Haha, yes, Earl Grey."

Hazel shared her laughter. It was funny.

The woman's laughter faded. "So you are American. I tell him"—she jerked her thumb at the serious man—" you were calling America talking about boyfriends, and he has a heart attack. That is a work phone."

"Oh my God. I'm so sorry."

"No, you fine. Chocolate cracker?"

"Yes, thank you."

The woman spread out a second meal of bread, pungent cheese, stringy meat, and dishes Hazel didn't recognize, but after everything she'd eaten underwater, this was nothing. Besides chocolate-covered crackers, there was a box of shortbread cookies and jam. Yum.

"Where are we?" Hazel asked around bites.

"Lapland, Finnmark. Many names."

Great, she could arrange Hazel's travel back to New York. "I'm so glad you speak English."

"You think I don't study in school?"

"They didn't."

"Yes, they lazy. They know I speak it, so they don't worry. Only speak the local three languages, ignore the rest of the world. They think this day's not coming. Ha. It came." She ate through an entire box of chocolate crackers and opened a second one. "Here. You don't eat this underwater."

Hazel was full, but she took another one.

She still clenched Lotar's necklace in her hand.

The woman inspected it. "So, you have the necklace of Oska and Lotar."

"Lotar," Hazel said, startled. "Wait, you recognize it? You were a sacred bride!"

"Jup."

And since no one had ever accused her of too much discretion, Hazel scrubbed her face and unburdened herself. "I do like Lotar, a lot, even though right now we're fighting. He kicked me out to hunt a traitor who's poisoning his brother, and his dad's blaming me for it."

She grunted.

Hazel sighed. "How do you know Lotar?"

"I'm his mama."

"Oh." God. "Oska, he's... I'm so sorry to tell you this way."

She waved. "We'll sort it out."

"We? You're going back to Syrenka?"

"No more signing treaties for my tribe, no more raising lazy boys to fulfill our traditions. My work is over. Now, it's vacation time."

The story came out.

Lotar's mother was one of those amazing women who fit into one year what most people struggled to cram into a lifetime. She'd grown up knowing her duty to lead her tribe as well as her duty to become a sacred bride, and so she'd checked off joining the mer and having Oska and Lotar right away. Then, in accordance with the All-Council ancient covenant, she'd been required to surface and never see them again. She'd gone on to marry a human husband and have a family to support her tribe.

It wasn't clear how many kids she had total, but they were all adults and held important positions. Anyway, brides or people who had a lot of exposure to Sea Opals always seemed younger than they really were.

"I saw your party, and I told my tribe I will go, join my first husband. But they say, no no, it won't happen, something will sabotage. But I say, just you wait. And here you are. Ha! Early retirement."

They had to wait while officials counted her reindeer. That was why the official had come with a cell phone. Because of the government. Anyway...

"And you?" Lotar's mother sipped her tea. "You return to New York or Syrenka?"

"Well, I..." Hazel toyed with the crumbs.

Lotar had ignored her wishes, opinions, and experience. He'd made a life-altering decision without consulting her. Even after all this time together, when he knew her inside and out, he thought she wasn't capable. She wasn't smart enough or good enough to figure out a solution with him.

And that was the crux.

He might *want* to be partners, but he didn't treat her as a partner.

So, what was she going to do about it?

"I don't know," she said finally. "If I go back, will he think he can dump me whenever it's convenient? I might have even agreed to come to the surface if we'd talked, but he didn't do that. So...yeah, I don't know."

If she returned to New York, she'd have to start over. The MerMatch office had closed. She'd need a new job, a new apartment to accommodate a baby and a new life.

But she didn't want to go back to New York. The All-Cities Gyre wasn't finished. The party invitations were still unsent, and although it was awesome that maybe more brides like Lotar's mother were out there silently planning to retire early, Hazel needed to do this herself. She wanted it. She was getting good at it. She'd earned it.

And she was starting to like it.

Plus there really was something rotten in the state of Denmark, and if she left now, she'd never see it excised.

Every single time she'd run into a serious problem with her partners, she'd accepted their treatment and moved on. Picked up the pieces and kept going. Searched for the next great business idea.

She'd never turned around and confronted anyone who had done her wrong.

She'd never demanded justice from the guys who'd stolen her prototype money and defrauded the Young Entrepreneurs.

She'd never called out the girls she'd planned a joint graduation party with for bailing on the actual work or organizing.

She'd never gotten anything from the women who'd encouraged her to invest in barista training or print up pet personal assistant business cards.

She'd never held anyone accountable and demanded an apology.

Or respect.

And sometimes that was because it was impossible.

But sometimes?

She hadn't even tried to push back.

Yes, closing statements had given her closure. They deserved a place in her toolbox, but they weren't the only tool. She'd accepted a lot and moved on, but she didn't want to move on from Lotar.

Not this time.

Lotar's mother put on another kettle. "My sons are the same above and below water. They think they know the best right way. But you know? My father had a saying: 'The snow falls, the wolf hunts, but you choose your destiny.' He always said that. 'You choose your destiny.'" She shook the half-empty box of chocolate crackers. "They don't have this down below, you know. Retirement will make me skinny."

"Oh, most queens run up to the surface. You can visit and get your chocolate fix."

"Visit? No." She snorted and gestured at the official, who'd entered the house again. "My tribe will save work for me, but they must resolve our problems now. Don't tell them I will come back."

The official shook off the snow and traded words in the other language with her. He handed over his cell phone.

Lotar's mother switched to English and chatted with the foundation staff, sharing Hazel's location, and looked up at Hazel. "Your friends call back to arrange the travel to New York. What do I tell them?"

You choose your destiny.

Lotar's mother had sure chosen hers.

Hazel still sat naked and abandoned in the middle of a stranger's kitchen in a foreign country. But the stranger was her mother-in-law, and she was also now quite stuffed with chocolate crackers and tea.

This wasn't about Lotar.

This was about Hazel.

Did she want to run to New York and the familiar that was different and start again?

Did she want to dive to Syrenka, unmask a traitor, and give Lotar a piece of her mind?

Did she want to start over as a reindeer herder in Lapland?

At this exact moment, with Lotar's mother holding the phone, literally anything seemed possible. All she had to do was decide.

"I'm going back," Hazel said.

Lotar's mother raised her brows.

"To Syrenka," she hastily clarified.

"Ah-ha." Lotar's mother handed Hazel the phone to finish updating Mel, the head of the foundation, about the Syrenka situation and her plans.

Mel, like Lotar's mother, had no judgment about her choice. She got Hazel what she needed to proceed.

While she finished the call, Lotar's mother washed up their dishes, pulled off her apron, and hung it on a peg above the sink. Hazel returned the government official's cell phone.

"Right. Brilliant." Lotar's mother brushed her hands. "Let's go."

Two snowmobiles roared up outside, and the thickly bundled drivers ferried Hazel and Lotar's mother to the seashore, not to where Hazel had come up, but to a large, weather-worn stone braced by the crashing waves and storm currents. A group of formally dressed men and women in thick coats and primary-blue-and-red embroidered fringes and hats greeted Lotar's mother. This must be the reindeer tribe. They were doing a send-off.

"Onto the ice floes," Lotar's mother joked to Hazel as she unbuttoned her thin housecoat and dress, stepped out of her boots, and let the wind whip her gray hair. A man gave her a blanket like Hazel's, and she wrapped it around herself before addressing her hurriedly gathered family and friends.

She spoke a bunch in her language, and there was a moment where she pointed at Hazel and everyone clapped. Good times. Then Lotar's mother finished with a big English, "Thanks again! Happy retirement! Big vacation."

They cheered, clapped, and stomped in a snow-muffled celebration.

She threw off her blanket, walked to the edge of the frozen shore, and dove into the frothing black water.

Wow.

Hazel dropped her blanket—er, should she fold it? Oh, never mind—and ran after her, tripping off the end into the sea.

The currents dragged her around, wild and scary, and she clawed her way to calmer water.

Lotar's mother emitted a thrilled shout. "This is living, yes, Hazel? This is the life!"

Her heart pounded. "Uh, yeah. Whew. And you threw off your blanket in front of everyone. It was so confident."

"Eh, you get older, you care less."

God, Hazel hoped that was true for her too.

Lotar's mother selected a current and swam into the deep. Puffy-headed beluga whales dogged their descent, silly and cute. She rolled out of the current and played with them.

"Ah, I think we should hurry."

Lotar's mother pshawed her. "We arrive when we arrive. And when we arrive?" She smacked a fist into her open palm. "We sort it out."

She'd spent her whole life taking care of business, and she wasn't going to stop now.

Hazel was the one who'd changed.

She'd spent her whole life accepting that she wasn't the one who could make things happen. She'd overinflated her failures and refused to recognize her successes. She'd let her partners determine her destiny. And never held them accountable.

That stopped now.

Lotar wasn't alone anymore. She had his back. Which meant he had better darned well have hers. She knew what she wanted now, and she would demand it.

Hopefully, it wasn't too late.

THIRTY-THREE

Lotar's father floated back and forth, pacing in the cell beneath the city. "How could you betray me?"

The room held ten or more prisoners, which was big enough to imprison a large raiding party or a whole family during a succession dispute.

Behind his father, the opening yawned to the rest of the ocean. A guard was stationed there.

"You. Oska's own brother."

Lotar wriggled his wrists, testing the bonds. He touched his index fingers to his nose, slid the hard knot over his teeth. It would not yield.

They had not bothered to bind his fins. The wrist manacles' woven tether was fed through the coral floor. He could barely sit up.

"Only finding the traitor could have moved me from my vigil. And to learn it was you..." His father choked.

If his father was here, it left his brother unguarded.

No one would suspect the first lieutenant. He could disperse the guards and stab Oska right through the heart.

Lotar had been stupid.

So stupid.

And now the one who paid would be Oska.

"You used to love Oska, but then you changed, wanting what he had, and now, to hurt him like this?" His father choked again. "I do not know you. You are not my son."

The familiar accusations sliced into his chest.

Just like in childhood.

Warlord Yashu floated down from the city and dismissed the guard.

Oh?

Perhaps help was coming.

Warlord Yashu floated inside the cell, his chest glowing with steady sympathy as Lotar's father ranted. In the past, he'd offered condolences. Kind words his father would never hear.

But not today.

Today, his father's lacerations fell onto a hardened heart.

Since childhood, one thing had changed.

"Why did you begin to hate your brother?" his father asked the ceiling.

Lotar would no longer remain silent.

"I have never hated my brother," Lotar vibrated. Soft, incisive, but undeniable.

His father blinked and lowered his bleary gaze, not used to Lotar answering back. He frowned. "Then why did you poison him?"

I did not.

That reply would never reach his father. "How clever of me to poison Oska so many times from afar and in front of you. How sad that my plan failed in such a stupid way."

"Yes. Well." His father rubbed his temples. Even in his exhausted, grieving state, he sensed the flaws. "I no longer know you. Your hatred ran so deep, you had to leave."

"I left out of fear."

"Fear?" His father puffed water out of his mouth. "Of what?"

"Fear that someday your accusations would become true."

"They are true. You always pushed yourself to make Oska look bad."

"I push myself to outperform everyone."

"But you will never be a prince. When you were a young fry, you understood the reason, but as you grew, your honorable intentions became twisted."

"That is what happened to you, Father."

"I have never changed. Only you changed."

"Father, I am not as exceptional as you believe. I will never be the stealthiest warrior in Syrenka, but any successes I have had, you converted to failure."

"You knew why, and you resented Oska—"

"I am the stealthiest warrior in Atlantis by infinite measure, but there, they do not curse me when I show my skills. They ask me to teach. They assign me the most difficult missions to scout."

"Are you bragging? Do you think this attitude will earn my forgiveness?"

"I came because the All-Cities Gyre leads to Syrenka, but I will not stay. I serve a new king now. King Kadir. My castle is in Atlantis. When I leave here, I will never return."

His father studied him. The dark shadows under his eyes emphasized his confusion.

"Until the next time," Warlord Yashu vibrated.

"Yes," his father said. "Your All-Cities Gyre is a guise. You have always wanted to be king."

"Never."

"You told me so when you were a young fry."

Lotar vibrated an incredulous bark of laughter. "When I was a young fry?"

"And you have acted that way ever since."

"Have I?"

"Yes. All the time."

"I do not remember, but desires change. I have a bride."

"You sent her away."

"Because you were not acting in your right mind," Lotar told him bluntly. "I will not endanger her, especially now, as she carries my young fry."

His father's eyes bugged. "She carries your young fry? She should have sheltered in your castle."

"My castle is in Atlantis."

"That is not the city of your ancestors."

"No, it is not, but it is *my* castle." He fixed his father with a hard gaze. "And my young fry will not be the first to grow up never knowing his grandfather."

His father floated in shock.

A warrior swam full speed to the cell. "I have an urgent message for the king."

"Is it about Prince Oska?" Warlord Yashu asked.

"No."

King Falki waved the messenger away without lifting his gaze from Lotar.

Warlord Yashu shooed the messenger away an appropriate distance to wait.

"You are not lying," his father finally said.

Lotar shook his head.

His father rubbed his chin, squeezed his eyes shut, and scrubbed his hollowed face.

This, then, was Lotar's closure. He had spoken his truth.

When he left Syrenka, he would not return. He would collect Hazel and they would continue on the All-Cities Gyre. And it might be sooner than he thought. A sensation of knowing pinged deep in his bones. Wasn't she closer than before, already on her way back to him?

"You are right." His father dropped his hands. "I have not been thinking clearly since the day First Lieutenant Anik brought my son's lifeless body. There are things I am missing. How did you transfer the poison to your bride?"

Lotar shook his head.

"And how did she transfer it without suffering its effects?"

"What you are missing"—Warlord Yashu crossed deeper into the cell—"is that Lotar should not have taken a bride before Oska. Oska is older and a prince. Lotar embarrasses his brother by even having a bride."

That wasn't the kind of thing Warlord Yashu would usually say. Even his father frowned at his oldest friend. "What?"

Warlord Yashu shrugged to show it wasn't his opinion. "It is what the others say."

"Let them say it." The king lifted his trident. "And they would be wrong. Many warriors received their brides out of order. I was ranked higher, yet I was away during the annual ceremony, so you received your bride before me."

Warlord Yashu nodded thoughtfully. "You are right. I had forgotten."

"Oska was furious when you left, Lotar." King Falki studied the ceiling of the prison. "He told me over and over that I had treated you unfairly. Me." His father shook his head with the ghost of mirth. "When all I have ever tried to be is fair. But he said that while championing one young fry was fair to the other warriors, it was not fair to *you*. And that if you did change and hate him, the reason was my unfairness."

"I never hated Oska."

"He said that as well." His father kneaded his face. "He said I crushed your strong heart. The heart Irina gave you. I knew you could endure my harsh words, and I took advantage, so I destroyed you. Why am I remembering these arguments now? I could not believe he was right. That would be torture."

"I am not destroyed," Lotar said simply. "And my heart is stronger now because of Hazel."

"Hazel..." Lotar's father knelt and gripped the line anchoring Lotar's wrists to the coral. "Do you not hate Oska? And me? For all the things I have said to you?"

A hard lump formed in Lotar's throat.

Lotar shook his head.

"There is a traitor here." His father rested his hands on his knees, the binding trailing from his lax fingers. "He has laughed at my grief, impersonated me on the echo points, and even sent secret messages to the All-Council army. Oska was investigating that when he was injured. But the traitor has made one mistake. He—*ungh*."

His father jolted and looked down in horror.

The central spine of a trident protruded through his father's chest.

No!

Warlord Yashu leaned over the king's curved back, the trident base in his firm hands. "It is you who have made the mistake, my old friend."

"You..." His father could barely vibrate.

Electric eels surged through Lotar's veins.

"Yes, I betrayed you." Warlord Yashu shook his head and barked a laugh. "How amusing to hear that again. I had no idea a queen's touch was so powerful, or I would never have let her anywhere near Oska. How close he came to getting out the truth. '...u betrayed me.' He meant 'Yashu,' but all I had to do was look at Lotar and the whole city turned on him. Again. All because you, Falki, trained them to believe that a second son was not the greatest blessing we have experienced since the sacred brides dwindled, but instead, that he should never have been born."

Lotar's father gripped Lotar's still-bound hands. His fingers trembled with weakness. He scratched at the bindings.

"I told your father many things since he turned to me for guidance," Warlord Yashu said conversationally to Lotar, "but that strange denial of you originated with him. Perhaps he feared that his blessing would be taken away if he embraced it. But his attempt was for naught because he will lose you both after all."

Lotar's heart thudded faster and faster.

He could barely hear.

His gaze tunneled in on his father and the sharp trident point jutting from his skin. The taste of coppery blood filled the cell and Lotar's mouth.

"I had to get rid of your bride, of course. But I could not allow you to leave. The elders were always in favor of making you a second prince. With Oska and Falki out of the way, they might make you king. And if you left again, you might someday come back. Or realize my deceptions. But..." Warlord Yashu's eyes lit. "Now, I think it is fitting that you trick your father into freeing you, steal his trident, and stab him in the back. Yes. And when I come to his defense..."

Warlord Yashu wagged the trident.

Lotar's father stared into Lotar's eyes. He looked furious. And his silent wish was not difficult to interpret.

Avenge me.

Warlord Yashu shoved Lotar's father down.

His father yanked Lotar's wrists to his chest as he fell.

The trident point scored Lotar's left forearm to the palm with a sharp bite.

The bonds slipped free, and his wrists separated.

His father collapsed on top of Lotar's torso. Warlord Yashu pinned his father—and also Lotar—to the cell floor.

"Now I will wrestle the trident free here." Warlord Yashu yanked the trident out, causing his father to spasm and blood to spray. "It is a shame that I had to drive you away, Lotar. I do feel guilty about that. You were always so good at everything. Amplifying your father's insecurities was tragically easy, and such a waste. You would have made my son an unstoppable first lieutenant. But..." He hefted the trident and aimed it at Lotar's head. "Now I have to kill you. In self-defense."

He brought the trident down in a killing blow.

Lotar jerked to the side.

Warlord Yashu grunted in surprise.

Lotar scrambled free.

A high, clear pitch filled his ears. This male had stabbed his father and poisoned his brother. He would *end* him.

Warlord Yashu kicked back, evaluating Lotar as they squared up to fight. "Give up. I have the only weapon."

He flexed his fingers. "I *am* the weapon."

Warlord Yashu hesitated.

Lotar attacked.

He dove at the elder, arms out to grapple the trident.

Warlord Yashu dove to the side and slashed. The king's blades sliced the water before his fingertips.

Lotar shifted his fins to feet and kicked off the floor, again diving at the elder.

Warlord Yashu kicked out of his way.

Lotar's fingertips brushed the base of the trident prongs.

Warlord Yashu jabbed the sharp points at him.

He hooked the base and yanked.

Warlord Yashu's eyes flew wide. He whirled and twisted, wrenching free. Then he kicked back, hard, deep into the interior, and held up the trident, his lungs sucking in water, the exertion clearly surprising him.

He had manipulated Lotar's father for years. The elders, advisers, and warriors even longer. He had been careful for so long.

And he alone had always seen Lotar for exactly who he was.

Now he saw the promise in Lotar's fury.

Lotar was going to take back his father's weapon and kill Warlord Yashu.

And the traitor could not stop him.

Warlord Yashu backed away, keeping the trident pointed straight at Lotar. He raised his vibrations to a shout. "Guards? The prisoner has gotten free. He has—oh no. Stop. Traitor! He has murdered the king!"

Curse it.

The shouts of answering warriors approached the jail cell.

Warlord Yashu smirked. "Your move, second son."

"I *will* end you." Lotar floated by the entrance, fading into the shadows. "You only delay your inevitable doom."

Warlord Yashu's smile faltered.

The warriors streamed in, surrounded his father, and spoke over each other. "The king! He is still alive but unconscious. Quick, the healer. We must get him to the Life Tree."

Lotar darted from the jail.

Warlord Yashu's vibration shouted after him. "There. He flees. Do not let him escape!"

Lotar veered from the Life Tree.

As soon as the warriors organized, they would spread Warlord Yashu's lie. And without any witnesses, they would condemn and execute Lotar, leaving Warlord Yashu all the time in the world to ensure his father and brother followed him into the blacknight sea. The assassin's plot would be complete.

Lotar needed a method to counteract the lies. Stop everyone, make them listen. Shield his father and brother so they could heal...

How foolish to think he could succeed by himself.

He had stumbled from trap to trap, making the same mistakes as in his youth, ignoring Hazel's greatest power: She spoke her truth fearlessly. Even more than her queen powers, her fierce words were his greatest allies. She was the defender he needed.

And he'd pushed her away.

Lotar needed Hazel.

He kicked through the open territory, leaving the city behind. The warriors would have escorted her along the old routes to the sacred island's shore. He pumped his legs, ignoring stealth for speed. If she returned in time—if she healed his father—the other warriors would learn the truth. At least enough to imprison Warlord Yashu and save Oska.

Lotar swam over the final rise.

And right into the line of the massive, heavily armed, conquering All-Council army.

THIRTY-FOUR

Lotar's mom swooped and twirled, sang, and darted after curiosities—taking, in Hazel's opinion, far too much time.

"We're almost there. We really should go," Hazel called as Lotar's mom chased after a wolffish with a snaggle toothed mouth.

She pinched its gelatinous cheek and swam on. "Young people always want to go faster. Old people relax. Enjoy the ride."

"I know, and I'm sorry to cut short your new retirement, but I can't help feeling like there's a disaster happening and we're not there to stop it."

"A disaster?" Lotar's mom squinted into the distance. "Such as a giant army surrounding the city? Yes, that's possible, true."

"What?"

Uh-oh.

Sure enough, masses upon masses of warriors filtered the glow of the Life Tree. It was as if the All-Council had realized they could not rule the oceans as they had before and so they'd combined forces into a super army.

And Lotar was trapped in a hostile city with a traitor.

Hazel's stomach dropped.

How would they break through?

Lotar's mother chased a flickering see-through tube fish. "Ooh."

Hazel's fear combined with irritation, and she snapped. "Would you please focus?"

"Bah." But Lotar's mother drifted back into line with a sigh. "This is your first time facing an army, huh?"

"It's not yours?"

Lotar's mother laughed uproariously. "Young people are so funny."

Oh, good Lord. "Well then, you tell me how to get through."

"Normally, it's a problem." Lotar's mother flexed her fingers. "But you say we have superpowers. Now I know kung fu. It's a movie, get it?" She laughed again.

At least one of them was having a good time.

Warriors surrounded the city like a sphere.

"There's no way in," Hazel vibrated. "We took too long."

Lotar's mom rubbed her jaw.

Movement flashed beneath her.

Hazel rotated down.

A familiar angular warrior moved like a shadow close to the coral.

She squeaked and dropped on him. "Lotar!"

He looked up. Shock changed to relief, and he rotated to catch her.

She zoomed into his arms.

He hugged her so tight she could barely vibrate. "I am so mad at you."

"I know." His soft vibration soothed her.

She would not be soothed. "We agreed to do this together. You undermined me, hurt me, and you broke your promise. And it doesn't matter that you had the best intentions because—"

He covered her mouth with his hot, hungry, demanding kiss.

She lived in this moment. He was alive. His arms welcomed her, and he wanted her.

And then he vibrated what she least expected to hear. "I was wrong."

She tore her mouth away to gaze into his sincere gray eyes. "You were?"

"In every way. I needed you. Need you."

Aw. Tenderness seeped into her heart. "I'm here."

"Praise the Life Tree." He hugged her again, so close, and his arms trembled.

He really meant it.

Her eyes burned with tears.

"Here." She tied the shell necklace around his neck. "This is yours. We're going to raise our baby together. Never take it off again, understand?"

"I vow it." He adjusted the tie and fitted her to his body. "Now we must fly. Warlord Yashu stabbed my father and blamed me. He will murder Father and Oska if we do not stop him."

"So we have to get inside."

"A coral tunnel runs beneath the city. I hid until the army passed over so they would not find the entrance." He glanced behind her. "Who is the other mer?"

"Huh? Oh. So, yeah, I also brought your mom."

His brows lifted. "Mama?"

"Lotar." His mother reached past Hazel and cupped his cheek. "You have grown into a fine man. Now take me to Syrenka. I need to sort something out."

It was not the tearful reunion Hazel had imagined, but that was fine. They were short on time.

Lotar skimmed over the surface of the coral, silent and careful, and ducked beneath a ledge. He twisted and contorted through the long, spike-filled cave, flying faster than she was comfortable. "What are those spikes?"

He veered within a hair's width. "Blackthorn coral."

She clung tighter.

"Do not fear. This is one of the many races I won."

Hazel closed her eyes. She trusted him.

They emerged beneath the king's castle. His mother lagged far behind. Lotar swam up to the dais of the Life Tree.

Elders argued. Warlord Yashu lurked nearby, dropping hints that surely spelled someone's doom.

Injured warriors rested at the Life Tree, the bodies slumped by the king and Oska. The healer moved from one warrior to the next, patching and binding. They must have skirmished with the army outside.

"So how do we heal your brother?" Hazel murmured. "Just sneak in? Or...?"

"Lotar!" First Lieutenant Anik flew with a unit of injured warriors toward the Life Tree. He darted for them, trident raised. "You dare show your face? After you betrayed us to the All-Council?"

"You are acting the jerk," Lotar told him. "Atlantis is anathema. We did not draw the All-Council army here."

"Lies!" Anik kicked forward with a jutting trident.

Hazel flashed up her shield. It glowed marshmallow white. "Back off."

His trident bounced off it.

The elders grew silent. Warlord Yashu's nostrils flared as he gripped his trident. He was a spider who lurked in shadows.

Anik jerked back. "What is this?"

"Powers that could save Syrenka," Lotar said evenly. "If it is worth saving."

Anik's eyes narrowed, then he frowned. "Who is that you snuck in?"

Lotar's mother kicked up to join them. "Ah, this is familiar."

Hazel craned her neck. "*This* is familiar?"

"Last time I came, there was more chaos."

"You snuck in a stranger?" Anik rasped in fury.

Hazel straightened. "She's the king's wife, okay? She's the prince's mom."

Anik blinked.

"No, no, no." Lotar's mom swam abreast of them. "I have a name."

"Oh, God. I'm so sorry."

"Irina." She nodded at the first lieutenant. "Nice to meet you."

Anik looked nonplussed.

But the elders murmured in shock, and Warlord Yashu's face drained of color. "You."

Irina grinned with devilish pleasure. "Yashu. Long time I've been thinking of you."

"Do not threaten me." He curled his lip. "The old king is not here to protect you."

"The old king made his rules not to protect me." She

flexed her fingers and rolled her shoulders like a warrior preparing for a fight. "He protected you."

So there was history.

Another warrior hurried across the open water between the first castles and the Life Tree. "Have the elders chosen a new king to parlay? The All-Council general will not wait."

The elders turned en masse toward Lotar.

Now, in their darkest hour, they put their faith not in Anik, but in him.

He straightened. Taller than before. Broader. Proud.

And Hazel snuggled close.

He held her to his side, ready to face the new challenge.

The head elder held out his hand to beseech him. "Warrior Lotar, the elders of Syrenka ask you to take the honor once bestowed upon King Falki and Prince Oska and become King Lo—"

"No!" Warlord Yashu swam forward. "You must select Anik. King Falki would have chosen him. He is the worthiest warrior."

There was an awkward pause.

"Warlord Yashu, do not question the ruling of the elders," the head elder said.

"But you have made a mistake. Lotar has not swum in these waters for years. He does not have the respect of his warriors."

"Lotar beat Anik fairly at every test of skill."

"Years ago."

"They remember, as we remember."

"But Lotar has murdered—"

"Father." Anik leveled his trident at his father. "Do not speak lies."

Huh.

Warlord Yashu licked his lips. His gaze skimmed over

Lotar, Hazel, and Irina. Something had given his plot away to Anik. Was his son was trying to save him from himself?

Did Anik know the full truth?

The head elder spoke into the silence. "Your protests, Warlord Yashu, come from the chest of a proud father, and so we will overlook your gross overstep today."

"But Anik is the most worthy of becoming king."

One elder intoned deeply, "Whoever faces the All-Council army will likely die, Warlord Yashu. They will kill him to make a point."

Sure, no wonder they wanted Lotar.

Lotar glanced down at her with a slight grin. Even though she hadn't spoken her snarky comment aloud, he must have guessed her thoughts. And she could almost hear his confidence.

Yes, nominate him to deal with the All-Council. Yes, the All-Council would kill any other warrior, but not Lotar.

He had Hazel.

She was a queen.

And the elders were no fools.

Warlord Yashu, perhaps sensing that his moment was slipping away, grasped for it. "The All-Council will not kill Anik. They will recognize his authority and disperse."

The elders regarded him like he was crazy.

"Why would they recognize his authority?" the head elder asked, then rotated to Anik for an explanation.

A shadow of dread crept across Anik's features.

Warlord Yashu urged his son to parlay. "Declare yourself and negotiate. You can convince them to leave with few demands and only small changes to our city. Claim your destiny as the rightful king."

Anik's eyes narrowed. "Few demands? Small changes?

Father, I am loyal to Syrenka. When you vibrate these words, I do not know you."

Warlord Yashu insisted. "Think. You can save Syrenka."

"I will negotiate the terms of the All-Council surrender, or I will fight." Anik lifted his trident. "To the end."

His warriors repeated his gesture and growled, "To the end!"

Warlord Yashu lifted his hands, his movements jerky, panicked. "No, my son. Do not act so recklessly. You must not leave it to this traitor. He murdered his own family. And now he has brought back his poisonous female—no, two females—to finish them."

Anik stared at his father for a long, hard moment.

Then he shook his head.

"Yes, my son," Warlord Yashu insisted.

But Anik kept shaking his head. A strange smile cracked his face, and he laughed, but the sound was brittle. "Do you know the last thing Prince Oska said to me before his solo patrol?"

"Son, concentrate."

"He said he wanted to see Lotar one more time."

Lotar stiffened.

"Yes. What a surprise, eh? Lotar?" Anik waved his trident at them. "My father said he saw your shadow nearby. Had you come to meet Prince Oska secretly and caused his death? Where were you? Where had you gone?"

"I told you already. We were never here," Hazel said.

"A troubling denial, yes, but you had no proof. And then, Lotar, you went straight to that bag of poison. I was so relieved. 'It was him,' I thought. 'His reign of terror stops now.'" Anik laughed again, that harsh, choking laugh. "And what should happen but while he was in jail, his message from the Dragao Azul echo point arrived."

Warlord Yashu's expression went lax.

Anik lowered his trident and slumped. "Father. Lotar was never near Syrenka. He could not have injured Prince Oska. He was on the surface with his bride."

The ocean fell silent.

Warlord Yashu frowned. "There has been a mistake."

"More than one." Anik lifted a finger. "Lotar. How did you know where to seek the poison bag?"

"I did not. I swept the area."

"I watched you circle with glee. 'Only the real poisoner would know to search for the bag here,' I thought." Anik slanted his gaze at his father. "How did you know where I should wait in ambush?"

"My son, I do not like the way you look at me. I am an honorable warrior with a long history of friendship—"

"Just answer, Father. Please."

Warlord Yashu shrugged one shoulder. "It was logical. As he said."

Anik's hope slid off his face into despair. "No more lies."

"I have never lied to you."

"No more mistakes, no more 'Maybe I heard something.' No more." Anik slashed his trident in frustration. "Prince Oska is my prince. A warrior I would die for. And *I will kill* whoever has hurt him. Even if that is..." Anik couldn't quite seem to accuse his father, but the implication hung in the heavy silence. "Now, tell me. How did you know where to find the poison?"

Warlord Yashu pursed his lips. "Son, Syrenka needs you—"

"Now!"

Warlord Yashu's brows drew together. "I am sorry to disappoint you, but I cannot tell you more. It was logical, and so I thought of it."

Anik squeezed his eyes shut and pinched the bridge of his nose. "I suppose I will die without learning whether my suspicions dishonor me or you."

"No, my son. You will not die. This is your time. I have laid out everything. Go forth and claim your rightful place as Syrenka's king."

"Starting with the All-Council? Very well. I will take on this mantle to parlay." He tossed a calculating look at Lotar. "Prince Oska is laughing at me. He said my brows had grown scales to cover my eyes. If he departs for the black-night sea first, do not fear. He will not be alone for long." To the other warriors, he lifted his trident. "Syrenka or death!"

His warriors roared.

"Hold." Lotar swam forward to block them.

The other warriors, including Anik, stopped in shock.

"You are not king. The elders offered that position to me." Lotar faced the elders. "And I accept."

LOTAR FACED down the shocked first lieutenant.

"All hail King Lotar," the head elder blurted before Warlord Yashu or anyone else could protest, and the rest of the elders agreed.

First Lieutenant Anik blinked rapidly and lowered his trident. The warriors behind him lowered their tridents as well, but no one moved out of formation. Despite the elders' choice, their loyalties aligned with the first lieutenant. And if First Lieutenant Anik turned against Lotar, so would the city's warriors.

"We are on the same side," he told his new first lieutenant.

Anik snorted. "Are we?"

"We are." Lotar released Hazel. "Heal my father."

"No." Warlord Yashu blocked her path, and guards formed behind him. "She cannot touch the king. She is not his bride."

"I *am* his bride, and I say fine," Irina said.

Warlord Yashu's lips flapped even though his words vibrated in his chest. "I will not allow it. She is a danger. A threat."

Hazel floated in the center between them.

Lotar was not an effective king if he could not take control.

But...

First Lieutenant Anik waved his trident at his father. "Move."

"You cannot do this, my son. You cannot allow her to touch the king. She will injure him as she injured Prince Oska."

"She never handled the poison. She never injured Prince Oska."

"My son, brides have ways—"

"Move."

When Warlord Yashu still blocked the way, First Lieutenant Anik ruthlessly ordered the guards to remove him. After a short, shocked hesitation, they obeyed. Warlord Yashu yelled and struggled, cursing them fluently.

Hazel looked at Lotar. He had only been king for a few moments and yet he had already shaken the city to its foundations. And this was only the beginning. He waved her forward.

"Okay." She swam on her short but effective fins for the Life Tree dais. "Um, I'm still kind of mad at him, though."

"Do your best." Lotar stared down the guards, who reluctantly moved aside, and she knelt at the king's side.

"K-king Lotar." The warrior from the front barely stumbled over his name. "The All-Council general is waiting for your parlay."

"Let him."

The warrior blanched. "They will destroy the outer castles."

"Syrenka can lose the outer castles."

The messenger gasped. The warriors moved restlessly behind Anik.

"He will kill Syrenka," someone muttered.

Warlord Yashu crossed his arms. "I told you."

First Lieutenant Anik curled his upper lip. "Is that your plan? Let the All-Council fell our castles? Get your revenge by watching our city die?"

"This is not my first time losing every castle to an unstoppable All-Council army," Lotar replied. "This is not my first time making a final stand at the Life Tree with few warriors and no allies. And this is not my first time defeating those armies, defending that Life Tree, and saving the city."

Anik's chin jerked back.

Lotar enunciated. "Do you have more experience than I?"

Anik held his gaze. Shoulders square, spine straight. Grip tight on his trident...but he clenched it tight to his side.

The Life Tree chimed.

Hazel knelt beside the king. White light shone on her hands and flowed into the king's injured back. She hummed as his color improved and his tattoos shimmered, iridescent with the Life Tree's energy.

The king groaned and straightened.

A tension long coiled in Lotar's belly released.

The king stretched, winced, and rested against the Life Tree. His lashes fluttered.

Hazel scooted back and sat on her heels. "Hey. I healed you."

He waved her away. "Not me. My son."

"How's that for a thank-you?" She prodded the poultice. "Hmm. Well, I must still be mad at you, because I feel like I could do better, but it's a start."

The healer knelt on the king's other side, nearly elbowing Hazel out of the way, and began poking and prodding beneath the bandages. "Hmm. Yes. Just like the rumors. It defies my old eyes."

"Then, King Falki will live?" the head elder asked.

"He will, although he is weak and faint. He cannot fight off an army." The healer nodded at Hazel with respect. "I treated the poison. Will you heal Prince Oska?"

"I can try, but..."

Hazel bounced onto her feet and stepped over the other injured warriors, singing quietly as she danced healing fingers over one and another, increasing his army one surprised yawn and stretch after another. She stopped at Oska and studied him.

"I still don't know why it didn't work the first time. If I try again and he chokes up, he might get reinjured even worse."

"What is wrong?" Lotar's mother asked.

"Warlord Yashu stabbed Oska," Lotar told her. "The healer could not fully clear the injury so Hazel's powers fail."

Across the open space, Warlord Yashu stiffened. "How

dare you accuse me? I am a loyal warrior, and I will die before admitting to treason."

"Yes, Yashu, I think you will." Irina flexed her fingers. "Anik. You are very brave, eh? To challenge the army and die for Syrenka."

He lifted his chin. "I have failed my prince and my king. I will not fail my city."

"You have not failed," Warlord Yashu counseled. "The king and prince failed. You will surpass them as king."

His son ignored him.

"Very brave." She nodded in approval and lifted her hand as if to high-five him. "But your death can have meaning. See?"

Her hand glowed.

A wall of energy blasted out, smacking First Lieutenant Anik in the chest. He flew back and hit the wide trunk of the Life Tree with a thump.

The Life Tree emitted a shattering sound. Resin pearls cascaded onto the warriors resting below. The warriors pushed off the dais and shifted to fins, clasping daggers, battle-ready.

First Lieutenant Anik's eyes bugged. His trident slipped out of his fingers and clattered to the dais. He slid down the trunk and landed in a heap on the other side of Lotar's slumped father.

The elders gaped.

Warlord Yashu froze.

"Hm." Irina flexed her fingers. "Maybe too much force."

The warriors advanced on Irina to battle the new threat.

Lotar held up his hand.

They stopped, suspended between grief and fury.

"Irina!" Hazel swam to the first lieutenant's side, as did the healer. "What did you do that for?"

"Now, he tells you how to fix Oska, or you do not heal his son," Irina said.

"That's insane." She closed her eyes. Her hands glowed.

"Hazel." Lotar waited until she opened her eyes again and looked at him. He subtly shook his head.

"But Anik's really hurt."

"I know."

"But..."

He willed her to think this through. Her desire to heal the first lieutenant was honorable. *Listen as my partner. Your wish is not wrong. I even agree with you. But consider our choices. Do not act on impulse now.*

Hazel clasped her hands. The glow faded. She wriggled unhappily on the mating gemstones. "It's not Anik's fault his dad is a backstabbing murderer."

"It does not matter," Irina said. "Yashu kills my son, I kill his son. That is fair."

"To you, maybe." Hazel crossed her arms. "Either way, it's still wrong."

Irina shrugged. "I speak the way Yashu understands. Eh, Yashu? Tell Hazel how to heal my Oska, or your Anik dies."

Warlord Yashu licked his lips. "I know nothing about Prince Oska's injury."

The first lieutenant spasmed, arching his back and moaning.

Warlord Yashu cried out and kicked to the Life Tree.

"Stop him," Lotar ordered.

Warriors blocked his path.

Warlord Yashu pushed against their tridents, cutting himself. "Let me through to my son!"

They blocked him, impervious to his curses and commands.

The healer checked First Lieutenant Anik's heart and palpated his ribs. A dark bruise had already formed over his sternum, and spots of blood drifted above his mouth.

"She crushed his body," the healer announced. "He will not survive."

Warlord Yashu snarled at Lotar. "How could you hold back a grieving father while his son dies? And when you have the means to heal him?"

Lotar met his honest grief with cold fury. "You must have asked yourself that question every moment of my father's vigil."

Warlord Yashu's eyes widened.

Hazel bounced unhappily. "Lotar…"

Yes, he understood.

And he agreed. Under Lotar's leadership, Hazel and the healer may have successfully undone the sabotage and healed Oska with no interference.

But Irina had acted. Time was of the essence. And her assessment of Warlord Yashu was not wrong.

"I could try to heal Oska anyway," Hazel said. "I don't want to wait so long that they both die."

"If they die, they die." Irina's eyes were cold as she fixed on Warlord Yashu. "I still have one son, so I win."

Rage flashed across Warlord Yashu's face. He whirled to Hazel. "Please. Heal my son. I beg you."

She glared at Warlord Yashu. "Why can't I heal Oska?"

Warlord Yashu curled his lip.

Anik made a choking sound and stilled.

Warlord Yashu gestured at Oska. "I lodged a coral spike in the shell necklace."

"His mom's necklace?"

"Yes."

"You're sick."

Warlord Yashu shrugged. Nothing mattered but his son.

The healer kicked to Oska's side and inspected the necklace. On the reverse, a cleverly hidden spine pierced skin. The healer carefully removed the dangerous necklace and handed it to a guard, who conveyed it to Lotar.

Lotar pried out the spine with a dagger, but the coral had ruined the necklace. The shell was crushed, leaving a gaping hole that could not be filled.

"Give me," Irina said.

He handed it to his mother, and she pressed it to her heart.

Hazel knelt at Oska's side. "That little spike couldn't have scratched through all those bandages, could it?"

Warlord Yashu said, "When I was left alone, I worked more slivers under the bandage."

The healer removed the bandages, exposing Oska's jagged, red, seeping wound. He used a medical tool to pinch out more small pieces of coral. "So they did not bubble up in the blood. You replaced them."

Warlord Yashu nodded.

The healer rubbed his brow. "That is a relief. I was beginning to question my competence."

Hazel spread her hands over Oska's wounds. Her chest glowed, her hands glowed, and a matching light glowed in his soul.

The light spread through his body. His color improved as his wound knit together faster and more completely than her last attempt. Oska hunched his shoulders, stretched, and yawned. His eyes opened on Hazel, and he frowned.

Then his gaze lifted to Lotar. A great smile broke over Oska's face. "I knew you would come. I knew. Warlord Yashu... He..." Oska waved at his injured chest. "I swam away from the blacknight sea. So many times. You stopped him?"

Lotar's chest squeezed.

His brother's faith was painful. He had been wiser than Lotar. And he had never stopped believing in Lotar's honor.

Lotar nodded.

Oska closed his eyes and sagged. His body paled and his iridescent sable tattoos dulled as though he'd fought all this way just to hear the answer and now he gave up and died.

The healer pinched his toe, but he did not respond.

"Oska." Irina floated to the edge of the dais. "Do not sleep now. This is a dangerous time. Our fight is not over."

Oska forced his eyes open with a moan. "Mama?"

Irina smiled. "Hi, my darling."

"You are here." Oska's color returned, and his tattoos shone. He straightened stiffly. "I dreamed about you."

She stroked his cheek. "You have grown. I am so proud."

He beamed.

The healer floated close, relieved. "Stretch your fins, but do not go far from the Life Tree. You will tire quickly and must replenish your strength."

Hazel pressed her hands to her bright, shining chest. "Aw."

"My son." Warlord Yashu waved at Hazel. "You promised."

"I did." She bounced over to First Lieutenant Anik, knelt by his side, and rubbed her hands together. "I'm still a bit angry at you, but I'll do my best."

First Lieutenant Anik pushed her hands away while trying to touch her as little as possible, rolled into a pained sitting position, and winced. "Save your strength for my warriors."

Warlord Yashu stilled.

"Huh?" She rested on her heels. "But your chest is crushed. Look at that bruise. Aren't you going to die?"

First Lieutenant Anik shook his head tiredly.

"I may have made a slight miscalculation." The healer nodded at Lotar in silent apology for his deception. "Perhaps the first lieutenant is not as injured as I had believed."

"Oh-ho." Irina smirked. "Perhaps Yashu is not the only one who smiles with one half of his face."

Lotar's father groaned. His lashes fluttered, and he squinted. "Oska? You are... Irina? Are you really here?"

"Early retirement." She crossed the dais, Oska limping behind, and rested beside King Falki. "I had to sort things out."

"I am glad to see you." He tried to roll more upright, but winced and instead settled her into his arms. "Did everyone survive? The sorting out."

"So far."

"Good." He covered her mouth with a tender kiss. "Oska was ill."

"Yes, yes. Lotar and Hazel saved him. And you. The All-Council army is here."

He winced again. "I must face them."

"You rest. Lotar is king now."

His father opened his eyes, sought Lotar, and focused.

Lotar straightened.

You will never be king. The words had echoed in these waters so many times.

And yet...

"King Lotar." His father held his gaze as one ruler to an equal. He accepted him, after all this time. "Save Syrenka."

———

So that was it, then?

Lotar simply held his father's gaze, locked in private communication, while his father hugged Irina and Oska floated close by. They still had a family unit while Lotar was out floating alone.

Well, not alone exactly.

He *was* king, and he had an entire army to fend off.

First Lieutenant Anik tried to roll forward and gave up with a pained whimper.

Great.

Hazel reached out and pressed her glowing hand against the first lieutenant's back. Pure white light glimmered through his torso, reflecting in his tattoos, and pooled in the chest.

He straightened as the light flowed into him, then frowned at Hazel and brushed at the glowing sparks. "I told you not to waste your strength on me."

"Yeah, but you're about to fight an army, so you should probably go into it without an existing injury. Besides, I don't take orders from you." She hopped up, shifted to fins, and swam to Lotar, her eyes bright and her chest glowing. "I accept suggestions from my partner. Partner."

He snugged her against his body. Gratitude curved his lips, and he traded a sweet kiss with her.

Sure, she'd disagreed with Irina's problem-solving, but after taking a moment to think things through, she'd understood Lotar's position. They were on the same page, aiming at the same goal, shooting fish in the same barrel. So to speak.

Anik was less injured than Oska and King Falki had been, so he could stand easily on the Sea Opals. His jaw flexed, and his eyes reddened. He swallowed hard and vibrated. "Father. I am disappointed."

Warlord Yashu nailed his son with a look. He was more than betrayed. He was wounded. "I did everything for you, my son."

Anik flinched. "I would rather serve Syrenka as the lowliest warrior than as the puppet king of the All-Council."

"You have undone decades of work. Decades. You must be king."

"Warlord Yashu." The head elder floated before the rest; they were all in agreement. "You tried to kill Prince Oska and King Falki. The punishment for treason is exile."

"You cannot exile me." Warlord Yashu glowered. "I promised a worthy king would rule Syrenka."

Anik twitched. "Father."

"No, you will not take this away from me." Warlord Yashu made his hands into claws. "None of you will take this away from me. I have made a pact. If you do not send Anik out as king, the All-Council army will destroy Syrenka."

The warriors exclaimed in shock.

"This is not what I want, Father," Anik snarled.

"It is what you deserve." Warlord Yashu's grin twisted into sick triumph. "And whether or not you like it, I have arranged it so you will get what you deserve."

The Life Tree shrieked.

At the edge of the city, the first castle groaned as army saws sliced into its stem. It turned black and collapsed to the seafloor, shattering coral.

The army had begun its attack.

THIRTY-FIVE

The pain of the city screamed through the Syrenkan warriors' veins.

Lotar's father arched in pain and Oska clasped his own chest.

But Lotar felt only a distant unease.

The elders had declared him king, but Syrenka was not his home. He was no longer fully linked with its Life Tree. He had given it up.

Now, his home was Atlantis.

And that meant he had the advantage.

"First Lieutenant Anik, gather your warriors." Lotar's vibrations cut through the chaos. "Leave a force to protect the Life Tree. The rest will come with me. You." He ordered the messenger. "Tell them to cease the attack. The king comes to parlay."

The messenger whirled and kicked, in agony but forcing himself to swim. He disappeared.

"These are all the warriors fit to fight." The first lieutenant gritted his teeth at the small group as though battling a migraine. "We cannot win. We are too few, and they are too many."

"We can win," Lotar said.

The first lieutenant looked at him like he was crazy.

Warlord Yashu laughed. "How can you win? There is an army destroying the city, and you will face them with a handful of warriors? You will be the downfall of Syrenka, Lotar. The disappointing second son Falki always said you were. No wonder he prefers to sleep at the Life Tree, so he will not see your crushing defeat."

"I will fight at your side, Lotar." Lotar's father rose with a groan and leaned on Irina. "Stay back where it is safe, my bride."

"Falki." She rested her head on his shoulder. "You know you cannot keep all the fun to yourself."

Oska paddled slowly. "I will make this stand with you, Lotar. As brothers."

His father rumbled, "As a family."

"See? Falki does not trust your abilities, Lotar. And he is right to doubt. You cannot win. Cede your position to Anik and let him preserve Syrenka while there are still castles to save."

"I do not join my son out of doubt." His father vibrated, slow and resonant, holding his gaze. "I join him because he is king. And if he says we will win? We will win."

Warlord Yashu sneered, but Falki turned away and faced Lotar. "Where do you want me?"

Oska waited for his assignment as well.

Lotar's heart swelled so large, it ached.

The city was on the brink of being torn apart, and finally his father looked at him as his son. Not his second son. His son and king.

"Swim close behind me and Hazel," Lotar said. "It will be most effective."

"Effective?" Warlord Yashu choked. "What do you mean, effective?"

But his father simply nodded and assumed the position, moving carefully but managing his injuries.

"Oska, you swim with Father and Mama."

Oska took his position, and Lotar sorted the rest of the warriors with First Lieutenant Anik. This was not unusual for a parlay. Lotar would speak to the general while also showing off their greatest warriors. The general would do the same.

"This is ridiculous," Warlord Yashu muttered. "You follow a warrior you have always treated badly. He wants to kill you and destroy the city."

The warriors and elders all regarded each other uncomfortably.

Lotar should probably bind the slimy male's chest so he could no longer vibrate his lies.

Hazel nudged him. "You should explain why he's wrong."

"Explain?"

She nodded, eyes twinkling. "You keep too many things inside. You're the king now. You can act like it."

Drawing attention to himself still made him uncomfortable.

But with Hazel at his side, he would conquer the world.

Or at least one All-Council super army.

He vibrated for attention. "Warriors of Syrenka. You are forgetting something."

His father turned to listen.

Even that made his heart squeeze.

And yet, even when his father had thought Lotar was a

jealous threat, he'd always given his full attention. Now, without Warlord Yashu's influence, his expression was open.

"Traitor Yashu has promised the All-Council a city in chaos. Unsolved assassinations, no first lieutenant, a newly chosen king. Instead, we present a stabilized city with experienced warriors." He looked at Hazel and his mother. "And two queens."

Irina grinned.

The head elder hummed. "Is it wise to bluff the All-Council general?"

"It is no bluff. You have not seen the power of a warrior with his queen."

And so they hadn't. They fell respectfully into line.

"Fine lies," Warlord Yashu muttered, and the warriors nearest him, making a final ring of protection around the Life Tree, frowned.

They could not wait until after dispersing the army to deal with the traitor.

Lotar motioned to his warriors. "Rearguard. Bring the traitor."

First Lieutenant Anik stiffened. "Overseeing the punishment of a traitor is the role of the first lieutenant."

Lotar's father murmured. "No king would ask a warrior to oversee the execution of his own father."

The first lieutenant stiffened further. "It is my role."

King Falki looked at Lotar.

Family relationships were complicated. First Lieutenant Anik felt guilt from being the center of his father's murderous plot. If this gave him the closure Hazel talked about, Lotar would not deny him. "Very well. Bring him, First Lieutenant Anik."

With stiff, trembling hands, First Lieutenant Anik

bound his father with bolas. His father did not fight. The son's soul fluctuated with harsh emotion, but his loyalty demanded unwavering obedience.

They kicked through the city. No more castles had fallen, and the army had reformed. They passed the nervous messenger, whose relief battled with anxiety at their small, injured numbers, and exited the last band of castles to face the All-Council army.

The army was vast. Hundreds of warriors loomed over them, weapons drawn, as they approached the point to parlay. A general kicked forward to meet them. A river of warriors fell in behind him.

They were outnumbered by so many.

But the All-Council army did not have two queens.

Hazel vibrated quietly. "And if all else goes wrong, I'll just summon the kraken."

It would not come to that.

But her vibration must have carried, because Irina responded. "You can summon her?"

"Well, maybe." Hazel jerked her thumb at the cluster of warriors floating with their general. "They don't know I can't."

Irina laughed.

King Falki smiled, and his chest glowed brighter.

They hung back at the prearranged area.

Lotar and Hazel kicked forward to meet the general and his entourage.

Hazel glowed brighter and more beautiful than ever before. Using her power successfully had energized her. She glowed, gorgeous and full of determination.

His heart squeezed.

How had he ever thought he was stronger alone?

Lotar stopped before the general.

"Syrenka king." The general bristled with weapons and harsh certainty. "The All-Council has accepted your request to settle the succession and will enforce your rule for as long as your fellow citizens need. In exchange—"

"No need." Lotar gestured behind him. "When I leave, my father, King Falki, will resume his duties."

The general squinted at Lotar's father. "King...Falki?"

"And my brother, Prince Oska, will succeed him."

Prince Oska waved. Both warriors were pale and gaunt, but they were also both upright, in full control, and not dead.

"This is not the information I received," the general said sharply.

"You should have investigated before making the long, pointless journey to our city. But as compensation, I gift you the honorless exile responsible."

First Lieutenant Anik dragged his father forward. His expression was immobile, but his soul light fluctuated. He had to hand over his father to certain death. It was a punishment no warrior should endure, and yet, he had insisted.

An All-Council warrior swam to meet him, collected Warlord Yashu's bola, and dragged him into the mass of the army.

The general raised an irritated brow. "What am I supposed to do with a useless exile?"

"That is your choice." Lotar lifted his trident. "But you have trespassed too long and destroyed one of our castles. If you withdraw immediately, we will let you go."

The general's lips cracked in amusement. "You will let *us* go?"

The vicious warriors behind him laughed uproariously.

Syrenka's warriors behind Lotar tensed.

The sheer volume of the All-Council army would unsettle him as well.

Except for one thing.

Hazel squinted at the general. She tapped her pursed lips.

The general cut off the laughter. "We will not withdraw. Your exile promised us our pick of the best warriors, the finest hunting grounds, and shelter to rest from the kraken. You will have to drive us out."

"Gladly." Lotar lowered his chin. "The army of Syrenka will hunt you across the ocean. We will fade into the reef, snipe you on patrol, pick you off one by one until only you remain on this side of the blacknight sea. Alone."

The All-Council warriors rustled and murmured.

The general's eyes widened.

Behind Lotar, his fellow warriors had faded into the ocean. Only Lotar's family remained visible, mostly because they were injured, but also for support.

The reputation of Syrenka. Ghosts of the ocean. Lurking, hidden, ready to strike.

"Your warriors may disappear, Syrenka king, but we are the net. You cannot escape." The general lifted one brow in challenge. "Perhaps I should tighten that net. Your warriors will reappear when I raze the city. Destroy the Life Tree. What would you say to that?"

Lotar gripped his trident.

Tension filled the ocean.

Hazel had the power to shield his family. They would retreat to the Life Tree. His mother would push the enemies back. And then they would—

"Hey." Hazel wagged her index finger at the general. "You. Don't I know you?"

The general's brows dropped. He motioned to his belli-cose second. "I thought this city had no queens."

"They did not. They do not."

"I see..." The general squinted. "At least two."

"Two?" His second curled his lip in a snarl and peered at the assembled warriors. Males who had never seen brides sometimes could not pick them out.

"I totally know you." Hazel craned her neck to get a good look. "Giru. Right?"

The general twitched. "Retreat."

His second jolted. The All-Council warriors behind him gaped.

"Yeah." Hazel shook her index finger. "You broke into our hospital one time. Aren't you with Nora?"

The general turned away. "We are leaving. Now."

His second chased him. "But General Giru, we fight only a few warriors."

"And two queens. I dislike those odds."

"But—"

"If you want to test your mettle, guard our retreat, but withdraw before you get too many skilled warriors killed."

Hazel pulled free and linked one hand with Lotar. "Oh, hey. Giru."

The general paused, dread affixed to his face.

"General!" his second snarled.

"Sorry. General." Hazel straightened formally. "We're having a party in Atlantis when the platform is done and you're all invited. Your moms might be there. Might. No promises, but Lotar's mom took early retirement, so you might get lucky."

General Giru turned fully to face Hazel. "You know I am an honorable general of the All-Council, sworn to defend the ancient covenant, and I will annihilate all who blaspheme it?"

"Right, but things are very 'it's complicated' right now. You've lurked in the ruins of lost cities, but have you ever visited a city full of new life? It's not too late to make a different choice." Her arms widened to encompass the rest of the general's warriors. "For anyone."

The army seethed down at her.

But she represented herself perfectly. She conveyed the invitation without hesitation or stumbling. She glowed with confidence.

Lotar was so proud.

"Anyway, if you want to see your mom or someone else, you don't have to sneak in. You're invited." She curled against Lotar.

"I have no mother," the fierce second snapped as though she'd issued a personal invitation to him.

"No? They found you in a row of cabbage?"

"In a seaweed forest."

"Oh. Uh, wow. I had no idea that happened."

"So there is no reason to invite me."

"Right. Gotcha."

General Giru shook his head at the whole exchange and kicked away. "We are leaving."

And just like that, the army withdrew.

The Syrenka warriors reappeared and watched in shock.

"We did not even raise a trident," Lotar's father said.

Lotar's mother gripped his father's trident. She slashed it experimentally. "Pity."

"I didn't have to summon the kraken." Hazel flexed her fingers. "If I can even do that."

"Is she near?" Lotar asked.

"I don't know. Maybe..." Hazel pointed. "There?"

Everyone turned to look.

It was an empty ocean.

Hazel deflated. "Haha. Never mind."

A distant shadow moved. Ripples in the ocean tossed sea creatures out of the way.

Lotar fitted her more snugly to his side. "Shield."

"What?"

"Against the current."

"She was there?" Hazel squeaked. Her soul glowed, and she threw the shield around the city just in time.

The chaotic tumble of debris whooshed over the top and carried on the other side. Syrenka's castles and Life Tree bobbed gently in place.

"This shielding is useful." Irina poked the white light until Hazel released it and it faded away like the swirl of bioluminescence. "Pushing is more fun. I must practice."

"By the time I see you at the party, you'll be an expert," Hazel assured her.

THIRTY-SIX

They returned to the city.

With Irina at his side, Lotar's father grew stronger. He focused on securing Syrenka, undoing any more sabotage, and double-checking everything that Warlord Yashu had touched with the elders. And he was careful not to exceed his authority since Lotar was still king.

Following his lead, the city warriors deferred to King Lotar with respect.

And every time Oska heard "King Lotar," he smiled.

In a short time, the city flourished, and the open ocean beckoned.

Once, Lotar had dreamed of becoming the second prince. Ruling with his father and brother. Enjoying the new respect and appreciation in his fellow warriors' eyes.

But now...Syrenka was not his city.

He had a mission to complete for *his* king.

And while this had filled a deeply held need, he knew it was time to go.

Hazel moved to him, sensing his thoughts as always, and nestled in his arms. "Ready?"

Lotar gazed upon the city's buzzing activity one last time, fixing it in his memory. It had been a home of great striving and great frustration, but he was glad to have returned, if only for a little while.

His brother broke free from the elders he'd been speaking with and swam to Lotar's side. He had always seen more than Lotar had realized.

Oska clasped his forearm. "You are leaving? I know you must. No one else could complete the All-Cities Gyre."

Lotar gripped his brother's forearm.

If only he had realized Oska was an ally, perhaps he would have endured. But Oska had been silent, like Lotar. They had both been young and uncertain. Now? They were true brothers.

"Will you come to Hazel's party?" Lotar asked.

"Very likely." Oska grinned. "You know what 'they' will say. You are an exceptional warrior. I must study your successes so I can improve."

"They" would never say such a thing, but Oska's genuine kindness buffeted Lotar's heart.

He squeezed Oska's forearm and released him. "May your spears be dulled by bounteous hunts and your castle walls burst from too many young fry."

"And you, brother. And you."

Then Lotar called for the rest of the warriors to gather around the Life Tree for his final announcement. "Elders of Syrenka. You honored me with the title of king. I return it to you now so you may return it to the rightful choice: King Falki."

His father accepted the announcement. He clasped Lotar's forearm. "You ruled well."

His chest tightened. "Thank you, Father."

He nodded and pulled back. Perhaps it was too late for them to ever have the close relationship his father enjoyed with Oska, but for Lotar, this was enough.

It was enough.

Hazel waved at Irina. "Enjoy that retirement."

"If you have another city under siege, you call me." Irina flexed her fingers. "I will come. You'll see."

"That reminds me. We've got three-quarters of the ocean to go." Hazel shook her head. "If all this happened in the first quarter, what's going to happen next?"

Irina laughed. "Relax, young person. It cannot be a siege every day."

"Thank God," Hazel said.

"Pity," Irina said at the same time, and Hazel choked.

The entire city escorted Lotar and Hazel to the edge of Syrenka's territory.

Lotar's father gave his final farewell. "Syrenka honors you, noble warrior. You have proved yourself, and the goodwill of Atlantis, on this stay." Irina rested a soothing hand on his shoulder, and he covered her hand with his. "You are welcome in Syrenka any time."

How different from the last time he had left.

The elders moved forward to wish him individual farewells, and then the rest of the warriors honored him as though he were a real hero.

Funny.

Only First Lieutenant Anik kept his distance. When Lotar's gaze flicked to him, he lowered his head in honor. They had so much in common, and yet they had both suspected each other. Perhaps they would never be friends. But they could respect each other as allies.

Lotar finally turned away, fitted Hazel to his side, and affirmed, "Ready."

She nestled against him. "Let's fly."

He kicked out of the territory and entered the Nord Est current flowing fast.

"You know, all things considered, meeting your parents went pretty well," Hazel mused. "It couldn't have gone better. I'm getting the swing of this undersea traveling."

He smiled.

A tiny thresher shark paced them.

"Oh my God, that is so cute! You and your shark sense, attracting all the baby sharks." She reached out and almost touched the thresher. It darted away. "Aw. Bye-bye, baby shark."

She was the adorable one.

And so much calmer now than when she'd jumped into the water in Mexico. He had changed, yes, but she had also come so far that their past selves were almost unrecognizable—

"Argh!" Hazel's soul light fluctuated wildly. She slammed both hands over her ears, squeezed her eyes shut, and gritted her teeth. "Quick. Sing me something. Anything."

"Sing?"

"It's an emergency!"

Perhaps they had not changed so much after all.

Lotar summoned his only song from memory and let the renewed lyrics, a melody so recently refreshed in his mind, wash over them as they continued on the greatest journey a single warrior had ever attempted in the modern era—with his quirky, caring, very determined queen.

EPILOGUE: HAZEL'S HOMECOMING

Almost two years later...

"Oh, he's awake." Hazel snuggled her little bub, safely sandwiched between her chest and Lotar's, as his pale blue eyes blinked open and his little mouth wrinkled in a yawn. "Perfect timing. Pause here."

Lotar slowed his long kicks and let the current carry him over the rise.

"Look, Tal." Hazel turned her fifteen-month-old to stare openmouthed at the city spread out below them. "Home at last."

Atlantis.

The city sparkled like a perfectly cut gemstone. Masses of coral stretched for the sky and created secret grottos filled with fairyland wonders. Castles unfurled in three concentric rings growing rapidly, and schools of fish fluttered between the healthy anchors like great flocks of birds. Silvery fish flitted below like shimmering butterflies, and powerful, sleek predators darted overhead. In the center, small but mighty, the Life Tree gleamed like a beacon calling them home.

The group of warriors that had escorted them from the territory's edge flew ahead. Excited shouts filled the ocean with a jubilant celebration.

Home.

Her heart swelled.

She was ready. So ready.

Lotar beamed at her.

Behind the glowing city, the great wreckage of the ancient Atlantis was slowly being fixed. Between the ruin and the new city, a scaffolding rose into the abyss, and multiple cables anchored near the ancient wreck. They secured the almost-completed, floating, not-oil platform overhead.

Here, the two races would reverse the past and once more live in harmony.

"This is what Mommy and Daddy have been doing for the past year," Hazel told her son. "Inviting others to our party."

"Gaaa." Tal yawned and chewed his fist.

"He's impressed," she told Lotar. "But this awake period isn't going to last. Let's go."

Lotar kicked for the largest central castle by the Life Tree. His smile remained firmly in place.

He hadn't stopped smiling since Tal was born. All his adorable worry leading up to Tal's birth had melted away once he'd held his son in his arms, and the later cities had welcomed them with amazement, generosity, and even tenderness. Few things united the mer like a young fry. And although most were scandalized that they traveled with a newborn, their safety-oriented moralizing was always softened by long, adoring gazes at baby Tal, so Hazel couldn't even get too upset.

Now a crowd flew from the battered Atlantis Life Tree to throng them. It was like being welcomed by the Macy's Thanksgiving Day Parade and getting crowned the leader.

They reached the king's castle, where King Kadir and Queen Elyssa welcomed them personally with a great feast. During and after the feast, Lotar greeted his old friends and showed off his son. Hazel met old friends and new ones. The preschool crowd screamed around the castle, echoing their parents.

"Tal?" Queen Elyssa touched his cheek. "He's so little. You went nontraditional, huh?"

"Well, his middle name is Halo, so he can be mer when he wants, but Lotar was okay with me choosing a more normal first name. So his full name is Talbot Halo Green."

"Adorable. Oh, big yawn." Elyssa cooed at Tal and tickled his rounded belly. "Have you seen your castle?"

"Not yet."

"Gailen will show you around. After all the work he's done, you're going to love it." Elyssa called over the orange-tattooed warrior, and he led her and Lotar through their still-celebrating friends to a larger castle at the outer edge of the concentric ring.

Even his castle was a loner.

Gailen led them through the long entrance tube to the inside. Lotar took baby Tal, who was fussing from being tired, so Hazel could focus on her new home.

Lush green gardens blanketed the floor, corridors and alcoves were hollowed out like a cozy hobbit's house, and rounded windows were filled with trailing window boxes of lovely seaweed. Light seemed to slant through the center of the courtyard, and the walls glowed.

"You have more rooms than the average mer because you have been gone so long." Gailen showed off the fully stocked pantry and cute hidden nooks. "So I could also take my time and let things grow. Those tall flowers are the herb I collected in Aiycaya. You can mash the white puff into a substance that the other humans say tastes like soft white cheese."

This was her home. An open, airy castle filled with light.

"You can change anything." Gailen pulled off a few yellowed nubs from the nearest window box seaweeds and tucked them into the dirt. "Let me know."

Hazel choked up. "No, no. It's what I've always wanted."

"Are you sure? I can—"

She threw her arms around him. "Thank you so much."

Gailen held stock-still. Even though the warriors had come a long way from the beginning, when they'd refused to touch a woman or else risk getting the offending parts cut off, they still weren't at the hugging-another-man's-wife stage.

She patted his shoulder and let go, recovering with a sniff. "Thank you."

He looked anywhere but at her and gripped the back of his neck. "I am glad you like it."

Lotar rocked baby Tal, a rueful smirk on his face. He did not mind Hazel's generous hugs, and he enjoyed the awkward reactions of the other mer.

"Anyway." Gailen dropped his hand and straightened. "Over there is the pedestal for your family's Life Tree seed. That corridor will lead to your Heart Chamber after you resonate with the castle for the first time. That hole over there belongs to your house guardian. And—"

"House guardian?" Hazel peered in the small hole. "I get a pet octopus?"

"She is blue. And unnamed, so you have the honor."

The others had named their pet octopuses things like Lassie, Scooby, Benji, and Wishbone. Time would tell if Hazel's was a Lady or a Bruiser.

And that was it.

Gailen took his leave. Hazel stretched, alone in a castle with her family for the first time in over two years.

Wow.

It was so quiet. And peaceful. And wonderful.

She moseyed from plant to plant and room to room, brushing her fingertips over the walls. They glimmered as though reacting to her touch. She was making it hers simply by being here.

A lot had happened in two years.

Flora had put her things in storage and canceled her lease. Except for the succulents. Those had gone to her friends and beautified the last remaining office of the foundation in the city.

Pia had gotten rejected from so many auditions, she'd lost her patience and written her own role in a solo musical. The first week it opened, she got scouted by an important choreographer and had now danced backup in a few commercials and music videos. Owen still went to every performance.

Zara had been more successful than she'd initially believed and had a decent list of former sacred brides from every city promising to attend. Some had refused, some had changed their minds, some had always planned to return to the world of the mer like Irina. It took a certain kind of person to go through what they had experienced, and they were strong.

But Hazel's real goal had been to outreach, and they had done it.

The ocean was more exotic than she'd realized. For a woman who'd come from a small potato town to New York, this trip had made her a real world traveler.

Lotar joined her. His arms were empty, and baby Tal snoozed peacefully in the middle of the courtyard, neutrally buoyant.

"Good job." She nestled in his arms. "Elyssa gave me the update."

"I too heard news from the warriors. But..." He teased his lips over hers and vibrated as she spoke. "We should open the Heart Chamber now. It is the most protected area in the castle."

And because of how soon they would be inundated with potentially unfriendly warriors, safety was first. "Gailen said we had to resonate with the castle."

Lotar vibrated an affirmative and cupped her heavy breast. His cock hardened against her thigh.

Oh.

Yeah.

She yielded to his kisses, slow at first, then rough and demanding. They had gotten few opportunities and she felt just as desperate.

He tongued her breasts, her nipples, and down her belly to her throbbing center.

She locked her knees over his shoulders, opening to him, and he stroked her needy interior right up to the first delicious back-arching orgasm and over the other side.

Yes, this was how she wanted it. Fast, hard, and now.

She twisted and clamped his torso, finding his hard cock, and teased her tongue across the trembling cap. He shuddered. She loved this part too. Driving him wild. He was always so tightly in control, always so focused on keeping her and their baby safe and happy that she loved this wildness. He was a wolf romping in the snow. A warrior finally home to rest and love his wife as only he knew how.

His long fingers dug into her thighs as she mercilessly revealed just how thoroughly she treasured him, and his vibrations changed to guttural hunger. He marked her belly, her inner thigh, her calf.

Each bruising kiss made her nipples tighten and her belly throb. She clawed him closer.

He spun her in the water, moving her body as fluidly beneath the surface as above, and planted his cock at her entrance.

She squeezed her thighs to draw him in, deep, and they undulated in her favorite dance. His gray eyes shimmered iridescent and his lips curled back from his teeth as he grunted, thrusting deep into her taut channel, sliding hard against her pleasure spot.

And then he slammed her into a second orgasm, and when he saw her eyes roll back with lust, he went harder, and she exploded with a third toe-curling, muscle-clenching, total-body release. Driving her body hard, yet always pacing her, he was relentless and exceptional.

But even an exceptional warrior needed his rest.

She clenched his gorgeous, taut buttocks. "Okay. You can go. Your turn—"

He groaned, and the release poured out of him. He slowed to soft undulations, sweet spurts, and lay still.

Lotar still moved her world. Heaven, earth, water, sky. They revolved around her warrior. Her husband. Her soul mate.

In the aftermath, she toyed with the spiral shell necklace at his throat. A similar shell in glacier white adorned her neck, Lotar had gifted an ochre-colored shell to Tal.

Sparkles flickered across the walls of the inner dome like reverse shooting stars. Their resonance revitalized the castle and, in turn, the Life Tree, because the mer were connected.

And all news mattered.

"What did you hear?" Hazel finally asked. "Did Ciran suggest a new role as you expected?"

"I will begin training warriors in stealth as soon as I wish."

Hazel squeezed him. "That's great! And you once thought you were unfit to be around kids."

He pressed a kiss to her shoulder. "There is more."

"Yeah? Tell me."

He had updates from his family, surprisingly. Syrenka rarely shared on the echo points, but the Atlantis warriors had heard Prince Oska had ascended to find a bride. No word yet on whether he'd succeeded, but Hazel could imagine the excitement when he showed up on the shoreline and ran into his half siblings on land.

First Lieutenant Anik had tried to resign several times, but King Falki and Queen Irina refused. Warlord Yashu's pride and Lotar's father's desire to protect had twisted into something toxic. Lotar's father had finally learned not to punish a son for his father's mistakes.

Lotar fell silent and looked over at Tal.

She pressed her palm flat over his heart. "You know what happens when love goes wrong. That's why it's not going to happen to you. You'll love Tal exactly right because love is like an ocean, and you've crossed them all. You are more capable than you believe."

His gaze returned to her, and he softened. "Because I have you."

"Of course." She nuzzled him. "You're my exceptional warrior."

He accepted her words, finally, and that was the most beautiful thing of all. That her love, her husband, could finally accept himself. The recognition of his talents and skills no longer tortured him. He could be himself at last.

"Hm?" He frowned suddenly, untangled from Hazel, and swam over to the pedestal.

It had been empty before, but now he closed his fingers around a Sea Opal that looked small in his grasp.

"The house guardian must have left it," he mused.

"Without us noticing? Jeez, she's as stealthy as you are."

He opened her palm and rested the Sea Opal—which to her was massive and heavy and filled up her whole hand—there. "From a warrior to his bride."

"I wondered why you never gave it to me." She hefted it. It was like a baseball and so beautiful. Icy gray with silvery streaks, it was a veritable wolf stone. "But now I see why. This rock would have anchored you to the seafloor."

He snorted and shook his head. "That is not why I left it."

"No?"

He snugged her against his body. "I did not want a bride. I preferred to swim alone."

And he was so certain he'd never change his mind.

She wrapped her arms around his shoulders and hugged him tight. "The next time we surface, I am going to buy a whole wardrobe of rich-woman Saturday lingerie."

He hugged her. "There is one more thing."

"I have a confession too. But you go."

"Queen Dannika has identified the leader of the Sons of Hercules."

"That's wonderful!" She danced. "And before the party."

But his sober gaze told her it wasn't wonderful. "The security officers from the other countries—Aiycaya's sacred island, others—traced the leader to the platform building company."

Her chest fell. "The building company? There's a traitor inside the platform building company?"

He nodded.

"But I just invited everyone to the platform to party!" She clapped her hands on her cheeks. "Do you know what would happen if the Sons of Hercules sabotage the platform? Right when everyone's here?"

It would mirror what had happened a thousand years ago. Humans and mer had gone to war. Ancient Atlantis had been destroyed, sunk, and the mer had disappeared beneath the waves and into legend.

But this time, no sacred island brides would save them from extinction. This time, the mer would fade out forever.

"Agh. I knew something would go wrong." She gripped her hair. "Tell me we're fixing it."

"It could be a lie spread by our enemies to halt the party. So your security officer, Starr, is investigating."

"Oh." Hazel dropped her hands. "Thank God. I mean, I've never met Starr face-to-face, but she's like a superhero. We're saved. Unless it's true. Oh my God, what if it's true, and the platform, which was supposed to be safe from the Sons of Hercules, is actually set up to be sabotaged by them?"

"Then we will work together to save the platform."

The end would depend on them.

To save the platform, stop another Great Catastrophe, and prevent another long war.

Plus she had a personal stake. Tal was sleeping peacefully. Lotar was exceptional, but the platform was huge. If it sank, could he be sure it wouldn't slide over and wipe out the new Atlantis? Her friends, her city, and her gorgeous new castle?

"Hazel." Lotar pressed her palms together, sensing her panic spiraling. "The ocean is deep. What happens on the surface is important, but what happens beneath the ocean is another matter. There is still hope. We can make many changes. Your connections with the other cities' kings are the beginning. Others are making similar connections. No matter what happens to the platform, we have changed. The surface world and the ocean. And this is another obstacle. We will overcome it. Together."

Gosh, those were the most words Lotar had ever spoken.

And the fire glimmering in his wolf-gray eyes proved that he believed in every word.

She linked hands with him. "Okay. You're right. It's a lot to take in, but we saved a whole city from a traitor who'd been working for decades, so we can definitely stop a saboteur who's only been working a couple of weeks."

He rubbed her shoulder and kissed her forehead. "What is your confession?"

"Yeah. There was something I had to tell you. Um, I might be pregnant again."

He blanched.

How funny that imagining the collapse of all they cared about and the extinction of the mer by humans was no big deal, but finding out he might be a father of two made him lose it.

She squeezed his fingers. "I promise you'll be so loving that no child will ever feel more important to you even for one moment. We'll have the same size birthday cake. My dad used to take a kitchen scale to measure out my and my brother's ice creams. We'll gift the same number of Christmas presents and the same dollar value. Erin's been tracking this for her kids for years. She has a spreadsheet. We will give them the same number of compliments. We'll love both of them, of course, but we'll also show it too. I promise you."

Lotar hugged her. His shoulders trembled, but he believed her.

"And if one of them is better at one thing, we'll celebrate. The winner is the winner. No talking down."

His arms tightened. His vibrations sounded broken but happy. "Yes. Yes."

She loved him.

There were always challenges. Apparently, in a few weeks, they'd either unmask a saboteur and pull off an amazing party, or their whole world would collapse.

But they would stand tall and meet those challenges together.

Hazel and her very exceptional warrior.

ABOUT THE AUTHOR

USA Today bestselling author Starla Night was born on a hot July at midnight. She hikes, scuba dives, and swims naked in the ocean. She writes about smokin' hot dragons and tattooed mermen at StarlaNight.com.